# *A Bestseller For Fifty Years!*

''Stands in a class apart for its high sense of spiritual values, as well as for its glowing background.''

—The Times, London

''A book of fine idealism, deep compassion and a spiritual quality pure and bright as flame.'' —New York Times

''Rich in timeless wisdom...a symbol of the best that the human spirit holds.'' —New York Post

''The book is, as it were, clairvoyant, so clear, so living are the pictures conjured: it reads like an unclouded dream, like something written out of the body and brought back.''

—The Observer

''Joan Grant constructs a remarkable story, not just an ordinary work of fiction, but a moving recreation of the life of ancient Egypt, written with such clarity, detail, and living presence that it is quite reasonable to believe that *Winged Pharaoh* is a 'far memory'—not a figment of imagination but a recollection. A rare treat.''

—Books of Light

# BOOKS BY JOAN GRANT

*Far Memory Books:*

Winged Pharaoh

Eyes of Horus

Lord of the Horizon

So Moses Was Born

Life as Carola

Return to Elysium

Scarlet Feather

---

Far Memory

---

The Scarlet Fish and Other Stories

Redskin Morning

---

The Laird and the Lady

Vague Vacation

A Lot To Remember

Many Lifetimes *(with Denys Kelsey)*

# WINGED PHARAOH

*by Joan Grant*

ARIEL PRESS
Columbus, Ohio

First published in Great Britain by Arthur Baker Ltd. 1937
First Ariel Press edition 1985
*Third Printing*

This book is made possible by a gift
to the Publications Fund of Light
by Grant and Chris Kurtz

WINGED PHARAOH

 Printed in the United States of America. Direct inquiries to: Ariel Press, P.O. Box 30975, Columbus, Ohio 43230.

ISBN 0-89804-140-6

to d.s.

# author's note

The Ancient Egyptians gave many names to their land. In this story of the time of the First Dynasty, it is called 'Kam' and also 'The Two Lands'; Sumer, the land of the forerunners of the Babylonians, is called 'Zuma'; and Crete, the centre of the Minoan civilisation, is called 'Minoas'. Except for the city of 'Men-atet-iss', which is Memphis, near Cairo, the locality of all sites is shown clearly enough for the purposes of the story. 'Abidwa' is the modern Abydos, and the 'Amphitheatre of Grain' is now the site of Tell el Amarna. 'The Narrow Land' is Sinai, and 'the Narrow Sea' is the Red Sea. There is no standard system for the spelling of Egyptian words and names; in my spelling the 'a' is pronounced long, as in 'calm'.

The emblems of Upper Egypt, 'The South', were the Lotus and the Reed; its crown, the White crown. The Red crown was of 'The North', whose emblems were the Papyrus and the Bee.

Though horses are introduced into this story, I am aware that no record has so far been found of the horse in Egypt prior to the XVIIIth Dynasty.

# TABLE OF CONTENTS

## PART I



## PART II

## PART III



## PART IV

## PART V



## PART VI



## PART VII

PART VIII

# Winged Pharaoh

CHAPTER ONE

# Into Exile

When the time came for me to return to Earth, a Messenger of the Great Overlords told me that I should be re-born in Kam; and the two who would fashion my new body would welcome me, for we had been companions aforetime and the ties between us were of love and not of hatred, which are the two threads that bind men most closely together upon Earth; and for my brother I should have one with whom I had travelled long upon the great journey.

When this was told to me, the sorrow, which all know when they must leave their true home and go to the place of mists upon another day's journey, was lightened: for I should have companions in my exile.

While my mother still sheltered me with her body, my father sought to find a gift that would tell her of the love that filled his heart. He could not tell her of his love in words, for words are but the fleeting shadows of reality. Carvers in turquoise nor workers in gold or ivory could please him with their finest craftsmanship. One day, as he was walking in the gardens of the palace in the cool of the evening, he thought of making a garden for my mother, a garden such as had never been seen before. Only by this could he symbolize his love. For nothing can be greater than its creator; and though a carving may be a song in stone, it is born of the sculptor; but the plants of the earth are the children of the Gods.

And so, in a curve like the young moon, he planted trees to shade her from the sun at noonday, and bushes with aromatic leaves to spice the air for her refreshment. And for the bowstring of this living bow, there was the lapping water of the lake, which stretched its silver to the setting sun, Amenti in the West. Then he mustered a host of grassy spears, which closed their ranks to make the smooth green lawns; and he starred them with little flowers, scarlet and yellow, violet, blue and white, which grew to make a carpet for her feet. From lands beyond the boundaries of Kam he brought the scarlet lilies of the Land of Gold, and trumpet vines that grow far to the south, where men walk in their own shadow; and from the north he summoned lemon trees, white oleanders and anemones, and flowers that keep their perfume for the moon, to fill the dusk with their drowsy sweetness. And honeysuckle entwined arbeeta flowers and the blue convolvulus to make her wreaths.

When I was twelve days old, my father for the first time took her to this garden that he had made for her. It was surrounded by a garden wall, and upon the lintel of the door of cedarwood were carved their names, Za Atet, and Merinesut, 'the beloved of Pharaoh's heart'. Together they went into the flowering shade, where the paths were secret as gazelle tracks through the reeds. When she reached the heart of the green quiet and saw a garden more beautiful than any she had dreamed, she said that here the petals of the flowers were as though the clouds of sunset had been carved in blossoms by the Sun-god Ra, who upon the Earth could never before have found such pleasure for his rays. And both agreed that it must have pleased the god to see his children here so glorified.

So they named this place Sekhet-a-ra, 'the meadow of Ra'. And to me also they gave this name.

My brother, who had returned to Earth three years before me, was called Neyah. For at his birth the Priest of Maat in attendance, seeing those who came to speed him on his way, had said: "Hence is one who is worthy to rule over the people of Kam, for the companions of his spirit are long in years.

And this child shall be called, Neyah, 'born with wisdom'; for his master bore this name when in the Old Land he listened to the voice that warned him of the coming of the Great Rain. And just as his master guided his people when the evil ones had disappeared beneath the waters, so shall this child guide the people of Kam when they are assailed by evil ones, who in their turn shall be engulfed by the sea.''

CHAPTER TWO

# ANUBIS

When I was very little and walking was still a new adventure, Maata took Neyah and me with her to the temple. Neyah held my hand going up the steps. Everything was very big, and it was cold after the hot sunshine in the courtyard. In one of the rooms there was an enormous wooden animal like a hunting-dog, painted black. I wanted to touch it, but Neyah said I mustn't, because it was the statue of a god, and it was called Anubis. And suddenly I felt much older than two, and as wise as Maata my nurse; and I thought I knew all about Anubis, but I couldn't find words to explain it to Neyah.

When we got home I told Mother about it; and she gave me a little statue of Anubis, just the same only child size, with a little painted wooden house for it to live in. And I kept it beside my bed, so that I could see it the first thing in the morning when I woke up. Mother said that Anubis was the bringer of dreams to children. Sometimes I dreamed of being grown up and doing lots of very important things. I couldn't quite remember them, but in the morning it seemed very unfamiliar to be only two.

Neyah didn't have to go to bed until long after me, because he was five. Quite often, before I went to sleep, he used to come and tell me stories. I had a very specially favourite story about a lion and a wild-cat and a hare. The hare lived with his mother in the reeds. He could run much faster than all his brothers and sisters, and although his mother warned him not to go too far from home, he didn't listen, for he thought he could run away from any danger however sudden. He used to creep out at night and look up at the moon, where he could see the Father of all the Hares, and he used to tell him all about the clever things he had done.

One day, when he was busy thinking about himself, a huge wild-cat sprang upon him; and she picked him up in her mouth and took him home to her cubs for their breakfast. But the cubs had had plenty of breakfast, so the wild-cat put him down at the entrance to her cave and told him that if he moved she would kill him at once. The poor hare was so frightened he kept quite, quite still. Then he looked up at the god of the hares, and he said, "Please, please look down out of the moon and help me. I made such a mistake about being clever. I'll always listen to people who know more than I do, if only you'll save me from this wild-cat."

The wild-cat listened to what he was saying, and she licked her whiskers and laughed to think that any hare, even if he lived in the moon, could attack a wild-cat.

Suddenly in the shadows outside the cave there was a great roaring, and an enormous lion sprang upon the wild-cat and ate her right up.

The little hare saw that his prayers had been answered, and he wasn't at all frightened of the lion, because he knew that the answer to a prayer is always good, whatever shape it comes in. So he went up to the lion and thanked him. The lion lay down so that the hare could climb on his back. And he nestled in the lion's mane while he rode back home to his mother.

When the little hare grew up, he told this story over and over again, and he always finished up by saying, "Look to the moon and you will see the wisest of us all."

CHAPTER THREE

# DREAM COUNTRY

One day, when I was three years old, I was with my mother by the swimming-pool. One end of it was quite shallow, and I could stand there alone. I took off my necklace of lapis and shell beads and my little white linen kilt, and played in the water, banging it with my hands, so that the drops leapt into the air. When I had finished with the water, I ran about in the sun without my clothes on; and I picked some flowers and made them into a bunch to give to Neyah, who was out with my father.

Then Maata came and said that it was time for me to go to bed. But I didn't want to go, and I said, "No, won't," because I wanted to stay with my mother in the sun. Maata looked very stern, and as tall as one of the pillars in the great hall. I jumped back into the pool and splashed very hard, so that she couldn't come near me without getting wet. And then Mother asked me to come out, so I did. Maata got cross, so I lay on my back and yelled very loud, "I won't go to sleep. I won't go to sleep. I won't." And I drummed my heels on the ground so that she would know I really meant it and stop bothering me. This was a good idea, because Mother told Maata to leave me alone with her. So Maata had to go; and I was very pleased.

Then Mother asked me why I didn't want to go to sleep. And I said, "Because it's dull, and because I'm enjoying myself having a lovely time."

And she said, "You can have a lovely time when you are asleep." I didn't quite know what she meant, until she pointed to my kilt, which was still lying by the edge of the pool, and went on, "Sometimes you wear that kilt and sometimes you don't. Just because you haven't got your kilt on it doesn't mean you have to be dull. When you want to get into the water you take your kilt off—you love being in the water, don't you? Well, when you go to sleep you take your body off and leave it in your bed, and then you go and have a lovely time; and you can do lots of exciting things you can't do when you're in your body, just the same as you can't go into the pool when you are in your kilt....Don't you ever have dreams?"

And I said, "Of course I do." Then she told me that dreams were memories of things I did when I left my body asleep...."When you are in bed, if you still want to bathe you can leave your body there, which will please Maata, and you can come and play in the pool, which will please yourself. And in the Dream Country, water is just as wet; and you can have even more fun playing there than when you are awake."

After she had told me that, I thought I had been very silly to mind having to go to sleep. So I gave her lots of kisses, and went to my room and told Maata I was sorry I'd been horrid. Then she stopped being a long way off like a pillar and became all near and friendly again.

When Mother came to say good-night she sat beside me and stroked my forehead with her cool hand as her soft voice caressed me,

Sleep, my daughter,
For the sun has drawn the curtains of the night,
Leaving the stars to watch you while you rest.
The sails of all the river boats are furled,
And the birds have folded their far-flying wings.
Lion cubs are sleeping in the mother's warmth,
And fish dream in the shelter of the reeds.
The flowers breathe out their perfume on the dusk,
And all is still, save the night-singing bird.
So sleep, my daughter, and close your drowsy lids;
Sleep with the world and let your spirit free.

And I curled up in my bed and tried to go to sleep very quickly so as to get to know more about the Dream Country.

CHAPTER FOUR

# neyah's newest adventure

Sometimes Maata used to take Neyah and me for walks along the river bank. It was quite a long way from the palace, so we usually went as far as the river in a litter. We used to see the fishing boats and want to go on them, but Maata wouldn't let us.

One day Neyah told me he wasn't going to have Maata interfering with what he wanted to do, and if I liked, he would let me join in his newest adventure. And I said, "Of course I'd like. It wouldn't be a proper adventure without me in it too."

So the next morning we got up very early when it was only just beginning to get light, and we put on our very oldest clothes so as to look like village children. First we climbed over the wall of the vineyard and picked four of the best bunches of grapes. Neyah carried them, and I took some figs and put them in the napkin with the four little loaves of bread that I'd hidden in my room the night before.

We walked a very long way, until we came to the river. A little way along the bank there were some fishermen getting their boats ready. Neyah went up to the oldest of them and asked if he would exchange some fish for the grapes. The man said that he would, but that we were too early, for he was only just setting out to spread his nets. Neyah pretended to be very surprised and said sadly, "We will have to wait until you come back, for we dare not go home without fish, or our uncle will be angry with us." And then he said, "Can my sister get into your boat just for a moment? She has always longed to go in one. And then we'll just sit on the bank and wait until you come back."

The fisherman seemed to be fond of children—he told us that he had five of his own. And he said, "If you are very good and sit in the bottom of the boat and don't get in my way, you can both come with me.''

So we thanked him very much, and jumped in quickly, before he could change his mind.

The nets were piled up in the bottom of the boat and smelt very fishy. The boat was very clumsy. It had no paintings on it, and the sail was stained and patched; but the wind soon took us out into the middle of the river. The nets were thrown over the sides, and they trailed out beside the boat while it moved slowly downstream.

The fisherman was a very nice man. I didn't like to ask him his name in case he asked us ours; and we hadn't arranged what we should say. He let Neyah hold the steering oar for a bit, and I made a face at Neyah to remind him that he mustn't show he knew how to do it, because we had both said we hadn't been in a boat before. Then I asked the fisherman if he would sing us one of the songs we had heard from the bank, but never clearly enough to hear the words.

He had a nice voice, very loud and deep. The song didn't have much tune, just two or three notes like a sort of chant.

> O my net! swing widely for your master.
> Call to the fish that you would give them shelter
> From the monsters of the river.
> O fish! leave the caverns of the reeds
> And drowse in the shadow of my boat.
> Blow softly, wind! so that my boat glides through the water
> Quiet as a naked girl swimming at sunset.
> O fish! hear me and join your brothers in my net
> So that it be weighted with silver
> So that all my family rejoice with me.

Then he called to the other man, who was right up in the front of the boat, hidden by the sail, and they started to pull in the nets, with Neyah and me helping. The fish poured over the side in a wriggling silver flood; they jumped and flapped against my legs and I would have liked to climb up on the side of the boat, only Neyah didn't seem to be minding it. He was helping the men to sort the fish into different kinds and to put them into reed baskets. I think if there had been any eels, I would have had to get out of the way, but luckily there weren't.

When we got back, there were several people on the bank waiting to get fish. For a moment I was afraid they might recognize us, but I looked at Neyah and was sure we were all right, because there were scales all stuck to his arms, and smears of fish blood on his forehead.

Neyah tried to give the fisherman the grapes as a present for taking us out in his boat, but he laughed very friendily and said, "You shall have four fine fish for the grapes, and two extra for helping me; and you can come out with me any time you like. Ask any fisherman where Das is, and they'll always tell you where to find me."

Then he threaded six fish on a reed through their gills and gave them to Neyah. We thanked him very much for everything and set off for home.

It seemed a much, much longer walk than it had on the way out. I got tireder and tireder, and the loop-thong of my sandal broke, and every time I walked it flapped, and then a stone got in and cut my foot. Neyah knew how tired I was, but he said it was just one of those things that thinking about made worse. And I said, "Well, you haven't got a sore foot; and when I've got a sore foot it's the thing I think about."

And Neyah said, "If you fuss about a foot, you'll never be able to come with me when I'm a warrior. Warriors are always getting spears stuck into them, and arrows, and quite often they get hit by maceheads, but they're so brave they hardly notice it. They certainly don't make a fuss."

After that I would have gone on walking until my feet were worn right off. It must be much easier being born a boy, because then you don't have to keep on pretending to be brave to get taken on adventures: you just go anyway.

Then Neyah said, "I'll tell you a new story. Listen very hard and you'll forget about being tired.

"In the middle of a garden there was a very large and beautiful pool. It was tiled in turquoise colour, and fresh water always ran into it through a little stone channel and out again through a grid at the other end.

"In it there lived a lot of very, very fat contented fishes; and one little scarlet fish. The big fat fishes ate up all the flies and all the worms, and they took for themselves all the nicest shadow caves, which the lotus leaves made. But the poor little scarlet fish had very little to eat and no private place where he could sleep out of the hot sunshine. He couldn't spend his time eating or being lazy in the shade, so he had to do a lot of thinking to keep himself from going sad. And he explored every bit of the pool until he knew just how many tiles were on the walls, and which lotus bud was going to open next.

"The fat fishes got greedier and greedier, and the little scarlet fish got thinner and thinner, until one day, when he was swimming past the grating, he knew that he was thin enough to swim right through it. It was rather a struggle getting through, and he lost quite a lot of his scales doing it, but at last he was free. He swam down the water-channels until he got to the great river; and he swam on and on down the great river until he came to the sea. And there he found lots of things that were very beautiful, and lots of things that were very frightening.

"Once he saw a fish so big that it could have drunk the whole of his home pool for breakfast and still have been thirsty. The great fish was swimming along with his mouth open, collecting his breakfast, just like a fisherman drawing in his net, and the poor little scarlet fish prayed very hard to the god of fishes; and the god heard him in spite of his being in such a dark place. And the god made the big fish have hiccoughs; and he hiccoughed the little scarlet fish back into the sea again.

"Then the little scarlet fish found a beautiful palace of coral in the clear, green depths of the sea; and beautiful little fishes with blue and gold spots brought him the most lovely fat worms on mother-of-pearl plates. He enjoyed it so much that he might have stayed there the rest of his life; but he wanted to go back to his own home pool and tell the fat fishes all the exciting things they were missing by being too big to go through the grating. So he left the sea and swam back up the river. And on the way he had many more adventures; and some were nearly as beautiful as the palace of coral, and some were nearly as dangerous as being swallowed by the great big fish. And he swam and he swam up the long river, and up the water-channels, until he came to his own grating, and now he was so thin from all his adventures, that he got through it quite easily.

"He thought everybody would be very surprised to see him again, but nobody had even noticed he had been away. He swam up to a big, very fat fish, who was the king fish of the pool, and he said, 'Stop eating and blowing bubbles, and listen to me, you fat and foolish fish! I have come to tell you of all the wonderful things that happened to me on the other side of the grating; and I shall teach you to grow thin, so that you, too, may go upon the same journey and become as wise as I am.'

"The fat fish swam towards the grating, and when he saw the bars were so close together that not even one of his fins could go between them, he blew two bubbles, slowly and scornfully, and said, 'Silly little scarlet fish! Do not disturb my meditations with your foolish chatter. I am much wiser than you are, for I am king of all the fish. How could you have got through the grating when even I cannot put a fin through it?'

"And the big fat fish swam back to the shadows under the lotus leaves. The little scarlet fish was very sad that nobody would listen to him; so he slipped through the grating and swam back towards the sea.

''Quite soon afterwards there was a drought, and the water-channel ceased to flow; the fish pool got lower and lower, and the fat fishes got more and more frightened, until they lay gasping in the mud at the bottom of the pool. And then they died.

''But the little scarlet fish was living very, very happily in the coral palace under the sea.''

It was such a lovely story that I had forgotten about my sore foot. When Neyah had finished, we were at the edge of the vineyards. I took off my sandals and walked along the water-channels beside the vines, and it washed the rest of the soreness out of my foot.

Then I remembered Maata and how cross she was going to be. So I said, ''Neyah, do you think we should bury the fish or give them away to one of the gardeners, so Maata won't know where we've been?''

And Neyah said, ''No, it was such a good adventure I'm going to tell Father about it. And anyway, I want to send a present to the fisherman, because he was so nice to us—but we won't let Maata see us till we find Father.''

We saw him coming out of the room that leads to the Hall of Audience. He still had on his ceremonial beard, which he wore only when sitting in judgment. It was fixed to the head-dress by two straps, hidden by the side-pieces. He took off his head-dress and gave it to the attendant, and said he was going for a bathe in the pool, and that we could go with him. He wasn't surprised to see us, so Maata couldn't have told him about losing us.

When we showed him the fish and told him all about our adventure, he wasn't at all cross, although he did say we ought not to have gone out without telling somebody. And Neyah said, ''I would have told Maata, but she would only have told me not to go, and I didn't want to be rude and disobey her.''

And Father said we could eat the fish that evening. Then Neyah asked him if we could have a present for the boatman, and he said we could go to Nu-setees and ask him to make us something.

Nu-setees had a lovely little gold fish for wearing round the neck; and he scribed my name and Neyah's on it.

Next morning we put on our best clothes and Harka took us in a chariot down to the river to give Das his present. When he realised who we were, he would have knelt upon the ground before us. But Neyah told him we were all fishermen together, and I tied the fish round his neck.

CHAPTER FIVE

# Baby Lion

When I was six I wanted a baby lion.

I had a black hound-puppy and two pigeons and a quail with a broken leg. Maata said to me, "Lions are fit playmates for warriors, but not for children."

One of the gardeners, Pakeewi, was my friend. He had only one eye and he had lost three fingers on his left hand, fighting for my father in the south. He worked in the vegetable garden, which was some way from the palace. Maata had a brother who worked there also, being the Overseer of the Gardeners; and while she talked to him, Pakeewi would tell of his travels to Neyah and me. He told us many stories of our father's deeds in battle. But when we asked Father about them, he laughed and said that, if reality were like a figurine, Pakeewi's stories were like the giant shadow that a lamp would throw of it upon a wall.

There was a little mud-brick house where Pakeewi kept his garden tools, and here he let us keep the animals that we were not allowed to take home. I had a horned toad, and two white rats with pink eyes, and a little jerboa, which had big gentle eyes and sat on its hind legs when I talked to it. Neyah kept a young wild-cat, which he was trying to tame, in a box with wooden bars in front of it; and he had a yellow sand-snake. I thought he was very brave to play with it; and so did he.... "I want a baby lion! If I had a baby lion and it grew into a very big lion and it still slept in my room, no boy could say I wasn't brave because I wouldn't play with snakes."

Pakeewi had a son called Serten, who was one of the boys who ran with the hunting-dogs; I had told him how much I wanted a baby lion, and he had promised to bring me one next time a wild lioness had to be killed for getting savage and left a cub.

One day I went to see Serten, and I found him sitting on the edge of a stone trough, polishing a bit of harness. When he saw me he looked round to see that no one was watching, and then he beckoned me to follow him quietly. He took me to an empty stable, and there, in the far corner, I saw a big mongrel bitch suckling a tiny lion cub with her own two puppies. It was very small, and its eyes were still shut. I stroked its dappled, golden wool. And I made Serten promise to bring it to me when I was alone for the night.

When Maata was putting me to bed, she seemed to take even longer than usual over combing my hair; but at last she left me. Nothing happened for such a long time that I was sure Serten had forgotten his promise. Then I heard a soft tapping on the shutter. I ran over to the window and saw Serten with the lion puppy in his arms. He handed it up to me and it whimpered a little; but it was very sleepy, and soon it curled up beside me under the warm cover of my bed.

When all was quiet, I did our secret whistle for Neyah. I must have woken him, for he came in looking very sleepy and rather cross. "Neyah, I've got a lion in my bed."

"Don't be silly, you're wide awake."

"It's not a dream-lion, it's a down-here lion." He still didn't believe me, so I pulled the cover off and showed it to him.

And he said, "Where *did* you get it?"

I told him; and then I said, "It's very brave of me to like lions sleeping on my bed!"

"Well, it's only a very little lion."

"It'll soon be a very big lion, and it will bite anyone who's ever horrid to me."

"They won't let you keep it when it's got its real teeth."

"Well, your snakes haven't got any sting."

And Neyah said, "That only makes you twice as cowardly not to touch them." And I got so angry, I cried.

Then Neyah was very nice and said he was sure it was a very fierce lion to anyone but me. And he sat on my bed and told me a story about a monkey and a crocodile until I went to sleep.

And this was the story of the monkey and the crocodile:

Long, long ago there was a family of monkeys who lived at the top of a tall tree in the middle of a forest. There was a mother monkey and a father monkey, two little girl monkeys and a little boy monkey. The two little girl monkeys were very good, and listened to all their mother told them: of how to swing by their tails, and how to keep to the thin branches, which wouldn't bear the weight of any dangerous animal that might hurt them. She taught them what fruit to eat, and what things would make them sick, and how to comb their fur with their fingers so that their coats should be smooth and tidy.

But the little boy monkey wouldn't listen to her, for he thought he was the cleverest monkey in the whole forest. He was too grand to play with his sisters, and he used to go for walks by himself on the tops of the trees.

One day, in the middle of the forest, he found a big clearing where there lived a lot of human beings. He thought they must be a very royal sort of monkey that he had never heard of before, and he said to himself, "These are my proper companions, and I will try to be just like them."

He saw that they hadn't got any tails, so he put his own tail over his arm as though he were carrying something. But because he was used to having it to climb with, he often fell out of trees and bumped himself quite badly. But that didn't teach him anything. And he saw, also, that the human beings had no fur on their bodies, and he tried to pluck out his coat so as to look more like them. But he made himself so sore, and the bare patches felt so cold, that he stopped doing that.

Then one day he saw one of the human beings alone in the forest. And he went up to him and said, "I should like to join your tribe of monkeys."

Now the human being was a very wise man, who knew the speech of animals, and he said, "We are not monkeys, we are men."

And the monkey said, "Well, I want to be a man too."

And the wise man said to him, "The time will come when all the animals in the forest will be men. Do not be impatient. When your time is ready you shall leave the companionship of monkeys and know the loneliness of man. Learn all there is to be learned as a monkey, and in so doing you will learn wisdom more speedily. And stop carrying your tail over your arm! If you do not use what the Gods have given you, one day you shall weep the lack of it."

This made the monkey very cross, for he still thought that men were a very special tribe of monkeys who considered themselves too grand to play with him—just as he was too grand to play with his sisters. And he chattered very rudely at the wise man and ran away into the forest.

One day he was walking by the river—still carrying his tail over his arm—and he saw a man paddling a raft, and he said to himself, "That same thing will I do also, and then at last they will believe I am their sort of monkey." In the water he saw what he thought was a log of wood, and he jumped on to it. It started to move along the water, and he felt very grand and important.

Suddenly the log of wood opened two very wicked eyes and looked at him. And he knew it for a crocodile. He was so frightened that he jumped into the water and swam away very fast.

But, just as he reached the bank, the crocodile bit his tail—right off!

And as he walked home to his mother all the monkeys, whom he had been too proud to play with, pointed and laughed and chattered at him. Nobody was at all sorry for him, except his mother, who of course still loved him in spite of his horridness.

Soon after, there was a great storm, and the tree they lived in swayed about so fiercely that the poor monkey who hadn't got a tail to hold on with fell off on to his head and was killed.

And before a year had passed, he was born again to the same mother. He learned to swing by his tail quicker than any child she had ever known; and he listened to everything she told him; and he became the nicest and friendliest monkey in all the forest.

For now he knew that wisdom and happiness can only be found by learning that which the wise Gods have arranged for one to be taught.

CHAPTER SIX

# ZEB THE LION BOY

I called my lion cub 'Natee', and until he was a year old he was allowed to sleep in my room on a mattress at the foot of my bed. Then my father decided he must be kept with the other tame lions where they lived in the court next to the hunting-dogs, but I was sure I could persuade him to let him stay with me.

I had been down by the marsh with Neyah. Very early

that morning he had woken me to tell me that I could go swan shooting with him.

We crept past Maata's window, in case she should hear us, and beyond the garden we found three boys, who were friends of Neyah's waiting for us. We had bow-cases slung over our shoulders, and little arrows for wild-fowl, in bark quivers. It was still dark, with a faint line of light on the horizon. When we got to the marsh we crawled through the reeds until we came to the lake. Then we lay on the damp earth at the edge of the shallow water, waiting for the birds to return from feeding.

It was getting light when we heard the curious creaking noise that wild swans make with their wings. It was a flight of about thirty, shaped like an arrowhead, and as they flew over us, we loosed our arrows at them. One dropped a tuft of feathers, but flew on unharmed.

Then we heard voices and knew it was the fowlers coming to search their snares, so we crept away very quietly. We didn't want to be seen, because we had promised not to go out without telling our attendants.

When I got back I found that Natee was not in my room, so I went to the lion court to see if he was there. No one was about. I unbolted the door of the courtyard and saw Natee asleep in the sun with a young lioness of about the same age as himself. I called him, and he swung across the court to me. One of the lion boys heard me; he came running up and said that Natee was to stay in the court, for he had been given orders that I was not to take him out unless I had somebody with me. I took Natee by the collar and started to lead him away, but the boy stood in the gateway and would not let me pass.

I ordered him out of my way, but he would not move. I saw a heavy whip of plaited hide lying on a bench by the wall, and I picked it up and lashed the boy again and again across the face and shoulders. He didn't cry out; he just stood there, looking at me. I was so angry that nothing existed for me but the boy standing in front of me and the weals the whip was cutting across his face and shoulders.

Then Natee sprang forward and knocked the boy down. Natee wasn't angry, but he was growling, and there was blood all down the boy's arm where Natee had mouthed him roughly; but the boy was frightened and lay on the ground, so I called to Natee and he followed me. Then I took him by the collar and led him to my room.

Natee was very glad to be back with me. I shut him in my room while I went to bathe, and when I got back he had chewed another hole in my mattress and pulled some of the feathers out; and he had gnawed the leg off my bed, which was a pity, because it was a very nice bed, and the legs of it were like antelopes' legs, with little gilt hooves. I loved Natee very much, but I scolded him sternly. He didn't mind at all, and licked my arm affectionately with his rough tongue.

Someone came to the door, which I had bolted, and said that my father wished to see me at once in the room where he set his seal.

He was looking at a papyrus roll when I went in. He had just come from giving audience and still wore ceremonial dress; and the Flail was on the table by his hand. When he saw me he did not smile; he looked like a statue, as if he was sitting in judgment. He said, "A whip in the hand of one of the Royal House is a symbol of justice. In your hand it was an instrument of injustice and of cowardice; for you struck one who was but showing his loyalty to Pharaoh and obeying the orders of your father. Moreover, you have injured a boy who, because of his rank and yours, could not strike back. To strike such a one is the action of an arrogant coward and is unworthy of our tradition. If you were a man, or in fact, if you were not a young girl-child, I should order you to be whipped. Then, had you done this wilfully, you would gain a just reward; and had you done it through ignorance, you would gain an experience that would remind you that he who raises a lash unjustly shall have weals upon his own back. As you are but a child, I hope that the flail of my anger will be sufficient to teach you this law."

It was the first time I had realised what I had done; and I thought how brave the boy had been, and how he had never moved all the time I was hitting him. I *so* wished I wasn't a girl, and that I could be beaten instead of seeing my father so cold and stern and far away. I tried to make myself angry, so that I shouldn't cry....I'm not a coward! I'll show him I'm not...and I put my wrist in my mouth and bit it until the blood ran through my teeth. It was very difficult to do, because it hurt, a lot! Then I held out my wrist with the blood on it and said, "That's quite as much as Natee bit the boy, and I'll go and tell him he can hit me back without remembering who I am, or that I'm a girl. I'm *not* a coward."

Then I turned and ran out of the room.

When I got back to my room Natee was gone. I bolted the door and lay face downwards on my bed, and I cried and I cried and I cried, and my mouth got full of feathers. Then I heard a tapping on the door, and I thought it was Neyah pretending to be Father. Neyah was the only person I didn't mind crying in front of, because he said it was only like having a stomach-ache and nothing to be ashamed of. So I unbolted the door. But it was not Neyah; it was my father. He had taken off his head-dress and his beard, and he was smiling. He took me in his arms and sat down on the bed with me on his lap. He never said anything about all the feathers, or about my bed being so rickety with its chewed leg. I was so relieved that he didn't hate me that I couldn't help crying three tears on his bare shoulder; and when I licked them off again, they tasted very salty.

Then he told me he had a much better idea about how to make the Scales true again between me and the lion boy. He said that although they could be adjusted by the lion boy hitting me, a much better adjustment could be made by my trying to undo the hurt of the whip. And he said that he had a special ointment that would take the pain out of the weals, and that he also would heal them. So I blew my nose very hard and washed my face in cold water, and then we went down to the court of the attendants. The boy, who was called Zeb, was lying on a bench. First I told him that I knew I had been wrong, and I asked him to forgive me. And Zeb said it didn't matter at all and the weals didn't hurt. I said, "Zeb, I'm very, very sorry." And he went down on one knee and took my hands; he held the backs of them against his eyes and said, "I will serve you truly with all my heart until I die." And my father told him that henceforward he should be one of my own attendants.

Then my father showed me how to put the ointment on his weals. And for five days I tended Zeb, until the weals had quite gone.

I explained to my father that I had lashed Zeb unthinkingly, because I was so angry, that I could think of nothing except that he stood in my way. It was when I was walking with him by the marsh; Shamba, his favourite lioness, who was more clever than any hunting-dog, was with us. My father said, "Sekeeta, your temper should be controlled by your will, as Shamba is controlled by mine. Trained anger, like a trained lion, is a faithful protector and a powerful weapon. With controlled anger a man can smite a wrong-doer as though he lashed him with a flail. And the fear of such anger is a protection for the weak against those who might hurt them if they did not fear it, just as no one would dare attack a month-old child if it were under Shamba's protection. But he whose temper is unmastered is like a child that is chained to a maddened he-goat. He must follow where it leads; through village middens, and through swamps, and even into a cage of wild leopards that would tear them both to pieces. And so, Sekeeta, remember: anger beneath your will is a flail in your hand, but uncontrolled anger is a lash upon your shoulders."

CHAPTER SEVEN

# SEERS IN JUDGMENT

Often Neyah would sit beside my father when he gave judgment, to prepare him for the time when, at the age of fourteen, he would be his co-ruler. Sometimes I would go too, so that I also might learn of his justice.

Ptah-kefer, who was one of the chief officials of the Royal Household, sat on the left side of the Hall of Audience, between the throne of Pharaoh and the table of the scribes. Being a seer priest of the highest grade of initiation, he wore the double scarlet feather, which were the Feathers of Maat, Goddess of Truth, meaning that from his body he could see two truths, the truth of Earth and the truth of the spirit.

Sometimes in his judgments my father would use Shamba, his lioness, in what he used to call 'the ordeal by lion.' He would tell a man whose heart he was weighing to walk up the room and put his hand in Shamba's mouth; and he would tell him that, if he were pure in heart, the lioness would mouth him gently, but that, if he were guilty, then she would crush his arm to pulp. If the man were innocent, he would approach Shamba, and her teeth would be so gentle that they would not have marked the feathers of a bird. And the innocent man would depart with yet another story to tell of the wisdom of Pharaoh, saying that it was so great that even the lioness at his feet was bathed in his glory and could weigh hearts as wisely as Tahuti. But if the man were guilty, before he reached Shamba my father would raise the Flail and pronounce judgment upon him. Neyah and I would keep our faces as calm as statues, although we knew that when Father had told Shamba to be at peace, if Set walked on Earth she would have been gentle with him; and when he had told her to attack, she would have torn out the throat of the great Ptah himself.

Once Father said to us: "Wise rulers know that many of their people are but children, although they may have the bodies of men; so he treats them as children, in ways that are within their understanding, so that they are obedient and content."

I asked him how he was always sure when a man had nothing to fear from Shamba. And he told me that Ptah-kefer watched the man as he walked up the room; and if he were afraid, then Ptah-kefer moved the ring on his finger. But my father said that if we wanted to know why he moved the ring, we had better ask him ourselves.

And Ptah-kefer told us, "With our earth eyes we cannot see patience, or anger, or jealousy, or greed; we can only see the reactions of them. But if I look at a man with the eyes of my spirit, I can see his thoughts, perhaps I should say his emotions, as colour; and the darker the colour, the more clouded he is by Earth; and the paler the colour, the nearer he is to the source of light, to which one day we must all attain.

"Jealousy and greed I see as a dull dark green; but true sympathy, which is compassion, is the pale green of the sky before dawn. Wisdom is a pale clear yellow, like sunshine on a white wall; deceit, and lust for riches, are clay-coloured, like the mud from which bricks are baked. And in the same way every kind of emotion has its special shade, and those that are most often experienced determine the colour of the light that shines from each one of us. But fear clouds the colours with a dirty grey, like oily smoke; and fierce impatience flecks them with a red, like little drops of blood. There are many other signs like these, by which I can judge a man; and if one walks toward Shamba with no hidden fear, then do I know that he has spoken truth."

I said, "But suppose the man was very silly and didn't like lions, the same as I don't like even very small and harmless snakes?"

"None who are not men of evil fear the justice of Pharaoh;

for they know that his Flail is but to protect them and the lion at his feet is part of his justice. He that would fear Pharaoh or Shamba must fear his own heart."

"Well, suppose he was a guilty man but he was very fond of lions, as I am, and he had one like Natee, then he couldn't be frightened of other people's tame lions."

"There are other ways by which I could tell a man guilty. Say, for instance, that two men disputed about a piece of land. If the colour of one man was heavy with greed, and the other had the turquoise blue of the poet or sculptor, and so much of it that I knew he thought too little of riches and might let his children go hungry and his wife patch her only tunic while he pondered on the small embellishments of Earth, then I would know that if he claimed the land, it was beause it was rightfully his, and not the greed of possessions.

"But it is seldom that your father needs my sight; for, of his wisdom and understanding, he can read the hearts of men; and though he sees not the colour of their thoughts, to him their characters are as clear as though he saw them written on a scroll.

"Long ago, when this earth was new, a wise man said, 'Let thy light so shine forth, that wheresoever thou goest, even if it be to the Caverns of the Underworld, those who are with thee shall fear no darkness, for thou shalt light them upon their journey.' And this light he talked of is the self-same light that shines from all of us, of which I have told you. When our feet have reached the end of our earth journey, then will the colours of Earth have been transmuted into the whiteness of pure light. But in this whiteness is all pure colour; and in it there are the colours of the three Wards of Earth: the pale clear yellow of Wisdom, which is all experience; the gentle green of Compassion, which is perfect understanding; the true scarlet of the Warriors of Maat, which is courage that is beyond fear."

CHAPTER EIGHT

# the legend of creation

One day I questioned Ptah-kefer about the stars, and he said, "There are other worlds like ours, numberless as the drops of water in the river. To try to conceive of such an immensity is foolish: for he that tries to stare the secrets from the sun grows blind and cannot see even what is beneath his hand."

Then he told me the Legend of Creation.

Long, long ago the Gods of Gods, who dwell so far ahead of us that we cannot conceive a thousandth part of their greatness, sent for their servant Ptah. And they gave him a bowl of Life, which, though he emptied it, was always full; and they told him that he must teach this Life how to gain wisdom, until at last it should become the pure flame of spirit with all experience. And they appointed him the overlord of Earth, a place of insentient sand and lifeless rock.

Then throughout Earth Ptah scattered Life, and the mountains began to feel the sun that scorched their sides, and the valleys knew the deep coldness of a winter night. And the time came when this Life returned to Ptah; and from his bowl he heard a faint voice, which said, "Now we know something of heat and cold. Let us go on."

Then Ptah clothed the hills with trees, and the valleys he covered with young grass and flowers; and into them he poured his bowl. And Life learned how plants thrust their roots through the ground in search of strength to unfurl their blossoms to the sun; how some clasped the rocks with tendrilled vines, and others threw their shade beside the lake. But all that they gained they shared among themselves, so that a blade of grass knew how great winds stir the branches of a tree, and the fierce cactus shared with the gentle moss its tenderness.

Then once more the bowl was filled by Life returning. Now it spoke with a stronger voice, and said, "We have learned our lessons through the plants; now we want bodies in which we can move and seek our destiny more speedily."

Then Ptah made animals upon Earth. First, simple ones like worms and snails; and then the bodies of hares and antelopes, of lions and zebras, singing-birds and fish.

Then again Life returned, and said, "Now we are wise; we can cross a desert at night; we can find water and shelter for ourselves; we have wandered far over Earth and learned a great diversity of things. Make us bodies worthy of ourselves."

And Ptah answered them, and said, "I have sent you forth into rocks, and into plants, and into animals. You have returned to me sharing one another's memory and experience, and sharing also the friendliness of growing things, which as animals you still have, though long to lose. Now I will make you bodies like my own, and for the first time you shall say, 'I am'; and in saying this must say, 'I am alone'. No longer can I lead you on your way. Now you must start upon a long journey, which does not end until you can greet me, not as your creator but as your brother."

And Life said, "We demand this chance, this right, to journey to your brotherhood."

Then Ptah created man. And man walked upon Earth, and he rejoiced in it. The grassy valleys were soft beneath his feet; his nostrils delighted in the scent of flowers, and the taste of fruits was pleasant on his tongue. While in hot noons he rested in the shade, gazelles would come and nuzzle in his hand; lions would walk with him beside cool streams; and he would test his fleetness with the deer.

But the words of Ptah kept echoing in his heart, saying "I am; I am alone," until his loneliness made him afraid. And he left the gentle places of Earth and ran despairingly in search of one to end his solitude, and in his anguish he cried upon the Gods.

And the great Min heard him and came down to Earth. Then he caused man to fall into a sleep, and while he slept, Min said, "No longer shall you walk in loneliness....Now you are man and woman, and you shall go upon your journey together. And the two of you I give the power, of your own bodies, to make others, which in their turn shall house the Life of Ptah. And when you see your children, you shall cherish them, even as your creator has cherished you."

And of each animal, also, he made a pair. And now more swiftly did all progress, with young to feed and shelter and protect. For even the plants shared in this godliness, and they thrust their roots deeper beneath the ground in search of water for their ripening seed.

In those early days all living things knew of their kinship, and on a cold night a little hare would lie for warmth against a mighty lion, and men were grateful to the plants and trees that sheltered them and gave them of their fruits.

For in those vanished days, when Earth was young, none had forgotten their creator.

CHAPTER NINE

# the Body

I was looking for Neyah one day, and I found him with my father in the room where the great rolls of papyrus are kept, on which the scribes record those things that are the fruits of wisdom; some were written many years ago, and some were of our own time. Wisdom knows neither youth nor age, for through all time it is the same.

Father was showing Neyah one of the new scrolls of Zertar. Zertar lived in the palace, where he recorded all that had been found out about the body of man, so that they who came after might learn how to care for it and house their spirits graciously.

On the papyrus there was a picture of a man without his skin on; it was painted in pale brown, and from the top of the skull red lines radiated throughout every part of his body.

Father was explaining that in the body there were little paths that carried feeling to the commander of the body, which was situated in the head; and that this was important knowledge: for if one of these paths was injured, a man might feel pain in his fingers while the injury was really in his arm. And this knowledge helped both healers-with-herbs and healers-with-the-knife when they had no seer to guide them. He said, "This outermost part of ourselves, although it is a part through which we gain experience, is to our real self only as the clothes we wear are to our body. It is called the *khat*, and it is written as a stranded fish: for when the spirit is joined to the body, the body is like a fish swimming in the river; but when the spirit is away from the body in sleep, the body is as helpless as a fish stranded on the bank."

And I asked, "When there are so many seers, why do you have to make pictures of the insides of people?"

"Although in the Royal City there is no lack of seers, there are always very few men who can go through the great ordeals necessary to attain this power; and even at the present time there are many people in Kam who might be hurt or ill where there is no seer. There are many countries where there are no seers or healers to succour the injured and the sick, where the priests are without power and the temples are not training-places. For such people—although it would not be as good as if they had seers—accurate knowledge of the working of bodies is of great value."

I was still looking at the picture, and I saw that in the top of the head, where the red lines sprang from, there was a tiny man, delicately drawn. I pointed to it, and said, "Have we really got a little copy of ourselves inside our heads, or is that just a way of writing?"

And Father said, "Yes, all human beings and animals have it. It is through this that the commands of the spirit are translated to the body. It cannot be seen except by a seer; if Ptah-kefer looked with the eyes of his spirit at this part of a man who was about to raise his arm, then, a flash of time before the earth arm was raised, he would see it being done by the arm of what is called the *ka-ibis*.

"Do you remember the soldier from the garrison of Na-Kish who was brought here to the temple? His captain sent him down in one of the empty grain boats. He had seen his wife seized and killed by a crocodile. The shock was so terrible that he became dumb, and he was sent here to see if we could cure him. Now this is what had happened to him: so great had been his fear and horror, that the force of his emotions ordering his body had injured his *ka-ibis*. And, just as a man whose shoulder muscles are torn cannot throw a spear, the *ka-ibis* could not translate the orders of this man's spirit to the speaking muscles of his throat, and he became dumb. But when Ptah-kefer saw what was wrong, the *ka-ibis* was strengthened with healing, until it was once more able to obey its orders.

"The *ka-ibis* is written as a man walking, an action which is an example of a man obeying his spirit through the channel of the *ka-ibis;* and sometimes it is written just as two legs, which means, as the scribe has taught you, 'to go' or 'to travel'.

"When the people of Athlanta first came to Kam they found the ibis; and they said that its black and white feathers symbolized the light of wisdom piercing the darkness of ignorance. And the cry of the ibis is 'Ah'; and they said, 'Here is a bird which speaks nothing but wisdom, and he that speaks nothing but wisdom speaks nothing but truth.' Now in the old land the great Tahuti, the God of Wisdom, the Weigher of Hearts, was always symbolized as the balanced scales, the same scales that you see in the places of justice in Kam to-day. Later the people called him Thoth, and they made statues of him with the head of an ibis; and he became known as the Keeper of the Great Records. For they said, 'As the ibis speaks only of truth, which is wisdom, so does Thoth record only those things that are permanent, which are wisdom and truth.' And so he has come to be known as the God of Scribes. To-day there are many people who have forgotten that Tahuti and Thoth are one god.

"And just as a scribe puts his thoughts into writing signs, so does this little man in the head turn thoughts into actions. And because it belongs to a part of us that, though it dies with the body, cannot be seen with earth eyes, as does the *ka*, we call it the *ka-ibis*."

Neyah had told me what the *ka* part of ourselves was, but I wasn't sure if I quite understood, so I asked Father to explain it.

"In the body there are many parts which make use of the things of Earth by which we live; our lungs purify us with the air we breathe; our bowels and stomach and many other organs transform our food and drink into fresh blood, which our heart pumps through us. But we have a greater need, which none of these can give us, and that need is life, that life which is everywhere, and which you have heard me call 'the life of Ptah.' It is too fine to contact the *khat*, and so we have a finer replica of ourselves, which is a network, like thousands of invisible veins; and through these channels flows this life of Ptah, without which we would die. This part of ourselves is called the *ka*, which means 'gatherer of life'. It cannot be seen by earth eyes, yet so important is it, that if these channels are injured and cannot carry life, then the body will die. Only when we sleep can the *ka* re-store itself with life—and that is why we can live longer without food than without sleep.

"The *ka* is written as two upstretched arms rising from a straight line. The line used to mean 'the horizon' and has come to mean 'Earth'; the upstretched arms with open hands symbolize one who is reaching upwards and gathering the life of Ptah. Hundreds of years ago there was a circle between and above the hands, symbolizing the source of life. But now we use the simpler form.''

CHAPTER TEN

# the healer with herbs

When my father became Pharaoh, twelve years before the death of the great Meniss, there was little knowledge in Kam of dealing with herbs. But under his guidance much old knowledge was remembered and much that was new was added to the store.

The people of the Land of Gold had much of the old knowledge of herbs, and many plants that were strange to our country were brought back from there by my father. Travellers from distant lands would bring him rare plants, for which he often gave three times their weight in gold. Although he loved flowers and trees, in the private garden that adjoined his own apartments there were only those plants that had healing virtue to men or animals. The leaves of some of them were dried, then boiled in water, and the liquid would cool fevers; some had roots that were pounded into dust and on the tongue would cure a disordered bowel; and there were some from which ointments were made to cure sores, or to heal the angry flesh round wounds. The bark of a low shrub with yellow flowers was made into a lotion for the eyes. There were tall poppies with crinkled, silky petals, from whose seeds a draught was made, which drowsily soothed pain; and a rare plant with a fleshy stalk, whose juice on linen, bandaged round the eyes, would take away the yellow crust that destroys sight.

Once my father said to me—it was after the stele had been erected which told of the building of the palace—"If far in the future men shall think of me, I hope that I shall be remembered, not as a warrior or as a builder, but as a man who healed with herbs. For it is greater to make a blind man see the stars again than to build mightily in stone."

He would often tell us that plants had much to teach us. "Mankind is often foolish: warriors throw down the sword to drive the plough; and fields remain untilled because the ploughman tries to paint frescoes on the cowshed wall; and the draughtsman throws away his reed, wishing to be the bearer of a sword. But plants are wiser; for they, in their several ways, gain each experience in its turn: the violet does not cringe under its leaves because it has no thorns upon its stalk; the verbena does not try to flower like the convolvulus, but it is content to yield refreshing scent from the rough greenness of its simple leaves."

One day we found Father kneeling beside one of his plants; its leaves were limp, and the flower-buds drooped to the ground. He was pointing his fingers at it as if he were healing a sick person, and when he had finished we asked him what he was doing.

And he told us, "This plant was dying for lack of life. Although the bodies of men and of animals collect new life when they are empty and the spirit has left them in sleep, plants cannot sleep or gather new life for themselves. And so Ptah made for each plant a little spirit to look after it, which does for the plant what our *ka* does for our body. These little plant-spirits take different forms, but all of them spin very fast round and round, faster than you can whirl a top with a cord." And he reminded us of the time we had seen a curious gust of wind, which had drawn up sand and little bits of stick, sucking them towards itself. "So does a plant-spirit collect life with which to feed the plant under its protection. The spirit of this plant was weak and could not spin, so, being a healer priest, I gathered life—the life of Ptah—and, by my will, drove it to where my fingers pointed. And now the little plant-spirit is once more strong enough to do its work.''

CHAPTER ELEVEN

# seership

Neyah's wild-cat never got tame, even after two years. He got a mate for it so it shouldn't be lonely, and had a special house built for it, which had a long run with grass and trees to make it feel natural. I don't know why Neyah was so fond of it. He used to spend hours trying to teach it to be a reliable friend. He always fed it himself, and at last it seemed really pleased to see him, and used to come running up to the gate when he called. But one day, for no reason except that it must have been feeling in a specially bad temper, the wild-cat gave him a terribly deep bite in the calf of his leg. Luckily Serten was cleaning out the run at the time, and he drove it off with a rake.

Neyah always hated being bothered when he had hurt himself, but this time he couldn't keep it private, for he could hardly walk, and blood was streaming down his leg. He went and told Father about it, because he knew Maata would fuss and would be sure to say, "I've told you a thousand times that horrid animal would turn on you one day.'' He didn't want to tell Mother, because seeing us hurt always made her anxious, although she never said so. Father was perfect when you had hurt yourself. He made me feel as if we were two warriors comparing wounds after a battle, so even if I had fallen out of a tree from sheer clumsiness, I would pretend I'd been wounded in a chariot charge. We used to make up imaginary stories about what we had done in battle; and I got so interested that there was no need to be brave.

When Father saw Neyah's leg, he sent for Ptah-kefer, who looked at it with the eyes of spirit. He said that a muscle was torn, but if it were healed twice a day, it would be well in about fifteen days. Father didn't send for a healer priest, but he drove the life of Ptah into Neyah's wound himself; then he put on an ointment and bandaged the leg with charged linen.

Neyah couldn't walk for several days. Ptah-kefer used to look at his leg every morning to see how it was getting on; and he often stayed and talked to us. He was very understanding with children, although he had none of his own. He was skilled at carving, and quite often he would help Neyah make things. Once he mended Neyah's model boat for me, when I had borrowed it after Neyah had told me not to, and I had broken it.

One day, when his leg was almost healed, Neyah asked him, "How can you see the wound in my leg when it is bandaged and you have your hand over your eyes? I know it's your seer's sight, but I don't quite understand how it works."

And Ptah-kefer answered, "I don't look at the body, I look at its life-bearing counterpart...."

And I said, "You mean the *ka*, the one that's written with two upstretched arms and a horizon?" Neyah frowned at me for interrupting. Ptah-kefer went on, "On Earth there is no stillness. Everything you can see has colour and is reflecting rays of light; some things throw the rays back faster than others do." He reached for the *checka* ball, with which I had been playing. "Let us pretend that this ball is a ray of light, and that that wall is the thing it is thrown against. Now if the wall were of stone, it would throw the ball right back to us: and that is as if a ray of light shone upon something that reflected it at the speed we call violet, for violet reflects light the fastest of all colours. If that wall were of wet mud, the ball would fall in the flower-bed at its foot: and that is as if a ray of light were reflected from something red, for red reflects light the slowest of all colours.

"Anything that reflects light faster than violet, our earth eyes cannot see. Now if that wall were of the substance of the *ka* it would throw the ball back right over the palace and across the vineyard, for the speed of light reflected from the *ka* is that much faster in comparison with anything that ordinary earth sight can see.

"Now when I am looking at a man's *ka* with the eyes of the spirit, I cover my eyes with my hand so that the slow light, which we know as colour, is cut off, and then with my trained sight I can look upon the swiftness of the *ka,* and yet it seems to be as still as a sleeping man, because my seer's sight travels at the same speed—perhaps I am not explaining clearly what I mean?"

Neyah said, "Oh, I understand. It's like this, isn't it? If I was looking out of the window and a cow walked past, I couldn't help seeing it, because it would be going at an ordinary speed; but if an arrow from a very strong bow went past, it would be going so quickly that I might not notice it—just as sometimes it's very difficult to see a dragon-fly moving...."

I interrupted, "If I'm looking through a doorway and a chariot gallops past, I can hardly see it, because it's going so quickly; but if there are two people galloping in two chariots abreast, they can see each other as clearly as if they were both standing still. And a seer just travels at the same speed as whatever he is looking at."

I think Ptah-kefer was pleased I was so good at understanding things. I wondered if he ever got impatient when people wouldn't listen to his wisdom and I said, "When people won't believe the truth, don't you want to do a big magic before them, so that they must realise their ignorance?"

Ptah-kefer laughed and said, "If you see a man who is starving, it is well to give him food. But if he refuses to eat of it thinking it is poisoned, do not force it between his teeth;

for food thus given may choke him instead of ending his hunger.

"And do not give a large bowl of food to a starving one, or he may gulp it too quickly and then suffer pain and say, 'That was a most grievous diet. In future I must avoid it.' Rather should you feed him gradually, a little at a time; and he must have milk before he is ready for strong meat. Then he will have great benefit from what you give him and will long for more with which to build his strength."

Then Ptah-kefer had to leave us, for it was the hour of audience. And I said to Neyah, "That shows it's no good trying to explain things to people who don't want to listen. Because in that story the food meant teaching, and the hungry man was an ignorant one."

And Neyah said, "Sekeeta, I'm very glad you realise that, because it's so very obviously true!"

I thought he was being grand and teasing me, but I wasn't quite sure, so I said, "Let's go off and have a bathe." And so we did.

CHAPTER TWELVE

# the soul

There was a stone pavilion at the end of my father's garden of herbs. It was open on one side, where the roof was supported by two fluted pillars. A record of all the plants in the garden was carved on its walls, and there were still many blank spaces, which would one day be filled. On the south wall were all those plants whose healing value lies in their leaves; on the east wall those that hold it in their flowers and seeds; and on the west wall those that hold it in their roots.

I went there one morning and found Neyah talking to the

stone-carver, who was cutting along the lines that had been drawn on the stone wall by a scribe under my father's direction. The scribe had drawn in black, and my father had corrected his drawing in two places with a red line.

Neyah had borrowed some tools from the carver and was practising on a thin piece of broken stone. I told him that I didn't think he was doing very well, and he said I could try and see if I could do it any better. I think I might have done, but I hit my finger and made it bleed; so I gave it back to Neyah. It was much more difficult than it looked. Neyah was so busy with his carving that he wouldn't talk to me. So without his noticing I worked his hair into little plaits at the back. He would probably be angry when he found out, but that would be much less dull than not being talked to. Then I heard voices. Neyah and I never teased each other except when we were alone, so I said, "Quick, Neyah run your fingers through your hair."

It was my father with Zertar. The carver asked my father if he had expressed the thought that he wished to be carved.

When they had finished discussing the carvings, we went with Father to the vineyard, where the red grapes were being harvested. The men picking them wore white loin-cloths, and the women coarse linen tunics, fastened on the left shoulder. When the tall rush baskets were filled, the women carried them on their heads to the wine-vats, where the grapes were tipped into a circular stone trough. Then they were crushed by a wooden roller, joined to a beam and pushed round by two white oxen. The vintagers were making wine for the palace, so the rollers were light and pressed out only the finest of the juice.

Then we went down the avenue of pomegranates to the orchard, where we sat in the shade of an old fig tree. I asked Father to tell us a story about something. And he said, "I will tell you about yourselves, for to 'know thyself' is of great importance. For only when a man can say, 'I know what I am, what I have, and what I have not', can he seek wisely for what he needs before his journey can be completed.

"I have told you about the body you live in—how it is made up of the *khat* and the *ka-ibis* and the *ka*. When you die this body returns to dust. Now that which wears this body is usually spoken of as the spirit, but really there are two parts of it: the soul which we need only as long as we must return to Earth; and the spirit, which is as enduring as time.

"Soul and spirit have five divisions, or, if you like, five attributes, just as the body has five senses. The first of these attributes is that with which we experience emotions, and with which we feel. If I touched you lightly while you were asleep, you would not feel it, because that part of you with which you feel is absent. But if your body is hurt while you are asleep, it calls for the protection of your spirit, and you awake. If the pain continues after you return, you know what has awakened you; but if the touch was so brief and gentle that the nerves of your body no longer recorded it when you have returned, then you would not know what had awakened you.

"To weep when you are unhappy is your body's way of expressing the emotion that you are experiencing in that part of your soul that is call the *ba*.

"When you are in your body your emotions are much less keen than when you are free of it. When Natee licks your bare hand you feel the roughness of his tongue; but if you wore a thick glove, you would feel it much less. When your body is awake it muffles feeling, just as your glove muffles the feeling of Natee's tongue on your hand."

And I said, "That must be why fear in a dream is far worse than anything you can ever be frightened of on Earth."

He nodded and went on, "Do you remember that story Pakeewi told you about himself and the two Nubians? How once, when he was with me in the Land of Gold, he got so angry with two Nubians, that, although he was only a little man, he knocked their heads together until they fell down as though dead. Afterwards Pakeewi admitted to you very shamefacedly that he had been full of beer. Well, too much beer or wine strips off that glove, so that the emotions are left naked; and anger can then be felt so strongly that it can make a little man act as though he were in the body of a giant.

"On that same expedition I was surrounded by the enemy, who numbered more than five hundred, and with me I had but seventy men. And with me also there was a Horus priest, and of his power he caused our warriors to know courage unmuffled by their bodies, so that they fought like warrior gods and fell upon the enemy, many of whom they killed, and the rest dropped their weapons and fled in terror.

"That is why the soldiers of our southern garrison sing together before battle; for it makes their bodies sit lightly upon them, and they fight with the strength of ten men to one sword."

And Neyah asked, "If your enemies in the Land of Gold had sung before battle, could the Horus priest still have made your seventy vanquish their five hundred?"

"He would have used a different magic. He would have held our enemies to their bodies, so that they were heavy with Earth. Then they would not have had the singleness of purpose that they had before; they would have known fear; they would have wondered why they were fighting, and what they were fighting for, and all those things which, though wise in their season, do not win battles.

"The *ba* is written sometimes as a winged human head, which is the older form, and sometimes as a human-faced bird. For the *ka-ibis* is the highest part of the body and it is in the head, and the *ba* is the first part of us that is conscious of leaving Earth and of being 'winged'.

"The *ba* is the first part of the soul; and the second part is that attribute you use when thinking of things of form, which are those things you know of through the five earth senses. With this attribute you think of a sunset, or of a lion; of the taste of baked quail; of the sound of a harp; of the smooth linen of your bed when you are tired; and of the smell of the bean-fields beside the river at noon. With this faculty also, you decide what words to speak or write; in what shape to carve or build; and when is the exact moment to speed an arrow to a flying bird.

"There is nothing fashioned by man that is not first fashioned by his thoughts; just as there is no living thing on Earth that has not first been born of the spirit of one of the Great Artificers. When the carver asked me if he had expressed my thought, he knew that there was a clear image in my mind of what I wished to be created in stone; and he hoped that he had translated it accurately. Before Neyah carves a boat, he has a picture in his mind of what he wants it to be when it is finished; he feels it is only hidden in the wood, waiting for his knife to free it. And when my plants are still beneath the ground, in my mind they flower, and sleeping branches put forth their leaves.

"Just as emotion is keener when we are asleep, so can we think more clearly of things of form when we are away from Earth. And that is why, before I make any decision of importance or even agree to the plans of a building, I sleep before I set my seal upon it.

"This attribute of thought is called the *nam*....'

Neyah asked how it was written. And Father took a piece of charcoal from a little quiver, which he often wore hanging from his belt, and in which he carried the reeds and charcoal of a scribe; and on the wall he drew a human mouth. "The words that come forth from our mouth belong to Earth, so when we talk of things of the spirit, they are but a poor conveyor of our thoughts; but when we talk of things of form, words can describe them accurately, for they both belong to Earth. And so the *nam* is written as a mouth, because it is that part of us with which we think of things that can be described in words.

"So now you know of your soul, which is the *ba* and the *nam*. The soul outlives the body; but when you need no longer be re-born on Earth, having learnt all that it can teach you, you will need your soul no longer: for then you will be master of emotion and you will have outgrown things of form."

CHAPTER THIRTEEN

# Horus the Hawk-headed

It was soon after the Festival of Horus that Ptah-kefer told me why the statues of the great Horus, the Hawk-headed, are carved as a man with the head of a hawk.

Long, long ago, when Earth was still unthreaded on the cord of time, Horus lived in a world as a man. The Gods dwell in splendour beyond our sight; but just as there is no plant that was not once a seed, so there is no god that was not once a man.

He was as gentle as dew falling on a meadow, and his strength was like the rising tide, which engulfs all that would bar its way.

His just anger could blast like the lightning; but when he brought peace the wildest storms abated, and the thunders dared not whisper across the mountains.

He was as patient as a climbing vine, and the jars of his memory stored all the wisdom of his world.

The flame of his spirit did not flicker in the coldest winds of circumstance, nor could the gentle breezes of joy disturb its still tranquillity: so had the sword of his will been tempered in the fire of life.

The Princes of Darkness loosed their arrows upon him, and it was as if rain fell upon a mountain; they challenged his will, and they were as dead leaves thrown upon a fire. They sent a mighty army against him, and under the eyes of Horus it was turned to stone.

The mightiest of the Lords of Evil he bound in their own darkness, until their hearts were changed. And he released those who had been imprisoned aforetime.

For his symbol he made the hawk, which can stay poised in the air and bind animals in the shackles of this trained will, just as the army that marched against Horus was frozen in its charge.

And that is why Horus has the body of a man, through which he attained this power, and the head of a hawk, which is his symbol of it.

CHAPTER FOURTEEN

# the wine-jars

After Neyah, my favourite person to play with was Neferteri. I thought we must have been friends lots of times before we were born this time in Kam. Her father was the Vizier and her mother was dead, so she lived in the palace.

She and I were playing at being dancing-girls. We were in the garden of fig trees, where there was a white wall on which we could watch our shadows to see which of us bent back further. I found that I could touch the ground with the tips of my fingers; Neferteri could put the whole of her hands on the ground.

I had a cousin staying in the palace. She was called Arbeeta, and we didn't like her much. She was rather fat, and awfully bad at running; she couldn't even dive into the swimming-pool, but walked down the steps as if she were an old woman going to wash clothes in the river. She wouldn't come and dance with us, although we told her she ought to try and make her body into a nice shape, and she had gone off to ask one of the sewing women to make a new tunic for her doll.

Then I heard Neyah whistling for me, so we stopped dancing. When he saw us he said, "They've been storing away the new vintage and they haven't sealed up the door yet. I've looked down the passage and it's as dark as the Palace of Set. Let's go and explore it—unless, of course, you think there might be snakes there."

I *did* think it was horrid of Neyah to keep on reminding me about not liking snakes. I said, "I think that's a lovely idea! We'll pretend it's the Caverns of the Underworld, and to get there we must walk along the True Path. The top of the fruit-garden wall will be very good for that." That would teach Neyah to tease me about snakes! The fruit-garden wall was twice as high as Father, and I knew Neyah hated walking along narrow places high up, although he would never say so.

He said, "I think that's rather a childish idea."

So I said quickly, "Of course, Neyah, if you think it's too difficult..."

"Of course it's not difficult, but I thought it might look a bit silly. Come on, I'll go first."

And he climbed up the fig tree and on to the wall, and we followed him. We walked along it, right round the orchard and the vegetable garden, and over that very difficult bit where one has to jump the gateway, until we got to the corner of the vineyard. There was an old vine growing up the wall near the wine-store, which was easy to climb down.

Ten steps led down to the door, which was right underground to keep it cool. The bolt was shot, but they had forgotten to seal it. The cellar ought to have been shut by my father's cupbearer and sealed with the Royal Seal.

Neyah left us there for a few moments. He came back with a little oil lamp, which he had borrowed from the cook of the Overseer of the Vineyard; it was only a wick in a little bowl of oil and it didn't give much light. We went through the door and shut it carefully behind us.

The wine-jars were taller than I was. They were marked with Father's name and the year and where they came from.

It wasn't my father's full name, but just Za Atet—a bundle of reeds, a feather, and a small half-circle; and after these the Reed and the Bee signs, to show it belonged to Pharaoh. The jars were in stands; I thought it was silly they weren't made so that they could stand up by themselves. It was very cold down there, and there was a strong smell of new wine; there were a few sherds on the ground, they must have dropped one of the jars and broken it.

The lamp threw huge shadows of us on the wall. Neyah started talking in his 'frightening' voice. I knew it was only a game, but it made my spine prickly.

"Who are you mortals who challenge the Caverns of the Underworld?"

"No, don't do that, Neyah!" I was glad Neferteri had told him to stop. I thought it so brave of her not to mind saying when she didn't like things.

Then Neyah said he was going to be Tahuti and the biggest wine-jars could be the Forty-Two Assessors. He pointed to the first wine-jar and said, "That one is 'Anger-without-cause'. Can you, Sekeeta, look at him and say, 'Thee have I conquered'?"

And I said, "Yes, I can."

"Sekeeta, you lie. Return to Earth. This morning you were angry with your attendant. You said she pulled your hair..."

"But she did!"

"But the tangles were of your own making, for you climbed trees without plaiting it. Also, yesterday, you tried to be as clever as your brother at carving in stone; when you very clumsily cut yourself you got into a rage and threw the chisel into the water. Pass on."

Then Neyah pretended that the next wine-jar said, "Is there one who sorrows because of you?"

I said, "No, there's not."

And Neyah made the jar say, "Miserable human! Thou liest. Return to Earth at once as the child of a cross-eyed

Nubian. Does not that girl-child, who is staying in your house, even now cry from her own dullness because you have only asked her to play at things that you know she cannot do and mocked her because she is fat?''

''But, Neyah, I mean Tahuti, she is so stupid...''

''Then your stating that which all know to be true is as foolish as one who points at the sun on a hot noon and says, 'See, the sun is shining.' So in talking of her stupidity you share it with her.''

Suddenly Neferteri said, ''Do you think they will remember about the door not being sealed and come and lock us in? It would feel awfully like being in a tomb.''

And Neyah said, ''Oh, we could easily shout. And even if nobody heard us we could live for ages on all this wine.''

I said, very firmly, ''I think we'd better get out now, Neyah, because this wine will be here for seven years; it was only put in to-day.''

It had been an exciting game, but I was very glad to get back in the sun again.

I felt I had been rather horrid to Arbeeta, so I went and found her and told her that she could give Natee his dinner.

CHAPTER FIFTEEN

# Chariots and Throwing-Spears

Every day, Neyah and I had lessons in spear-throwing and in the flying of arrows. Benater would set up a big line target divided into twenty red and white squares. In each square there was a rough drawing of an animal, and just before we launched a spear, Benater named the animal that we must transfix. We never knew until the last instant where we had to aim, just as when hunting a running antelope.

Our spears were shafted with light palmwood, weighted at one end with a small stone macehead to balance the heavy leaf-shaped copper blade. A spear is held above and behind the right shoulder, with the weight of the body far back on the right foot. For the spear to fly from the hand like an arrow from a bow-string, body and arm must launch forward together in perfect rhythm.

One evening when Neyah and I were practicing together, I got a blister on my hand, so we had to stop. We went down to the stables and got Neyah's favourite horse, Meri-naga, who was a beautiful shining black, and harnessed him to a light hunting-chariot. It was made of painted linen stretched over a wooden frame, and the floor was woven with strips of leather to make it less bumpy when going fast over rough ground. We drove to the place where the chariot horses are trained. Here, in a long oval, there are posts driven into the ground, and between them the charioteers must wheel their horses at full gallop without letting horse or chariot touch a post. We went three times round the oval. Meri-naga was very fast, and he turned as swiftly as a swallow; I had to hold on to the chariot rail to avoid being thrown out.

Then we drove down the track to the river to look at a private fish-trap of Neyah's. There was nothing in it, and he said it was because we hadn't put it in deep enough water. The trap was a new idea of his. I didn't think it was a very good one, because the neck of it was so narrow that, if a fish was clever enough to find its way in, it would be clever enough to find its way out again. But I didn't say anything, for it had taken him a long time to make. We waded into the water and set it again, further out from the bank.

It was a very still evening; there was no wind and the river was like a silver mirror. Meri-naga was eating grass; we could hear the sharp sound he made tearing it up with his teeth. There was a sailing-boat far out on the water, and we could hear the fisherman calling for a wind. The Gods didn't listen to him, and they left the river undisturbed even by a breeze.

Neyah cut a reed and started carving it. I lay on the bank, outstretched upon the ground. In the deep quiet of evening, it seemed that Earth was like a sailing-boat becalmed on a mighty sea that was the sky; and if a great storm arose, and it was night, we should be driven across the universe and out strip the stars, until they looked like the manes of celestial horses streaming in the wind.

I asked Neyah what he most wanted to do when he grew up, and he said, "Oh, I want to be able to govern people and have wise laws, and lead armies with the wisdom of a serpent and the courage of a lion."

And I said, "I want to do lots of strange things...things that I don't quite understand myself yet. Sometimes every-day things seem very important, and Kam seems a large country beyond whose boundaries few would ever wish to travel. And then sometimes, in my bed at night I look out of my window at the stars and think what a little place earth is, and that our country is like a grain of sand, and that I am so small that if an ant walked over me, it would not even think its path was rough. Knowing this littleness, I long to see beyond.... It's like your wild-cat looking through its bars and hearing the jackals barking at night, knowing that they are seeing things it can only guess about...."

"Don't move, Sekeeta! There's a gazelle coming down to drink, you can just see it in the deep shadow." It sent ripples across the water as it drank. Then it lifted its head and listened as though startled, and sprang away through the reeds.

It was getting dark, and Neyah said we must go home. On the way we heard a ploughman singing as he led his oxen back to their pasture. It was a ploughing song that I was very fond of:

Pull on your yokes, my oxen, pull on your yokes.
Run straightly, O plough! so that my field is furrowed

smooth as a comb divides a woman's hair.
Earth, open your womb to my scattered corn, shelter it in your warmth and bring it forth under the sun.
Listen, O seed! to the singing-birds, and spring upwards to hear them more clearly.
Water, run quickly through the channels, and pour sap into my plants.
Warm them, O sun! warm them with your life-giving rays.
Be gentle, wind, to my ripening corn, so that the heavy ear does not bear down its slender stalk.
Cut through the stalks, my sickle, cut through the stalks as the young moon cleaves the darkness, so that my threshing-floor is deep with gold.
Pound in the mortar, pestle, and grind my flour, so that my house lacks not the dust of life.
Burn strongly, fire, let the oven be hot and my bread be well baked, so that I may eat of it and be strong
To yoke my oxen.

His voice faded into the dusk as we drove slowly homeward, and before we reached the palace the road was deep in the silver water of the moon.

CHAPTER SIXTEEN

# the spirit

One morning before sunrise, Neyah and I went with Father to the little pavilion beside the marsh, to watch the morning flight of birds.

Neyah had brought some tablets of baked clay, and with a reed and black ink he had drawn a flying swan in a few strokes. When I tried to draw birds they looked dead, and quite often they didn't look like birds at all. As I watched him, I wondered why this was. We had the same parents; we were very alike; I was always with him; and the same drawing-scribe had given us lessons. And I wondered, also, why it was that, when I got angry, I wanted to throw things at people and say all that was in my mind; but when Neyah was angry, he seemed to go away inside himself, and sometimes his eyes would say all the things that his lips held back, and sometimes they would be like curtained windows.

Father asked me my thoughts, and I told them to him. And while we were eating our breakfast of fruit, he said, "Before I can answer the questions in your thoughts, I must tell you of your spirit.

"As I have already taught you, we are made of body, soul, and spirit. The body is the *khat*, the *ka-ibis*, and the *ka*. This is the outer covering of our soul and spirit, through which we gain experience on Earth, and when the body dies, the *ka* and the *ka-ibis* die also. Our soul is the *ba* and the *nam*, and these we have need of as long as our spirit must be re-born upon Earth, and that is until we have learnt to master our emotions, our thoughts, and our will. And that leaves spirit, which is the only part of ourselves that endures for ever.

"While we are on Earth we can think of much that is permanent, and we do this every time we think of those things which the *nam* does not embrace."

I asked, "How can I be sure that something I think about belongs to the *nam* part of myself?"

And he said, "All things that can be apprehended by the five senses of the body are things of form, and therefore of the *nam*. But you cannot see, or taste, or touch, qualities. You cannot smell courage, or hear patience, for they are beyond the limitations of form as we know it. When you think of qualities, you think of them with a part of your spirit called the *za*. You know the divisions of the body and of the soul, and how they are written. The *za,* with which we think of things that are permanent, is written as a circle with grid lines inside it, like a sieve. For just as a sieve can sift stones from dust, so does the *za* sift the dust of Earth, which is blown upon the wind and is no more seen, from the rocks of Truth, which endure through time."

And I asked Father why he didn't write his name as a sieve; and he said it could be written so, although usually in his seal he put the reed bundle, or the snake and the arm, which were the sound signs for his name. The great Meniss had called him Za, saying that it was a good name for a ruler who could sift truth from falsehood, and so give justice.

"The *za* is the first part of your spirit. The second part of your spirit is that wherein is stored the memory of every experience that you have undergone since that moment when, having gained all experience possible in the realm of animals, you are first born a human being and could say, 'I am I'. And it is the voice of this, your own individual experience, that says to you, 'To do this is wise; here is safety, there lies danger.'"

I said, "Yes, Father, but I have never been bitten by a snake, and yet I fear them; and Neyah has never fallen from a height, yet he fears them."

Neyah started to protest, but I said, "It's no good your trying to pretend, Neyah, I know quite well." And he wriggled his toes, as he always did when he had to admit something, and said reluctantly, "Heights do give me rather a horrid feeling, but you needn't have said so."

Father smiled and went on, "Through your many lives the two of you have undergone different experiences, and these experiences will have brought their several results. Those that were happy you will wish to repeat, and those that brought pain or sorrow you will avoid. But until you have both reached the end of the journey, there must always be those things Neyah has learnt, which you lack, and other things you have learnt, which he lacks.

"'The actions or the fears of another are easy to understand when they are the same as your own. But when one sees another do something that makes the inward voice of memory say, 'That is wrong,' an ignorant man would say, 'He has sinned as I would never sin; he is beneath me and unworthy of my compassion'. But they who say this are foolish, for they have forgotten truth, even as they have forgotten themselves: for that inward voice is born of their own suffering as a result of that same fault, which they now condemn. If they listened wisely to that voice, not only would they know that their feet had once been in the same mire, but also they would remember the path that had led them back to firm ground. And in remembering the path, they would be able to point the way to the one whom they, in their foolishness, had called a sinner, but whom a wise man would have known as a fellow-traveller who, for a little time, had lost his way on the great journey. And in that knowledge is compassion; and compassion is the fruit of experience."

And Neyah said, "But, Father, if I see a man doing something that I know is wrong, surely I should try to stop him and not just feel compassion for him?"

"I said compassion, not pity. By pity I mean he who goes to a sorrowing one and sits beside him, weeping; or he who, seeing a gaping wound, says, 'Oh! the blood, the pain, I cannot bear to see such suffering', and sits lamenting beside the wounded one; and lamenting so loudly that the sufferer's groans are drowned in the cries of pity, which is often just self-pity that he should be brought so near to another's pain and sorrow. But pity is the first step to the gaining of compassion.

"Now a man who has true compassion, if he finds one bowed down with sorrow, knows what has caused those tears to flow, and, knowing it, knows how to stem them. For he realises, and he may even remember, that he, too, has shed many tears, and in his time has thought that night was eternal and knew no dawn. He will show him that all sorrow must one day turn to joy, and when the weeping one would wipe away his tears, he will find that they have already dried upon his cheeks. And the wise man does not increase the burdens of others by the noise of lamentation, but tries to heal their wounds, or, if they are too deep for earthly help, he comforts the spirit as it leaves its tired body.

"And so, Neyah and Sekeeta, listen to the voice of your memory. If you wish your journey to be swift, let your actions be such that in future the voice cries out, 'This is right, this is the way', rather than 'Go not there, for that is wrong'. But few there are on the long journey who do not often leave the right path; for strange it is, that though a man finds his way beset with thorns, he often struggles there, because his pride will not let him admit that he has lost his way; although, if he would but listen, there are those who call to him to turn back and follow in the foot-prints they have left.

"My children, the day may come when you will rule. Always remember that all in your country, and all people of the many races and colours that dwell on Earth, be they friend or enemy, equals or slaves, all are fellow-travellers on the same long journey, and one day they shall be with you in that great brotherhood to which all must attain."

Father was sitting very still, with his hands clasped round his knees, looking far away to the horizon. I think he spoke to us not as children, but as our true selves. Then he moved and said that we have been having far too solemn a conversation. And he would have talked of other things, but Neyah wouldn't let him, and asked how the memory part of the spirit was written.

Father took the reed from Neyah's hand and drew a jar.... "For a jar holds fluids, which of all earthly substances are nearest to that which has not earthly form. When a man is born for the first time, his jar of memory is empty; gradually through his many lives it is filled. At first, much of that which fills it belongs to Earth, and the water in the jar is muddy. Later those things that are not part of the perfect whole still cloud the now clearer water of the jar. But when the spirit is cleansed of Earth, and has gained all experience, the muddy water will be clear, and it will be as if the jar were filled with liquid light.

"'And it is called the *maat*, 'truth': for truth is those burnished qualities that remain after the spirit has freed itself from Earth and can take passage in the Boat of Time."

CHAPTER SEVENTEEN

# my mother's anniversary

Very early on the morning of my mother's anniversary I went into Neyah's room and woke him up, so that we could both have another look at our present before we took it to her room.

It was a lovely bracelet of golden moon-daisies joined together with amethyst and turquoise beads; and Nusetees the goldsmith had said it was the finest work he had ever done. Neyah had painted a little wooden box to hold it, which he had made himself. It had a border of green and scarlet stripes, and a picture of the fish-pool with lotuses and some very alive fishes.

The mist was still rising from the swimming-pool outside her window. I had made a special poem for her, and I kept on saying it over in my head so I shouldn't forget it:

The garden through the cold night
    Longs for the warmth of the sun.
The fish on the river bank
    Longs to be back in the water.
A pigeon with a broken wing
    Longs to fly from a high branch.
The traveller on a dark night

Longs for the light of the moon.
But Earth longed a thousand times more
For you to be born on it again.

I wished I could have found better words to tell her how much I loved her.

Then she called us into her room. After we had kissed her, we gave her our bracelet. She said it was the most beautiful bracelet she had ever seen, and she would wear it always. Then I told her my poem. And she said it was a more lovely poem than any she had heard—even the best ones of Thenapt, the song-maker.

She was so beautiful. Her hair was black and soft; she didn't wear it in plaits when she slept, as most people did; sometimes she let me comb it for her with her ivory comb.

Then Father came in and sat on the edge of her bed, and Mother told me to say my poem again for him. So I did; and he said he could add another two lines to it, for he had been a thousand times more joyful than Earth when she was born—although when he was awake he didn't know it: for when he first saw her he was almost grown up, being six years old, and she was the very young baby of his favourite aunt, and was being carried by her nurse in the sycamore grove of the old palace.

Then Mother said, "We can have the whole day to ourselves until the audience in the evening. What shall we all do?" And we all thought; and while we were deciding to go out in Father's sailing-boat on the lake, I heard Natee grumbling outside the door, and I let him in. Mother told me I could bring him too, if I liked. And Neyah said, "Lions aren't a good idea in boats."

And I said, "Lions are a good idea anywhere. In fact, they're the best idea Ptah ever had."

Then Mother sent Neyah and me to the kitchens to choose whatever food we wanted taken down to the boat. We chose a cold goose and lots of radishes and figs; a jar of grape juice, some honey-cakes, and pomegranates, which are dull-tasting, but good if you are thirsty; and Neyah added twelve hard-boiled ducks' eggs and some small buttered loaves. It looked an awful lot; but I said it was a good idea to have plenty of food in boats, in case a storm should arise and blow us to a far distant land. And Neyah said, "However big the storm, it wouldn't be a very far distant land, because you can sail right across the lake in two hours with a fair wind."

I told him to stop being grand and trying to make exciting things ordinary.

It was lovely on the lake, the wind was just right for sailing. We saw a hippopotamus in the distance. I've always hated them for killing our great-great uncle. I suppose he was really too old to have been hunting them when he was eighty-seven. He was the greatest king that ever lived, and the wisest man, and the greatest warrior.

We saw a cloud of birds travelling north, and Father told us how in summer they went to a country such a long way away that we would never go there when we were awake. He had only been there in a dream himself. In the winter it's all white with coldness; and there are days and days together when Ra doesn't drive away the clouds. I hoped we should never be born in a country like that.

Neyah and I had swimming races; he went faster, but I made much less splash. Natee was so good; he curled up in the bottom of the boat and was no trouble at all, except once he got rather excited, and then the boat wobbled about as if there really was a storm coming.

When the sun was high, we landed on a little island and had our food under some trees. Natee was very useful; he ate up all the things we would have had to take back again.

On the way home the wind dropped, and Father and Neyah rowed, while Mother sang a rower's song to them, so that they kept in time.

It was such a lovely day! I did so wish I could always be nine.

# PART TWO

## CHAPTER ONE

# ney-sey-ra

When Natee was three years old he ran away. For many days no one could find him, and I thought I should never see him again. But on the twelfth day he came back, followed by a young wild lioness. He led her straight to the lion court, and although she was shy of people, she followed him to his stall; and he growled and roared at any lion that tried to come near him. At first Zeb was the only person whom she would allow to approach her, but even when she got used to people she was never allowed to roam about alone.

The royal lions were usually descended from generations that had been the companions of human beings, and it was very seldom that a wild lion was tamed, unless it was brought in as a tiny cub.

I called Natee's mate 'Simma'. Just before she was expecting cubs, she disappeared. Natee was very unhappy without her. He refused to eat, and he moaned and whimpered to himself all night. Zeb told me that he thought Natee might find Simma, for he would pick up her scent, on which he dared not put the hound-dogs lest they frightened her.

So Zeb went out at night, when a lion can follow a scent easier than in the hot sun. He would take no one with him; for he said that Simma would know his voice and follow it, while from anyone else she would run further.

I got up very early the next morning and went down to the lion court to see if Zeb had returned. But he was still away. I walked northwards to where, beyond the cultivation, there were hills of sand by the edge of the marsh. I had been walking for about half an hour along the path where I had often taken Natee for his walk, when suddenly I saw him galloping towards me.

He took my kilt in his teeth and pulled it as though he wanted me to follow him. Round his neck there was a strip of linen, and I saw it was marked with red. I untied it and spread it on the ground. At first I thought the mark was just a wavy line made by a finger dipped in blood. But then I saw it was the drawing of a snake, and on its head were two strokes, which meant it was a horned viper; and I knew that Zeb had been bitten by a snake and had sent Natee to bring help.

I was nearer to the temple than the palace, so I ran there very fast, and Natee followed me. I found Zertar just leaving the courtyard. He sent at once for three litters, each with two swift runners. He said that would be the quickest way to reach Zeb, because he could not be far away, as some of the blood on the strip of linen had not yet dried hard. Zertar took with him a box of salves and a *smaoo,* a little animal that is quicker than a snake and plays with them just as a cat plays with a mouse—which is why they call it a snake-cat.

When Zertar was ready, I let go of Natee's collar, and he ran on ahead, sometimes looking back to make sure that we were following. The runners were swift and in less than an hour we had left the cultivation and were among the waves of sand on the north border of the marsh where there are vast stretches of high reeds.

We found Zeb lying at the edge of them. At first I thought he was dead; but when Natee, who had run ahead of us, started licking him, he stirred. Zeb had been bitten in the left ankle, and he had lashed the wound deeply with his knife. It had bled a lot, but not enough, for his leg was swollen and turning black.

Zertar told me to try and make him drink some cane-spirit. While I was doing this he took the *smaoo* and made a small cut in its leg, letting its blood drip into a little cup, which didn't seem to hurt, for it licked his hand while he was doing it. Zertar told one of the litter-runners to bind its leg, and then he made two little slits in Zeb's flesh, one above the wound the snake had made, and one on the left breast, just above the heart. On these he bound two small pads of linen dipped in the blood of the *smaoo;* the rest of it he poured into Zeb's mouth, who now had strength enough to swallow. Next Zertar took an evil-smelling ointment from a jar, which he smeared on the snake bite. Then, after wrapping Zeb in woollen cloaks, they lifted him on to one of the litters and set off to the palace.

I called Natee, but he would not obey. He went back towards the reeds, as if he wanted me to follow him. When he saw I wasn't going to, he came and took my hand very gently between his teeth and tried to lead me along. So I went with him; and in the clearing, on a bed of dry sand, I saw Simma with two little cubs. She curled her lips as though to snarl at me, but Natee rumbled at her and then she let me stroke her. Her two little cubs were even smaller than Natee was when he had first slept on my bed. I took off Natee's collar so he would know that he no longer owed allegiance to me and was free to come back to the palace or stay with Simma. When I left him he followed me to the edge of the reeds and stood watching me as I went away, before he trotted back to his own family.

The runners of my litter caught up with Zeb before he reached the palace. He was put in one of the rooms near to where Zertar worked; for all in the palace who were ill Zertar would try to heal, with knife or herb.

Ptah-kefer came and looked at Zeb, and he said he could not tell for another day if he would live. His lips were a better colour, but he was still quiet and cold, and did not answer when I spoke to him.

So I left him; and I walked through the gardens, feeling very sad, for I loved my faithful servant and grieved to think that he might die, and Natee had left me for a better companion. I decided to go to the temple and pray for Zeb. So I picked some lilies, striped white and scarlet, to take with me, and I sent for my litter.

There was no one in the temple forecourt, for the sun was high and it was the time when people rested in the shade. I went to the Sanctuary of Ptah and put my flowers on the white steps of his statue. Standing before him with my hands upstretched, though I said no words aloud, I called so hard to Ptah to hear me that on his throne of stars he must have heard my voice. I told him about the snake, and asked him from his bounty of life to give some more to Zeb, and to let him stay with me. Then I knelt and touched his foot with my forehead, for love of him and in humility.

As I left the cool shade of the sanctuary, the sunlight in the outer court seemed solid as a golden wall. A young priest was walking across the courtyard; I knew by his robe he was a high-priest of Anubis. I had seen him in the temple before, and had heard that he had passed his initiation very young, when only twenty-three. His name was Ney-sey-ra.

He came and talked to me. He spoke as if he had known me for a long time, and I felt I was talking to a friend, though one much wiser than myself. He seemed to know that I had had no food that day, for, without my saying anything, he took me into one of the private gardens and brought me some honey-cakes and figs and a cup of wine, which he said would make me feel less tired.

As I ate I talked to him; and although it was for the first time, it was as though we continued a conversation that we had started the day before. I told him about Zeb, and Natee, and Simma's cubs; and he said that I had been wise to let Natee free, because an unwilling captive could never be a friend. But he thought Natee would return to me when the cubs were older; for he had changed his habits to my will because I understood his heart.

I asked Ney-sey-ra about the snake-cat, and why Zertar had put its blood on Zeb. And he told me, "Some men think that snake-cats take but little harm from the poison even of a cobra, and that they have a special virtue in their blood, which takes the evil from the venom. Zertar is trying to discover if a little of this blood, mingled with that of one who has been bitten, imparts some of its own quality to the poisoned one so that he can overcome the poison in his veins.''

And I told him of the ointment; and he said it was made of the fat of whatever sort of snake had given the bite, and he himself thought that both that and the blood of the snake-cat were of little value.

Then I said that I must go back to the palace and find out how Zeb was.

Ney-sey-ra smiled and said, ''I can find that out for you without your moving from the bench.'' And he picked up the silver bowl in which I had rinsed my fingers and held it between his hands just where a shaft of light pierced through the canopy of vines beneath which we were sitting. Then as though he were looking through a window into a room and describing what he saw, he said, ''Zeb is asleep. Ptah has filled his body with new life. He will awake an hour after sunset, and then he should be given milk and wine. Then he will sleep again, and when he wakes to-morrow, all will know that he will live. In twenty days he will be well again and have but a little scar upon his leg.''

I had never seen this power of 'looking' used before, yet it did not seem strange to me. Without speaking, Ney-sey-ra got up and plucked a lotus growing in the pool, and then he said, ''Do you remember?''

And I remembered that I had dreamed of this the night before. And in my dream he had shown me an open lotus like the one he now held in his hand, and he had told me that just as a lotus opens its petals until its golden heart reflects the brilliance of the sun, so must I open the gateway of my memory until on Earth I could reflect the Light. Then in my dream he had pointed to a half-opened bud, which though it showed its blue petals, still had them folded round its heart; and this, he had told me, was a symbol of what I was now.

The memory of my dream had come back to me in less time than it takes a bird to move its wing, and I went and plucked a lotus that showed its blue, and said, "This is what I am", and pointing to the flower that he held, "That is what I long to be."

And then he smiled and said, "I am a high-priest and you shall be a queen; but what is more pleasing to my heart is that I can teach you all you wish to know. Much have I taught your spirit while you have slept; soon I shall also teach you here on Earth."

Before I left him, he told me that henceforward I should say this prayer before I slept:

"Master, of thy wisdom, teach me to be a flame for the benighted ones, so that I may warm their hearts and light their darkness, until of their own knowledge they can kindle their own fire, and having kindled it can leave the darkness and dwell at last in the light of the sun."

On the twentieth day Zeb could walk again; and three months later Natee returned to me. Simma and her cubs followed him as he led them to the lion-court gate and into his special stall, which had been kept ready for him. And my father allowed him to go with me wherever I liked, as he did when he was a cub.

CHAPTER TWO

# Lion Hunt

I was ten years old, and for the first time I was going with my father upon a lion hunt. For a long time Benater had been giving me lessons with the throwing-spear, and at last Harka, Overseer of the Royal Chariots, had said that I was skilled enough in the driving of chariots.

I wanted to go on a lion hunt to show Neyah that I could share in all the things he did, so that when we grew up, if he went on an expedition against a warring country, he would take me with him into battle.

I wished we were hunting leopards or crocodiles, and not lions, even though we hunted only old ones that attacked people working in the fields because they couldn't catch deer any more. I hoped that the one we killed wouldn't look even a little like Natee; but if Father, who loved Shamba, didn't mind killing bad lions, I knew I was silly to worry that the ones we killed might be even very distant relations of Natee.

There was a foreigner staying at the palace, a barbarian from the north-east; at least, Neyah said he was. I hadn't seen him yet.

I wore a boy's hunting-dress, like Neyah's: the striped linen head-dress, a pectoral of thick quilting embroidered in rays of fine gold work, wide gold armlets, and a linen kilt with a gold-studded leather belt to hold my hunting-knife.

When I was ready I went to the outer court, where the chariots waited. There were forty of them lined up in a long row. Father's horse and Neyah's and mine had ostrich plumes upon their heads, of scarlet and green, which were my father's colours. At the end of each horse was its charioteer, who would hold the spear until the noble who drove the chariot was ready for it, then he would take the reins until the lion was killed. On the other side of the courtyard were the hunting-dogs, black, with pointed ears, like jackals, and they were held by the hound-boys, two in each leash.

My mother joined me at the top of the steps. She was wearing a blue dress embroidered with scarlet fishes and wavy water-lines of silver: her cloak was of the new violet dye, which is made from shell-fish and comes from across the sea to the north. She wore a wreath of scarlet arbeeta flowers; they have a very sweet smell, and her favourite unguent was scented with them.

Her eyes looked a little anxious, and I hoped she was not

worried about my going out hunting. I knew she wouldn't tell me if she were, for once I heard her say that if a mother was foolish enough to let her secret fears for her children shadow her day, she must not let this foolishness shadow the days of others. Maata was not like that. Once, when Neyah and I went out sailing, our boat got stuck on a mud-bank and we didn't get back till late at night. Maata was terribly angry with us, just because she felt frightened herself. She never realised how unfair it was of her; it hadn't been our fault at all, and we had had no food all day except a bunch of grapes we had happened to pick on our way down to the boat. Mother wasn't a bit cross; she said how clever we had been to get off the bank at all, and she gave us a specially lovely supper in her room, although it was long past our bedtime.

I asked Mother what the barbarian was like, and she laughed and said, "You mustn't call him that, because he is a king in his own country, even if he is a foreigner here. His name is Sardok..." And then she stopped because we heard people coming. It was Father and the guests for the hunt. When he saw me dressed as a prince, he put his arm round my shoulder and said to the man beside him, "See, I have another son!" I hoped Neyah heard.

Neyah was going along the line of horses, inspecting the harness. As though it needed it! Dear Neyah—he can't help being a little grand sometimes.

I thought Harka was coming with me, but Father told him to go with the barbarian. I looked at Sardok and thought, "You may be a king in your own country, but here you are a fat man, very fat." He had a great black beard all curled and greased like a decorated he-goat; and his hair was in ringlets, so heavily perfumed that you could smell him further away than a wild-cat.

Then we got into our chariots. Serten came with me; I had always been fond of him for giving me Natee. My horse was black and white like an ibis, so I had named him Moonshadow. Father headed the line of chariots out of the courtyard, Sardok went next, because he was the chief guest, and then Neyah and I. I waved to Mother before I went out of the gate, and wheeled my chariot very fast through the pylon so she should see how good I was at driving and not worry about me.

We went for about half an hour up river to the plain of Arbaw, which is a great marsh, dry at this season, where there were two old lions who took cattle when they went down to drink. The hound-boys had gone ahead along the river bank. When we reached the place to where they were going to drive the lions, the chariots were ranged in a great semi-circle, with Father in the middle, Sardok on one side of him, and myself on the other. When a lion breaks cover, the two chariots between which it runs challenge each other, and between them lies the glory of the swift.

In front of us there was a wide belt of high papyrus reeds where the trackers had reported the lions to be sleeping in the heat of the day. We could hear the dogs working through the reeds and the shouting of the hound-boys, who carried flaming torches of dry palm-wood, coated with resin, which gave off a heavy black smoke to frighten the lions. I saw the smoke nearing us. Some of the horses were getting very excited and pawing the ground, but Moon-shadow was being very good. Serten said he was as steady with a lion as any other horse with its own stable-dog. I suppose he had become used to Natee coming out with us. I wished I didn't keep on thinking of Natee.

Suddenly there was a great roaring, and a lion broke from the reeds with four hound-dogs yelping behind him. I was so excited I could hardly breathe. It seemed to be coming straight at me, I had the reins in my hands ready to give them to Serten. Then at the last minute it swerved and went between Father and Sardok. Father let Sardok go ahead. Sardok was clumsy and swerved his horse so fast that it stumbled, and when he threw his spear he missed the lion altogether. It turned and sprang at him, but he cringed down and the lion landed on Harka and knocked him on to the ground. Father, who was close behind, leaped from his galloping chariot straight on to the lion. He dared not use his spear because of Harka, and he forced his arm under the lion's head and drove his knife into his neck.

Neyah and I both reached Father just as he was pulling the dead lion off Harka. I had thought Father was going to be killed, and I knew Neyah had too, because he looked very pale. I felt so proud of Father, but I didn't say anything for fear of crying. Harka was still alive, but his left arm was badly torn. I sat on the ground and took his head on my lap. He opened his eyes and tried to smile at me, and then he closed them again. Father felt his heart and said that he still lived.

Sardok had got out of his chariot. I hoped that the scorn Neyah and I felt for him showed in our eyes, so he would know that although he was a king, in spirit he was a very little man. He said to Father, "That was a great risk to take for a servant."

Father's voice was like granite as he answered, "No man would have done less for his friend."

How dared Sardok speak of Harka like that! Harka, who was worth a thousand fat barbarians; Harka, who had loved us all since we were children, and who had taught my father to drive. Sardok must have felt our contempt, for he walked away and talked to one of his own people.

CHAPTER THREE

# the healer with the knife

The lion had hurt Harka very badly. Father said it would be safer for him to be taken home, not in a chariot, but lying full-stretched on one of the carrying-platforms, which had been meant for a dead lion. There were four bearers to this litter, and though they ran swiftly, it went smoothly, so even was the rhythm of their stride.

I went ahead in a chariot to tell my mother what had happened, so that she could summon healers from the temple. For a lion bite is like the bite of a copper sword, and it must be healed quickly or the flesh will die round the wound while the person still lives. I wished Father and Neyah weren't going on with the hunt. I knew just how Mother must feel when Neyah and I were out doing the sort of things that seem so dangerous when you're not doing them yourself.

A room in my father's private apartments was prepared. A high narrow bed, such as is used for rubbing, was put in the middle of the room and covered with several thicknesses of linen sheets. Beside it on a table were two jars of salves, made from my father's herbs, some bowls of water, and a jar of cane-spirit, which, although it feels like fire, is cleansing for a dirty wound.

Ptah-kefer and the healer in attendance on the Royal Household were both waiting in the room when Harka was carried in. I asked my mother if I could stay with Harka. At first she would have refused me, thinking I was too young; but I said that if I was old enough to see him hurt, then I was old enough to see him cured.

When I was little, the sight of blood made my bowels cringe up inside me, and my hands and forehead damp; so I had watched unseen when the tribute bulls were slaughtered for the butcher, until the sight of spilled blood stirred me no more than wine running from a cracked jar. Yet as I watched them bringing in Harka, I found that this weakness, which I thought to have conquered, was still there, and the sight of blood running from a friend was very different to that from a bull.

Harka's face was a curious purple colour; one side of it twitched, while the other was smooth. Ptah-kefer, covering his eyes with his hand, stooped over the wounds: he remained still for a moment, and then he beckoned to the healer, and they went to the doorway and talked quietly together. I heard him say that Harka's skull had been crushed and was pressing on the brain, and unless the piece of bone was lifted, one side of his body would always be still, and that the skill of Zertar was needed.

When Zertar came, he brought with him what looked like goldsmith's tools. Usually work such as this is done in the temple, but it was decided that it would be better for Harka to stay here instead of being moved again.

Poor Harka! I went up to him and took his hand. He gripped mine, so I knew he had not yet left his body. The wounds on his side and shoulder had been covered with cloths of wet linen; but the bright blood soon stained them.

Another priest came into the room, a high-priest of Anubis. He sat in a chair at the far end of the room, and seemed to sleep, while the healer pointed the fingers of healing between Harka's eyes and forced him to leave his body. I knew that although the priest of Anubis seemed to sleep, his spirit waited to take Harka far away from pain when he left his body, so that they might work upon his body and mend it as though they but stitched up a tear in an empty cloak.

I felt Harka's hand grow limp, and I knew that he was beyond the reach of pain and I could no longer help him by staying. But I thought that it was right for me to learn all that I could of Zertar's skill.

First he shaved the hair from the side of Harka's head, and on the smooth-shaven skin Ptah-kefer marked the place where the skull pressed. Then Zertar took a small leaf-shaped knife and made three cuts like three sides of a square, and, with two things like eyebrow pluckers, he drew back a flap of skin. Then the pluckers were held by the healer, who with his power tightened the veins so that little blood should flow. Two silver mirrors, held in high stands, reflected strong sunlight on to Harka's head. I could see the white bone of the skull, and there was a dent in it surrounded by fine cracks, like an egg that has been cracked by a spoon. Zertar took a little metal cylinder, the edge of which was notched with fine teeth like a saw, and, placing it against the skull, he spun it quickly between his hands, just as a goldsmith drills a hard stone bead. Then he moved and I could not see Harka's head; but they were still working on it.

Ptah-kefer, who all this time had been watching with the eyes of his spirit, told the healer to drive the life of Ptah into Harka's heart, for it was getting weak. When the healer moved to do it, I saw that an ivory plate had been fitted across the hole that Zertar had drilled; it was held to the fractured skull by little pins of gold. Then the flap of skin was put back and covered with a film of clear wax to keep it in place until the cuts were healed. When the wax had hardened, a pad of specially charged linen, which would ensure its healing cleanly, was put over the wound. And then his head was tightly bandaged.

The wounds on his shoulder and side were washed with cane-spirit to remove any bits of filth that might have been upon the lion's claws, and then they were bathed in water that had been charged with the life of Ptah. After this they were spread with a green herbal salve, which my father had found stopped the pain of bandages sticking to an open wound; and Zertar bandaged the arm and shoulder so that Harka could not move them and tear a muscle that Ptah-kefer said was frayed.

Cloths that had been steeped in a cooling lotion were laid on Harka's forehead, and a heated stone, wrapped in a towel, was put at his feet, under the woollen covers. When all was finished, the Anubis priest allowed Harka to return to his body, and suddenly I felt his hand which I still held, tighten on mine. Harka opened his eyes; his face was smooth again and did not twitch. He looked dazed, and said, "Za... Za Atet...my lord, my master. is he safe?"

I told him that my father was unhurt, and then dear Harka was at peace; and I stayed beside him until he went to sleep.

CHAPTER FOUR

# Dream of Zuma

That night there was a banquet in honour of Sardok, King of Zuma.

Sardok, who sat at my father's right hand, wore a crown of gold and enamel, high and fluted, as though a bundle of reeds, narrowing towards the top, had been covered with gold leaf and three times bound with jewelled thongs. His long straight robe was scalloped in three tiers and pleated to look like feathers. Over this he wore a cloak of dark red wool caught on the shoulder with a long gold pin, at the head of which was a large cylinder seal minutely carved from amethyst. His fingernails and toenails were painted like a woman's; his greased hair hung in ringlets to his shoulders, and his long black beard was curled elaborately and shone with grease. His hooked nose was fleshy and his skin a muddy yellow, not smooth like ours, but pitted like the holes of mud-worms on the river bank. He had bracelets of cornelian and onyx beads on his arms and a wide ring on each big toe.

I remembered Harka and wished it had been Sardok's body that the lion had torn.

Four of Sardok's nobles ate with us, the rest of his followers being servants or soldiers. Their faces were not clear-cut like ours, not as though cleanly carved in stone, but as if they were wax images that had begun to melt in the sun.

I wasn't old enough to stay until the end of the banquet, and when I left, Neyah came with me because he wanted me to tell him about Harka. When I was in bed he came into my room and listened while I told him every detail of what had happened.

My thoughts kept straying back to Sardok, and I said, "I know Sardok is evil."

"Yes, and I know he's cruel. I saw him lash his horse after he had made it fall. It wasn't the horse's fault. If he's the king of Zuma, it must be a dreadful country to live in."

I had found that answers to things sometimes came to me in a dream, so that, when I awoke, that which had been obscure before I slept, was clear to me. Neyah and I had often talked of this, and we had found it very useful. Once Neyah lost one of Father's seals, which he had borrowed and forgotten to return; and although we searched and searched, we could not find it. But that night I dreamed that it had fallen under the straw of the wild-cat's cage, and I woke Neyah and told him. And very early, when it was just dawn, we went and looked, and there, buried in the straw, we found the seal. No one had heard us, or ever discovered how in the night Neyah had got those scratches on his hands. Neyah put back the seal, and no one knew that he had borrowed it for us to play a game in which he was Pharaoh and I was a captive king.

But as a fish when sleeping in a pool shows every scale and detail of its fins, and when it is startled flicks its tail and disappears, so does a dream, which is clear in every detail when you waken, often vanish, unless some record of it is quickly made. So when there was something special that we wanted to know, Neyah would bring his mattress into my room and sleep on the floor, so that on waking I could tell him what I had dreamed; and then we would both remember all the details of it. We had tried sleeping in the same bed, but it was too narrow and we both fell out.

That night, Neyah came and shared my room, and before I slept I sent out a call that I might go to Zuma, the land of Sardok.

And much I saw. And when I returned to my body, I told Neyah, "First it was as though I travelled like a bird, and spread out beneath me I saw a country where the horizon in every direction was of green corn, rippling under the wind like the waters of the lake. Across this huge expanse of green ran straight rivers, straight as knife-cuts. There were so many of them! They seemed in ordered pattern, I think they must have been canals such as we have, but each was twenty times as wide and much, much longer. On these canals were many villages, built of a different sort of brick from ours, and smaller—and most squalid. There were flies everywhere, and the people seemed afraid, and did not sing.

"I went to the temple of a great city. Although there were large buildings there, I saw no stone. The temple was surrounded by a high oval wall, and at the main gateway there was a table with crude clay figures on it, which were sold to people who came to the temple with some special petition to their god. Some gave a tall basket of corn, and some two kids, and others five strange birds, which cannot fly, but stretch out their necks and scuttle; they have yellow legs, and shabby feathers, and little beady eyes.

"In the temple, I saw no one who could teach; those who should have been priests seemed but the attendants of a statue of a god; a god called Mardok, shaped like a man, yet with fanged teeth over his lips, and claws instead of hands and feet. In front of him the one who wanted to pray must break the figurine that he had bought at the gate. All they seemed to do was to cringe before the statue. I don't know why they were there: they could not have left the temple wiser or stronger than when they came: they must have felt more debased. I saw no women there; it may be that the women are too wise to wish to go, or that their men think they are unworthy.

"Then I saw a ceremonial rite, which was held at the sowing of the crops—it was in the courtyard of the king's palace. An enormous white bull was brought in, it looked as though it were eager for a cow....No, Neyah, I can't tell you about that."

Neyah said, "Don't be silly, go on."

"While eight men held the bull by its legs, a man in a long red robe took a knife from a gold sheath and cut off the thing that the bull waters through and the bag that hangs behind, and gave them to the king, who held them high above his head, while the blood ran down his arms. Then he carried these things round the court, where there were many earthen jars of seed, and into each he dropped something of the bull. There must have been at least two hundred jars. And when he had been round to all of them, he dropped the rest into a green stone bowl, which afterwards was to be taken to the chief temple and set before the god. After this the people were allowed into the courtyard; and those of them who wished to have children surged forward to dabble their fingers in the dead bull and taste its blood.

"Then I went a little further back in time and saw the burial of their last king. For I thought that if they had any goodness, these people would show it then. They have tombs of mud-brick, and I don't think they embalm the bodies of their dead. Oh, Neyah, this is a terrible country! Everything I see is horrible to tell you about. In my spirit I went into the royal tomb, which in our country would have been *sealed in splendour*, but here it was grey with horror and fear, such sickly greyness that it must entrap the souls of those who are buried here, like insects in a web. And here, laid out in ordered rows, were the bodies of young girls and the bodies of young men. I was told that they had been held down while a long pin was driven behind their eyes and into their brains, leaving them unscarred as though they still lived. And their priests allow these things; and of their power they can force these earthly slaves to tend their evil king where he lives, bound to Earth.

"The rulers of these people must be destroyed! Oh, Neyah, I wish that Sardok were not our guest, so that to-night you could stab him while he slept."

"And so make myself lower than a Zuma! No warrior of Kam would kill a man who was defenceless. I wish I could challenge him to single combat—chariots and spears, or even arrows at twenty paces."

"No, Neyah, it would be wiser to stab him while he slept, because he is too big for you to fight yet. Why should you give an evil one a chance to fight? If you see a poisonous snake you crush it; you don't put your hand under its fangs so that it may have an equal chance of hurting you!"

"Sekeeta! You have been brought up almost as a prince. You think that you can go into battle with me and be the companion of warriors. Have you learnt so little that you would attack an enemy by bribing a servant to poison his wine because you had not the courage to challenge him to battle?"

"All right, say I'm a woman if you like, or child or girl who cannot understand things that men understand. If a thing is evil, stamp it out, kill it, destroy it any way you can; whichever way is quickest and most sure is best."

"If you ruled Kam, its name would soon be tarnished, when your guests were stabbed in sleep."

"Neyah, when I grow up I will learn power. Somehow I will learn to free trapped souls who died in fear. And I will learn to fight the evil ones with magic, and break their wills so that their bondaged people shall be free."

Next morning Neyah and I decided that we must warn Father about Sardok and the land of Zuma.

We found him with my mother beside their bathing pool. They had been swimming, and they wore thin woollen cloaks, for the morning was still cool. His was of scarlet and hers of pale green. They were eating fruit from a flat alabaster dish, and Mother gave us each a bunch of grapes. We sat beside them, cross-legged, and Neyah said, "Father, Sekeeta has had a dream about the Zumas. They are dreadful people. Sardok is an evil one, and you should not stretch out a hand in greeting to him, but your mace should smite his skull and split it in two."

Father laughed and said that Neyah was a ferocious host. But he questioned me about my dream, and I told him all about it, except about the bull, which I thought Mother would not have liked me to have seen.

Father said, "I know Sardok for what he is, and that in his heart he plots against us. But when asked if he might visit us, I welcomed him, because I hoped that if the King of Zuma saw how Kam flourished under Pharaoh and a true priesthood, he might take back the teachings of Kam to Zuma, and in time the Light might shine upon them."

Then Neyah asked if it was right to let the soldiers of Sardok and his servants mix with ours, for they might teach them evil things.

And Father said that his attendants and warriors were strong men and needed no protection from evil. He pointed to the sky, where wheeled a vulture, and said, "The strong do not fear the contact of evil, for they are like the vulture, who dies not when he eats filth, but, of his special strength, thrives upon it, and after such a meal can fly to greater heights."

And then Mother questioned me about my dream, and when I told her that I often had dreams as true as this one, she seemed more pleased than if I had done some difficult lesson perfectly. This made Neyah so pleased that he told the story about my finding the seal, quite forgetting that Father did not know that he had ever borrowed it. Father listened gravely to the story and said to me, "That must have been a true dream. Such things will be more precious to you than her voice is to a sweet singer or his hands are to a sculptor."

As they walked towards their apartments to prepare for the day, I heard my father say, "Those two together shall rule after us," and I think it was then that they decided that Neyah and I should be co-rulers; for it was less than a month later that my father, at the Festival of Ptah, announced us to the people.

That night my mother came to my room and talked to me about my dreams; and before I slept she said to me, "Cherish memory above all things, for memory of yourself, which is the Silver Key, will stop your feet straying upon a path that you have found leads not to freedom. Memory will teach you humility, without which there can be no pride that is true. In memory you will remember fear, without which there can be no courage that is truly born of understanding. With memory you will learn compassion, which is the heart of strength.

"One day you will possess the Golden Key, which unlocks the memories of others. And this will show you that there is no pit into which you may fall, from which others have not climbed; no great mountain, though it may seem too steep, that others have not conquered, even as you must conquer; no pain that has not passed, and no sorrow that has not lifted the shadow of its wing, letting the sunshine dry the tears of the weeping one.

"All upon Earth are travelling towards their freedom and must one day reach the great gate where the last shackle is struck from their feet. Then shall all be equal in the light of the last sunset and the first sunrise; and the greatest priest and the poorest crippled prisoner shall be joined in the Brotherhood of the Gods.

"So I say unto you, my daughter, remember your spirit."

CHAPTER FIVE

# Royal Progress

Later in this same year Father took Neyah and me with him on his Royal Progress, in which he went up river as far as the southern garrison of Na-kish. My mother remained in the Royal City, for when he went upon a journey it was in her hands alone that my father placed the authority of the Royal Seal.

When I knew that Father was taking me as well as Neyah, I was very excited, for I had never been further south than Abidwa, and even that was when I was much younger. My clothes were packed in five trunks, which had curved lids; three were of painted wood and two were of leather studded with nails.

The Royal Barge was of fifty oars. The oarsmen sat on the narrow deck on either side of our rooms, whose walls were of cool reed-matting, with coloured linen curtains hung inside. At the stern of the boat, just in front of the great steering oar, there were mats and cushions for us to sit on, and when the sun was high it was covered with an awning striped in green and scarlet.

Sometimes we played a game with coloured pegs, which fitted into a chequered board; or I practised on a four-stringed harp while Neyah made a model of the barge, carving it from cedarwood, with thin strips of ivory for oars. Often we stopped at villages along the bank, and then the headman brought to Pharaoh a tally of all the people and animals under his care, and of the height of corn in the granaries. In some places my father gave judgment; and he always took us with him.

In one village there were two men who disputed the ownership of a wild-ass, which both claimed to have seen first. One man was more prosperous than the other, yet he kept crying out about his poverty and the number of his children and the poorness of his fields; and he protested that his was far the greater need. My father knew he lied, and he said, "You tell me your need is the greater because you are poor and this other man is evil and a liar. I shall give judgment and adjust your wrong. You, who are the poor man, shall have the wild-ass; and to show how much you are favoured, you and this other man shall exchange all your possessions."

Then the man cried out in great self-pity, and said that he had been robbed. At this my father pretended to be surprised, "Robbed! When I have given to you the great possessions of your neighbour, which you so greatly envied? See, he is content under my judgment, although he has got for his share the fields and herds that you yourself claim to be the poorest in the land."

Afterwards my father said to us, "Sometimes a man must lose all that he has before he realises the value of what he has lost; even as some, who loudly bewail about a scratch, need a cut from a sword before they appreciate a healthy body."

At another village my father inspected all the animals; and he saw that one man's oxen were in bad condition and had deep sores upon their shoulders from an ill-fitting yoke. He told their owner that this was not well, thinking perhaps that he was ignorant or stupid and had not seen the hurt of his animals. But the man protested that his oxen were thin because they were too lazy to eat, that the work they did in the fields was light enough for a child and that he envied his oxen their contentment. And my father said, "There is no need to envy them—you shall share it with them. You shall be yoked to the plough and draw it back and forwards under the hot sun until the field is furrowed." And the oxen my father took away from him and gave to another, whose beasts were sleek and well cared for.

Some days later we came to a village where there was much grumbling among the people. This was found to be due to the arrogance of the headman, so my father deprived him of his office and appointed another in his stead.

When we asked him how he decided which man to give the office to, he told us, "It seemed that three men had equal claims, until I saw their gardens. In one garden the plants sprang strongly from the earth; but in the other two, the plants were wilting from lack of water, although the river flowed within fifty cubits of them. A man whose plants wilt within reach of water must be both lazy and a fool; and he shows ingratitude to the Weather-goddess under whose protection are all things that grow from the soil. A man is greater than the cow, whose milk he drinks; and the cow is greater than the pasture: yet, lowly as the pasture seems, if that should perish, then all the links in the chain of life that leads from it would perish also. So remember this, and in gratitude succour all growing things.''

Sometimes, when we had anchored for the night, Neyah and I used to fish from the stern of the barge. We had bronze hooks, baited with mud-worms or lumps of putrid meat. Once Neyah caught a large eel, and a sailor said it was the spirit of one who had died on purpose in the river. We didn't believe him, but Neyah cut the line and lost the hook, and the eel fell back into the water like a long silver snake.

But what we liked best was when we went with Father to shoot wild-fowl in the reeds at sunset. His long arrows went much further than ours. I have seen him fly an arrow through the outstretched neck of a fast-flying swan.

We stayed at Abidwa, which was the royal city in the time of the Meniss, for five days. I got very tired of being there after the first two days, for I had to spend all my time with girls and women. They sat up very straight in their best clothes and talked about buildings and new embroideries for dresses. There was one girl, she was the chief noble's daughter, who was like a very rich doll, the kind that is too good to play with. I said to Neyah, ''Do you think she's a real person underneath?''

And he said, ''She's only behaving like this because she keeps on remembering you are Pharaoh's daughter.''

''Do you think, if I put a lizard in her bed, she would forget who I am, and be more use to play with?''

And he got quite angry and said, ''If you go putting lizards in people's beds I won't have you as my co-ruler.''

''Well, if you get cross with me I shan't have you as *my* co-ruler.'' And we nearly had a quarrel, but just in time Neyah remembered something funny he wanted to tell me. ''In the house where I'm staying, instead of lying down in a bath in the floor and having people to rub you with oil afterwards, you have to go into a little room, like a box without a lid, and suddenly somebody pours water over you from the other side of the wall. It's not a very good idea, because it's always either too hot or too cold.''

The day we left Abidwa, there was a procession down to the river. Father led the way in a chariot, standing in it alone; and after him came Neyah and I in a double chariot with two horses.

The north winds were strong, so the oarsmen rested in the shade of the curving sail; and in four days we reached Nekht-an, the chief city of the South. It had been founded by Na-mer, who before the Two Lands were united had subjugated the King of the North for ten years. He called this city Nekht-an, 'the place that shall be remembered for its power'. It was in rivalry to this that the capital of the North was called Iss-an, 'the place that shall be remembered for its wisdom'.

The country here is very different from that nearer the Delta. After several days we came to a place where the river runs between rocky hills; here there is a great quarry of red granite, which had been discovered three years before because of a dream of my father's. In his dream he had remembered that hundreds of years before he had been a vizier under Na-mer, and that it was here that the stone for the King's sarcophagus was quarried. As the dream was fragmentary, my father authorized a priest of Anubis to search his records, so that this place might be found again. And so, three years before our present journey, my father returned to this same quarry that he had last seen in the reign of Na-mer. And he caused this place to be called Za-an, 'the place of the memory of Za'.

I had never before seen stone of this colour. A block of it was being cut for a statue of my father and my mother, which was to be set up in the Temple of Atet in the Royal City.

Then we came to the First Cataract, which the sailors call 'The Hill of Angry Water'. We stayed here three days for the ceremony of the official birth of 'The Gentle Slope of Smooth Water', a canal, where in future boats could pass up and down the river without danger from the cataract.

When we arrived the canal was dry. Part of it was cut out

of the rock, but in some places the walls were of dressed stone. There was a path on each side of it for the teams of oxen that would draw the boats upstream, and at the top of the cutting two great pillars of stone still joined the solid rock; from them ran deepcut grooves, filled with grease, in which slid heavy stones attached to ropes thicker than a man's arm. These ropes passed round the pillars and were tied to a boat going downstream; as the heavy stones were drawn up, so would the boat quietly descend. This method was only used when the river was high, or when boats were so heavily laden that they would be swamped if they did not ride smoothly.

The head of the canal was closed by a wall of heavy timbers, in front of which were hundreds of bags filled with sand, each with a long rope attached to it.

Most of the timbers had been removed before the day of the ceremony. Five thousand workmen waited by the ropes, and at Pharaoh's signal they pulled away the bags of sand that held back the water, which then plunged down the canal. And while some of the river went onward to dash itself upon the rocks of its customary channel, the rest of it glided smoothly upon this gentle hill of stone, until at last the sliding silver joined the quiet waters below the fall.

Then in the Royal Barge we passed up this mighty roadway of Pharaoh, to the chanting of the men who had built it.

That night at sunset there was a feast, and all who had worked to make these things come to pass sat down together in companionship; Neyah and I sat beside Father on a lion-skin by one of the many fires. Oxen and gazelles were roasted whole; and there were jars of beer and wine, and platters of cakes and honey and baked fish. The men sang their working songs, in which they tell their picks to split the rock, or the soil to leap into their carrying-baskets; just as the people of the fields sing to their oxen to thresh out the grain. And when the fires burnt low, dawn was already in the sky.

The next morning we returned to the barge, and we journeyed five days upstream to Na-kish.

This garrison, which guards the southern boundary of Kam, is on the west bank of the river. It is irregular in shape, having the semblance of a crouching lion, for it follows the outline of the outcrop of rock on which it is built. The walls, between the six square towers, are faced with baked brick, glazed like pottery, and rise sheer from the natural rock; they are higher than five men standing upon each other's shoulders, and of the thickness of a tall man when he lies down in sleep. They surround a courtyard, where five hundred cattle and a thousand goats can be driven to safety. Leading up to the entrance is a narrow ramp, with a sheer drop on either side, which three swordsmen could defend against an army. The gateway is approached through a tunnel cut in the rock, which is closed in times of danger by three drop-gates of stone. These are each lifted by twenty raw-hide rope, which run over metal staples to a flat rimless wheel of sixteen spokes, on each of which two men must bear their strength to turn it. In the middle of the main courtyard is a well of sweet water, and round it are the storehouses, in which are kept wine and grain and other food that grows not here; and also arrows and maceheads and the blades of spears.

Na-kish is garrisoned by two thousand soldiers from the north, and eight thousand other soldiers, whose land this is. They are half as high again as other men, or so they seem; their bodies are black as bitumen and shine like statues of polished ebony. Their heads are shaven except for a tuft of hair on the top of their long skulls; and in their smiling faces their teeth look whiter than ivory or shell. They wear nothing but a breechclout held by a leather thong about their waists. These are our people, and they guard Kam from others of their colour, who are not of their race nor of their hearts, being cruel and treacherous and skilled in sorcery—that food of filth of little evil ones. Also do they guard us against invasion from Punt in the south-east.

The garrison must be strong, for here is stored the tribute that comes from peoples to the south of Kam: the gold and ivory, the precious woods and dyes, copper and silver, and marble of the sky; amethyst and wine-stone and rare plants; awaiting the yearly journey on the new rising river. Then when the river ebbs, the boats return heavy with grain to trade with the people beyond our boundaries.

It is well that gold should be protected by strong walls, for stone and gold are of the same company. And why should a wall of men risk their lives for the youngest things of Earth? Yet if these warriors heard that a child suffered from cruelty, then would they bring retribution with their spears, and, if need be, fight until not one of them was left alive to protect the mighty Laws of Kam.

Neyah told me that when he had grown his strength, it was with these people that he wished to gain his captaincy; he would learn their minds and try to win their hearts, so they would follow him to victory if hostile neighbours challenged us to war.

And I, too, loved these people; and the songs they sang at home about their fires. In their songs were curious harmonies, which stirred the heart like none that I had heard; some would drone like bees as loud as lions, as though a tempest blew on mighty reeds and thunders muttered to a moaning sea.

We stayed there for nine days, and on the tenth day we started downstream on our homeward journey to Men-atet-iss.

CHAPTER SIX

# Death of Za Atet

When I was eleven, Kam was invaded by Sardok, King of Zuma, who had come as a guest with treachery in his heart to learn the paths of our country and our strength in war.

His men are yellow-skinned and bearded, their skins greasy, for they eat of unclean food; their bodies are coarse and hairy, fat as a white sow heavy with young. And they know much of evil.

They had a horde of dead slaves, who had been tortured so that in their dying they could be enslaved away from Earth and obey their dark masters. These slaves attacked those of us who in sleep watched over our country. But this availed them not, and from the temple news was brought that the Zumas were upon our north-eastern frontier, in the Narrow Land between the Two Waters.

The northern garrison challenged them. But our chariots were few, for our horses came from Zuma, who would trade us only stallions; and the chariots of Sardok mowed us down as corn falls to the sickle of the harvester.

Then the Zumas poured into our country like a destroying torrent: the fields were laid in waste, and the people of the villages fled from their homes, and they that fled not were engulfed in pain.

Five times the Royal Army under Pharaoh battered against the wall of the invader. Sardok would be driven back, and then more troops would swell the ranks that we had thinned; until the Zumas seemed like a wounded leopard that slinks back to lick its wounds only to launch forth a fiercer fury.

Then all the men of Kam who could hold a spear or swing a mace were called to the standard by my father. And the women of the land yoked the oxen and furrowed the fields; they set the bird-snares and cast the fishing-nets, so that the warriors should not know hunger, and when they returned they should find no famine.

For five months the wings of destruction shadowed Kam, and then it was decided that the whole strength of Kam should be thrown against Sardok in one mighty battle. If he triumphed, then would our country be in darkness, and the Light of our temples would gutter like a candle in the wind.

The day came when all our forces were arrayed against the Zumas, and behind the invader was the sea. News was brought from the temple that the battle had been joined.

That night Kam would know victory or defeat.

I wished I had been born a son to follow my father, like Neyah, to battle; or that I were a priest, that my spirit could be there—even to know defeat would be better than this suspense. Time passed so slowly, each moment seemed like a drop of icy water falling upon my forehead.

Then I remembered that sometimes, when looking on bright water, I had seen visions, vivid as in a true dream. I went to the garden and knelt beside the pool; and I prayed to Ptah of his compassion to clear my eyes. The last rays of the sun were falling on the surface of the water, as on a dark shield. I looked at the light....

I could see great armies in conflict....

I could see horses plunging, crushing many beneath their hooves who were not yet beyond their pain. I saw a man whose entrails tripped him as he tried to fight, and another with a spear sticking from his mouth.

I knew that the air was singing with the flights of arrows from Neyah's archers, and that there was a great noise, a screaming of stallions and the shouting and groans of men; yet I saw only the picture, and all was quiet.

The picture changed....I saw the chariot of Pharaoh leading the thundering charge; like the prow of a boat he cleaved the Zuma line, and it parted before him like the waves of a storm. Our warriors swept onward, with the Zuma host fleeing before them....Now they could retreat no further, for behind them was the sea....But we drove them on until they were engulfed by the waters, even as the rain engulfed the evil ones of the Old Land. This was no war of people against people, but of Light against Darkness, and to the Shadow we show no clemency.

Then I saw my father's chariot. His standard of the scarlet feather was planted beside it. But it was empty.

Again the scene changed....

I saw my father—he was smiling. Strange...I could hear....I heard his voice. He said, "My daughter, tell your mother that, knowing victory, my body died from a spear, and my spirit left it like a wild bird freed from the snare of the fowler. Tell her to sleep early to-night so that we may walk here together, for I have much to say to her. Tell her to grieve not at my freedom, but to share it with me. Tell her that she but steps from her sleeping body to my arms.

"And to Neyah say this:

"Much of rulership have I taught him upon Earth and much will I teach him away from Earth. Tell him to listen to wisdom, whether it be from the lips of an old man or a young hound-boy, for it is not earthly work or earthly years that gives speech that is fruitful to the ear. Tell him to rule as I have tried to rule: sharing his strength with the weak until they become strong; sharing his courage with the frightened ones until they become brave; sharing his honesty with thieving ones until they become true. Tell him to try to be to his people as his own master is to him.

"And to you, my daughter, I say this:

"When you are twelve, go to the Temple of Atet and learn to be one who can say unto the people, 'I, of my own knowledge, tell you that this is the truth'. Then, when your speech is proven, return and help your brother to guide his people, even as your mother and your father together have guided them."

CHAPTER SEVEN

# Freedom Regained

I knew that I should have been like my mother, who would not dim my father's glory with her tears. But when my sorrow was too heavy to be borne alone, I would go to the temple; and Ney-sey-ra would talk to me of death, until I saw it truly, as a gentle thing. And before the funeral of my father, he said to me, "If you were in a prison, little Sekeeta, and with you there was one you loved, and one day the door of the prison was opened and he was set free, then, although against you there were still bars, you would rejoice that he had regained a freedom that you had both longed for, and you would try to quench the tears of your loneliness with the thought of his joy.

"And if at night, while the world slept, you could fly through the window of your prison and share in his freedom, where you and your dear companion could be together, and where your eyes, undimmed by the shadows of the prison, could see him while he still held you in arms unshackled by fetters, then you would not shadow your time together by weeping because each day you must return to the four walls that had once enclosed you both.

"When your father was on Earth, you told him of all the things you had done throughout each day; and if you saw him in the evening, you did not sorrow because all through the day he must sit in audience or think upon the guiding of his country. That hour of being with him has now become but a little further from the sunset hour. Sorrow not because you do not hear his footstep at noon, for you have but to draw the curtains of sleep to walk with him.

"We are all travellers upon a long journey, and we pass through many countries. We may find gardens and tranquil rivers where for a time we are happy; yet in our hearts we know that we are exiles and long to return to our true home. When the Overlords of Earth send us forth upon our journey, they judge the span of time of our exile. And when that span is reached, whether it be the hour of a child that outlives its birth, or the day of an old man who for ninety years has watched his body age, then will the traveller see before him the doorway of his home.

CHAPTER EIGHT

# Funeral of Pharaoh

Za Atet was the son of the eldest daughter of the first sister of Meniss. His mother's tomb had been built where for a time Meniss had thought to make his new capital, northwards of the Royal City. She was drowned when sailing in a small boat near the First Cataract; her body was never recovered, and so her tomb was left empty.

When Meniss and my father, in co-rulership, built the new city of Men-atet-iss, they decided that the resting-place of their bodies should be at Abidwa, where the Light had been rekindled. When my father died, his tomb was still unfinished, though his plans for it showed where every brick was to be placed.

His body was embalmed in a temple of the Delta, and until his tomb was ready, it rested in the unsealed tomb of his mother. His sarcophagus was of cedarwood, carved and painted in his semblance, wearing the sphinx head-dress, and holding the Crook and the Flail.

And while he lay there, his soldiers guarded him. Always a chariot stood beside the door, as though it waited for his swift command; and every day his sword and spear were burnished, as though he were but sleeping in his tent before he armed for battle.

Upon the first day of the second month of the Inundation he started on his last journey to Abidwa. The great funerary barge was in the likeness of the Boat of the Gods. It was towed by ropes that went beneath the surface of the water to another barge, which led the procession, so that it seemed to move alone. On it he lay in his sarcophagus under a green and scarlet canopy, and none but he was on the boat, save Neyah, who stood at the steering oar. For nine days Za Atet journeyed, and each day from one hour after sunrise until sunset Neyah must steer, and could not rest or eat. Far down the river stretched the other boats—the Royal Household; his warriors; his priests; and his scribes. And on the banks were gathered his people, who had come from all his lands to see the splendid passing of their Pharaoh. They had wreathed themselves in flowers to honour him, that had died to free his people from the Shadow.

My mother's eyes were never dimmed with tears; yet when she smiled there was a sorrow on her mouth, and I knew that her days were exiles between sleep. She had said that his people must share in his joy of freedom from Earth and be of courage and not weep that he had gone ahead of them beyond their sight. And so his last journey to Abidwa was not of sorrow, but like a triumph on a victory.

At Abidwa his bier was drawn by twelve white oxen yoked in pairs; they were garlanded with scarlet poppies, the flower of warriors, and with golden corn for garnered wisdom. And thus he led a mighty river of his people along the avenue of sycamores, lined with the soldiers of his southern lands, who sang their warrior songs, as when they sang them before he led them in the battle-line.

This great Pharaoh's tomb was not a sepulchre of sculptured stone, but it was like the room in which he had set his seal; and the white walls were in the likeness of the shelves where he had kept his wide papyrus rolls. Behind Za Atet's final resting-place were the tombs of those that had worked with him and been his friends. Yet this seemed no city of the dead, for it was lapped with lawns, like smooth green water islanded with flowers. For he had said that when his last garden was no longer green and none should come to tend the paths that he had planned, then would his memory have faded from men's hearts; and he wished not for the little immortality of stone when he would know the glories of the West.

Then past the semblance of their almighty dead, his people filed....

Now all had bidden him their earth farewell, and the floor was deep with the flowers they brought as that final tribute he had wished. No food or wine, no furniture, no swords; no gold or ivory, no carven stone; but only the growing things that he had loved. And then the doors of cedarwood were sealed.

And we left him there in his serenity.

## PART THREE

### CHAPTER ONE

# young pharaoh

After my father's funeral, on the evening we got back to the palace Neyah and I went to the Pavilion of Plants and talked together.

Only a year ago we had been children, but now he had grown almost to a man's stature. He looked so much older, and even his voice was tired as he said, "It isn't only you and I, Sekeeta, who have lost our father, but it's all his people. They knew that every one of them could go to him for justice and counsel, and for his wisdom and his kindliness. Now he is not here any more....

"I knew that one day I should be Pharaoh, but I thought that I should rule with him for years; and gradually he would let me do more and more; and when he was old he might have wanted me to rule alone, but I should still have had him behind me. Now his people have only me to guide them. I shan't even have you to rule with me—for such a long time. Oh, Sekeeta, do hurry up in the temple! It can't really take years, if you work frightfully hard."

"I wish I hadn't got to go to the temple. I wish the priest could do all that sort of thing, so that I could stay with you. But when I'm a priest, I shall be able to remember being with Father all the time, instead of only sometimes."

"Father's judgments were always right. When he ruled, Justice and Pharaoh and the Scales of Tahuti were three ways of saying the same thing. He had all these thousands and thousands of people to look after, yet everyone who talked to him felt that they alone filled Pharaoh's heart. His soldiers were his brother warriors: he knew their names, even if he hadn't seen them for years, and he remembered how many children they had, and where their homes were. It wasn't just an army that he led; all the men fought for him because he was their friend. A child could talk to him and be sure of his understanding as if he were a child himself. Do you remember, Sekeeta, how, whenever we went and asked him something, even if he was tired after a long audience, or working at something very important with Zertar, he never answered with just half his mind, he always gave everything of himself?

"How can I ever be worthy to hold his Crook and Flail, to sit in his Hall of Audience, to wear his Double Crown?"

"Neyah, I know—not only in my heart, but with the sort of certain 'know' that comes from outside oneself—that you will be another Atet. Remember what he said to me after he was killed, 'Tell Neyah that much have I taught him on Earth and much will I teach him away from Earth'. He will be helping you all the time; you have only to think of him and he will be beside you to give you counsel. And have you forgotten what was said of you when you were born, 'He shall guide his people when they that assail them are engulfed beneath the waters, even as were the evil ones in the Old Land'? This has been fulfilled, just as the other words shall be true of you, 'This child shall be called Neyah, for the companions of his spirit are long in years, and he is worthy to rule over Kam'."

"But Father wasn't impatient, as I am. He could live in the present and see it clearly, undistorted by the past or the future. When he was sitting in audience, he thought of nothing except of how to bring the clearest judgment upon what was before him. He never let half his mind be thinking that there were still twelve cases to be heard, or how hot it was, or that he wanted to go sailing at noon; or any of the other things that always creep into my mind....

"When he was here with us in the evenings, it wasn't Pharaoh, or a captain-of-captains, or a high-priest of Ptah: it was just a father talking to his children, or a man tending his plants, or a healer-with-herbs searching for yet another secret of the Great Artificers."

"Do you remember, Neyah, long ago when he said, 'If men remember me, I hope it will be not as a warrior, or as a builder, but as a healer-with-herbs'? Yet he built many temples, and he died upon the greatest victory. Under him our people called themselves no longer the 'People of the Two Lands', but the 'People of Kam'; and the Bee and the Reed became two eyes that see one thing.

"And when we are afraid of failing, Neyah, we will say in our hearts, 'For Atet and Light'; for we are his children, and we must follow him and be not afraid."

CHAPTER TWO

# Last Day of Childhood

On the day before I went into the temple, I went with my mother to the Meadow of Ra; and I stayed there long with her, for I knew that this was the last day of my childhood.

I sat at her feet and rested my head against her knees, while her hands caressed my forehead like the cool winds of sunset. My heart was sorrowful, for I thought that never again should Neyah and I know the happiness of children together; for he must rule; and he would find other companions, and some might be dearer to him than I. No longer could the love of my mother be as sandals upon my two feet, for I must learn wisdom myself, so that, shod in truth, I could bear burdens across the heavy places of Earth.

And as the shadows grew long, my mother talked to me, and the weight of tears upon my heart was lightened. "If you were blind, my Sekeeta, there is nothing that you would not do, there is nothing that you would leave undone, if it might let you see the stars again. Long have you worked before in this life I first held you in my arms, so that you might see from this poor misty land we call Earth to realities where all truth endures. When you were a child and frightened by a dream, remember the comfort a lamp could give to you by driving back the darkness that you feared. One day of your own knowledge you shall be a lamp, and others, who fear the twilight of this world, shall look to you to light them on their way. When you were little I taught you this prayer, 'Master of thy wisdom let me grow into a great tree so that the weary may rest in my shade and go upon their journey refreshed, and the storm-ridden may regain their strength in the shelter of my boughs' Now like a tree you shall grow upwards to the Light, and your knowledge shall be the roots that withstand the bitter winds of time that in the future may assail your strength.

"Far in the future there may come a time of little knowledge in the land, a time when men have forgotten that death and sleep are one, a time when men have cloaked the face of truth, and walk in fear, and know not where they walk. But if you can cross the Causeway to the Gods, then you shall never know the loneliness of those poor lost ones, crying in the mist, who cannot see the stars for their own tears.

"For love of you I would take all the joys that this Earth holds and put them in your hands. I would keep every sorrow from your path that there should be laughter ever in your heart. Yet would I give you a far richer gift—but it is a gift that you yourself must find. Even if you could have all the joys of Earth, they would last such a little span of time; for chariots break, and lions must die; and sailing-boats shall no more fly the wind; and even the loveliest bodies return to dust.

"But what you learn in a temple will endure when Earth is a link in a half-forgotten chain. Wisdom and love are mightier than time: there may be deserts where this garden is, forgotten mounds for temple sanctuaries; yet will the love in our hearts be with us still, and you will have learnt how to remember it."

CHAPTER THREE

# First Days in the Temple

I said good-bye to Mother and Neyah on the night before I went into the temple. I couldn't tell them how much I minded leaving them, lest they should feel they were sending me into exile. That night Natee slept in my room. When I woke in the morning, I saw standing open beside my bed the plain wooden chest in which were packed the few possessions that I should take with me. No longer should I wear fine linen embroidered in gold and coloured threads, or cloaks clasped with golden lion-heads; now my tunics would be of coarse white linen and my cloaks tied with a violet cord.

Then for the first time I put on the tunic of a temple pupil. It felt harsh to my skin, and my sandals of plain leather were such as only a servant would wear in the palace. I opened the box of painted cedarwood in which I kept my necklaces and bracelets, and I thought how long it would be before I saw them again. Though such things are unimportant, when one looks upon them perhaps for the last time they take on a new significance; just as one may have a garden and see in it the weeds and the flowers that are wilted, yet when one knows that one must leave it, it seems beautiful and without blemish.

When I said good-bye to Natee, he put his great paws on my shoulder and licked my face. I told him I couldn't help not taking him with me, and that Zeb had promised to bring him to meet me in a little wood near to the temple so that I could take him for walks. But he knew that I was sad, and he would not be comforted; he whimpered as he always did when he was unhappy. Then I shut him in my room, so that he couldn't follow me. I wished he were a cub again and could stop himself being unhappy by doing something he wasn't allowed to do, like eating my sandals or tearing the feathers out of a pillow.

I went to the temple alone, so that none of the pupils should know that I was of the Royal House; for in a temple there is no rank, save the grades of initiation.

When I went through the pylon, which had the Scales of Tahuti carved upon the lintel, there were still many people in the forecourt, sitting on the grass in the shade of the sycamore trees as they waited for their friends who had gone into the sanctuaries. I went across the forecourt, up the three wide steps and across the pillared terrace into the cloistered courtyard.

Ney-sey-ra was coming out of the Hall of the Sanctuaries, talking to another priest, and when I saw him I forgot that I had dreaded leaving the palace.

I sat down on the grass beside the pool, waiting till he should be ready for me. The lotuses, with their open hearts like golden suns in the blue sky of their petals, reminded me of the first time I had met Ney-sey-ra.

Soon he joined me, and as we stood looking down at the pool, he said, "Every temple has a lotus pool, for the lotus has always been the symbol of a true priest. Though its roots grow in the mud beneath the water, it opens in the sunlight, and through its stalk the root knows of what the flower has seen.

"Mankind between birth and death knows of the earth-body; and that is the roots of the lotus. All leave their bodies when they sleep, but few there are whose memory of what they do away from Earth is not washed away by the Waters of Forgetfulness. Some go to the places from whence the

Light shines; but only those who have a channel of memory, which is the stalk of the lotus, can bring back to Earth what they have seen in the Light.

"The bud of the lotus can sense the light and know of its presence, but it is not opened to it. Yet has it gone far in the journey. This is the symbol of one in his first life of temple training. The bud opening to show its petals is the symbol of one who has passed the fine test of an initiate; and the fully opened flower is one who holds all power that one who is still on Earth can possess."

Then he told me that he would take me to Hak-kab, who looked after all the girls in the temple.

The entrance to the pupils' part of the temple was on the west side of the forecourt—opposite the entrance to the priests' quarters. I had often been to Ney-sey-ra's house, but this was the first time I had seen the place that for many years would be my home.

Hak-kab was old and very thin. She looked a little like Maata, but her eyes were hard. She called to a girl, who was inlaying the lid of a box with bitumen and shell, and left me with her. The girl asked my name, and I told her, Sekeeta. She showed me the pupils' rooms, which were built in rows on three sides of a long swimming-pool bordered with grass and shaded on the fourth side by pomegranate trees. Beyond the trees were the two-roomed houses of the younger priestesses, each with a garden like a room open to the sky. Dividing us from the boys' part of the temple was a long building where we had our food and could meet each other and play games and talk.

It all looked very bare and strange after the palace. I felt very miserable. The future stretched before me like a long grey road, and what it led to was so far ahead that I couldn't see it.

The girl told me it was the hour for swimming. I took off my tunic and joined the others in the pool. It was the first time I had ever bathed with anyone except Neyah and our friends, and I didn't like being in the same water as thirty people I had never seen before.

Some of them played a game, which they seemed to be fond of. Three girls stood in a row at one end of the pool, while another threw in a plate, and then they dived in and raced to see who got it first.

In the afternoon Hak-kab told me that I was to be one of the four girls who garlanded the Meniss pillars of the Hall of Sanctuaries with flowers. She explained to me that the pillars were copies in stone of the reeded pillars of the little temple where Meniss was trained during the long exile. But as Meniss was my great-great uncle, I knew that already. She said that I could go outside the temple when I liked, as long as I was in my room by sunset.

The rest of the day I wandered about and nobody talked to me. I wondered if I should ever get used to living with a lot of girls, and I longed for Neyah to come in his chariot and take me away.

In the evening I went out into the forecourt and listened to one of the temple story-tellers, who tell old legends and tales of wisdom to any who come to listen. Men and women and children were sitting round him on the grass. I sat between a goatherd and his son, who carried a newborn kid in his arms. The story-teller was just beginning another story.

"There was once a man who walked upon stones until his bare feet bled. He was offered sandals, but would not put them on.

"Then he found himself in a swift river and thought that he was drowning; but when strong hands would have pulled him into a boat, he tried to swim away from them.

"When he was sitting on a scorching rock at noon-day, he saw before him cool trees beside a pool; and they invited him to rest in their shade, but he ran further into the desert.

"He tried to draw music from a splintered reed; and he was given a flute of rare wood and ivory, but he broke it across his knee and threw away the pieces.

"When he was starving, a platter of his favourite food appeared before him; but he buried it in the ground and tried to stifle his hunger by licking a stone.

"And when the weather grew cold and he had only a few rags to hide his nakedness, they offered him fresh linen and a soft woollen cloak, but he would not wear them, and shivered in the storm.

"This story may seem hard to believe, yet if you think his foolishness passes understanding, do you not know one who is afraid to die? For if you do, you know one still more foolish than the man in this story I have just told you."

And so ended my sad day.

But as time passed I got used to being in the temple.

The walls of my little room were of mud plaster painted white. They were very thick, so that no sound should call me back to Earth until I was ready to return. The bed had Anubis heads carved at its head and foot, and there was no other furniture except a chest to hold my clothes. There was a window high in the wall, and in a niche below it I kept a bowl of flowers, which were the last things I looked upon before I slept, instead of upon a white wall as was usual. Beside my bed I kept a tablet of wax, on which as soon as I returned to Earth I wrote that which would remind me of my dreams. And I had a little cylinder of stone with which I smoothed the wax before I slept, preparing it for the morning, just as I must smooth all the thoughts of Earth from my mind, so that it would be free to record those things I did and saw away from it.

At night, before I set my spirit free, I said this prayer:

"Anubis, teach me to become a maker of paths, so that I may be as thy symbol, the jackal, which can cross a desert on a night with no stars and leave a track which others may follow in the light. And by thy wisdom may I cross the chasm between this world and thine, and lead my people to thy country of peace."

And in the morning, when I had recorded my little journey in the way of Anubis, I prayed to Ptah:

"Ptah, may my body be a vessel for thy life, so that on Earth I may be strong to do thy work."

And at noonday I prayed to Horus:

"Horus, of thy wisdom let my life be the whetstone which sharpens my will, so that I may become a sword in thy army."

Every morning I went to Ney-sey-ra and told him what I had recorded on my tablet. Often I would have met him in a dream in which he had told me that on waking I was to take him something to show that I had remembered meeting him; it might be a flower, or a pigeon's feather, or a coloured bead. Sometimes I remembered exactly what he had told me, but at first I made mistakes; perhaps I would wake up remembering that I was to take him a flower, and I might take a poppy when he had told me to take a convolvulus. Then, when memory was clearer, it might be that I remembered it was an ear of wheat that I was to bring; and, thinking that that was clear memory, I would take one to him, only to find that I should have brought an ear from the garland round the third pillar in the Hall of Sanctuaries.

In this way and in many others did he help me to train my memory. He would tell me of things of Earth and of things away from Earth. And sometimes he told me stories of the Gods, and of great warriors in the Light, and of Pharaohs. And much that he told me was new to me; but that which I had heard before lived in his words, as when he told me the story of the great Meniss.

CHAPTER FOUR

# the story of meniss

For two hundred and eighty years Meniss was rightful ruler of Kam: although many in turn held that name, it was as if one man renewed his body, as if his earth life were unbroken, so well did each continue the work of his predecessor. And Meniss shall be remembered through time as one great ruler.

The first Pharaoh to bear this name was one nearing the end of the long journey. Of his wisdom he planned much for the welfare of his country, but he knew that his body could not house his spirit long enough for these plans to be carried to fruition. So he chose one of his sons, who was a dreamer of true dreams, and taught him much while they were still on Earth; and after he died they met while the body of the second Meniss slept. And the elder counselled his son, so that the young Pharaoh had not only his own wisdom to guide him, but that of his father also.

And the time came when he was told by his father that there were many priests in Kam who were unworthy of their office. So he ordered his soldiers to drive them from the temples. But these priests of the Shadow, who reflected not the Light, but obscured it, had great earthly power: for their temples were rich, and the people had so long looked to them for truth that they knew not falsehood when they heard it from their lips. And the priests told the people that their Pharaoh was possessed of an evil spirit, and that to save their country they must destroy him.

It was decided to kill Pharaoh and his loyal soldiers on the first day of the Festival of Horus.

The young Meniss knew of this plan from his father, yet he still hoped that the Shadow might be lifted from his people. On the first day of the festival he sat alone upon the great single throne. Before him the dark floor of polished stone stretched to the open doors of the Hall of Audience, between a double row of round undecorated columns. Across the courtyard he could see the pylon of the gateway. There were no soldiers in the courtyard; for he said that if Pharaoh should need protection from his people, it would be as if a father feared his own children. So he waited there alone, to see whether this trust that he showed others would prove his truth to them who doubted him; whether it would teach them that where there is no fear there can be no treachery, and when there is courage there can be no betrayal.

But when he saw that those who came before him to bring tribute, brought not offerings, but daggers in their hands, he sat immobile, waiting for his death; so still, that he who stabbed him to the heart paused with upraised knife before he struck, thinking it was a statue.

Before his death, Meniss had sent his infant son secretly by night to a small fertile island among the sands, which lay fifteen days' swift journey towards the setting sun from Abidwa. Here, as his father had told him, was a small temple of Tahuti, where the Light shone unobscured. And with the infant went his nurse, who had been to him as his mother, who had died in giving birth to him; and with them also went the Looker of the Royal Household and her husband, who was a healer priest, and fifteen soldiers of the Bodyguard, under a captain. They travelled upon large white asses, for carrying litters or ox-carts would have been too slow.

Here, in this little settlement of people, the boy grew up; and he married the daughter of the priestess and the healer; and a son was born to them, who in his turn took the name of Meniss. And when the son was sixteen he too married, and his son bore the name, so that the line of Meniss should be carried on unbroken, until the name of Meniss should once more be borne by a reigning Pharaoh. For ten generations these people dwelt here, and they were like a small clear flame in a great sea of darkness.

Everyone, from the high-priest to the children, cultivated

the fields. They had no fish, and very little meat, except that of young male calves; for there was only sufficient pasture for cows that gave their milk, and not enough for bullocks to be fattened. They grew corn, beans and lentils, cucumber, radishes and garlic, melons and dates and pomegranates. They had goats from whose milk they made white cheeses; and sometimes they snared wild-fowl, during the passing of the great bird migrations, which stopped for rest and water on the little lake. This lake was always clear and cool, and from it came all the water of the settlement.

The houses were of mud-brick, roofed with a palm-leaf thatch, for there was no stone. There was no linen, except that which had been there before the death of the second Meniss; and there was no fresh papyrus, except some that was made from the fibre of the bark of palm trees; but this lasted not, and crumbled; and the scribes wrote upon clay tablets.

The people of this settlement multiplied themselves. And they lived as upon a little world of their own: for, beyond their near horizon, the high-priest made a great invisible wall of protection, so that any who came that way turned from their path and travelled outside this secret circle, yet knew not that their path had branched.

The Meniss were trained as priests of Anubis, so that when the word came, they might be ready to return and free their country. And all the children were examined by a seer when they were five years old, and according to the paths on which they walked, they were trained how best to help their country. Some went to the temple and learnt how, in their several ways, to bring back true knowledge to Earth, or to charge sick bodies with new life. When the time came these would drive out the false priests, so that once again the people could go to the temples and hear that which they needed for the growth of their spirit from the lips of one who could say to them, 'I, of my own knowledge, tell thee that this is Truth'.

And it was decreed...Others shall fly straight arrows and

master the sword and spear, so that their muscles, smoothly as oil, obey their will. Their strength shall protect the weak and their might in battle shall protect their people from evil. They shall be true warriors, to whom a wounded enemy is a friend: and to the women of their enemy they shall give comfort and protection; and when they go to a new country, it shall be to build, not to destroy; to free, and not to chain; to give peace, and not fear; to give light unto their darkness.

And there shall be those who administer the land. They shall see that the balances in the market-places are true, so that each woman, or child, or husbandman, who brings the work of their hands in change for another's, shall share contentment with the other.

They shall see that water runs freely to each garden and that none obstructs its flow of life.

They shall teach the people how best to tend their fields, so that the stalks of grain sway with the weight of the ear.

They shall see that none works his servant, be he man or animal, beyond his strength.

They shall see that no animal suffers from its master, unless he too receives an equal share of pain.

They shall see that no child fears an upraised hand or cries in hunger.

They shall see that the scribes record with truth that which they are told.

They shall see that the corn in the granaries falls not below ten cubits' height, so that the people walk not in fear of famine.

They shall see that, if a lesser man cannot adjust a wrong, the path to Pharaoh be not obstructed.

And they shall be wise and impartial in all their works, so that the people in the land may say, 'See, the scales in the market-places and in the places of judgment are as true as the Great Scales of Tahuti'.

When the twelfth Meniss was nineteen years old, the father of his line told him in a dream that the time was come when Meniss should rule again. And he was told to dress as a herdsman and go to Abidwa and mingle with the people, so that he might see what had befallen them under the Shadow.

And Meniss journeyed to Abidwa. He saw that in the great temple the statues of Anubis, Horus, and Ptah had been torn down and statues of Sekhmet put in their place. Walls had been built between the pillars, and all was dark except for a ray of light that shone through the roof and lit the eyes of Sekhmet, so that it seemed alive with the power of evil. Where had once sat a priest in counsel, now lolled the fat, swollen body of a boy with misshapened head; and from his lips came babblings at the bidding of the evil spirit who possessed his weakened body; and the dais on which he sat was stale with blood of many sacrifices. In what had once been the temple bathing-pool now crocodiles were kept, and to them were thrown any who dared cry out against the priests.

Then Meniss mingled with the people in the market-place, and he saw that the grain upon the scales was weighted by a stone; and that the fruit was sound only upon the top of the baskets, and the rest was blemished and rotten. And he saw, also, that the fields of the poor were barren for lack of water, because the channels were controlled by those more powerful. And he saw cattle whose backs festered with running sores. Filth and rotting food lay in the streets, so that the air was choking-thick with flies, which clustered round the eyes of children and shared their scanty food, even between a baby's lips and its tired mother's thin and flaccid breast.

Everywhere he heard murmurings of unrest, yet each who spoke, spoke fearfully, lest in his hearing might be a temple spy.

Then Meniss went to the soldiers' courts, and he found that the captains wore gold pectorals, for they had become rich by bribes. But soldiers are simple people without guile, and evil teaching is soon forgotten by them and dies, as when a poisonous weed is planted in dry sand. And Meniss talked to them, saying he was a captain from the rebellious North.

And they said that if they had a rightful leader again, they would follow him against the evil priests. And Meniss told them that in a secret place, their true Pharaoh waited to lead them from oppression; and that they would know him, for he would wear the White Crown of old and carry in his hand the Crook and Flail of Meniss. And the soldiers promised him that when they saw their true Pharaoh, they would follow him and sweep evil from their land as cleansing fire purges a field from blight.

And Meniss heard that at the next full moon the priests were placing yet another puppet king upon the throne. So he talked to his high-priest in a dream, telling his people to journey swiftly to Abidwa and wait for him outside the city, where he would join them.

And the people came. Then Meniss for the first time took up the Flail and buckled about him the golden belt, which had been rescued from the body of his great father by one who loved him and who had brought it at peril to the settlement.

Dressed as Pharaoh, and followed by two hundred warriors, he entered the soldiers' courts; and they welcomed him as their leader. Then through the city he led them, and men and women cried their joy at a deliverer. When he reached the temple, he halted his followers and went up the steps, alone. There, with his priests beside him, stood the high-priest of Sekhmet. And as the people watched in a deep silence, Meniss and the high-priest challenged each other's will. Standing immobile, they fought with power, their wills burning through their eyes like white-hot rods. They never moved, though sweat of effort cloaked them. At last, the high-priest wavered, and as though mighty hands down-pressed upon his shoulders, he sank at Pharaoh's feet and lay grovelling on the steps.

Then did the other priests of Sekhmet, seeing the greatest of them bowed to shame, his will broken like a splintered sword, try to escape. But their way was barred by a fence of levelled spears, which, slowly advancing, silent as a rising flood, drove them towards the pool, until their feet found space beneath their backward footsteps and they joined their victims with the crocodiles.

The last Meniss ruled his country gently and wisely for fifty-seven years, and during his reign the plans of the first Meniss flowered. His people flourished under the Light like corn-fields in the sun, for the temples were true temples, where the parched in spirit could quench their thirst in the waters of wisdom; the justice of the land was the Scales of Tahuti, and the granaries were filled ten cubits high, and none walked in fear of famine, either of truth or of bread.

And though Meniss grew long in earth years, until he died he was a master of chariots and a mighty spearman; and when he died, all his people unto the youngest of them felt the loneliness of one whose father has left Earth.

I had heard the story of Meniss when I was a child, but when Ney-sey-ra told it to me it was as though the scenes were taking place before my eyes. I asked him why this should be, and he answered, "I have read the records of these things, therefore in the jar of my memory they are also recorded. Last night while we slept, I shared this part of my memory with you, and so this story has now become a part of your reality."

I asked him how memory could be shared, and he said, "Think of two bowls of water, in each of which swims a fish. The fish symbolizes pure spirit, and the water symbolizes the memory of all experiences that the spirit has undergone. Every spirit is limited by its own experience, just as the world of the fish is limited by the water in which it swims. Now imagine that these two bowls of water are poured into a large vessel, so that each fish can swim as freely in the water from the other bowl, as in its own. Even so can our memories become one at will and your spirit can share my experience. But the time has not yet come when you can do this unaided."

CHAPTER FIVE

# Night in the Sanctuary of Anubis

When I had been three years in the temple, Ney-sey-ra told me that henceforward, on the night of each full moon, he would watch the progress of my memory while I slept in one of the rooms of peace beside the Sanctuary of Anubis. These rooms are cleansed with power, so that no spirit can enter into them unless its body is there also. This is done as a protection, so that no evil one, who might wish to soot the Mirrors of the Gods, can wait to attack them at the moment of their return to their bodies, which is the moment when the spirit is most vulnerable and when memory is most difficult to hold.

While I slept Ney-sey-ra would take me to many places away from Earth, and he would watch how I worked in the Light under his direction. And in the morning, as soon as I awoke, I would tell him how much I had remembered; and he would tell me what I had reflected truly, what I had distorted with my Earth thoughts, and of what I had brought back no record.

On the first night I spent in the sanctuary it was long before I slept. I was alone in the temple, for the pupils' quarters and the houses of the priests were outside the inner wall. A thick curtain closed my room from the sanctuary. There was no window, and when I put out the lamp, which I could not re-kindle, the darkness was heavy upon me. I thought of the darkness, and of the statues staring between the pillars. I heard a rustling sound and was frightened; I hoped it was only a bird that had flown into the sanctuary. Never before had I realised how dark a room could be; it made no difference if my eyes were shut or open. I had never slept with even a curtained window, and now it felt as if the walls were closing in on me till the room was small as a sarcophagus. I nearly ran out into the friendly moonlight of the courtyard, but I knew that if I did, Ney-sey-ra would be disappointed in me. I wondered if I should ever be strong enough to undergo initiation, when I must be alone in darkness and silence for four days and four nights, and before returning to my body, must undergo the great ordeals which might kill me if I failed.

I heard the rustling again, and deep in my heart I thought it was a snake and not a bird: the sound echoed, and I could not tell where it came from. I said loudly, "Sekeeta, you're being a coward!" so that I should have to prove to myself that I was not. Then I wished I had not spoken aloud, because the silence seemed to rush in on me: it was so still, it was like fingers pressing on my ears. I hoped Ney-sey-ra was asleep, so that he would be waiting for me. I thought of him very hard and prayed at the same time to Horus for courage....

When I awoke, Ney-sey-ra was sitting beside the bed waiting to hear my memory. But I was so pleased to see him and to realise the night was over, that the memory of my dreams flashed away and was gone. I thought Ney-sey-ra would have been disappointed, but I should have known his understanding. And he told me that many temple pupils, after their first night alone in the sanctuary, realising a little of what initiation meant, went back to their families and left the work of priests to others.

CHAPTER SIX

# First Trial of Memory

The next time I slept in the sanctuary, I had much to tell Ney-sey-ra when I returned to my body.

"First I went to the house of a poor woman who had a sick child. She knew not from what it suffered, and she thought it was dying. When from exhaustion she slept on the floor beside the bed, I told her that her child had eaten of a poisonous plant while leading the goats to pasture; and that she must give it a cupful of sweet oil to drink and put cloth wrung from hot water on its stomach to ease the pain; that in three hours she must give it bread crumbled in warm milk, and soon the poison would be gone and her child be well again.''

Ney-sey-ra asked me, ''Was the child a boy or girl? What country did they live in?''

''I think it was a boy; I am not sure. I do not know the country; there were hills covered in short grass.''

''It was a boy, and the land was Minoas, five days' rowing from the island of their king.''

''Next I went to a man who starved his oxen and stalled them belly-deep in filth; and clustering flies were feasting on their sores. I made him see a white bull with golden horns, who said to him, 'I am the God of Oxen. For your cruelty to my people, until every sore upon them is healed, you shall spend your sleep in lying down in filth and on your shoulders you shall wear a yoke.' I cannot remember where or who he was.''

''His name was Shezzak and he was a Zuma. For five nights you have been to him and told him to be compassionate. But he would not listen; and so he needed stronger teaching than words: for he could not understand his oxen's pain until he shared it with them.''

''Then I went somewhere, I know not where, and tried to go along a narrow path, but my way was barred by a frightful creature like a monstrous crocodile. And as it rushed at me, I turned and fled, and I woke in terror.''

''That was a creation of an evil one, to send you back to your body and stop your work. I know the fear that such things can instil, but next time you see one you must try to walk on, and will that it should crumble at your feet. If it is too strong for you, call to me for aid. Use your courage as a sword and as a shield, and they who challenge it shall run from you: for all things of the Darkness fear the Light."

"Then I slept again, and I went to the Place of Children and showed two little crippled boys that there they need not limp, but could run races one with the other...and there was more, which I cannot remember. I think I told them stories. And I built a little girl a house of sand."

"You have often been to this place before, as you remember, and played with children who smiled in their sleep because of the happiness of which they dreamed."

"And lastly, I remember going to a man who had just died, to tell him he was free of Earth. But he laughed at me and said I was mad. He picked up a stone and threw it at a tree and said, 'Do you still think I am a ghost? Ghosts are but part of man's imaginings, or at best misty shapes that sob upon the wind. I am alive—you fool to call me dead! Even my wound has healed and shows no scar'. But though I talked gently to him, he only laughed. And I said, 'You say that we are still on Earth: watch me fly, here I am lighter than a bird'. And of my will I rose above him. But still he laughed, and he said this was a trick, or else some strange fantastic dream and that he must be sleeping after too much wine.... He had been murdered in a wine-house brawl on the island where the sea ships of Minoas are built, and his name was Prax-ares."

Ney-sey-ra said, "That is well remembered. You have brought it back clearly and in detail, with nothing added or misunderstood. When next you sleep, go to him again, until he wakens to reality and knows where he is."

"Why should he not believe that he had died?"

"People of his country know not what death is. They think that when their nostrils no longer draw breath, they shall have reached the end of consciousness. So finding themselves still living, they think it must be upon Earth that they live. And in so thinking, they are bound by the limitations of Earth, from which they should be free....But he will listen, though it may take time."

CHAPTER SEVEN

# the Great Artificers

When I asked Ney-sey-ra how the Great Artificers created vessels for life on Earth, he told me, ''Before any living thing first comes to Earth, it must be conceived within the mind of its creator. He must fashion it from thought in all its complexity and at one time. Then he must clothe it with the substance of Earth before it becomes visible in the eyes of man.

''When a scribe draws a picture, he draws first one line and then another, until all the separate lines together make the picture that he sees in his mind. If he worked like an artificer, he would have to hold the picture in his mind, complete and perfect in every detail, and in a flash of time project it on to the wall. Yet the drawing-scribe has only to see his vision lengthwise and heightwise. So now think of a sculptor. In his mind he knows the statue he wishes to create, and with his chisel he frees it from the block of stone before him. If he had to create a statue in a flash of time, he would have to hold every aspect of it in his mind, as though a thousand interlacing circles encompassed it and every part of every rim of them were at the same moment the place from which he saw it. And statues are but the outer shell; they have not texture, save the wood or stone, no flesh, or heart, or channels for their life.

''Now think what an artificer must do if he would make the body of a lion. Not only must he know all that the eye can see, but also all the elaborate workings of veins and stomach, heart and lungs and bowel, muscles and blood, and a thousand other things that must be there before a lion can live: the thousand thousand hairs that make its coat and all the royal splendour of its mane; those magic mirrors that are living eyes, which let its spirit know of sound; and its nostrils, which bring it knowledge on the wind.

''Now close your eyes and visualise that lion—and your vision must be more embracing than the sun: for though the sun can bathe a stone in light, half of it is shadowed. But the artificer must know each hair-tip, each drop of blood, bathed equally in the brilliant light of his will, so that he sees it in its entirety, all at one time. Then he is but a quarter on his way. Now with his power he must mould it into earthly form, so that it can hold the life for which he made it. Does it sound difficult?''

''So difficult!''

''And therefore worthy of the Gods who do it.''

''I am glad they do not waste their time by doing things that I can understand....Would it be much easier to make an ant?''

''Perhaps a little. But though an ant looks small to us, size—away from Earth—is but a manner of thought. So there one cannot say that a lion is bigger than an ant, except when thinking of them in terms of Earth. Though an ant is shorter than you little finger-nail, its design exactly fulfils the purpose for which it was made, and if you could see it the same size as yourself, you would know it to be very complex.

CHAPTER EIGHT

# THE DWELLER IN THE CORN

One day I walked along the path through the cultivation and went among the corn, gathering scarlet poppies, the flower of warriors, to weave about the pillars in the temple; for it was the anniversary of my father's great victory. The sun was hot and I had walked far; and being tired, I lay down in the shade of the growing corn and went to sleep.

I found myself in a great forest; and the smooth trunks of

the trees soared above me to the sky. I walked onward through the growing colonnades, and I saw an animal, which was as large as a lion, but with the semblance of a field-mouse. We could talk together, for I knew its thoughts. I asked it what it was called and it told me 'The Dweller in the Corn'. Then I knew that I had left my body, and that the forest through which I walked was the corn-field in which I had gone to sleep.

I put out my hand and touched the mouse; and the mouse suffered me to caress her as though she were my favourite horse. Her eyes were larger than a gazelle's and her whiskers were like rods of silver. Then I asked her where she lived, and the mouse led me up the smooth pillar of a corn stalk and showed me her nest. I stood beside her in the soft and rounded warmth, which swayed with the ripple of a passing wind. And the mouse told me of the Danger Shadow of the Fields: how a brother might be still, in fear, when death fell from the sky. And she warned me to keep in the shelter and not to cross an open space till it was dark.

Then I left the mouse and went on my way; and above me the wind curved out the silken sails of scarlet petals.

And then before me I saw a grassy wall, and I looked over it, and I saw it was a nest with three great eggs. Suddenly the air about me was stirred by wings, and the mother quail had come back to her nest. She seemed not to see me, nor to feel my hand smoothing the feathers of her head. I knew she was listening for the tapping chicks to start breaking their way out of the eggs, for she had sat long upon them and yearned to see their hungry mouths open in greeting when she brought them food.

When I awoke I pondered on my dream. Why do we not remember that there is only size when we think in terms of earthly form? Zeb, who would rather cut off his right hand than injure Natee, thinks nothing of seeing a hawk swoop on a mouse. A moth is as worthily the work of Ptah as a swift horse. To think that size relates to godliness is as though one listened to a man for his stature and not for his words. Tall buildings are not more lovely than a flower, nor twenty harps sweeter than a singing bird. We should think of all things as though they were as ourselves, for once we shared their life, in our first journey from the hands of Ptah.

CHAPTER NINE

# the temple scribe

In my fifth year in the temple, there were twelve pupils in the way of Anubis, and forty who were learning to be lookers.

A looker is trained to leave her body by looking at a bright spot of light, sometimes at a flame, but usually at sunlight reflected in a cup of polished silver. Although she has left her body, to her it seems as if the things she sees away from Earth are a vision pictured in her cup. Lookers can see only to the spirit counterpart of Earth. They watch over the borders of our country, so that an invasion should not find us unprepared. They are also used to send messages between temples; and by this means news can travel many days' journey in the span of time that it takes a priest to leave his body and make a distant looking-girl see a vision in her cup. For some messages there are symbols, which are recognised in all temples. Every big town has its symbol. If a looking-girl at Abidwa saw first a crook and then a locust, she would know that there was a pestilence in the Royal City. If she saw an ibex and a stripped husk of corn, she would know that the garrison of Na-kish needed more grain. At the chief temples, in time of danger, three girls look into three sides of a pyramid of silver, and if all see the same vision, then it is known that their sight is clear and unobstructed.

Of these forty pupils, there were three training to be 'Lookers of Maat'. And of these, I was one. And Ney-sey-ra taught me how to leave my body, first by looking at a bright light, and then by my will, unaided, until I could travel as freely as if my body slept, yet at the same time make my tongue record what I did and saw away from it. I travelled not only to the counterpart of Earth, but to all those places to which my spirit could reach upon a sleep journey. And Ney-sey-ra taught me also how to read my own records; until I could look back across a vista of the years and see myself when I had lived in other countries and spoken other tongues; remember a hundred childhoods and a hundred deaths as clearly as if each past moment were the living present.

Although I could remember that I had made my body speak when I was away from it, when I returned I could not remember in detail what I had said. So my words were recorded by a scribe, and when he read them to me, I knew whether I had recorded clearly what I had seen.

Among the scribes was one, Thoth-terra-das, who was my friend; and often we talked together when our work was done. He was old, and had been a temple scribe for forty years. Though he had no priestly training, he had recorded much of wisdom, for he was a scribe of priests. Words to him were like colours to a drawing-scribe, and with them he painted things that he had seen, so that other men could look upon them through his eyes.

He would tell me to search for words as if I were a goldsmith matching beads to make a necklace, balancing their colour, sound, and shape, and smoothly stringing them upon my thread of thought, so that they should delight both mind and ear.

Once he said to me, "The Goddess of Truth in her celestial sphere walks naked in beauty, but when she comes to Earth she must disguise herself in words. There have been wise men who have seen her face, yet dressed her in plain tunics of coarse wool, hiding the silver beauty of her hands in falling sleeves of sober-coloured stuff. They should have spun for her fine linen robes, so that her radiance could shine forth on men as light shines through an alabaster lamp.

"Though I am old and long have been a scribe, I have but heard her spoken of by priests; yet was their wisdom heavy on their tongue and could not show her image to my heart. They have the knowledge, I the net of words. If we could only share each other's skill, then would men see her rare beatitude and all would follow on the path she leads.

"So I but string my words upon the thread of gratitude for the loveliness of Earth—the slumberous murmuration of the sea; the patient pattern of an ancient vine; the muted gold of sunlight through a mist; the mountain's still impatience for the sky—into a necklace carven of my thoughts, unwarmed by the touch of her that I make it for.

"Sekeeta, in a little span of years your gateway will be open to her sphere. Remember that words may be the only link between many dwelling here on Earth and a perfection that they cannot see. So pray to Ptah to make you wise in words, so Truth may walk on Earth serenely crowned."

And he inspired me with a love for words. For to say, 'Death is kind', is not enough; men should be told of it until they feel it is their lost love that they hasten to. And I would show Thoth-terra-das the little tributes I had made to what my heart found beautiful and true.

I have a beloved.
Yet I know not how long is the path that leads to her door.
But when she opens it to me,
I shall hear music sweeter than harps or flutes.
If I am hungry,
She will give me fruit.
More delectable than figs or pomegranates
And food smoother than honey on the tongue.
If I am thirsty,

She will give me cool wine
More refreshing than any in the royal cellars.
If I am weary,
She will anoint me with scented oils
And put sandals finer than Pharaoh's upon my feet.
If I am sorrowful,
She will make my tears be of joy.
As I hasten towards her,
I hope that each turn in the path
Will show her waiting for me,
Her arms outstretched in greeting:
For I long to dwell in peace in her house.
My beloved is very beautiful,
Her eyes are gentle,
And her hands that succour me are strong.
I have longed for her through my lonely days on Earth.
For she has welcomed me after many journeys.
And the name of my beloved is Death.

Thoth-terra-das was quite pleased with my poem, but he said it was too long and it would have been better if it had ended:

...I hope that each turn of the path
Will show her arms outstretched in greeting:
For I long to dwell in peace in her house.
Do you not know the name of my beloved?
Her name is Death.

I said, "I am not sure that I agree. But if you want a short poem, here is one:

A starving man dreamt he sat at a feast
A blind musician dreamt he saw the stars,
A vanquished warrior dreamt of victory,
And when they woke they found that it was true,
For in their sleep the three of them had died.

And he said, "I find that very pleasing. Always remember, it is better to make a bracelet that fits the wrist, than a necklace so long that the wearer stumbles over it."

CHAPTER TEN

# SECOND TRIAL OF MEMORY

As time passed my memory became clearer and more detailed. One evening, before I slept beside the sanctuary, Ney-sey-ra told me to return to Earth two hours after sunrise. And in the morning as I opened my eyes I saw him sitting beside me, waiting to hear what I should tell him....

"First I went to the wife of a farmer, who though good of heart was foolish of tongue. She loved her husband, yet she would upbraid him if he were lazy, or too full of beer, or if, when he had been irrigating his fields, he left not his sandals outside the door, but covered the matting of her floors with mud. Her husband saw not her love, because it was obscured from him by a thicket of thorny words. So he thought long on the girl who tended the milch cows, and who was comely and spoke to him only with admiration on her tongue. Before she slept the woman had prayed that her husband's love might return to her.

"I took her to a place where there was a wall of baked brick; and the wall was just so high that she could see over the top of it. Upon the far side she saw her husband sleeping in the cool of a fig tree; behind him stood his idle plough, and beside him was an empty jar of beer. And she called out to him and said, 'Lazy one! If your plough went as quickly as beer runs down your throat, you would be a rich man and your sleeping would be a sign of merit, instead of laziness.'

And as she spoke another row of bricks appeared upon the wall.

"I said to her, 'Sebek, do you see that wall which has grown up between you and your husband until you can no longer reach him and now he is even hidden from your sight? Each brick of it is but a foolish word of yours; and even as you can no longer see him because of it, so can he no longer see you; and, of his loneliness, he has taken unto himself the girl who tends the cows. Henceforward, think well before you speak. Say only those things that you would like to hear said to you by one you love. Build no more upon this barrier and you shall find it crumbling before the love in your heart, as a wall of unbaked mud crumbles before the inundation.'

"I think she will remember what I told her, for the picture that I made her see was better than if I had counselled her only with words. She lives in the Delta a day's journey from the sea. Her house has five rooms, and three sycamores are before her door. Is that truly recorded?"

"Yes. And you answered her prayer with wisdom."

"Then I went to the country that lies westward across the great ocean where Athlanta was. There, in a great forest, journeyed a man who searched for gold. When he was last born on Earth he had been a noble; but he had thought not of the welfare of his people, and they that should have been to him as his own children suffered grievously of his neglect. The drainage channels were uncleared; and where there should have been rich fields, there were swamps where fever came with the evening. When he died he knew that he had thrown away his chance of succouring those to whom he should have been a friend. And he asked that he, who had let his people die of fever, should on Earth cure others who suffered as they had suffered.

"In this his next life, he was born the eldest son of a master road-builder. When he was eighteen he left the house of his father and set out upon a long journey; for he knew that there was something that he must find, though upon Earth he knew not what it was, and he thought that it was gold, with which he could succor his fellow-men. For many weeks he journeyed through great forests, where fiercely growing plants made walls that shut away the sun. Then, he, too, fell ill of the fever, and first he longed for warm coverings, when his body shook with cold; and then when he burned with fever, he longed for the cool sea at sunset and for the juice of fruits in a cool pitcher. And he thought that he would die and that he would have found nothing to cure even his own suffering.

"'Because of his fever he could see beyond the things of Earth as if for a time he were a seer. So I took upon me his semblance, and he thought he saw a vision of what he must do to cure his sickness. I went to a tree, the *kahan* tree, which grew near to where he was lying, and I took the bark of it and boiled it in water in an earthen pot over his cooking fire; and when it was long boiled I drank of it and cried out, 'Behold! the fever has left my bones and I am whole.'

"'Then he saw me no longer. But I watched him crawl towards the tree, and I knew that he had remembered his vision. He has found a cure for the fever that once others suffered because of him, and so shall the Scales be adjusted."

Ney-sey-ra was pleased; and I was glad that I had been the instrument by which that man had found what he had sought so long. And through his prayers the Gods had shown him how to find one of the wonders that they have made upon the Earth for the assistance of mankind.

"'Then I went to a woman who was upon her deathbed. She lived many days' journey beyond the most northern outposts of the people of Minoas. The people of her country have no knowledge, and they think that when they die, though the memory of life may linger round the body for a short time, soon it must return to the earth from whence it came, just as water, which has for a time been shaped by a jar, loses its separateness when it is thrown back into the river.

"'This woman had a son who longed to see beyond his

horizon to new lands; so he left his home and journeyed to far countries. For a time he lived with the fishermen who collect the shell-fish from which they make the violet dye. While he worked there, he met the steersman of one of our ships that bring dye and cedarwood to Kam. And the steersman talked to the boy of the Light and reawakened memory in him, so that he knew that the words he heard were true.

''When after many months, he returned to his home, he thought that his village would rejoice with him in his knowledge, that the widows would cease to weep and the mothers be comforted that their dead children were not lost to them. But the people listened not to him, and they called him a dreamer and a fool; and they said he was a coward that turned his back on reality.

''But the boy's mother listened to him, for she loved the sound of his voice. Yet did she say, 'There is no proof of these things. Think not on death, for to think on death is to think on nothingness, and that be the thought of fools.' The boy was sorrowful, and often he prayed to the Gods that his mother should not die uncomforted, lest she should walk bodiless on Earth.

The boy left his village and went among many people, but he found that few there were who listened to him.

''When I went to the woman, the time of her going was almost reached. She longed to see her son once more before she died, and her eyes were upon the door, hoping that it might open and that she would see him again, returned from another journey. But the boy was awake, for he was upon a boat upon a rough sea, where none had time for sleep because of the storm. So I took upon myself his semblance and let the mother see me walk through the opened door. And she saw not the rest of her family, who wept beside her bed, but only me, who walked towards her. Then those who watched beside her saw her sit upright and hold out her arms and they heard her cry, 'My son, you have returned to me'.

''And as they saw her fall back dead upon the bed, she

walked with me out into the sunshine through the open doorway. And I left her resting in a place of peace, until her son should greet her when he slept."

CHAPTER ELEVEN

# Scarlet Poppies

By the time I was seventeen I had learnt how to read my records. In the space of five days I lived five lives. In three of them I was a man, and in two a woman. All were turbulent, and I had died in battle, or in a pestilence, or in a famine; and in none of them had my path led through quiet fields, but always had I travelled through deserts of unrest in the shadow of thunder-clouds.

I wondered why I should remember so little of quietness and of peace. So I asked Ney-sey-ra, and he told me, "Think of this life, Sekeeta. Which days spring to your mind? The days of strife, the days of sorrow, the days when you learnt something that made you wiser."

And as he spoke, before me was the day that I had lashed Zeb, the day I had met Ney-sey-ra, the day when Harka was hurt, the day of the great battle, the day of the funeral of my father.

Ney-sey-ra knew my thoughts, and he said, "Life is a teacher. Sometimes he whispers of joy in the cool of the evening, and sometimes he speaks in a voice that thunders about our ears. But always he tells us to take courage and remember that our tears water the corn that grows seven cubits high. In many days have you known peace and quietude, and in many lives; yet are the moments of greatest joy or grief as clear in your memory as a single scarlet poppy against a sheaf of golden corn. So do you first record those lives with which you learnt courage, wisdom, or compassion: for they are in brilliant colours. The other things that you must learn, though they are stored in your memory for you to find, have not the bold challenge to memory that wisdom and courage have. You may learn patience through many lives as a ploughman, or as a woman working in the fields; yet those lives will not hasten to be remembered, for they distil their wisdom quietly as a violet spreads her fragrance while she shelters under her leaves. It is easy to remember those times when, heralded by trumpets, you knocked upon the gates of death with uplifted sword scarlet from your enemies; or when you crept towards them through a land of famine when only the vultures hungered not. But for each of these, a hundred times have the gates of death opened smoothly before you, swinging wide upon their hinges as you walked through them and knew their sweet familiarity as the doorway of your home. And this you remember not: for it is the sound of the mighty waterfall, and not the quiet river sliding between its banks; the day of great storm when the arrows of lightning are loosed upon mankind that you remember, and not the gentle evenings when you walked alone in the dusk.

"In the future when again you remember how to turn the Silver Key, it will be my voice that you will hear, for wisdom speaks with a louder voice than any other. And you will remember how to remember."

CHAPTER TWELVE

# ARBEETA'S WEDDING

When I was seventeen I went with my mother and Neyah to Abidwa, where we stayed at the house of my mother's sister, for the marriage of her daughter, Arbeeta, to the eldest son of the Vizier. I had not seen Arbeeta for three years, but as children we had often played together when she stayed with us at the palace, and Neyah and I had always thought of her as rather a dull little girl.

I found her changed, for she had become beautiful because of her happiness. She showed me the house she would live in and the rooms that her children would have when they were born. And always she said, 'This is how we planned it—do you like this garden we have made?' just as though she and her husband were one person. It brought home to me the loneliness of my life. For me there was none of this shared security; I should never become beautiful, as she had done, because of the love of a man; for the things of a woman's heart were not for me in this life.

After her marriage festival was over, we returned to our city and I lived again in the temple. But often I found my thoughts dwelling on what I had seen at Abidwa. And in my heart was envy of Arbeeta's shared security, and though I knew this was unworthy, I could not drive it forth. So I went to Ney-sey-ra and told him of my thoughts that troubled me.

And he said to me, "All who feel envy are looking to one who seems to have more than they, instead of looking to one who longs to be as they are. The cripple envies the swift runner and forgets the blind man who longs to share his sight; the musician envies the night-singing bird and thinks not of the giraffe, which makes no sound; the merchant envies the noble in his painted litter and thinks not of those who walk hungry past his stall. There may be ten thousand in this land who envy Pharaoh, but they do not know the loneliness of kings. The very things that you are finding difficult are the proud heritage that you have earned, and for you to wish you were not born to them is as though a musician were to throw away his harp."

"But, Ney-sey-ra! For years and years and years I've worked to bring back memory; other queens have ruled, and Pharaohs, who were not temple-trained....When I am away from the temple, even for a little time, the earth-fever gets into my blood and makes me feel that priestly things are too hard. It is so difficult when one is young."

"The joys of youth are sweet, but they soon pass, like flighting birds across a summer sky. But what you are gaining here is wisdom. That is permanent, and you will still have it when your body is old."

"But any in the land can come to the temple to hear truth; all can bring their troubles to a priest, whose wisdom will show them their own hearts. Yet I must work to gain it for myself."

"There is a strength and peace that only self can give to self; and therein lies the value of your striving. There is nothing that life on Earth cannot take away from you, save your own wisdom. Here in Kam, where there are many priests, the Light shines and all may bathe in it. But in the past, evil has swept Earth and there were no priests to light their fellow-men through the dark valleys of their troubled years. These things have been, and they may come again. You may be born in a country of the blind, where there are puppets dressed in robes of priests, who mouth forgotten words that bring not comfort even to themselves. But though there be no other in the land who walks not in the Shadow, yet will the wisdom I have taught you here be with you still, and you can never feel the loneliness that those who have sought not for themselves shall know. Then can your voice speak to the multitude. And some there may be who heard it here in Kam, and they shall seek it to quench their spirit's thirst for truth, so they no longer starve in a waste of words, as they shall do in the temples of that time.

"But always, my pupil, you must speak of Truth. Cry to the Gods, 'For Atet and the Light', and I shall hear you, even if I am far away from the Earth. Fear not to die for what you know to be true, though evil ones should burn you for your words. And in your burning, look towards the stars and you shall feel me clasp you by the hand."

"But why should these things happen? Why should the Light not shine, always?"

"I remember what happened before Athlanta fell. Men of themselves create their time on Earth: if they sow evil, they must return to gather their harvest, and the fair meadows become a wilderness. The future is in the hands of mankind. When they allow the Light to shine upon them, they walk in peace; but in the Darkness they cannot see their way and they fall into destruction. If the time comes when men have forgotten the Light, then will they live in a land where there is more despair than in a city where all are dying of a pestilence. Children in spirit shall hold the Crook and Flail, and they shall have a terror of true priests and when one speaks shall silence him with fire. When they have broken the Mirrors of the Gods they will have brought a desolation upon Earth. Then Death shall walk through the streets, not as a beloved guest but in that guise of the long dead which chills the heart with fear. And there shall be wars, not of the Light against Darkness, but of people against people, who will have lost the nobility of leopards, which kill only when they are hungry. They shall slay not even for the lust of destruction, but because their thoughts are dead and the jars of their memory are sealed so that they die of thirst unquenched by waters of their own memory. The granaries shall be filled, yet the people shall starve. There shall be great temples, but the bread of wisdom and the wine of truth shall not be found there.

"In their affliction the people shall cry out to the Gods whom for so long they have denied, and for many years their voices shall die upon the wind and leave no echo. But at last, when they think that their darkness is of a tomb, upon the horizon they shall see a small clear flame, and they shall hasten towards it and it shall fill their hearts. Then, as the sun drives forth the shadows of the night, the Light shall return and they shall cherish it, and Earth be so brilliant that it shall be ready to become a moon."

And as he spoke he cleansed my heart and I no longer

yearned for Arbeeta's life, but only wished for strength to shield the land of Kam from Darkness....Anubis, whose priestess I shall one day be, give me the courage to use thy wisdom well, that I may be thy servant worthily.

CHAPTER THIRTEEN

# NEFERTERI

I had a close friend in the temple. Neferteri, who used to live in the palace when I was a child. She was two years older than I. At the age of thirteen she was betrothed to a young noble, but he was killed in the same battle as was my father. On the same day that he died, but before she had heard of his death, she was knocked down by a chariot. The horse, maddened by the sting of a hornet, galloped down a narrow street between high, mud-brick walls where Neferteri was walking; and the swaying chariot knocked her down and the wheel went over her and injured her back.

For five days she lay as if she slept, and when at last she returned to her body, her legs no longer obeyed her. And when she awoke, she knew that her betrothed had died, and yet she grieved not, for she remembered all that they had done together away from Earth. But the next time that she awoke, she remembered only vague fragmentary dreams. So she wished to go into the temple to train her memory. The priests thought it would be too great a strain on her, for only those who are strong in body are taken into the temples. But my mother thought that in the temple Neferteri would find, not that her burden would be made more heavy, but that it would be lightened. So when she grew stronger and could walk again, although her right foot was twisted, and cold as the claw of a bird, she became a pupil of Ney-sey-ra.

Neferteri stayed in the temple until I was nineteen. Often when I had been away at the palace, I would cry out to her that the temple training was too long and wearisome. Before she talked to me, the colour and the pageantry of the palace were bright before my eyes, and the walls of my little room seemed narrow as a tomb. Then Neferteri would talk to me, until the music of festivals sounded remote, and the walls of my room seemed to fold back like a door, a door which led to as yet undreamed-of-splendour; and hot impatience left me, and again I knew that time passes as quickly as sand slips through closed fingers.

When I was nineteen, Neferteri died. She had known for three days that her time on Earth was drawing to its close. Her spirit had burned too brightly for her body, as burning oil would crack a thin shell bowl.

I sat alone beside her in her room. She felt no pain, and the hand I held in mine was quiet and cool. Sometimes she smiled and talked to one who stood beyond the bed, where I saw but the wall.

Then dawn showed through the window, and I turned to pinch the wick which spluttered in the last few drops of oil. But when for a moment I would have left her side, I felt her faint hold tighten on my hand, and she said, "That little lamp is to the sun as what I've done to what I've longed to do. Soon we both must go, but each of us shall leave the Earth a little darker for our going."

When the lamp went out, the room was filled with the pink light of dawn. And in it I was all alone.

CHAPTER FOURTEEN

# temple counsellors

Every day in the temples of Kam, two hours after sunrise and in the evening, those who are sufficiently experienced, although not yet initiate priests, wait in the room of peace beside the sanctuaries; and to them come any in the land who seek wise counsel for the guiding of their hearts. If a counsellor finds that the burden brought to him is too heavy to lighten unaided, then does he pass it on to one of greater wisdom.

In villages where there is no temple, always is there a priest to whom the people can take their troubles, so that there is no one in Kam who need be without a wise friend and counsellor.

When I was nineteen Ney-sey-ra adjudged that I was ready to become a counsellor of the Temple of Atet. In this work I learnt much that was of great value to me, for because of my office, the people showed me their hearts and told me of their troubles, with nothing added and with nothing unrevealed.

On the first morning, there came to me a man who wept and said that he was afflicted of the Gods. After much questioning, I found that he was a fruit-seller in the market, and that he had dealt dishonestly with many people, selling them baskets of fruit that was about to spoil. He said that an old woman had put a curse upon him for defrauding her; and every night when he slept, rotten figs rained down upon him, and, weighted with their sodden pulp, he awoke screaming out that he was being stifled. He regretted that he had done wrong, and he asked me to remove the curse and to forgive him.

And I said to him, "The curse was put on you because of your dishonesty. A priest cannot adjust the Scales of Tahuti.

Only you can adjust a wrong that you have done. Secretly by night you must put baskets of fresh fruit before the doors of all whom you have defrauded. Then, when you have done this, you will find your dreams are calm again.''

Next there came a man who told me that sometimes his young wife looked at him with unfamiliar eyes and spoke to him in a tongue that was strange; and sometimes she lay writhing upon the floor. Afterwards she would forget that she had done these things, and he dared not tell her what she had done, for fear of frightening her.

I thought that there might be some evil one trying to possess this woman's body. So I took him to the room of Ney-sey-ra, who told the man to bring his wife to him and he would armour her against attack.

When I got back to the sanctuary, I found a little boy waiting for me. At first he was shy, but soon he was talking to me as if we were children together.

He said, ''I've been to the Sanctuary of Ptah and prayed to him, but I thought I'd like to tell you about it as well, in case he didn't hear me. You see, I'm not quite sure if it's the sort of thing he likes being bothered about.''

I told him that Ptah always liked being bothered about things. And the little boy looked much happier, and went on, ''My father is dead and my mother is a linen-weaver, and we live with my uncle. I've got a pet rat, she's very beautiful and she's called Tee-tee, and I love her; but I have to keep her hidden in a box behind the kindling wood, except when I'm out and then I always take her with me. And now she's ill, and I daren't tell my uncle because he hates rats and kills them and nails them up to a tree by their tails to frighten other rats away. And I asked Ptah to make Tee-tee well again. Do you think he'll mind?''

And I told the little boy to bring Tee-tee to the temple and that one of Ptah's own servants would heal her.

That evening the little boy returned, and he brought with him some flowers he had picked in the fields as a present to

Ptah. And he told me that he hadn't needed to bring Tee-tee with him, because Ptah had answered him so quickly that, when he got home, not only was Tee-tee well again, but she had six tiny baby rats with her in her box.

CHAPTER FIFTEEN

# septes

Some there may be who, being in their first incarnation of training, came only twice a year to the temple to be examined as to their progress in their work, which they did in their own homes. Only when it was hoped that they would be ready to pass one of the three grades of initiation did they live in the temple.

When I was nineteen a girl called Septes, who had been expected to pass the first test of lookers, was driven from the temple. Although we all knew that she was disgraced, none were told what she had done to merit her being despised by all who knew her: for they that are banished from a temple for being unworthy are the lowest in the land.

I asked Ney-sey-ra what Septes had done. And he told me that she had been lying with one of the stonemasons who were working on the new court.

I said, "Here there are priests and priestesses who are married and have born children. They are married, and this girl was not. But an action to be right must be right always; and that which is wrong cannot be altered by ceremony. How is it that she is unworthy, while Na-saw and her husband are honoured?"

And he said, "Sekeeta, you are right. Ceremony cannot change a wrong. But it should be a symbol of an inward rightness. The spirits of Na-saw and her husband love each other and are glad that their bodies should be united upon Earth and that children should be born both of their bodies and their spirits. Septes knew that it was not well for her to lie with this man; for had she loved him, she would have wished to make him her husband and to share his life, even though he was a poor man and she the daughter of a noble. But though she knew she loved him not, yet her body was eager for his, and her pulses clamoured for him so loudly that she did not listen to the voice of her spirit. One whose will is not strong enough to order his own body is not ready to be trained how to sharpen a will that is so easily mastered.''

I asked Ney-sey-ra what made a woman an adulteress. And he said, ''There are two kinds of adultery. The first is a woman who lies with a man when the voice of her own experience tells her that it is unwise. This is wrong because, in being mastered by her body, she has weakened her will. But all of us when we are young in spirit pass through this stage, and we must reap unhappiness from it, just as they who cannot control their anger or their greed must reap the consequences, which are often most unpleasant. But what is meant by the law against adultery—I mean not the laws of man, but one of the great laws that are not written upon Earth—is a woman who lies with a man although the voice both of her body and her spirit cry out against it, and who does this for gold, or worldly gain. And in the degrees of the gain so do the consequences of her action increase: a woman who is hungry and lies with a man for a meal has done little against the law; but she who lies with a man for great riches—perhaps it may be that she marries a noble or a rich merchant—has done much against it and she will spend many tears in its adjustment.''

And I said, ''When I was at the palace for the Festival of Anubis, the Vizier of the Tortoise Land was at the feast, and with him was his wife, the daughter of a rich merchant. I noticed that when she looked at him there was hatred in her eyes. She was conscious of her new nobility, as one who had it by right would never be. If she married the Vizier to gain position as his wife, is she then one with the women who dwell near the soldiers' courts?''

Ney-sey-ra said, ''If what you say of her is true, and the Vizier dwells not in her heart but only in her bed, then it would be unjust to the soldiers' women to compare her with them, for they may love the men they take to bed.''

''What of the woman who lies with a man to get food for a child or for someone she loves?''

''If she does it, not for her own gain, but so that she may give to another, then she has done no wrong. In sacrificing herself so that another may not go hungry, she has done as well as one who shields a friend in battle. Remember, Se-keeta, it is unwise to judge until you are in a position to know the hearts of those you would pronounce upon. Even though you know all the circumstances of an action, you must also know the age of the spirit of the doer. There is no wrong in a lion not recognizing his cub when it is two years old, but all would cry out against a man who turned against his child; for a man is older than a lion and therefore has greater responsibilities.

''For a young one to be obscured by the pleasuring of his body is a little matter. But in one whose will is trained it would be a degradation for that will to be clouded by Earth. That is why adultery for one in a temple is accounted a sin: not because it is wrong for a woman to lie with a man, but because it is wrong for her to do so against the voice of her experience. It would be unworthy for one in a temple to lie with one with whom she—or he—did not wish to share her life. If they knew that their spirits also walked together, then would they wish to proclaim it by vowing their unity before a priest.

''Remember always that in anything you may do, if in the truest weighing of your heart you find there is no shame, then that action cannot be unworthy, and so, for you, must be right. At the end of the journey, for all of us must come a time when we look back over all our lives and see all that has helped us on our way and all that has retarded us. But every action of which we can say in true sincerity, 'That I did, not for myself, but because I loved another better', must be a step along the true path. Even one who joins the train of Set because his master leaves the Brotherhood gains in the loyalty that he has shown, if he has followed after one he loved and not for what he hoped to gain for himself. Sometimes to help others, men break little laws. If a woman steals bread when she can find no other way to get it for her hungry child, though in the eyes of man she is a thief, before the Gods she is higher than another who from fear lets her child starve. And although she will owe the baker the loaf of bread, which in some life or time she must repay, she will find that what she has gained in courage is like a piece of gold beside a grain of sand."

"Then is thieving well, so long as it is for another?"

"Only if all other ways of getting food have failed. But first one must be willing to do any work, to carry water, or to clean out a filthy byre, or anything one's hand may find to do; and even then only after one has prayed that one may not have to become a thief."

I asked what the next life would be of a woman such as the wife of the Vizier of the Tortoise, and he said, "Without knowing all the circumstances, of her I cannot tell you. But once a woman came to the temple for help, and to give it I had to look up her records. I found that in a previous life she had been a beautiful dancing-girl; and she had married the son of a noble for what he could give her, although she had no love or charity for him in her heart. In this present life she was the daughter of a captain of the Northern Garrison. Her body became filled with longing for one of the officials of the court of Sardok when he visited your father the year before their invasion of our country. Against the wishes of her father she returned to Zuma as his wife. When she was far from her own people, she found he was a cruel and bitter man, who delighted to humiliate her before her guests, for he hated the people of Kam. Yet, although she feared and despised him, she could not throw off her deep longing for him; and because of this she suffered anything he did to her. Only at his death did she return to Kam. And she found that her father had been killed in the last battle against Zumas; and she had no relatives to whom she could go. Now she looks after the motherless children of the Overseer of the Vineyard. So she who once had taken everything and given not even gratitude in exchange, in this life gave herself and all her heart, but received nothing."

And I asked why she had felt this passion for the Zuma.

"It may be that she had some debt to pay to him. Or it may be that this attraction of the body was decreed by the Gods for the adjustment of the Scales and the gaining of experience. Sometimes this is done so that, because of it, people will undergo things which otherwise they would refuse to suffer, and sometimes so that two people who are chained together by hatred may free themselves from their bonds: for in every marriage, however unhappy, something of tolerance and understanding is learnt. Bodies may seek bodies through the will of the Gods, but the call of spirit to spirit can be only from shared experience. And a true marriage is where two who journey together along the same path help and comfort each other in their exile."

CHAPTER SIXTEEN

# the wheel of time

I had been dreaming about Athlanta, and when I woke I was surprised to find that I was in Kam, five thousand years further on in time than when I was away from my body.

After I had told Ney-sey-ra of my dream, I asked him why

there should be this timelessness away from Earth. And he said that he would explain it to me, but first he wished to see whether I could put my knowledge into words for myself. So I sent for Thoth-terra-das to record my speech. After I left my body, I travelled to where I could see time clearly. And when I returned, Thoth-terra-das read my words to me.

"On Earth I see Time as a straight line. Upon it, the present is a point from which, in opposite directions, stretch the past and the future, marked into divisions of the years like thumb-joints on the the taut string of the drawing-scribe. On Earth I see the horizon also as a straight line. When I am free of my body, I can see Earth as a sphere and Time as a circle. Upon this circle are the years marked, and if one travels along it, then is the distance between any two points greater or lesser according to the distance that one travels, just as it is on Earth. But I can reach to a place where it is as though the circle of time were the rim of a wheel, and I upon the hub of it. From me radiate the spokes, which are of equal length, whether they go to a point in time of what I have been, what I am, or what I shall become. While I am here, that moment I was first born as man—though it was before this little Earth—and that moment when I left the body that I dwell in now, and that future time when I shall be reborn, are at the same distance from me; for where I am is within and beyond Time, for it is the centre of a circle where past, present, and future, join and are eternal. When my future and my past are joined, then will my circle be complete, and I shall be free of the limitations of Earth. And when the circle of Earth is complete, Earth will have fulfilled its purpose. And it shall be a moon unto another world."

Ney-sey-ra told me that I had well expressed the truth, and, in so doing, had gained knowledge of the bonds of Time and learnt how to free myself from them more speedily; which would help me in my work.

This knowledge made many things more clear to me. On Earth, memory struggles through the mists of years and we are often forgetful of experience that strives to tell us what is the right path; but from the hub of the Wheel of Time, all things are clear and there is no need to remember what we have learnt, for all our wisdom is with us at one place and time, pure and unshaken in the endless now.

And I asked Ney-sey-ra, "Away from Earth I can see the past as clearly as the present, why can I not see my future?"

And he said, "The past is solid, for what has been done cannot be changed. But every action that you do is changing a future, which is fluid and can be altered, into a past, which is permanent. Your to-morrow, or your life when next you are born, is like a pool in which you are reflected. At any moment it can be known what state the pool of your future is in, but by your free will you can make the storms upon it become quiet, or change its placid surface into waves. That is why so few prophecies come to pass. Look at that gardener carrying a water-jar. I can prophesy that he will cross the courtyard with his jar unspilled, but that is the future which his present actions form. But if he stumbles, or throws down the jar of his own will, then his present future is changed, for by his action he has brought another result into being; and so my prophecy would have been wrong. It is true to say that with the knowledge of all circumstances a picture of a future can be built up. But this is a picture which few are allowed to see, for it might influence a man's actions. One who had a great store of good to reap, seeing a future clear and undisturbed and thinking himself secure, might let weeds grow in his field and spoil his harvest. Or another, seeing the famine he must have, might in his despair abandon his fields and so bereave himself of even his few ears of corn.

"Think not of the future except to mould it by the present in which you live; and sow the seed that you will wish to reap."

CHAPTER SEVENTEEN

# The Widow

One day, as I was returning to the temple through the bean-fields, I saw a woman coming towards me along the path. She stared before her as if she were blind; and grief had carved her face into a mask of sorrow. I asked her if she could tell me the way to the house of Ketchet, the linen-weaver; for I wanted to break in upon her loneliness. She said that she would put me on the path to his house. And as we walked together, I asked Ptah that if I could comfort this woman, she would tell me of her grief.

And as if she were talking to herself, she spoke. "Only a week ago I was the happiest woman in Kam, and now I am the most desolate on Earth. Since childhood my husband and I have known each other, for our fathers were brothers; and when I was fifteen and he but two years older, we were married. Always were we together, and five years ago we had a son, and for the three of us our days were joyful. Often my husband took our son with him in his boat, for he was a fisherman. Then in a sudden storm their boat capsized, and when the boat drifted to the bank, their bodies were found tangled in the net. Why must I live alone with grief? My Earth is broken. Why does it look the same, why do I see the sun and hear the birds, when heart and love and life are buried in the ground and lost for ever? Why should the Gods have so afflicted me—how can stone statues be so hard and cruel?"

I said, "If you shut your eyes, the sun does not vanish from the sky; still does it warm you with its rays. For a little time, on Earth you cannot see the two beloved of your heart, yet they are there beside you, and when you sleep then are you with them."

"Such things are easy to say. Why should I believe them? You talk as if you were a priest, but you are only a girl, younger than myself. Don't listen when they tell you of the littleness of death. Even if I believed the priests, what help would it be to me? To me—I never dream! For me sleep is nothingness, even so must be death: an end of consciousness, an end of hope."

"But if you could remember your life beyond sleep, remember it more clearly than what you did yesterday, wouldn't that teach you that what the priests told you was true?"

"That is easy to say. As well ask me if I should believe my husband lived if I saw him coming towards me along this path and heard his voice and felt his hand in mine. Both are impossible, so why torment me with thoughts of visions I shall never see?"

"Will you do one thing for me with your heart? Before you sleep, think not of your husband and your child as when you saw them dead. Think of them living, think of little happy things you did together, the sound of the laughter of your son, of your husband mending his nets at noonday in the shade with you beside him. Do not shroud yourself from him with sorrow, and I will help you to remember being with him, so that when you wake you will know he is alive. I do not ask you to believe these things, but I will give you proof, so you can judge them for yourself. Meet me here to-morrow three hours after dawn and I shall have good tidings for your heart."

I knew that she did not believe me; yet she promised that she would wait for me.

That night when I slept, I went to her and found her still caught in her web of tears. She was standing by the upturned boat where she had found it drifted to the bank, frozen in horror as she saw the dead bodies shrouded together in the heavy net beneath the water. And beside her were her husband and her child, entreating her to speak to them and to show they were alive, trying to break through the cobwebbed greyness that enveloped her.

I bathed her still figure in a shaft of light, and the vision of death before her disappeared, and her cloak of greyness vanished like mist under the sun. And as though she were awakening after a deep sleep, she saw her husband and her son, and her face was lit with a radiance greater than that of a blind man who regains his sight. Then I took them to a place of grassy banks and flowers and waterfalls and splendid trees. Here are a thousand counterparts of Earth, where, in the places they have known happiness, people meet their loved ones who have died; and here, far nearer than they were on Earth, do they forget their hours of loneliness. But from this country of reality, each day for a little time they must return to Earth: and it seems shorter than if they but left their lover's side to fill a water-jar from a river running by the house. Before I left her, I made the sign of the circle upon her forehead and told her that on Earth she would remember; and I told her that when we met upon the morrow, I would do unto her this same thing, lest she might think this was but a dream and not a memory of reality.

When in the morning I met her, she would have knelt at my feet in gratitude. And when I marked her upon the forehead, her tears were of joy. And she said to me, "You have taken me up out of a tomb and given me life. Once I disbelieved what the priests told me, and now I need not believe them, for I know that what they say is true. And every day I shall pray that I may be able to do for another what you have done for me."

CHAPTER EIGHTEEN

# Hykso-diomenes

During the last year that I was in the temple, work was begun on two new cloistered courtyards, which Neyah was adding to the Temple of Atet. The walls were to be not of brick covered with plaster, but of stone. And they were to be carved with scenes from the life of the people of Kam: with fishermen at their nets and bird-snarers in their marshes, vintagers pressing out the grapes and herdsmen with their flocks. They were to be deep-cut in stone, so that they should endure like the plants in the pavilion of my father. There were to be no chariots of Pharaoh or royal tribute bearers, for it was in the temple, where all are ranked by the weighing of their hearts.

The architect of the new buildings was the son of a noble of the Delta, and he was called Hykso-diomenes. His hair was the colour of burnished copper, and his eyes were yellow like a lion's eyes, but with dark flecks in them.

His work brought him often to the temple, for both the design of the building and the lining in of all the frescoes were done by him, and the stone-carving was carried out under his direction. He had a house near to the temple, and there he kept long papyrus rolls of sketches and designs, some to be frescoes and others to be carved in low relief. In the courtyard he had a model of the new building, made of palmwood and hardened wax. This he had made to show others what was still in his mind, so that all who were working on the building could see what it was that grew beneath their hands; and knowing what they built, they would work the better for sharing in the knowledge of the finished whole.

Much of his time, when he was not at the temple, was spent in the fields, or by the marshes, drawing animals and birds.

Often I talked to this man, who I called Dio; for I wished to learn of the art of building, so that the temples and palaces, which I might cause to rise when I was Pharaoh, should be worthy landmarks of my journey.

Sometimes I told him of the things that I had seen away from Earth, but I found he listened as though I were making a pretty story for a child. He believed that men perish when their bodies die and that their immortality is only through their children, or in men's memory. He would talk of children as though each generation increased the father's store of knowledge, just as a tree each harvest bears a heavier crop of fruit, flowering more freely on its lengthened boughs. In his philosophy the spirit of a child springs from the mind of its parents to think their burnished thoughts; and when its body leaves its mother's womb, then for the first time it sees the sun; and in the child its parents find their immortality. Though he saw no ordered pattern of life, he was content. He thought that what I told him were pleasant fancies, as when his servant put a crumb of food before her household goddess before she ate. And I told him that his beliefs were as if he had forgotten all yesterdays and denied all to-morrows.

To Dio, time sped so quickly that he could almost hear the sweeping shadows hurry across the sand. To him, life and time were measured, and in the dark sea of eternal nothing his life was like a little lamp of oil, which for a small space let him see, and feel, and be alive; and when the oil was gone, his body cold, the great unruffled sea of nothingness lay undisturbed.

He said, "To have a building, conceived within the mind, and then born like a child through heavy labour, and to see it in its calm purity of line, that is the greatest man can hope for: that of their minds they should achieve something of beauty that endures, so that ahead in time others may see and say, 'He knew, just as I know, that beauty is permanent, though bodies go back to dust'."

I had never met one who thought like this. Evil I knew,

and good. Yet he was neither. Young ones I knew, too young to understand more than the simple rules of right and wrong. But this man had been well tempered in the fire of life. So this strange obscurity I could not understand; and I tried to remove it with my will, and with my wit, and with my heart and mind. Just as a blind musician brings sweeter music than does his brother who can see the stars, so perhaps do those on Earth see beauty in form more clearly when the eyes of the spirit are closed with leaden seals.

How do they live, these people? How can they laugh, and sing, and praise the stars, thinking each day the sun that rises brings them yet nearer to a timeless dark? Why do they try to steer their lives, when they think the endless river a stagnant pool? Why, when they do not see the ordered pattern of life, do they not rail against the blind injustice which for them ousts the Gods? For they think themselves a grain in a great sandstorm of blinded forces seeking disordered doom.

CHAPTER NINETEEN

# DREAM OF MINOAS

Sometimes Dio would tell me legends of his mother's country, which was Minoas, the Island Kingdom in the Northern Sea; how their gods lived in the stars, and, if men failed in tribute to them, they would strike them down with rods of lightning. There they worship bulls, for, they say, without milk babies would die; if babies die, then all mankind will perish. And milk comes from the cow, yet the cow gives nothing until the lusty bull thrusts springing seed to swell her placid flanks. These people wrestle with their sacred bulls, vaulting between the razor danger of their horns, so that the watchers cheer to see a fellow mortal outwit the god.

And trying more closely to understand Dio's heart I visited Minoas in a dream....

It is more richly green than Kam, and vineyards crowd great steps down to the sea. Their temples have elaborate pageantry, yet they are but a mask that hides a face that is not there. Their gods are only puppet gods of stone, forgotten symbols of that which never was. Their temples ring with music to the deaf, and incense rises to nostrils that cannot scent. They seek truth from lips of carven stone, and deck themselves with roses for blind eyes. And, of the people's will, these things of form shall raise great monuments to earth beauty; yet, if true knowledge does not come to them, their buildings shall be like a ruined hall, where only lizards cross the broken flooı and lost altars crack beneath the sky.

In these temples there are no true dreamers, but the priests distil a draught of herbs, in which are poppy seeds, and they give this to any who come to the temple—if they can pay. He who drinks it has strange dreams, for it opens the eyes of the spirit, though to no place which it is desirable to see. Then, when he wakens, the sleeper describes his dreams to the priests, who, being men of wit, experience, and earthly knowledge—though having no true wisdom—interpret his dreams, saying that they have hidden meanings, and twisting a fevered vision until the poor dreamer thinks it a message from the Gods.

And in one temple, the Temple of Praxitlares, there was a high-priest who, though small of spirit, was most lusty of body. The priests of this country are celibate, as are the priestesses; and strangely, here they think it more important to keep their virginity than to open the gateways of their spirit. Yet the sower of this high-priest was impatient that his seed remained stored in his granaries, and often he longed to plant it in a fruitful furrow.

Now in the temple there was a statue, which was hollow; and in the secret chamber beneath it the high-priest would hide himself, and from there his voice would echo as though it were the statue that spoke. And the people revered it as an oracle.

There were days when to this oracle came virgins, who would ask it to describe to them the men who were to be their lovers or their husbands. They would wreathe the plinth of the statue with flowers, for he was the embodiment of all their hopes, being carved in the form of a young man of great beauty, with a straight nose in one with his forehead, full lips curved like a bow, and tightly curling hair.

One day while the girls were bowed before the statue, the priest's voice spoke through it and said:

"I am a god, yet sometimes, when I am tempted by beauty such as yours, I come to Earth. But if I should come to you in my true godly form, then would you die as though you were plunged in fire. Nor can I take all outward semblance of a man, for that would be as though gold should cloak itself in filth. But I shall take the semblance of a swan, and ten of you, whom among yourselves you judge to be most fair, shall lie with me to enhance your beauty; and when men see you they will think it is a goddess that walks on Earth; and the proudest shall kneel at your feet in supplication that you should be their wives.

"And so to-night, which is the dark of the moon, secretly you shall come to the third sanctuary behind the temple. Each shall enter alone. Then you shall feel my swan's wings brush your face, and each may keep one feather from my wing. And if in any of you there be some greater spark of godhead than in other mortals, then shall that one feel the god beneath the swan, and, in the darkness, to her I will appear in my most sacred semblance, as a man.

"Let no word of this escape your lips, lest you profane the message of the gods by letting it be heard by other mortals. To-night I shall await you as a swan, and perhaps to one of you as man." Then the girls returned to their homes. And they spent that day in busy longing, smoothing their bodies with fragrant oil.

As they walked up to the temple through the moonless dark, their pulses sang with an expectant joy. The high-priest waited in the inner sanctuary, and as each girl entered alone, he threw about her a feathered cloak, so that she felt as though a great swan clasped her in its wings. And while she lay upon a silken couch, she thought she must be a goddess to have reached with a god this pinnacle of bliss, where past and future were lost in feathered flames.

Then through the secret door of the sanctuary each in her turn found herself alone upon the mountain-side, holding a single feather in her hand. And one was drowsy with her memories and slept beneath a tree through the warm night. Her body had shown her as yet undreamed-of-joys, and the future hid from her its heaviness and the sharp cruelties of birth.

CHAPTER TWENTY

# The Blind Goddess

Dio was building a temple wherein Truth is housed, yet he could not see her walking through the courts or hear her voice in the quiet sanctuaries. Although I could not give him of my knowledge, there were many things of Earth he gave to me. He showed me that though a bird is carved in stone, its feathers may seem warm beneath the hand; and a carved baby donkey has all the sprawled unsteadiness of youth. In a hunting frieze, the stalking muscles slide smooth beneath the skin of a young leopard; and the deer surprised at drinking stands rigid with quick fear. He showed me that a dancer's posture may be caught so that she stirs the pulse with her smooth rhythm, though long still in death. And though a dead fish dulls, when netted in stone its slippery silver lasts a thousand years.

One day, while I was watching Dio carving the frieze of fisherman pulling in their loaded nets, I thought in my heart, "When I am Pharaoh I shall cause the buildings in Dio's mind to grow upon Earth. I shall send messengers to bring scribes and workers in stone to Men-atet-iss. I shall work in granite as others have worked in clay and brick. The pillars shall soar about men like the stalks of corn about a field-mouse, yet the craftsmanship in stone shall have the precision of goldsmiths' work. The scribes shall write so that the eye as well as the heart delights in their message, and the walls shall be painted as though they were mirrors in which the beauty of the Two Lands is reflected. In dreams I have visited countries where there are great temples empty of teaching, and others where there is teaching in buildings that are un-beautiful. But in Kam the Light shall be housed worthily: a flame in a lamp of flawless alabaster."

I wanted to tell Dio what I would do for him in the future, but if he had known that Pharaoh was my brother and that I had been born on the royal birth-chair, I feared that he would shut the doors of his heart to me. I hoped that one day they would be wide open to me and I could enter though I wore the White Crown.

As I watched the stone under Dio's hand turning to fishes trapped in the nets, I thought of the Great Artificers. And I told him of them, and of how they wrought in flesh as he in stone. "Although those who see your carven fish will share your memory of them, the thoughts of the Gods can come alive on Earth and follow out their master's plans for them. Some fish are made to drowse contentedly in pools, shading their noondays under lotus leaves, and others journey the watery highways to the sea."

I saw that my words had made no ripple in his thoughts, although he loved to listen to my voice.

"Dio, you think the Earth is not made by Ptah. How do

you think ants learned to build their citied hills? Why does the lotus live only in water, and the scarlet poppy spring among the corn?"

"The lotus has come from a thousand thousand years of plants where land was wet; the plants that needed the warmth of the sun upon their roots died out, and so we do not know of them; but lotuses adapted themselves and shot up long stems so that their flowers might blossom in the air."

"Do you think that this plant growing by the wall, of its own will designed its sheltering leaves to hide its buds from the hot sun? Do you deny the Great Artificers and hold that all things create and change themselves?"

And Dio said: "It must be so. I have heard that in countries to the north animals grow thicker coats in winter to protect themselves; and there are many things like that; those that conform to change survive, the others die. So we only see those that succeed, and those that perish are forgotten."

"Do you think, then, that a plant possesses a more keenly tempered will than a woman? For you say this plant designed its leaves at will. I have known women who wanted to have red hair, and though for thirty years they longed for it, still did their hair spring obstinately black—although the rest of it succumbed to dye. You talk of Nature, whom you think a blind goddess, the twin-sister of Chance, but to change the form of any living thing so that its seed shall reproduce that change can only be done by the artificers. It pleases you to deny the Gods. Yet you do not deny them; you call their power by other names. One day you will find out that you but play with words, and though you think you simplify the world, you but shroud truth in small complexities.

"You think that the convolvulus once grew along the ground, where taller plants kept it from the sun, and then of its own will it put out tendrilled arms to save itself from death in the green shade. Do you think that the violet made its scent, and the fish its multiplicity of scales? You would not expect the stone under your hand to flow into patterns untouched by a chisel unguided by your thought. Why do you give the flowers this godliness, the fish this wit, this clarity of thought to achieve this beauty of themselves? You who love order and beauty of design, with every stone meticulously placed, why do you look for chaos in the universe and try to make the smooth rhythm of the world into a lost drunkard staggering along a road that leads to nothingness?''

Dio smiled and said, ''Sekeeta, why will you always ponder on strange immensities? Leave all these thoughts until you need their warmth when you feel cold wind blowing from your tomb. Why spoil the joy of a sycamore tree at noon when it patterns the dust in shadows? What does it matter who made it or why it is there? Rejoice in the sunshine, and do not think of it as one of your ponderous gods; think of the river as clear water in which we can bathe, and not as a symbol of interminable life. While you are young, rejoice and think not of the past. Be grateful for beauty and do not always compare it to a vision, which you think puts it in the shadow. Delight in music, and do not listen for echoes from the stars. When you are old you may have to bemuse your loneliness with memories, but now you do not need them, for the present is glorious before your eyes.

''One day I shall take you from this ancient land where people are grave with too much wisdom, and take you to Minoas where their hearts sing with youth.''

## CHAPTER TWENTY-ONE

# DIO

When thoughts of the future would have clouded my days, I put them from me, for the flowers of the present were sweet under my feet. When I woke in the morning, I found that my heart was filled with joy, for the sun shone upon a land where Dio and I were together. No longer did I ask Thoth-terra-das to tell me stories of the old wisdom or of great warriors in the Light; but he told me of lovers who, strong in their love, were mighty as the Gods.

Though Dio and I did not speak of love, we knew that it was living in our hearts. He knew that I would not leave the temple until after my initiation, but he thought that then I would be free to share his life. I was like three people housed in one body; I longed to join Neyah as Pharaoh; but when I was with Dio, I wanted only freedom to find a rich contentment as his wife. Our hours together were clear as a dream untarnished by Earth, free of the shadow of the hurrying days; for I protected my thoughts, so that they should be unspoilt by the fear that this happiness would be cut short if I should die in my initiation.

When the time of my initiation drew near, my mother, who of her wisdom knew my heart, ordered Dio to be sent for six months to the South to choose new stone for the temple statues. And though I sorrowed that he was to journey from me, I was glad that he would be away from the temple at the time of my initiation.

On the eve of his going, he told me on the evening of the sixth full moon from then he would return and we should meet down by the marsh, where we had walked so often in the past; and he said that then he would at last be free to tell me of all that was in his heart.

I wondered whether when he returned he would hold me in his arms, or whether my body would be housed in my sarcophagus, with pulses unstirred by the melody of love, the breath of life no longer in nostrils cold to the scent of bitumen and myrrh.

Soon after he had travelled south, Dio sent me a poem beautifully scribed in colours on a little roll of papyrus:

I am a sculptor that has lost his hands,
  And an orchard where no water flows;
I am a sailing-boat on a still day,
  And a bird that cannot move its wings;
I am a lotus in a dried-up pool,
  And a bow whose string is broken;
I am a sanctuary without a god,
  And a night-sky without stars:
For I had to leave you upon a long journey
  And you gave me not your heart to take with me.

And later he sent to me:

The seed is planted
  And the grain springs from the furrow.
The fisherman casts his net
  And it is leaping with fish.
The vintagers press out the grapes
  And the wine-jars are filled.
The throwing-stick flies through the air
  And the bird falls to the hunter.
The night is long.
  But the day is rekindled by the dawn.
The noonday sun is hot,
  But the shadows grow long in the cool
    of the evening.
I have given you my heart,
  But will you give me yours?

# PART FOUR

## CHAPTER ONE

# Prelude to Initiation

The Place of Initiation was across the great lake, towards Amenti in the West. It had been built long before our time. It was like a pyramid, though the sides were not smooth, being built in three great steps, symbolising body, soul, spirit. When it sheltered one who away from Earth was proving the flame of his spirit, on the top of it would be kindled a beacon-fire. From the lake a water-channel of stone led to the entrance, where a shaft pierced through to the chamber of initiation, which was shaped like a sarcophagus with a pointed lid. The shaft was closed by three great drop-stones, so that it was sealed like a tomb; for it was as though the initiate died and was born again with wisdom. And many there were who failed in the great ordeals, and this symbolism of the tomb became true upon them.

The one to undergo initiation would cross the lake upon a gilded boat, in the likeness of the Boat of the Dead, followed by a procession of boats, as at the funeral of a Pharaoh. If they returned with their wings proven, then would the procession homeward be as the return of a great warrior from a victory. And this homeward crossing of the waters was a symbol of a Winged One crossing the Waters of Forgetfulness.

For seven days before my initiation my mother stayed with me in the temple and shared my room; and I spent my days with her in rest and gentle conversation. At night my sleep was deeply healing, for Ney-sey-ra of his wisdom let me bring back no memory, so that I should be strong for the great ordeals. And on waking and on lying down in the evening, a healer filled me with the life of Ptah, so that my body should take no hurt when for four nights and days I must forsake it.

On the last morning, I slept until high noon. Then my mother dressed me in the white linen robe of a priestess; and about my waist she put the gold belt of an initiate, and upon my finger she put an amulet carved with the signs of a priest of Anubis. When I returned, these would be my heritage, or they would clothe my body for burial: for if I died I should be buried with the honours of a warrior vanquished in battle. My face was painted in gold, like a death-mask; and on my feet were the golden sandals of one who can walk across the Causeway to the Gods.

When all was ready my mother kissed me upon the forehead and told me that she but waited to welcome me in victory. Then I lay upon a bier, whose sides were in the form of two jackals of Anubis, and it was borne by four priests through long avenues of people—I had seen others go upon this journey and I knew what must be about me, though my eyes were shut. The sun beat down on my closed eyelids, which must not flicker: for how could they who watched me believe that I was a Mirror of the Gods if even my body did not obey my will?

When I reached the lake my bier was put upon the Boat of the Dead, at whose prow was an Anubis head, and at whose stern was a gilded Ape of Thoth holding the steering-oar. Then I heard the creaking of the oars and knew that the leading boat had left the shore.

I thought of all that Ney-sey-ra had told me of what I was so soon to undergo....I must go to the places where are the Dwellers upon the Heights. I must walk through the Caverns of the Underworld, alone. I must give wise counsel to those who know not, and make them listen. I must fight a great one upon the left-hand path, no longer as one of a great company, but standing alone. I must undergo the great ordeals, in which I shall see my oldest fears in their most horrible reality; and I must combat them, not with the wisdom that I have away from Earth, but bound in my earthly limitations. These things that will bar my path I shall not know for the creations of another's will, for it is my will upon Earth that must be tempered before I can bear the name of priest. And if when I return I can record what I have seen, then shall I be a Priest of Anubis.

Ra was shining his long rays before the sound of the oars had stopped and I had entered the final watery road. Then, as my bier was lifted from the boat, I heard the echoing footsteps of the priests going down the shaft, and I felt the chill of stone upon me.

When the bier came to rest, all the old terror, a thousand times increased, of my first night in the temple as a child swept down upon me. My courage flickered like a draughty lamp. I longed to cry out that I could not face the perils I must undergo. Yet pride is sometimes the strongest of our shields, and it saved me from thus betraying Ney-sey-ra.

Then I heard the whisper of their robes, as they left me, so utterly alone. One by one the drop-stones fell and closed me in this living tomb, which echoed to their fall, and it was as though I were in a mighty gong.

Wrapped in this living silence, I knew that now I must be as the dead: no longer could my body be a friendly refuge to which I could fly when the Powers of Evil were too strong for me to combat. Would it ever obey me gently and pleasantly again, or would it hold me an unwilling captive? Should I be as Hekket, who failed yet did not die, and who sits in the courtyard with blind eyes and wet sagging lips?

Fear stood beside me in the dark. I drove him from me with my will, and I seemed to hear the thin rattle of his bones....

I must think of quiet, gentle things, to make me still.

I will think of cooking-fires, with their smoke gently rising at sunset; think of them until I can feel their warmth and their shelter.

I will think of birds leaving the reeds at sunrise upon a

quiet morning, until I can hear the whirring of their wings through peace.

I will think of flowers, smoothly unfurling their petals to the new day.

I will think of children lightly breathing beside their mothers in gentle sleep.

I will think of warriors, their swords shining with the Light for which they fight; their courage shall be my shield and the memory of them shall give me strength. And the love of my mother shall be as a cloak about me.

I will remember the wisdom of Ney-sey-ra, my teacher, and his words shall be to me as is the guidance of the stars to a traveller across the desert by night.

CHAPTER TWO

# the torturers

And then I went to the Caverns of the Underworld.

Here all is grey, and no light shines unto this place where people expiate those crimes which are too manifold to be freed on Earth. Many times they have been taught, by reaping the bitter harvest they have sown, that their actions were against the Laws of the Gods. Yet they listened not; and now, chained in the shackles they have forged themselves, they suffer in all intensity and in one time what they once did to others upon Earth.

First I went to the place of torturers. Here upon the rims of mighty wheels are men outstretched and tied by their hands and feet to ropes, which pull them backwards into a hoop of pain. And stretching them into this agony are twenty of their fellow torturers. When the tortured one has reached the utmost pinnacle of pain, then he must join the others straining on the rope, while another takes his place upon the wheel.

They know that they are dead, and they wear that image of death which they hold in their minds; some are like skeletons, and some have shreds of putrefying flesh upon their bones, and some are like corpses bloated in the sun.

There is no sound of groans or shrieks of pain, but only the sullen creaking of the ropes and the sharp crack of arms being torn out of joint.

Among them there was a woman who had reached the limit of the experience that she must undergo to free herself of her old evil. She had been the leader of a tribe of woman warriors, whom she had joined because her lover had deserted her. To avenge her pain upon his fellow-men, when she took a prisoner in battle or captured a herdsman as he tended his flocks, she would tie his hands to a tree and his feet to an ox; then would she beat the ox with thorned rods until, maddened with pain, it broke its living bond.

When I took her by the hand, I felt the rustle of her long-dead bones; and as I led her from this hell, I saw her beautiful in youth, as she had been two thousand years before. And now she will sleep until she is reborn, compassionate to all who suffer pain.

Then I went to one who had been a priest of evil in the land they call Peru. In his temple of dark sacrifice, upon a mighty tower shaped like a cone, he had torn the living hearts from thousands of slaves, splitting them open with a leaf-shaped knife, and had felt their hearts' blood beating in his hands.

Now he lies naked, bound upon his own altar, watching a figure like unto himself make dedication to an evil one. Then does he feel the knife first mark his skin in a thin line of scarlet, and then, as it rips upwards through his breast, he feels taloned fingers clawing for his heart. Ten thousand times, again ten thousand times he feels this done to him by one he knows is what he once had been. Yet does he think it is some horrid twin, and he knows not that he sees but a vision of himself and it is his own cruelty that tortures him.

Then I saw one who had been the chief of a great tribe in a country of marshes. The people who were in his power feared him greatly, for those who angered him he punished with the death by water. They were weighted by heavy stones in the shallow water at the edge of the marsh, and into their mouths were put two hollow reeds, a thumb-joint in thickness, through which they could suck air. Every day the mouth of the reed was made smaller with wet clay, so that they must struggle ever more fiercely to appease the torment of their lungs; but some lived three days and four nights before they died. When the time came that the chief died, his body was put into a stone coffin. But before he was buried, his people, who for so long had hated him, revolted; and they carried his coffin not to the burial-place, but to where he had tortured others. There they sank it into the muddy water, and into his mouth they put two hollow reeds. And they thought it was but an empty puppet upon which they took their vengeance.

But though he was dead, his spirit was still bound in his body. Chained in the semblance of the newly dead, he fought for air, though long ago his body had joined the slime at the bottom of the marsh.

I went to him and took him up out of the water. And I told him that his time had come to be born again on Earth, and that he would be a fisherman and become wise in the ways of the sea. And he who had killed people through water would learn to feed others with its fish.

Then I went to one of the Dragon People, who had sought to find the tones and depths of pain, and had delighted to play the discords of cruelty upon the living bodies of others.

First every tooth is wrenched out of his jaws. Then are his nails pulled from his fingers and the bleeding stumps fretted against coarse wool. Then each hair is plucked from his head, one by one, and it is as though his scalp were assailed by stinging flies. Then joint by joint his fingers are cut off and plunged into boiling fat to check the blood. Then are his lids meticulously slit, so that horror is before his ever open eyes. Then is his body eaten by hungry rats, and as they fatten on his cringing flesh, they seem those that he once skinned alive.

Then I saw one who had burnt others and made fire the enemy of man. Now fire has forsaken him and he is alone in a land of grinding cold. Naked he wanders over ice that cuts his feet like knives. And the cold holds his veins in the crushing grip of its icy fingers. Often he sees before him a camp fire and runs towards it longing for warmth, but as he reaches it, it turns to icicles.

Here he must stay until he will never again misuse fire, which man should cherish as his friend: for it is the first gift, unshared by animals, that Earth gives to all mankind.

Then I went to where there were animals writhing in their pain. Oxen with gaping sores upon their sides; and starving dogs, some with their ribs crushed in by heavy blows; a monkey with its paws cut off; and a bird without its wings.

And as I watched, I saw there were human beings looking through their eyes, prisoned in the likeness of them who should have been their little brothers, but who had been their slaves.

CHAPTER THREE

# The Speakers of Evil

Then I went to that place where those whose tongues had been a poisoned weapon suffer the pain that their venom gave to others. Among them are not those whose speech was foolish or without thought, but only those who maliciously echoed the cruelty in their hearts.

First I saw a man who lay upon his face, and upon the soles of his feet fell the cutting blows of a thin rod, faster than the hooves of a running ibex. He had stolen a flawless pearl, and to conceal what he had done he had accused his servant of the theft. And the servant had been beaten until he died.

Then I saw a woman who had been one of the lesser wives of the king of an eastern people. The royal wife had been as pure in heart as she was in body; but for jealousy of her this concubine had filled the king's heart with hatred, telling him that when he was away from the palace, the royal wife pleasured herself with any whom she found desirable, even if they were of low caste. The queen was too proud to defend herself, and because her husband believed this of her, she wished for nothing except that he should put her to death. The king was blinded by his jealousy, and he drove her forth from her body, not with a dagger or with poison, but by rape. And to the concubine he gave fifty sacks of gold pieces.

Now the concubine lies stretched upon the ground, her widespread hands and ankles tied to wooden posts. Beside her there is a jar, and one by one the gold pieces that once she delighted to run through her fingers fall into it; and each time she hears the chink of gold, again she suffers this unending rape: an Asiatic of the lowest caste; a filthy leper rotting with his sores; a slave, his limbs deep-eaten by his chains.

Then I saw a woman whose presence in a house had always disturbed the quiet of them who shared it with her, until it was as though their rest was tormented with stinging insects. Now she is beset with hornets. They have stung her hands until they are like the webbed feet of a duck; her eyes are narrow slits in the swollen flesh of her lids, her tongue is thick between her cracked lips, and she is bearded with flies.

Then I saw a man who, when he had met people who were in trouble, instead of speaking to them with words that would have been a healing ointment to their wounds, in his self-righteousness had told them that they were unworthy of his sympathy, for their sufferings were of their own making. Now he who would not comfort others is in a desert with no shade, and the sun beats down upon him until his skin is cracked like river mud before the inundation. Before him he sees palm trees, which surround a well of cool water, and in the shade there sits a man with two jars. He knows that in one of them is a healing ointment, and he goes to this stranger sitting in the shade and asks him to anoint his wounds. But it is from the other jar that his wounds are anointed, and it is filled with salt, which licks over his skin with a tongue of fire. Then he is driven forth to wander again under the sun, to learn that, though it is true that a man who is lost upon a desert would not be lost if he had stayed at home, yet if a fellow-traveller leaves him to wander unguided, he in his turn shall look for comfort and find it not.

Then I saw those who had mocked children and others who could not answer to their wordy spears. They stand naked in the market-place and cannot control their hands or feet, which make idiot gestures and bespatter their own bodies with filth, so that the passers mock them in their turn.

Then I saw a man who had slit the tongues of those he had made the unwilling holders of his secrets, lest they should betray him as he had betrayed others. Now he lies blistering upon a rock, while water-carriers pass, who, if he could but make a sound, would pour sweet water into his parched mouth. But he is dumb.

Then I saw another, who had stood in shadows and looked upon sacred things that were not for his eyes and then revealed them. Now, as he lies rigid upon the ground, he watches the vultures wheeling in the air, until one swoops and tears out both his eyes. Then for an instant he is in the dark, and then again he sees the wheeling birds, until one down-plunges with darkness in its beak.

Then I saw the place where all must go who have betrayed a proven friend. This is one of the greatest of sins: for he who would betray a friend is a betrayer of the Brotherhood. He shall go upon his journey without a friend, and fear shall be his only companion. Such as he shall walk through a bleak and bitter land, where before them stretches a seemingly endless path between sombre rocks and withered, arid wastes; and above them is a canopy of mist, for upon them no sun or stars shall shine. At their backs there plods a horrid shape, the embodiment of their most secret fears; and though they strive to hurry through this place, their straining feet are bound by clinging slime.

Here they shall remain until one, of whose companionship they are no longer worthy, shall of his compassion fetch them from this place to rejoin the brotherhood of man.

CHAPTER FOUR

## the false priest

Then I went to one who had been a priest of Anubis in the little temple of Athlanta. He was the only true dreamer in that temple, where the Light should have shone, but he had blunted his will and had lost his sleep-memory: for he had become a sooted mirror that no longer reflected the light. He was too lazy to strive to recapture his lost power, yet he was too proud to admit of his failure. So he recounted that which was not true, and which was but a weaving of his earth thoughts. And when the time came that the Prophecy of Doom was heard by all true priests, those who came to his temple received it not, and with their false priest perished beneath the water.

For more than two thousand years he has dwelt alone in a temple whose courts echo to his solitary footsteps. Here there are statues of gods whose faces he knows not. He prays to them, although he knows that their ears are deaf and their hearts are of stone, for he can reach no others. And he prays to them that there may be one still left in this land of desolation who may come to him; for he thinks that all the world perished because of his sin.

Often he stands at the gate of the temple, looking out upon an endless plain. Sometimes he sees a loved child running towards him and he thinks that his prayers are answered; but as he touches it, it is as though his hands were white-hot, for the child shrivels before him, and he holds but a figurine of charred wood. Sometimes he sees one walking toward him in the robe of a true priest; but as he clasps his hand in greeting, he finds that he holds the whitened bones of the long drowned. Sometimes he sees his mother walking towards him with infinite compassion on her face, but when he touches her, he finds waterweeds dripping between his fingers. Sometimes upon the barren plain he sees in the distance flowers growing; but as he runs toward them, they turn to a reef of coral that cuts his feet.

When I came to him, he stood before me not daring to stretch out his hand, lest I should turn to ashes at his touch. I put my hands upon his shoulders, and his drowned face was lit with a radiance. And I said to him, "Your time has come. You will return to Earth to train your memory, and it will take you five lives to gain that perfection which once you should have had. But your great loneliness is ended. In five months you will be born from your mother's womb and feel the gentle comfort of her arms. For your companions you will have three brothers. And when you are seven, a seer will come to your house and he will say that in your twelfth year you must go to the temple to be trained. And the time shall come when you shall bring wisdom to those on Earth; and you shall express your knowledge in such words that you shall be known as 'the priest of the silver tongue'."

CHAPTER FIVE

# TREASURE ON EARTH

Then I went to that place where are those who upon Earth had made a graven image of their possessions and worshipped it as their god.

I saw a man who had been master of a great vineyard. The love of plants can be a bringer of peace to the heart, but it had filled this man's thoughts and encompassed his spirit.

Now he is imprisoned in his house by the vines that he loved too much. They have shrouded the walls and thrust open the doors and the shutters of the windows. They creep across the floors, and their clustering leaves have shut out the light until the air of the room is like dark water heavy with the weight of the sea. Savage with growth they strain towards him like leeches on a jungle path. He tries to scream, but he is as voiceless as a fish. He thinks that soon their tendrils, groping towards him with their blind green fingers will twine about him and ensnare him, even as his love for them had once ensnared his heart.

On Earth he had known no enemies save the insects that assailed his vines, and he could see the sky only as a background for the pattern of their leaves. To him life was the putting forth of their shoots, and death the decay in their branches. He ordered that when he died he should be buried under the great vine, which grew upon the wall of his house, so that his body might be food for its strength. His vines were his father and his mother, his children and his gods; and he prayed that they should grow as no other vines had grown throughout the history of the Earth.

And when he died the Gods had granted him his prayer.

Then I saw a man who upon Earth had filled his house with rare treasures. He had been jealous of the pleasure that their beauty might give to others who saw them, yet he invited people to his house so that they might envy him his possessions. He liked to see their fingers clasping the smooth curve of his goblets, for he thought their hearts sorrowed that their own wine could not be so graciously enfolded. He liked them to walk across his floors of cedar-wood so that the floors of their own houses should seem like the beaten mud of a fisherman's hut. He liked them to sleep between the gilded leopards of his beds so that they should think of their own as a wooden bench covered with straw. He would walk round his house and stroke the precious woods of his furniture, and fondle his figurines of ivory as if they were the head of a favourite hunting-dog; and if his finger found a grain of dust upon a table, he ordered his servants to be beaten. He could not see the stars, for his eyes were filled with the beauty of the frescoes upon his walls; he could not see the beauty of a tree, for to him a thing must be possessed before it could be beautiful. And of his house he made a temple where he reigned alone, and of his possessions he made his only god.

When he died his spirit could not travel beyond the walls of his house, and the things that had filled his heart made him their slave. He would see a figurine of ivory begin to crack, and only when he took it in his hands was it whole again; white ants would attack his furniture, and only when he polished it with a soft cloth was it unflawed. Now he runs backwards and forwards between the rooms of his house, trying to save his possessions from dissolution. He thirsts, and his wine flagons are dry. He hungers, and his gold dishes are empty. He longs to sleep, but he dares not rest, for he thinks that by morning all the things he cherishes will have crumbled.

When I went to release him, he was trying to sweep out the dust that shrouded the floor of his favourite room. It swirled about him in a choking cloud, and only where he stood did the polished cedarwood shine through the grey. As I walked towards him, the dust curled back and withered like foam on a beach, and before me there was a smooth pathway like moonlight across the sea. And I said to him, "On Earth you built yourself a tomb, not for your body, but for your spirit: and in your spirit you have lived in it. Now the time has come for you to be free."

Then I took him by the hand and led him from this prison that he had made, and I showed him the part of Earth where he would be re-born, a country whose white cliffs, rising from the sea, gave to it the name of The White Island. I told him that here he would find little to distract him from realities or to remind him of what he had loved too much before. His heart was thirsty for wisdom, but though he knew of his thirst, he thought that it was a thirst of the body. So, to appease it, I gave him water in an earthen cup. And when he had quenched his thirst he broke the earthen cup lest he should become too fond of it.

CHAPTER SIX

# the pitiful ones

Then I went to that place where are those who upon Earth know not true gods, but worship a blind figure of injustice whom they call Fate; and they are guided not by their will, but are driven by the reins of their own imagination.

Among them are those who fear famine. Although the granaries are full and their sleeping bodies are satisfied with food, here they are like skeletons with hunger, and round them are empty grain-jars, and even their water pitchers are cracked and broken.

And here, also, are some who on Earth have but a little fever, yet here they suffer the torments of all the illnesses of the flesh that they have seen or heard of, and they spend their nights sweating in an agony that is of their own creation.

And here are some who, though their land is at peace, fear death in battle; and though their sleeping bodies are safe upon the bed-places of their own houses, every night their flesh is pierced by arrows and their skulls staved in by the maces of their enemies.

And here are some who upon Earth have well watered fields deep in grain, and fat cows whose milk hisses from heavy udders, yet here they wring their hands as they walk over the desolation of their barren fields, or watch their sick cattle dying in the byre.

To these I went, and I told them that they were being as cruel to themselves as a scribe who cut off his right hand, or a gardener who destroyed his most precious plants; and I told them that of their own craven fear they created the realities that they dreaded, so that the wise compassion of the Gods was kept from them by barriers of their own building.

Few there were who listened to me, but to one I talked who night after night for years had lived death. On Earth he was a soldier of the garrison of Na-kish, and he was on an expedition in the deep forests to the south. I knew that round his camp there was an ambush of the pygmy people. I told him to return to Earth and to lead his twenty men through a narrow defile down to the river where they might yet escape this closing net. I put my hands upon his shoulders and said, "You shall have the courage for which you have prayed, and you shall no longer visit this shadow-land, but belong to the companionship of the brave." And his fear-ridden eyes grew calm; and he returned to his body and left my sight. I knew that before the sun again set over Kam the time of his return from exile would be reached, and that in his dying he would find that he no longer suffered a thousand deaths; rather would he walk clear-eyed and fearless into the Light.

Then I talked to a man who feared pain and disease, and I told him no longer to think about his ills, but to fill his courtyard with all the suffering and the crippled who crossed his path. And in succouring those who needed it, he might attain to the courage of those who felt deep pain and rent not the air with lamentations, but smiled their courage.

And I told a rich man who feared to starve, no longer to guard his granaries, but to share his plenty with the poor; and that in so doing he might share the satisfaction of those whom he had fed, and learn that it is better to lie hungry upon straw and to find refreshment away from Earth than to live in fear of famine and in sleep to suffer it.

These three listened to me. Yet there were many who refused my words and strove not for that courage which would free them. And they stayed among the pitiful ones who dwell in prisons they have built around themselves.

CHAPTER SEVEN

# the house of the gods

Then I saw before me the Great Building Splendid with Pillars. And it shone with light, as though it were of alabaster translucent with a living flame.

Before it were two great lions, which in size and savagery were as an earth lion is to a kitten; and they towered above me as though I had but the stature of a field-mouse. I knew that I must walk towards them smoothly and in rhythm, my steps unhurried, for they would know my heart and it must be filled with peace. I must be upright in my strength and without fear. And as I walked towards them, they no longer towered above me, and they became as earth lions. And as I passed between them, they lay upon the ground, gentle as lion cubs in my father's courtyard.

I mounted the steps and passed across the colonnaded terrace under the great lintel. And before me stood the Keeper of the Gate, and he asked me to tell him what was written upon the lintel. When I looked upon it, it was smooth; and then, written in letters of fire, I read, 'Peace and Truth and Wisdom be one, and from them shines the everlasting Light which casts no shadow'.

Then did the doors open before me.

Here I saw many things that are strange, yet I thought they were not strange; I saw many things that my earth eyes know not, yet they had a sweet familiarity: for here I was as a tree knowing all that is part of my growth through the ages, and not as I am upon Earth, where I am as a leaf upon a branch.

Then I entered a great hall where many were seated at a long table, which was white, like polished stone, like pearl, like ivory, and yet like none of these: for it gave forth a faint light. And the Watchers can look upon it and see any part of Earth as though lit in a mirror.

These great ones are beyond form as we know it, yet did I see them in the semblance of man. And in their faces is the wisdom of age and the glory of youth; they are neither man nor woman, yet they have the knowledge, they have the beauty, they have the strength, they have the understanding of these two in one.

Here all is light, which is a living substance.

CHAPTER EIGHT

# The Place of Records

Then I went to the Place of Records, where the Keepers of the Great Scales of Tahuti take those of mankind who cannot themselves look into the past; and here they show them those things that are reflected in their future, so that upon Earth they know what, of their free will, they should do to adjust the balance.

It is like a great hall of audience and the walls are of a smooth whiteness, yet they who come here see it as though it were a place of earth records, in the form that in their own countries such things are kept.

Some there are who see it as a storehouse of clay tablets, and to some the records are carved upon sheets of gold, or scribed in bright colours upon a vellum page; some see them in the likeness of papyrus rolls, or frescoed upon a temple wall.

In whatever form they see them, among the records there is one on which they see their true name, and none other can they read; and when they hold it in their hands, they see what they must know for the hastening of their long journey; like a vision in a looking-bowl, like sleep-memory, yet clearer.

I saw an old man of the Dragon People. He held in his hand a tablet of white jade, and in it he saw himself as he was in his last life, when he was the son of a gardener and his work was to tend the peonies of his master. But he sorrowed when their petals fell, and he longed to capture their beauty upon silk. His master knew of this and he took the boy into his house and had him trained in the way of a scribe. That boy is now a man of riches and his house is the dwelling-place of things of great beauty, of jade and ivory, chalcedony and bronze and fragile porcelain that is smooth as oil. And the man who was once the master that befriended him is poor and works in the rice fields. And in the morning the man who read from the tablet will meet him as they go to the temple, and they will talk to each other of the gentle philosophies of these people; and they will walk home together and forget that one wears an embroidered robe and the other a coat of blue cotton. And their friendship will have been renewed.

Then I saw a woman who is barren. She was shown how once she had had a child that died when it was six years old. And in the morning, when she rides upon her litter through the streets, she will see a little boy playing in the dust; and though she will not remember him, she will find there is love for him in her heart. And when she finds that his parents are dead and that he lives with his great-uncle, a silversmith, who is grudging of his charity, she will give the old man a bag of gold and take the child with her. And they will be happy together, for her son who died two hundred years ago will have returned to dwell in her house.

Then I saw a boy who, when last he lived, had been tortured to make him betray a friend. And his body had triumphed over his will, and he had spoken against his heart. And this had shadowed his days, for he had known himself a coward. Now he is the son of a goatherd in Minoas, and he is happy in his gentle life, smooth as the pastures that he walks among. Yet he will go to the Court of Sacred Bulls and there learn to temper his body to his will, so that it obeys him without fear, until Courage has marked him upon the forehead for her son.

CHAPTER NINE

# the place of weather

Then I went to the place from whence the weather of Earth is ruled.

Here, at the bidding of their master's will, the roaming thunders slip their leash of fire; and raging tempests race across the sky, bending great forests like a field of grass, warning mankind of the flail in Wadon's hand.

Here are the winds that cry to ocean deeps to leave their quiet and rage like mountain tops, reaching towards the tempest-driven skies that cloud the face of Ra from mortal man.

Here is the peace of drowsy summer wind that ruffles the wide seas of ripening grain, and the young freshness of the evening breeze that heralds the rising of the summer moon.

Here are the swelling sails of sullen clouds that cloak the Earth in melancholy rain, and morning mists that shade it from the sun like a thick canopy of vines at noon.

Here is the crystal panoply of snow that shrouds the imperfections of the Earth in whiteness, wherein every colour sleeps, yet leaps to life when challenged by the sun.

Here is that little death of creeping cold that stills the throbbing heart of Earth in an immense sarcophagus of ice: from whence at last it shall arise new-born, when Ra shall beat upon the coffin lid.

CHAPTEN TEN

# the place of melody

Then I went to that place wherein is all melody.

Here, amidst essence of sweet sound, the joy of hearing is intensified, and I can feel these splendid harmonies as water knows the urgent river's quest for foam-capped mountains of tumultuous seas, and shares the mist of leisurely cascades and the calm tranquillity of pools beneath the moon.

On Earth there is only an echo of this sound. But here the frosty voices of the stars, clearly across the chasms of the night, sing with cold brilliance of immensities; and songs of triumph, blazing like the sun, leap with the challenge of exulting fire; and the songs mothers sing to bring their children sleep are sweet as the shadows of warm-scented dusk. The melody of every lover's heart, who throughout time has longed to match his love with silver strings to leaping ecstasy, is here in all its manifold delights. And the slow tears of grief become distilled, until the sorrow of the world is caught into a glistening sigh of summer rain.

And here are sweeping galaxies of sound, which weave together intricate designs, patterned with turquoise, violet, blue, and rose; saffron, vermilion, amethyst, and green: making a fabric of celestial song.

Here is the source from whence all music flows. But only scattered silver drops reach Earth; as liquid notes from strings of harp or lute, or bubbling from the night-bird's trembling throat that stirs the perfume of the sleeping flowers.

Musicians there are who come here in their sleep and pray to keep memory when their bodies wake; and then on Earth they weep on the shadow sound that all the instruments of man but give: for to try and echo with a thousand flutes how music lives in its magnificence were as if a fisherman should cast his net to ensnare the golden brilliance of the sun.

Musician, come not here if you be wise! Or you may be tempted to cry out to Ptah, "When I return to Earth let me be deaf, so in the quietness of my body's shell I may relisten to my memories."

CHAPTER ELEVEN

# the place of scent

Then I went to where scent discovers all its harmonies.

Here is the dark red perfume of the rose; the drowsy quiet of bean-fields in the dusk; the gentle death of autumn in deep woods; and the clean smell of ploughland after rain.

The friendly wood-smoke of a cooking-fire; the satisfying smell of baking bread; the earth-forgotten green of new-cut grass; the moon-drunk sweetness of night-blooming flowers.

The warmth of clover murmurous with bees; the sleepy peace of avenues of limes; the tuberose's languorous caress; the chill austerity of alpine flowers.

The yellow warmth of primroses at noon; the scent of water running over stones; the lonely sorrow of the river mist; the smooth white smell of linen, and of snow.

The dusty wisdom of papyrus rolls; and the warm spice of cedarwood and myrrh; the hot impatient smell of spikenard; and tarnished silver's half-remembered dreams.

The clear sharp energy of lemon rind; the lover's ecstasy of orange trees; the melancholy smell of winter nights; and hyacinths' azure echo of the spring.

The salty challenge of wind-driven spray—that wander-urging message of the sea; the gentle memories of sundried flowers; the still abandonment of fields at noon.

The moth-winged purple of new gathered grapes; the easy laughter of a jar of beer; the excitement of a gallop-sweated horse; and the proud splendour of the manes of lions.

The acrid keenness of a copper sword; and the brave smell of torches in the wind; the musky pomp of ceremonial robes; and the solemnity of bitumen.

Here can our nostrils so delight our hearts that we forget colour and are blind to sound.

CHAPTER TWELVE

# Where Prayers are Answered

Then I went to the place where true prayers are answered, though the time has not yet come for their fulfillment upon Earth.

Here it is where they who are living in a land of famine eat until they hunger no longer; and the parched quench their thirst from cool streams.

Here the arms of women who have wept for their barrenness are no longer empty, for each pillows a child's head in the crook of her elbow; and lonely children are cherished and know themselves loved.

Here do the blind see through the dark curtains of their lids; and the deaf hear sweet music and listen to the voices of their friends.

Here do the lame glory in swift running; and the dumb find words smooth upon their tongues.

Here do children find their broken toys mended and their lost pets returned to them.

Here dwellers in deserts make gardens where, in a night, flowers spring from the soil, and they rest beneath shade-trees that they have planted; and they who are benighted in a forest find themselves in an encampment of friends.

Here they who sleep upon storm-driven ships are rocked by the smooth swells of placid seas; and ships becalmed upon wide oceans cleave through the water with a following wind.

Here the poor sculptor sees his statue shining before him unflawed by his clumsy chisel; and the musician feels the strings of his harp rippling under his fingers like a field of corn in the North Wind.

Here does pain turn to peace, and fear to quietness; and lovers find that death or the distances of Earth can make no barrier between them: for here they are together, to the rejoicing of their hearts.

CHAPTER THIRTEEN

# the teachers

Then I went to the place of the teachers. Here they talk to those who are children in spirit and who, while they are on Earth, know not why they are there, or to what horizon their journey leads.

I saw a beach beside a dark blue sea, and palm trees of a different shape to ours, with large rough-rinded fruit among the leaves. These people are copper-skinned and beautiful. The women's hair falls round them like a cloak, and they are garlanded and wreathed with flowers. One, who wears a form like theirs so they will know him as their counsellor, is talking to them beneath a soaring tree, which grows beside the calm water within the reef, where fish of scarlet, violet, green, and gold, flit through the clearness of the coloured sea like fighting birds through the blue depths of the mid-summer sky. And he tells them of the further beauties they shall find when, in the great canoe rowed by the paddles of their many lives, they shall outstrip the limits of the sea and weave triumphal garlands from those flowers that grow beyond their world, and whose reflection stains the sunset clouds.

Then I went to another island in the west, where a great snow-capped mountain seeks the clouds, which these people think is the dwelling of the gods. And here are many flowering almond trees, and others with white blossoms like the snow. Here the teacher is like a man heavy with earth years, but with a calm serenity of brow. His face is the colour of dark ivory, and he wears a robe of saffron-coloured silk, embroidered with flowers in green and silver threads. He tells those who sit with him in the flowering shade to think not of the splendour of the temple, though its roofs be gold and the celestial dragon silver-toothed, but to listen only to true words, for it is better to eat rice from a wooden bowl than to drink poison from a cup of jade.

Then I went to another part of Earth. Here there is a mighty waterfall whose surging rhythm echoes through a gorge, where flaming rocks, the colour of the dawn, climb upward to hold converse with the sky. And here the trees have aromatic smells like precious gums and the sweet-burning wood, and their trunks are clearly spaced like colonnades. These people have faces like our own, but thinner lips and darker, copper skins. They live in caves and spear the streams for fish and cook their food over an open fire, yet in their walk they hold the proud heritage of kings. Their warriors wear a scarlet feather in their hair, and it holds a different meaning than in Kam, for here it means 'one who bows not to fear'. And should the wearer fail in his appointed task, he must dare the rapids in his frail bark canoe; and if he can steer it among the foaming rocks, his people welcome him again. But if the waters claim him as their own, then he is free to join the mighty hunters in their spirit-land.

Here is earth courage tempered to its keenest edge; and if it be gained by climbing a sheer rock, or in single combat against another of the brave who owns allegiance to a warring tribe, the manner of the gaining matters not. And in this gain of bodily control the power of will is mightily increased. He that teaches them wears a yellow feather, which to them symbolizes wisdom brought from beyond Earth. Though they have no priesthood such as ours, among them there are some whom we would call priests of Anubis; for they bring wisdom to their tribe through dreams. Each time they bring back memory to guide their people they may wear another feather; and so some, oldest and wisest and so acknowledged chiefs, have feathered head-dresses reaching nearly to the ground.

These people I know, for I have lived with them, though long ago across a sea of time.

Then I went to the White Island, where they know much wisdom. Here there are many who listen, for upon Earth they have teachers who go among the people from a place called A-vey-baru, where priests are trained in the way of Anubis. Their temple is encircled by a great ditch, and the walls are of single stones, unhewn, joined to each other by wood and clay covered with white plaster. With such awe do the people look upon this place that when they sleep they come here to learn those things which it is well for them to know.

Here the changing seasons of the year are marked with a sharp division, unlike ours. Now was the time when the land grew cold in sleep; and the deep forests, which clothe the swelling hills, had leaves that, before they stripped the branches bare, were like a shield of cooper, lit by fire; and woodland paths were deep in rustling gold, which sought to keep the earth from bitter wind. And as I watched I saw the seasons change, and winter trees traced patterns on the sky, more intricate than any scribe's design; and over them there came a verdant mist, which crept across the valleys, through the woods, and licked along the branches like green fire, until the trees unfolded their new leaves and summer brought its canopy of shade.

These people know little of men's art; yet do they know of beauty through their eyes, and instead of harps and flutes have singing-birds, which hover in the air as though they rested upon the springing jet of their celestial song.

Here come many who have found their paths hedged in by the complexities of life; for here there is nothing to disturb their thoughts: no carven temples, no effigies of gods; no dancing girls, no wines, no palace feasts; rather, a stark simplicity where, in the silence of their wooded groves, they may approach their gods among the trees, seeing them more clearly in the boughs than in the greatest of the sculptor's art.

Here there are no divisions of rank or wealth; each man is judged solely by what he knows. And those who are young and know not for themselves follow the guidance of their priests, as happy children follow them they love.

CHAPTER FOURTEEN

# the land of peace

Then I went to the dwellers in the Land of Peace, who are reaping the joy that they have sown on Earth.

Here are people of all times and of all nations who have

weighed their hearts against the Feather of Truth and gone into freedom through the open gateway of Tahuti.

Here, in the light of their beatitude, do they know the happiness for which they longed, until a greater longing fills their hearts: to journey onwards through the stars.

Here they re-live their moments of great joy, unshadowed by the future's hurrying wings, unclouded by the sorrow of the past, clothed in the semblance of their glorious days.

Here are some who last were born on Earth ten thousand years before Athlanta fell, and others are resting in their garnered peace before they must again take up the sword.

Here the beauty of a painter's thoughts is untrammelled by the bonds of wood and paint. And here are temples roofed with gold and jade, which far-off Dragon People longed to build.

Here are sailing ships upon the wide seas, which fair winds harbour at the Islands of the West that long-dead mariners have sought to find: for they did dream of their spice-laden air and knew not such beauty could not live on Earth.

Here swimmers can find the secrets of the seas, share with the fishes the translucent depths, questing for beauty through the coral groves.

Here is a man who longed to be a bird and rest upon the wind his outstretched wings. Here he shares swiftness with the flying swan, and crests the sunrise in an eagle's flight.

Here I saw people I know not on Earth, yet once I walked in their far-distant lands and had a body like unto their own. The old Athlanta and the older land, both have I lived in, and both here I knew, as though I should return there when I woke.

CHAPTER FIFTEEN

# Ishtak

Then, standing alone, I fought with Ishtak, who for five thousand years had led his followers in the train of Set.

Once we had been brothers. But when last we met upon Earth, he was a priest of power in the southern province of Athlanta. He remembered our old friendship, and if I would have joined him, he would have given to me a wide dominion; but I knew that his power was wielded not for the Light, but against it; and I listened not to his words. I joined a band of wandering soldiers, who by the power of their swords protected many people, whom they met upon their journeyings, from the oppression of the priests. Then, while my body was still young, it was killed in battle, and though my bones bleached where my body had fallen, I died in freedom.

When Ishtak had tempted me to join his host, I had told him that the time would come when I too would gain power, and then I would challenge him to combat, and by my strength make him return to the Light.

And now the time was come when I must fulfil my challenge; and if his strength was greater than mine, then would my body die; but if I triumphed, then would he lead his host out of the Shadow.

We wore the likeness of our last meeting upon Earth. He was mighty in stature, his face proud and unyielding as a colossus of granite, his skin dusky as a blue grape; and he wore a robe of purple embroidered with black and crimson symbols. I was as a young man of the red-brown people, and I wore a kilt of the warrior scarlet and the gold fillet of a captain.

We fought with naked will and not with swords. We stood alone upon a mountain-top, alone on an island in a cloudy sea of nothingness. Behind him were ranged the thousands of his host to watch their master as he fought for them: yet did I see them as dark thunderclouds. Behind me, down through the empty depths of space, there shone a shaft of scarlet light.

I felt that in the universe I was alone, fighting against this dark stupendous power. I drove forth my will like lightning-rods, yet did his eyes stare back unflinchingly. Both past and future were lost to me; only the eternal present of our strife. I thought my last endurance had been reached. I knew no gods, no powers. I was alone. Yet must my will refuse to bow to his.... Again I drove forth my shafts of molten fire to meet the white-hot challenge of his eyes....

The vivid purple that shone from him flickered and grew dull, and the massing clouds behind him were pierced by shafts of light. Then in the last upsurging of my will he swayed and fell defenceless at my feet.

And I saw him as a young boy, as when we had been brothers together. It seemed that he was dying and that I had killed him, although I knew that he but returned to Earth. There he will learn humility; and when in its pure white flame his pride is tempered, then will he be most splendid in the Light.

Before he vanished from my sight he gave a last command to his followers: to return and walk in the path that the Over-lords of Earth had decreed for them. And the clouds rolled back and I saw before me a vast plain, and across it there passed the great army of Ishtak, marching into exile.

CHAPTER SIXTEEN

# the seven great ordeals

Then did I undergo the seven great ordeals.

No longer could I look across the seas of time, wise in the garnerings of my long journey: for in this testing of my will I was bound to the present, encompassed by the limitations of Earth and enshrouded in its fears.

Before me I saw a vast swamp of quaking mud, which clogged the eyes and nostrils and the open mouths of the long-dead that it had drowned. From its dark surface there stretched the arms of skeletons, their clutching fingers transfixed in their despair; and fetid bubbles broke its dark expanse, the dying breath of those it had engulfed. Upon it there were tufts of withered reeds; and as I stepped upon them, they sank under me, sucked beneath the ooze. Yet did I will my footsteps to be light, and before each tuft sank down I reached the next. The swamp seemed to stretch before me out of sight, and for an endless time I laboured there. And then I felt firm ground beneath my feet and I knew that I had triumphed in the first ordeal.

Then before me in the mountain-side I saw a cave, and from it a passage-way led steeply down into a darkness piercing with bats that swept about me with their leathern wings. Lit by a faint phosphorescence, which came from bodies whose putrefying flesh fouled the scant air with heavy sickening stench, the shaft slanted more steeply down. It narrowed, until I had to crawl, and further, until I lay upon my face and could only drag my body through the cleft by digging my fingers into the rock. I went forward in a darkness closer than a tomb, and I thought that I should be entrapped to linger eternally in the crushing shroud of a mighty mountain cleaving to the earth. Here time stood still, yet seemed eternity. I found my way barred by solid rock, but with my will I drove my desperate hands to claw their way against it. And not until my fingers were stumps of splintered bone did it yield before me. Then I fought myself into the freedom of the outer air. And I had triumphed in the second ordeal.

Then before me I saw a plain of fire, and the air was dark with smoke of burning flesh. Through the blazing pillars of hungry flames I saw charred bodies still twisting in their pain; and as I thought of the pain that they endured, it seemed that my skin would crack beneath the heat and show my bones black in my blistered flesh. Yet I went into this tumult of devouring flames: and they parted before me, and they died low, as when a grass fire reaches the river. I walked forward upon a pathway of glowing ashes, yet their scarlet marked not my feet with blood. At last I felt a cool wind blowing upon me, and there was no longer the voice of fire about my ears. And I had triumphed in the third ordeal.

Then I stood upon the bank of a wide river, and I knew that I must cross it. But as I looked upon it I saw that the water churned with crocodiles. I nearly fled in terror from this place, for I remembered how once I had seen a crocodile snatch a man and crunch him like a twig between its jaws. They floated like logs along the river bank and watched me with their heavy-lidded eyes; and then the water was still, but for the ripples as they swam toward me like fish hungry for millet in a pool. Then did I keep them frozen with my will until they floated like a chain of rafts. And I crossed the river on their rigid backs, but only the ones before my eyes were stilled, and those behind me flailed their scaly tails in anger and lashed the water in their fierce pursuit. And as I felt the horror of their breath, I reached the safety of the other bank and knew I had triumphed in the fourth ordeal.

Then before me I saw a narrow road, avenued by archers. Between them lay the people they had slain, quivered with arrows; and others who crawled onwards in their agony, making the path scarlet with their blood. As I walked between this singing death, I knew that if a single arrow pierced my side, I should have failed and my earth-body die. My only armour was to show no fear, and I walked forward with unhurried steps, the wind of arrows hot against my cheek, buzzing like angry bees about me. Slowly I walked along this path of death, until at last I found that the air was quiet, and I stood alone upon a grassy plain. And I had triumphed in the fifth ordeal.

Then before me I saw a mighty cliff soaring above me stark against the clouds, grey as the caverns where the light shines not. And at its foot lay mutilated shapes of broken bodies fallen from the heights, their pulped flesh riven by the splintered bones. I knew that I must scale this precipice which stretched above me like a polished wall. Yet as I looked I saw that there were cracks in its smooth surface to which I could cling with desperate fingers. My body seemed heavier than stone as ever upwards I forced myself to climb. Sometimes the rock gave way beneath my hand and I was left hanging by a finger-joint. My muscles stretched into shrill cords of pain, yet slowly ever upwards I crept on, until the skin hung tattered on my arms and fleshless fingers held my draining strength. And when I felt that the draw of the abyss beneath me must enslave my will, with a last desperate effort I reached the summit of this barrier and flung myself full stretched upon the ground, rejoicing in this blessed anchorage. Then I saw that my body was unscarred; and I had triumphed in the sixth ordeal.

Then before me was the last ordeal, which to me was greater than all the others I had passed; for it encompassed the essence of all my fears. I saw before me a great pit, and islanded in a rustling sea of snakes a mighty cobra reared upon its coils. Vipers writhed and slithered across the floor, weaving an endless pattern of venomed death. Yet must I walk across their chaining coils and crush the cobra between my hands. Its eyes glittered scarlet, and its mighty hood shone with the brilliance of its armoured scales. It seemed that for an endless span of time I stood with horror naked in my eyes.

Then I walked down into this hissing pit, and the vipers drew back before me in vicious waves. And I seized the cobra below its swaying head and held it from me as it tried to strike. Ten thousand times, again ten thousand times I thought that I had reached the final refuge of my desperate will. It seemed that time was endless and Earth grown cold, until under the last onslaught of my will the mighty serpent slid down upon its coils. And I was with its dead body in an empty pit.

CHAPTER SEVENTEEN

# the winged one

Then was the air alive with music, and I was no longer in this cold grey land. Bathed in a great shaft of yellow light I saw before me Ney-sey-ra, and in his voice there was melody of joy as he said, "Now you have joined the Winged Ones. Now you are free to come and go at will, to walk in the Caverns of the Underworld, to light them and be unshadowed by their fear. You have heard melody where music lives, and looked upon beauty in her house of light. And all these things you shall record on Earth, so that the hearts of your people shall rejoice, so that the hearts of the wicked shall know fear, so that they shall retrace their steps to find the path which leads them to the freedom of the stars.

"Unfurl your wings and glide gently back to Earth, like a white dove returning to its home, bearing the message of the Winged Ones."

Then I returned to my body, which for four days and four nights had lain upon the sarcophagus of white limestone in the Place of Initiation. My lids were heavy upon my eyes, and my body was slow to obey my will, as if it were exhausted after a long fever. Then I saw that I was no longer in darkness, for Thoth-terra-das waited beside me to record my speech, and the light of a little oil lamp challenged the shadows. The memory of all that I had undergone crowded upon me like the waters of a river, and I prayed to Ptah that it should be as clear as drops of silver in measured words.

I told Toth-terra-das of beauty beyond the imaginings of Earth, of melodies that Earth ears cannot hear, of colour that dims the sunset's brilliance, of quiet enfolding the still heart of peace. And I told him of fear that walks not on Earth's path, of pain that is beyond our bodies' span, of tears that mortal eyes can never weep.

When my tongue had told him my memories, I heard footsteps coming towards me down the shaft, and I saw Ney-sey-ra, robed in his earthly form. And when I saw the joy upon his face, I knew I had been his pupil worthily.

Before he would let me move he made me rest, and he gave me a draught of herbs and wine to drink; and a healer came and filled me with new life, so that my heavy weariness grew light.

Then did Ney-sey-ra lead me by the hand, as I had led others to the Place of Rest, and through the shaft I saw a golden wall that was the sunlight of the land of Kam. Awaiting me was a great multitude, dressed for a festival, with wreaths of flowers; and the stone causeway leading to the lake was avenued with gilt triumphal masts, streaming their pennants of scarlet, of yellow, and of green.

Then, holding the steering-oar of the Boat of Time, I led a great fleet of boats across the lake, like a warrior returning from a victory. The water about us was starred with brilliant flowers, and the air was joyous with the voices of my people as they sang the triumph of a Winged One:

> We rejoice,
> For we walked upon a dark night
> And now our sky is brilliant with stars.

We rejoice,
For we walked in a barren land of grey mist
And now Ra is ascendant in his glory.

We rejoice,
For we were beset by the spears of our enemies
And now they are vanquished and we walk in freedom.

We rejoice,
For our tongues were muffled in the soundless caverns
And now we are singing upon the clear heights.

We rejoice,
For we walked in the fear of famine
And now the bread is baking in our ovens
And our wine-jars are overflowing.

We rejoice,
For we walked on stones between the thorn-trees
And now a Bearer of Sandals has come to us
And led us to quiet pastures.

We rejoice,
For we were children crying in the shadows
And now we are cherished
And our dusk has been lighted by a flame.

We rejoice,
For we were in the darkness of the ground
And now we are as trees
And we listen to the message of the dove
That is nesting in our branches.

We rejoice,
For we were thirsty
And now we drink of the River of Life.

We rejoice,
For we were lonely
And now we are the little brothers of one who loves us.

We rejoice,
For we were afraid
And now we are strong in the shelter of a sword.

We rejoice,
For we were lost in a bewilderment of paths
And now we follow a Winged One to freedom.

# PART FIVE

## CHAPTER ONE

# Marriage of Pharaoh

Only after my initiation did I realize that for long years I had thought of it as a great abyss across my path. Now I had passed over it on a causeway of my own building, and with the Golden Sandals upon my feet I could go upon my journey fearless of the mountains before me.

My marriage to Neyah was set for the fifteenth day after my initiation, and on the eve of it I returned to the palace. That night I talked long with Neyah, and our hearts rejoiced that together we should be Pharaoh. Though we loved each other, our marriage was but a symbol of our rulership as one Pharaoh. Sometimes I longed to be as other women, to whom a husband is nearer even than a brother and is the father of their children. And I asked Neyah whether he would not rather have had a queen who was a real wife and not his sister.

And he said, "There is no one with whom I would share rulership save you. For years I have longed for the day when you would join me on the throne and we could be together again as we were when we were children. To rule is lonely, Sekeeta. I have companions of the chase, warriors to lead, counsellors and viziers; yet to all of them, however near they are, I am Pharaoh. Only between you and me is there no barrier."

Yet I wondered if there was not some woman that he loved with his body as well as with his heart. I asked him this, and he said, "Haven't you been to the women's quarters and seen my lesser wives? There are four of them; and I have two daughters and a son. But though I am fond of my wives, I would put none of them upon the throne. Pharaoh must rule with one who is his equal. And though Sesket—she is the mother of my son—is gentle and very beautiful, I would not rely upon her judgment even for the decoration of my sandals. But to you, my sister, I would leave the ruling of my country."

I remembered that I had seen Sesket at the Festival of Horus. I had known that she lived in the palace, but I had not realized that she was Neyah's wife. Suddenly I felt resentful that another woman's child should rule after me, and I said, "Neyah, you have children by other women. What if I had a child by another man?"

Neyah frowned as he always used to do when he was pretending not to understand me. "You are the Royal Wife, so if you had a child it would be the first heir; for it would be judged to be mine as well, through the intervention of the Gods. But Sekeeta, if you are wise you will let no man put you to bed; for it is the nature of women to like their lovers to be masterful, and Pharaoh can acknowledge no master except the Gods. And you would find that when women are with child they get so bound up in their own bellies that their wisdom is muffled."

When I would have protested, he went on, "Ten years have you trained yourself for rulership; it would be foolish to let your wisdom be obscured by doing those things that make up the lives of women whose horizon is an ointment jar, and who rule over nothing but their sleeping place—and even that they hope to lose by conquest. Sekeeta, it is better to hold the Flail than to put a napkin on a crying child; and to sit upon the throne beneath Tahuti's Scales than to lie upon a bed beneath a man."

"Those are easy words. You are Pharaoh and may have a hundred women, yet you grudge me one man...."

"Not a hundred women! I have only four; and two of them are only wives in name: one is eleven and the other is nine. They are daughters of two of my viziers, and I never see them except to give them toys and to know that they are happy in my house.''

''Perhaps I shall listen to your wisdom, Neyah, or it may be that I shall be guided by the same laws that you keep. For though I am your wife by ceremony, you have other earthly realities. Perhaps I shall not only share your throne: I may share your privileges as well.''

''You should use the memory that for so long you have trained, and try to find some record of your own to show you the foolishness of that idea better than my arguments have done.''

And then he said he must go, for I must sleep long that night, as the morrow's ceremonies were tiring.

Before he went he put his hands upon my shoulders and seemed about to say something. But he left me without speaking, and I did not see him again before the ceremony.

On the morning of the day that I became Pharaoh, I prayed long to the Gods that in my hands the Crook and the Flail should be true symbols of their wisdom, of their justice, and of their compassion; and that when I gave the Oath of Pharaoh I should find true words to convey my thoughts, and that my speech should be clear and unfaltering.

Away from Earth I had talked with my father, and I knew that he was glad that his wish to see me rule with Neyah would have come to pass before I slept again.

My wedding-dress was of fine linen, pleated across the breasts and shoulders and reaching my feet. It was embroidered with bees, reeds, and lotuses; and round the hem were seven rows of gold threads, which make it stand out like the bell of a flower. I wore the five-rayed pectoral, each bead of which was shaped like a leaf, the symbol of one earth life. The first row was of faience, symbolizing the *khat,* the second of copper, for the *ba,* the third of silver, the *nam;* the fourth of electrum, the *za;* and the fifth of thrice refined gold, the *maat*. Each link of my gold bracelets was in the form of a double-headed lion, symbolizing all-seeing earthly power. I wore the fillet of the Golden Cobra, which could only be worn by one who had overthrown the cobra of the seventh ordeal, and in so doing had added its strength to their will.

In the royal litter of twenty-four bearers I headed the marriage procession to the temple. Children strewed my way with flowers. Zeb, with Natee and Simma at his side, followed me carrying my standard. Then came three captains of the Royal Bodyguard, each with his hundred men: bowmen, macebearers, and spearmen. Behind them were two hundred musicians, some who sang and some who played upon flute, harp, or reed. Then, in litters of four bearers, came the women of the Royal Household and the wives of nobles according to their rank. Girls followed leading white oxen garlanded with the scarlet lilies that I had dedicated to Ptah in memory of the day when I first met Ney-sey-ra. And lastly came the bearers of gifts from the Two Lands: tusks of ivory and collars of gold; jars of unguents and alabaster flasks of precious oils; necklaces of lapis lazuli, of carved cornelian, and of wine-stone; silver and malachite and leopard-skins.

Round the forecourt of the Temple of Atet were ranged the captains of the armies, their burnished shields, blazing like the suns, making a wall of light.

A statue of Ptah, of gilded cedarwood, had been set at the foot of the pillared terrace; and before the gateway to the inner courtyard was the great double throne of red granite, upon which was the seated statue of Za Atet. A great company of priests, wearing their ceremonial robes of office, was assembled on the steps of the terrace: the Seers with the scarlet double feather of Maat; the Priests of Horus with the folded wings of the hawk framing their faces; the Priests of Ptah with the gold key of life: the Lookers with their winged moon-disc; the Priests of Anubis with their yellow cloaks clasped by two gold jackal heads. Their white robes, brilliant in the sunlight, were bordered with lines of violet, one for each life of temple training that they had undergone.

Neyah, holding the Flail and wearing the Red Crown, waited for me before the statue, and beside him was my mother, who wore the White Crown and held the Crook.

First Neyah and I made ceremonial offering to Ptah. Then, followed by the priests, my mother led us across the inner courtyard by the Hall of Sanctuaries. Neyah and I went alone to the Sanctuary of Ptah, for all when they are united before the Gods are alone except for the priest, who is their symbol.

The high-priest stood above and behind the statue so that it should seem that it was Ptah who spoke to us.

First he called us by our true names, and then he said:

"You who at your birth were called Neyah, and who as Pharaoh are the second to bear the name Za Atet; and you who at your birth were called Sekhet-a-ra, and who as Pharaoh shall bear the name Zat Atet, Wife and Daughter of Za Atet; henceforward you shall show, to all people, that on Earth you travel upon the same path, even as your spirits have travelled together through the spheres.

"If one of you grows weary, then shall the other give him of his strength. If one of you should lose the way, then shall the other show him the way to freedom. If one of you is assailed by the arrows of evil, then shall the other be his shield.

"You shall be unto each other as the Crook is to the Flail, as the arrow is to the bowstring, as the steering-oar is to the Boat of Time.

"Together you shall be father to a great people, and you shall cherish them even as I, Ptah, have cherished you. You shall be the ears with which they hear wisdom, the mouth with which they speak wisdom, the eyes with which they see the fruits of wisdom upon Earth.

"Now is your sun at noonday; and when your life is at sunset and you return to your true home, then let my heart rejoice in your day's journey.

"Henceforward Za Atet and Zat Atet are Pharaoh."

Then before the priests in the Hall of Sanctuaries my mother took off the White Crown and placed it upon my head.

As Neyah and I came out into the Court of the Pool of Lotuses, I thought of the time when as a child I had waited there for Ney-sey-ra on the day that I entered the temple to become his pupil.

Now in the forecourt there was assembled a great multitude, who waited, silent as a field of corn rippled by the breeze, to hear me take my oath before the Gods. Standing before the statue of Ptah and before my mother, who was seated on the granite throne beside the statue of the great Za Atet, I gave the Oath of Pharaoh:

"Mighty Ptah, hear my voice! so that throughout the Brotherhood of the Gods you may testify that these words spring from my heart and spirit and are the truth.

"With this Crook I will shepherd my people so that their feet stray not from the true path, but march swiftly to the Great River where they may take seat in the Boat of Time and ferry across to dwell in the Land of Peace.

"With this Flail I will drive back invaders of my country. It shall be the protection of the innocent, and wrongdoers shall fear it, so that they change their hearts and retrace their steps to the path of freedom.

"By the power of the Golden Cobra I will assail the forces of evil. The temples of Kam shall be as lamps in which the light shines strongly, so that none shall walk in darkness. The courtyards of the temples shall echo to the feet of the Bearers of Golden Sandals, so that many tongues shall speak with true knowledge of your country.

"No child shall know fear or hunger, or be without a parent; no man or woman shall be without a friend; and none shall suffer when their body is no longer strong enough to do their work: for to all my people I will be as a father.

"I will be the eyes of the blind and a clear voice to the deaf; I will be a healing ointment to the wounded and a draught of herbs to the sick; I will be a staff to the weak and a shield to those who are beset with enemies.

"I will remember always that all on Earth were given life by you, and remembering this shall know that all my people are my kinsmen.

"The gateway of my spirit shall be ever open to your wisdom, so that the Light of the Gods may shine forth upon my people and they be guided by your hand on mine.

"Ptah, by whose life I walk upon the Earth; Horus, who trained my will for rulership; Anubis, who showed me the Causeway to the Gods; to all of you I pledge my sacred oath: I will keep the balance of Tahuti's Scales."

Then my people with one great voice acclaimed me Pharaoh, and my thoughts again returned to the day that I had first entered the temple; and it seemed that I could see a sad little girl, who I knew was myself, going for the first time through the gateway to the pupils' quarters.

After the vizier of every nome had sworn fealty to me, Neyah and I, together Pharaoh, returned to the palace, standing in a chariot of two white horses. The way was lined with our people, and the air about us sang with their joy.

That night we gave a great banquet in the Hall of Audience to the priests, viziers, nobles, and captains, who had come from throughout the Two Lands to welcome Pharaoh. About the palace stretched the pavilions where this company was housed; and outside the walls oxen were roasted over fires and a thousand jars of palace wine were drunk; and there were baked fish, and ducks, and geese; sweetmeats, and cakes, and spiced white loaves, and beer: so that the multitude joined in the feast.

When the banquet was over and we could be alone, I found that my thoughts ran too swiftly for me to escape them in sleep. So I went to Neyah's room, and I found that he was awake. We talked for some time of the many happenings of the day. Then Neyah said, "We are both too restless to sleep. Shall we go down to the lake and sail? There is a full moon to-night and a good breeze; look how it is blowing out the curtain.''

I went back to my room and put on a plain tunic and left my hair free. We went out through the garden, where the moon shining through the fig trees made shadows clear-cut as the black and white plumage of an ibis. I picked some figs to take with us. When we were children we used to feel that it made it more of an adventure if we took something to eat, even if we weren't hungry; and I remembered how we used to pretend that we were explorers in a new land; and fruit became the animals we had speared for food, and a flask of water was a soldier's ration on a desert march.

A sentry saw us, but in the darkness he took us for a pair of lovers, and he laughed and wished us happy memories.

The boat was moored to a wooden platform among the reeds. We untied it and poled it through the shallow water until we were out of the shelter of the bank. The sail filled as soon as we unrolled it, and as it gathered strength, we slid smoothly out on to the lake. We saw a hippopotamus and steered away from it, for sometimes they will upset a boat if they have young with them, as this one had.

Then we threw over the stone and took off our clothes and swam for a long time in the moonlight. The water was as refreshing as cool linen on the skin. Usually I didn't like bathing in the lake, for sometimes there were crocodiles even in the deep water; but that night I didn't think about them.

When we climbed back into the boat, we pulled up the stone and drifted on the wind.

Here in the quiet darkness it seemed that Pharaoh was not ourselves, but two far-away people whom we had seen at the marriage ceremony.

When I am away from my body and look down to where I must return when I wake, there is an unreality about Earth: my body seems no more part of myself than does a dress, which takes on the line of my body only while I am wearing it. Here it seemed that only Neyah and Sekeeta were real, and that Pharaoh was as far from us as are the temple statues from the Gods they symbolize.

And I said, "For ten years I have worked to let the things of Earth be light upon me. I have thought of priestly things and been much alone so that I could hear the voice of my spirit. I have striven to open the gateway of my memory, and I have bathed in the light that shone through the ever widening gate. I have lived with people to whom ceremonies of palaces and courtiers are but toys for children. It will be difficult for me to remember that to the ears of many people, words sound wiser if they are spoken by one wearing the robe of ceremony. In a queen, unthinking actions grow long as the shadows at sunset; a small courtesy becomes a noble graciousness, and a small impatience the lash of a royal anger."

"It should be easier for you than it is for me, Sekeeta. You have but to sleep and you awake refreshed with memory. Sometimes I dream; but often sleep is a dark curtain that is drawn between my lying down at night and my waking in the morning."

"But, Neyah, your body is an armour for your thoughts. They do not leap from your mouth as mine do. Your speech is guarded by your wisdom; people hear from you only what you think is well for their ears. Too often I say what is in my heart; I think my hearers are ready for it, but often I misjudge their age. All the years I was with Ney-sey-ra I was a pupil of one of great wisdom; one who never over-tried my strength, and who always knew what food my spirit needed. But now a great people look to me for guidance. I must never seem unsure, or they would fear to follow me. I must never be impatient or unwise, or they would doubt the justice of Pharaoh."

"We have each other, Sekeeta, we shall always have each other. We need never be lonely, as I have been lonely for so many years."

"Neyah, we will be so strong in each other that we shall be like two great pillars. Kam shall be the lintel, and together with our people we will be a gateway to the Light."

"In memory of this day we will not set up a stele; but we will build a pylon to the courtyard of the palace. Upon one side there shall be your name, and upon the other mine. And upon the lintel there shall be the Reed and the Bee, and the Lotus and the Papyrus, the Sun at Noonday, and the Scales of Tahuti. And there shall be no doors, for it shall be an ever open gateway to Pharaoh. And they who come after us will know that in our time we upheld Justice and Truth in the Two Lands."

CHAPTER TWO

# Daily Life

When rulership was new to me, the ceremony of my days seemed like the games that Neyah and I used to play when we were children, when wine-jars had become the Forty-two Assessors, when a reed cut from the river bank was the Flail of Pharaoh, and the trees bowing in the wind were his people in homage.

I still woke soon after dawn and recorded on my tablet any memory of what I had done away from Earth that would aid me in what I must do throughout the day. Adjoining my apartments I had a little sanctuary copied from the room in which I used to sleep in the temple. In it there was no furniture, and the white walls were undecorated except by the flowers in a niche under the high window. Here, upon waking and before I slept, I prayed to the Gods that I might be worthy of my heritage, and that to all my people I might give wisdom, justice, and compassion.

Then I would swim with Neyah in the private pool of the garden of herbs of Za Atet, upon which our rooms opened. After we had swum together, I lay on a high narrow couch while Pakee rubbed my body with scented oils until my muscles were smooth under her fingers. Then she would sponge me with cool lotion from a silver bowl, and while I rested with all my muscles relaxed, my hands and feet were tended, the nails painted vermilion, or, if it was a day of festival, covered with gold-leaf.

In the temple I had but a single comb and a little copper mirror, in which my reflection was blurred as if I saw it in a wind-rippled pool. Now my ivory combs were carved with my seal as a Winged Pharaoh: the hawk of the trained will upon the triumphal boat, above the wings of a Winged One; then, below this, my Horus name, Zat, written as a snake, next to the key of life and flanked by two rods of power, power wielded upon Earth and away from Earth. This seal was carved on my ointment jars, which were also a gift from my mother upon my marriage day. And I had jars of salves and unguents, and alabaster flasks of scented oils; silver hand-mirrors with handles of carved ivory, and stone palettes for grinding the malachite with which I shaded my eyelids. I had little sticks of hard black greese, sharpened like the reeds of a drawing-scribe, with which I lengthened my eyes like the statue of a goddess, and I shaped my brows with pluckers of silver so that they sloped upwards like the wings of a flying bird. Pakee would comb my hair, which was cut to shoulder length, and polish it with fine linen cloths until it was as smooth as the shining coat of a black stallion.

Sometimes I wore the sphinx head-dress of linen or a wig of little woollen plaits, gold tipped; but usually I bound my hair with a wreath of flowers or netted it in narrow turquoise beads. For ceremonies I wore the gold fillet of the Royal Cobra, or the White Crown, which, though it was made of layers of starched linen, was heavy upon my head.

If the day was hot, Neyah and I took our first meal in the

Pavilion of Plants; or if it was cool, in one of our private rooms. We drank milk from alabaster cups and ate fruit from dishes inlaid with lapis lazuli; ripe dates and figs, melons and apricots and grapes. And we rinsed our hands in a bowl of scented water and dried them on napkins embroidered with gazelles or scarlet fish, or patterned with vine leaves.

Every second day Neyah or I gave audience until an hour before high noon, or if he was away from the Royal City, I gave audience four days in every seven. The one who was not in audience sat in council in the Room of Seals with viziers and overseers, and all others who came for the decree of Pharaoh. Messengers would come to us from distant cities, bringing news about the harvest, about the welfare of the people, and of their care. All that affects the people of Kam, be it a roadway, a system of water-channels, the building of a new temple or of the dwellings where the old pass their days in gentle quietude, the planting of the highways with trees so that the traveller may walk in the shade, or the planning of gardens that are shared among the people: all these things receive the Seal of Pharaoh, for the people of Kam are to Pharaoh as his palace. Their joy is his contentment, and their sorrows are the tears of his heart.

To all matters that had to do with temples, I set my seal with my priest name Meri-neyt, the Beloved of Ney-sey-ra, the name which he had given to me, his pupil, after my initiation. The name Ney-sey-ra means 'born a priest of the Light,' for at his birth it was known that before returning to Earth he was already a fully initiated priest. He wrote his name with the symbol of the Goddess Neyt, the goddess of those who are born ancient of days. This is a sheaf of corn, bound with a thong to show that the wisdom which it symbolizes has been garnered; and across the sheaf are the two arrows of the trained will, one pointing to Earth and one away from Earth, showing that in both places can this will be directed. At the Festival of Neyt her symbol is carried on a standard, and in the writing-sign of her name the pole of the standard is shown supporting the sheaf. So upon my seal there was the plough, 'meri', meaning 'beloved', for as the plough furrows a field before the harvest, so does love make the heart fruitful; and this was followed by Ney-sey-ra's seal.

One of the names of the great Meniss was Za-ab, the Wise of Heart, and his seal for this name was a bundle of reeds and papyrus tied with a scarlet thong: for he had united the North, the Land of the Papyrus, with the South, the Land of the Reed, by the wisdom of his heart and the scarlet of a warrior. This seal was also used by my father. But Neyah and I used it in two forms: either the field of papyrus or the field of reeds; and this was often followed by a young bird, meaning 'earth-child', and Za in the form of a sieve: Pharaoh Son of Horus, Za son of Za.

My father had also written his name by the snake and the arm, which are the sound signals for Za. Neyah and I used the snake alone.

These seals could be enclosed in a pillared square, to show that we had gained entry into the House of the Gods, the Great Building Splendid with Pillars. Above this square was the hawk, the symbol of trained will, showing that this was the Horus name of Pharaoh. Sometimes, in addition to the Horus name, we would write, Atet: the feather, 'a,' that same feather which is wisdom, and the half-circle, the sign for 't'. If I wished to show that it was I who had set the seal, I would use my own form of it, in which there was the priest-symbol of a drop of water, which showed that, just as rain falls from the heavens, so had I brought the water of my *maat* down to Earth. This sign, which means 'remembered wisdom', is also the sound sign for 'tet'.

Rey-hetep was the Vizier of the Royal Household. His scribes kept the records of all tribute, and under his counsel it was allotted for the welfare of Kam. The Overseer of the Royal Household had held his office since the time of my father. He was in authority over all the palace servants; over the twenty cooks and all the kitchen boys; the hundred serving women, the linen-weavers, the washers of clothes, and the water-carriers. Harka was still Overseer of the Chariots, and in his care were all the royal animals: the horses and lions, the hunting-dogs and cattle, the asses and geese and ducks and milch-goats. Pharaoh's Cupbearer was also the Master of the Vineyard. At his decree the vines were planted, the grapes harvested and pressed in the vats, and the wine-jars stored in the cellars. The Overseer of the Gardeners was the brother of Maata. Under his direction were the three hundred men and women who worked in the gardens and orchards of the palace and on the grain-lands of Pharaoh.

Yet all these sometimes came to Pharaoh for counsel, to tell him that a new plant had flowered for the first time, or that the foreign grapes prospered; that a mare was in foal, or that a blight had fallen upon a cornfield. And to all these things did Pharaoh give his ear and his heart.

In the hot weather all in the palace slept for two hours at noonday. And as Ra grew gentle upon his journey, sometimes Neyah and I would sail together on the lake or go upon the hunt with our nobles, spearing crocodiles or flying our throwing sticks at a wild-fowl in the marshes. And we would race our chariots against the captains, but none were so skilled in this as Neyah, for when the reins were between his fingers a horse would turn like a flying swallow, and at his voice would outstrip the wind.

Often there were banquets in the great hall of the palace, but the evenings that I loved were those when Neyah and I were alone together. We would tell each other all that we had done throughout the day; and when I had sat in judgment I would tell him of what had been brought before me and ask what judgments he would have given. And it was as if the long years I had been away from him had passed as quickly as a shadow moves a cubit over the ground. Our hearts were near to each other, and our thoughts were matched like twin-paced horses in a chariot.

Now that I was Pharaoh, my mother no longer lived in the palace. Though she had been weary of rulership, she shared the guardianship of Kam with Neyah until I took up the Flail. Then she was free to leave the life of ceremony and to live in the house that was the most beloved to her of any dwelling-place upon the Earth; for here it was that she had lived with my father in the days of their youth. This little palace, which had been built by Meniss, was circled by sycamore trees, and its lawns opened on to the lake. Neyah and I often went to see her there, and though our day might have been long and we weary with responsibility, we were as children that are happy, while we walked in her tranquillity.

CHAPTER THREE

# Pharaoh in Audience

Every night before I sat in audience, I sent out this call: "Master, if to-morrow there be that before me which of my own experience I cannot judge truly, may I be shown away from Earth that which is necessary for my understanding: so that I can see the truth, and the Scales beneath which I sit remain a true symbol of justice."

One morning, on waking, I knew that I must judge between two women: one I should remember by the five gold bracelets that she would be wearing on her left arm; the other, who was the innocent one, would have a white scar, shaped like an arrow-head, on her right temple.

The throne in the Hall of Audience was made of gilded wood, and its feet were lion-pawed. When I sat alone in audience, I held the Crook and the Flail; when Neyah and I were together, I held the Golden Lotus. On each side of the room there was a table at which sat the scribes who kept the records of all judgments. With them were those who read out the history of the case that was to be heard. This custom had been introduced by Neyah in the fifth year of his reign. Before then, every disputant had told his own story in his own time, and sometimes a man would talk for an hour and still leave his hearers with little knowledge of what he wished to say. So now to each one a scribe was allotted, who could put a long confused story into a few words.

The first case read out to me was between the widow of a rich noble from Abidwa and a girl who had a child, but who was unmarried. The child's father—who had died before it was born—was the son of the rich widow; and she was claiming the right to take her grandson and bring him up in her own household, saying that it was his proper home, for the child's mother was a prostitute and had no claim either on the child or on her charity.

The mother of the child wished to keep it with her, saying that, having inherited a small farm-land, she had the means to clothe it and feed it, and that she would bring the child up in accordance with the teachings of the Light.

I ordered the two women to be brought in.

One was a woman of about forty-five. She was over-richly dressed; her mouth was bitter, her hands soft and fat. And on her left arm were five gold bracelets. The other, a young girl, wore a white tunic of coarse linen and a blue cloak, which was draped over her head and hid her hair, but I could see that there was a scar upon her temple.

The noble's widow was plainly in awe of me and was unsure of ceremony. I knew that she wished that she were at the palace for a festival, which she could attribute to her nobility, and not for justice, when all are equal. Her face was not of the pure race. Perhaps she was the daughter of some rich trader; by the shape of her nose she must have had a strain of Zuma blood. Her fat hands were restless, she twisted her necklaces in her fingers, and her bracelets jingled on her arms.

Yet she felt secure in her respectability and her riches, and had no fear of the claim of one whom she considered a prostitute.

The girl stood very still, her arms hanging at her sides. She had the proud carriage of women who are used to carrying jars upon their heads. Her eyes never left my face. She was calm, for she knew that I should give true judgment and that, knowing her heart, I should leave the child in her keeping.

I spoke to the girl, and asked, "Why did you have this child?"

And she answered me, "Daughter of Horus, Bearer of Double Wisdom, Weigher of Hearts, and Mirror of the Truth! I loved his father, the husband of my heart; yet I could not share his house as wife, for I have few possessions and my husband's mother wished him to marry one of noble blood, who could bring treasures to enrich his house. Although we could not be one before the priests, yet were our bodies joined on Earth, and when we slept we were fearless before the Gods and in our hearts we knew no shame.

"When he fell ill, before our child was born, a servant told me that he often called for me. Yet they would not let me see him, though I waited in the garden and spoke to his mother and begged her, very humbly, that I might go to see my beloved and comfort him. She saw that I was big with child, and told me that I was a creature of the night, who by my presence made her garden fouler than a village midden. Yet when her son died, leaving no other child, she had me spied upon until my child was born, then sent her servants to my house to try to take my son away from me."

I asked her what she could give her son.

"He shall have food and shelter, sun and air, the river to bathe in, plants to grow, and animals to play with; and when he is older he shall have a field to plough and a cow to milk and take to pasture; and he shall learn the ways of boats, and how to cast a fishing-net. I will teach him gentleness and truth, so that he may look in a mirror and be unafraid of what his eyes read from his own eyes. And I will teach him to keep his body pure and strong; and that the greatest happiness on Earth is to find another more beloved than oneself.''

And all that this girl said I knew was true, for I had heard it in my dream.

Then I turned to the other woman, and I asked her what she could give her grandson.

She railed against the girl, saying that she was a liar and a prostitute, of whom her son had taken careless pleasure for an hour; and only from the kindness of her heart had she decided that, in duty to her son, she must protect his child from living with such a woman; and that, being of noble birth, she could not have her grandson ploughing a field and living like a servant. Then she said what riches would be his: orchards and vineyards, serving-maids and gold; which, she being a widow, all belonged to her, and when she died would go to the child, whom she would make her heir.

When she had finished I waited a moment before I spoke. She was so sure I would decide in her favour. She did not realize that I saw her heart and knew its worth. Then I said to her, ''In your house the child would have all that he needed for the comfort of his body. He would have a gilded bed, but where would his spirit go to when he lay upon it? You have shown that you know nothing of how to assist the growth of the spirit of a child.

''You think that riches are more important than love, for you wish to give the child possessions, and yet take it from its mother. This shows that you are a fool.

''If you acknowledge the child as your grandson, then should his mother be as a daughter to you. But in your self-righteousness you look down upon the girl. Thinking that she has sinned—and therefore that your son has shared her sin—you should have done all that was in your power to compensate her for what your son had brought her to. But instead, you wish to rob her of her child. And so you are a thief.

"You would drive your son's love from your door. So you are without compassion.

"Yet you, who are a thieving fool without compassion, dare to despise one who has known unselfish love for a man and for a child. This shows you have no wisdom and small experience.

"And lastly, you dared not go for judgment in your own city: for there they know that, but for your pride of position, the girl would have been the wife of your son. And so you brought your case to me, thinking that I, Pharaoh, would be deceived by you. This shows that, thief, and fool, without compassion, having no knowledge or experience, you dare to hold your ruler in contempt, thinking to keep your petty truth from me.

"For this you should be whipped upon the feet.

"Instead, you shall give to the mother of your grandson that part of all your possessions which would have been hers if she had been your son's wife before the priests, instead of only in her heart and thus before the Gods. As well as this, you shall give her two ass-loads of gold and one of silver. And when you see less food upon your table, and fewer serving-maids about your house, it may remind you that I am Pharaoh, and the Truth."

Then there was brought before me a man who was kinsman to the Vizier of the Lands of the Jackal. He was a rich noble called Shalnuk, and he had demanded the right of being heard by Pharaoh.

He had diverted the water-channels to his own vineyards, where he tried to grow three vines where one should have flourished. And the farm-lands between the borders of his estate and the river dried up, and all the grain perished.

When I found that he had done this not of his ignorance, but because he thought that the little fields below him mattered not and the hearts of the farmers were beyond the boundaries of his compassion, I gave judgment upon him:

"You have sinned because you did not understand what it was that you did to others. In the green shade of your garden you forgot the sorrow of the parched fields. As understanding is the fruit of experience, and understanding is what you lack, you shall eat of the fruit that is unfamiliar to you. You shall live in the hut of a ploughman and have a rich field and two oxen to draw your plough. Beside your new home there shall be a grain-bin six cubits high and three cubits across the circle. When this is filled with the grain that you have reaped from your sowing, then shall your own lands be returned to you."

But though in three months this bin could have been filled, for three years Shalnuk laboured. When his grain began to gild the stalks, the plant-spirits of the grain were called away, so that it rotted and fell unripened from the ear. Thus did he labour under the hot sun, until his field was watered with the tears of his heart and he shared the sorrow of all who had suffered because of him. Then, when hope had all but died in him, his corn ripened and his granary was filled. And once again the floors of his house heard the footsteps of their master. And now in the Land of the Jackal there is no kinder overlord to his people.

CHAPTER FOUR

# the poisoner

One day, while Neyah and I were walking together through the vineyards in the young darkness soon after sunset, he said that he had just heard the proof of the wisdom of one of his judgments. And he told me of Benshater, who had been the chief scribe of the Vizier of the Land of the Hawk. Three months before, soon after I became Pharaoh, the vizier had died, and the messenger who had brought the news of his death brought also a petition from Benshater that he should be appointed to the office. Neyah was about to set his seal to the new title when he remembered that I had told him of a dream in which I had seen a golden hawk lying dead and bloated in the sun as if it had died of poison. Although at the time neither of us had thought the dream was of any importance, now Neyah saw its significance, for the standard of the dead vizier was a golden hawk upon a blue ground. So Neyah sent back the messenger empty-handed, saying that the candidate for office must come to the Royal City before the title could be granted.

When Benshater came before him in audience, Neyah found that he was a scholar as well as a scribe; and so well did his face mask the evilness of his heart, and so plausible was his tongue, that he might have deceived even Pharaoh. But the seer who was watching him reported that the light of his *ba* was so heavy with cruelty, greed, and jealousy, that not only was he unworthy to guide others, but his light would throw a shadow in a dark pit. To every question Benshater made smooth answer, and Neyah saw that he was too clever to betray himself. So he told him to return on the following day to hear the decision of Pharaoh. Then Neyah asked Ney-sey-ra to look into the jar of Benshater's memory: for in the water of his *maat* would be the reflection of those earthly deeds that had filled it.

Ney-sey-ra did so, and he told Neyah that Benshater had poisoned the vizier. And he told him, also, the name of the poison; that it had been given in the spiced milk that the vizier drank instead of wine or beer; and the days on which it had been administered, which were fifteen.

On the next day Benshater came before Neyah, thinking to receive great honour and the titles and office of vizier; but instead he heard the history of his crime. Neyah recounted to him in detail all that his evil had brought to pass, and Benshater thought that he had been betrayed by some hidden watcher of his crime, for he knew of no other way in which it could have been discovered. And he fell upon his face before Pharaoh and screamed for mercy.

Then Neyah gave judgment upon him: "You who have given a slow and painful death to one whom you should have honoured, shall die in the same manner in which because of you, he died. You shall not know the time of your release. You shall be kept in a dark prison, where your guilty heart will conjure pictures of your sins and of your victim, and you will cringe from these your sole companions. Lest your body should grow weak, you shall be exercised at night, but your eyes shall be bandaged, for they are unworthy to look upon the stars. Twice a day food shall be brought to you, and while you eat you shall have a lamp. For many days you may enjoy your food, but one day, although it will have tasted the same, when you have eaten of it your bowels will twist within you as though they were trying to wring your spirit from your body. But you will recover, and you will grow strong again before this same thing shall happen to you; and it shall happen many, many times, until at last while you are racked with pain, you will implore the Gods to make your torment yet more unbearable so that your spirit may be free of it.

"You may think to avoid your punishment by refusing to eat the food that is sent to you, but you do not know the power of hunger; it would need a stronger will than yours to starve to death while your quivering nostrils savoured choice dishes from the royal kitchens. You will remember that many dishes will give you nothing but a pleasant feeling of repletion; and, when the pangs of hunger grow keen, it is easy to forget that food might be poisoned. Even if you can resist hunger, thirst is a greater torment; you will find that there are few who would choose to die of thirst when to their hand there is a goblet of warm, spiced milk; and until the day you die you shall drink no other liquid than that in which your master drank his death."

Neyah paused in his story, and I told him that I thought it

was a worthy judgment. He laughed and said that I had heard but a quarter of its wisdom. "This morning Benshater was found rigid in death, his bitten lips drawn back, his body twisted as though it still writhed in a last agony, and his blind eyes staring as though at some shape of horror. And yet, my sister, of my wisdom there has been no trace of poison in his food. If he had but known it, for nearly three months he has shared the dishes of our household and sometimes even those served to our own table. Yet having always before him the picture of a terrible death, which in his spirit he must have undergone ten thousand times, at last his body was so encompassed by his mind that he died, most suitably, a victim of the memory of his own evil."

CHAPTER FIVE

# TRIBUTE

Twice every year the people of Kam make a free gift of a twelfth part of what they have gathered during the past six months. This tribute is used for the common welfare of the country, excepting a tenth part, which belongs to the priests, and a tenth part, which belongs to Pharaoh.

The wealth of Kam is administered by the viziers, who barter those things of which we have too much with other countries which have things that we lack. At every big city there are the Watchers of the River, who record the height of the water; and by the rising of the river they know whether the harvest will fill the granaries and there will be grain for barter, or whether there is a danger of famine, and gold and ivory must be turned into bread.

Those of our people who have grain-lands, or animals, or

anything that time does not destroy quickly, give a portion in tribute: a twelfth of their harvests, or animals from their herds, or linen of their weaving. Fishermen, and others whose goods perish, give each day a twelfth part to the temple or to the poor as a free gift. And those who work for another and who are without possessions work one month in twelve for Pharaoh, on the grain-lands or in the brick-fields or in the making of roads and water-channels.

Throughout the land tribute is received at the temples, save in the Royal City, where it is brought to Pharaoh. In the first year of my reign Neyah and I received tribute from the steps of the outer courtyard of the palace. We were seated on two thrones of ceremony, which were covered with zebra-skins. Below us were the scribes, who kept the tallies of all that was brought. On the left side of the courtyard were those officials who would take the tribute into their care, the Overseer of the Granaries, the Royal Herdsman, the Vizier of Pharaoh, and the Overseer of the Royal Household.

In the order of tribute there was no degree of rank, for before Pharaoh all the people of Kam are equal. A farmer, with two little donkeys loaded with sacks of grain, was followed by a noble, whose porters carried tusks of ivory; then came a woman with two ducks in a wicker cage, followed by a merchant, who brought six flagons of *sheptees* oil; then a little girl with a bunch of radishes and a string of onions; a boy with a she-goat and twin kids; a man carrying two bales of raw wool; a noble with four collars of gold; then a kinswoman of the Royal House with two tame gazelles and her servants bearing unguents in six jars inlaid with gold and lapis lazuli; a man leading a red and white bull; and a woman with linen napkins finely embroidered; a noble from the South with gold and malachite; then six carts filled with grain, and two others with wine-jars of a rare vintage.

Tribute is used first for the welfare of the dwellers in the temples; for the food and linen of the priests, for the temple servants, and for the journeys of the seers and healers that go about the country; so that the life of no priest is burdened by the small complexities of Earth.

Secondly it is used to look after children who have no parents, and old people who can no longer work in the fields. Either they live in the house of a friend, who is then given sufficient grain from the granaries for their bread and for barter, or they live in houses that have been specially built for them by Pharaoh. Each city has a house for children set in gardens where they can play together and learn the care of plants, and a farm where they are taught of their brothers the animals. Some learn to be fishermen or to build in brick. The girls learn to weave linen, to make clothing, to cook, and to look after a house. They are cared for by childless women who long for children.

Those of the sick who have a family to look after them are visited by the healers in their own homes; but if they are alone, they are taken to the temple and there they remain until they are strong again.

Thirdly the tribute is used for the maintenance of the armies of the garrisons and for the fleets of Kam, both trade ships and ships of war.

## CHAPTER SIX

# the festival of min

When the waters of the inundation had subsided and left the fields strong with new life for the sowing, the Festival of Min was celebrated to mark the opening of a new cycle of fertility.

Neyah and I drove to the Temple of Atet in two state chariots, followed by the nobles and the captains, and by the viziers in their carrying-litters. I wore the White Crown of the South, and Neyah the Red Crown of the North.

In the forecourt of the temple were three hundred grain-jars arranged in thirty rows of ten. In the days of my father, who had been a healer priest as well as Pharaoh, it was he that charged the first jar of grain with life. But now it was a high-priest of Ptah who by his will caused the plant-spirits of the grain to spin strongly, so that the seed should thrust quickly from the soil and bear crops for a rich harvest. The high-priest went between the rows of jars, followed by nine young healer priests. The first jar of each group he himself charged with the life of Ptah, while the young priests with him each charged another.

After the Safeguarding of the Grain, the jars were loaded upon carts, each drawn by three white oxen garlanded with flowers, their horns tipped with gold and painted in green and scarlet. Then the statue of Min, in his semblance of creative man, was brought from the temple on a litter of wood covered with gold-leaf. Neyah and I led the procession, in which the statue was carried by forty young priests, round the royal boundaries of Men-atet-iss. The owner of each field waited to receive the grain as we passed, and at once began sowing, so that, behind the procession, the grain scattered over the earth in a shower of gold. Our way was lined with people. There were children with goats, and women with cages of ducks; and some had brought their cows so that the shadow of Min should fall upon them and they be fruitful. As the procession passed them, the people chanted the Invocation to Min:

> "Min, who took compassion on the loneliness of man and made of him our first parents, give of your fertility to the Land of Kam. Let the earth receive the seed into her womb and bring it forth beautiful in the sight of Ra. Let the branches of our fruit trees be strong to bear the harvest of our orchards. Let our vines jewel their leaves with amethysts. Let our bulls be lusty, so that our cows delight to

give their milk. Let our goats bring forth twin kids, and the river hurry with fish. Let our ducks lead forth a fleet of chicks upon our pools, and the reeds whisper with wild-fowl. May the Land of Kam be your dwelling-place, so that you shall send those beloved of your heart to be our children."

While the sun was still high a festival banquet was held in the great hall of the palace. Neyah and I, with nobles, viziers, and captains-of-captains, were seated on chairs of state at one end of the hall; in front of us the floor was clear, and at the other end of the hall the great entrance was hidden by a stretched white curtain, upon which many shadow scenes were enacted throughout the banquet. Bearers of tribute passed in procession; with the collars of gold and the tusks of ivory; with deer and small cattle, slung by their feet on poles, and fruit piled high upon flat baskets. And young boys leading hunting-dogs and tame leopards straining in leash. An ever moving frieze of black and white.

I wore a wreath of stephanotis flowers, and my pale green dress was embroidered in gold with ears of wheat, symbolizing the fresh young green the river waters bring, soon to be gilded by the sun. Each bead of my rayed pectoral was carved as a different flower or fruit. Neyah's clothes were blue, embroidered with fish and birds and deer, to symbolize the river from which animals draw life beneath the moon.

The other guests were ranged down each side of the banqueting hall. Beside each chair was a low table, on which the food was set, and on every table there was a lotus flower. They sat with those to whom they wished to talk; some in little groups, and some in pairs, and some sat alone, content to feast their eyes and stomach undisturbed. Some of the women wore pleated dresses of transparent linen, through which one could see their breasts and the pleasant curve of their bellies. For if a young girl's breasts are pleasing, it is well that they should be seen, indeed it would be as foolish to cover them as for a red-haired woman to wear a black wig; but foolish as it is to hide beauty, it is yet more foolish to show that which is no longer beautiful.

While we ate, musicians played to us. The music they gave did not inflame, as do the chants of soldiers entering battle, rather was it refreshing to the ear, as is water to a dusty garden. Reed pipes and flutes entwined their melodies with the ripple of harps, cooling the air with their silver music like clear water falling from a height in measured cadences.

The Vizier of the Land of the Hare, who was over seventy, sat alone, for he liked the enjoyment of his food to be uninterrupted. His cooks were famous for their skill, and they blended subtleties of taste as a painting-scribe ponders on his colours. To him the exact span of time that the oven must caress a quail for it to be worthy of his palate was as the length of each line of a poem is to a song-maker.

To the right of the vizier, the wife of one of the captains of the Royal Bodyguard was sitting with her husband and another woman. I noticed that three times she beckoned to the serving-girl who carried a great bowl of honey-flavored cream, in which were ripe dates and slices of orange dried to sweetness in the sun. I wondered how long it would be before she realised that sometimes a love for rich sweetmeats and for the wearing of transparent linen do not walk happily together.

Ptah-kefer sat at my right hand. He told me a very long story of how, when he was a little boy, he and his brother had been sailing to the south of Nekht-an when the river was at flood. Their boat had struck a rock and they had been stranded on an island for three days before their father found them. I didn't listen very closely, because I had heard it several times before. There was a long and deep friendship between us, and though often we would talk together and he would give me of his wisdom, he enjoyed far more to talk of the little things of Earth. To him a childish adventure was more interesting to talk about than a great triumph over an evil one. To most people, life upon Earth is their work and the life of the spirit is their refreshment: but to great Sandal Bearers, such as Ptah-kefer, the Causeway to the Gods is the road over which they carry their burdens, and Earth is where they find their relaxation.

There was a pleasant smell of the sunny warmth of fruit and the heavy sweetness of flowers. The serving-girls, wearing tunics of green linen and wreaths of young green wheat, went among the guests with platters of food. There were little birds wrapped in vine leaves; and young gazelles each roasted whole upon a silver spit; fresh dates, served on a bed of smoking rice; and young corn, cut when the cob was at a finger's length, served with quails each cooked with a fig inside it, which was my favourite dish.

Sesket, the mother of Neyah's son, was at the royal table. She spoke very little, and when she ate she reminded me of a gazelle drinking from a pool where it can scent a lioness. Her eyes were large and the lids clearly cut. They were soft, and as if she were timid as well as stupid. I wondered why Neyah loved her. Perhaps his strength enjoyed her gentleness, like Natee, who allows a stable-cat to share his stall.

Another of the secondary wives was here, Tetab. I watched her eating grapes. As her brown fingers stretched out to take them from a dish, I thought of my monkey grabbing for a honeycomb. But I am very fond of my monkey; and though I searched my heart, for Tetab I could find no trace of affection. Her eyes were bold, and round as polished pebbles of onyx. When she saw me looking at her, she veiled them with her lids. Neyah must have been sorry that he held her father in such honour that he took his daughter into his household.

Girls went among the guests with flat rush baskets filled with wreaths of flowers, so that the women could choose fresh ones as those they wore wilted in the heat. The Overseer of the Watchers of the River had emptied his goblet too often for wisdom, and when one of the girls passed him he took a honeysuckle wreath and tried to put it on the head of the woman beside him. He was clumsy and disarranged her wig, and it showed the shaven hairline by which she had tried to heighten her forehead. He would be told that it is unwise to forget that the banqueting hall of Pharaoh is neither his own home or the wine-house of the garrison.

Then young girls, naked and slender as reeds, danced the Shadow Dance of the North Wind. First they stood quiet as a field of corn upon a still day, and muted drums murmured of the drowsy heat. Then the reed pipes whispered of the evening breeze, and the dancers' arms rippled like a breeze-stirred meadow when the grass is high. Then they moved gently, as leaves flutter with the first breathings of a storm. The wind strengthened to the melody of harps, and they swayed like papyrus bowing to the marsh. And as the music heralded the storm, they were like trees whose branches clasp great winds and scatter their leaves as tempest-driven offerings to the racing clouds. Thunder muttered to the surge of drums, until it seemed that we were encompassed by a mighty storm. And as the music drifted into peace, the dancers' rhythm turned to gentleness. Then the music enfolded quietness, and they were still, as trees upon a silent evening.

Before the banquet ended, a toast was given, which had been written by the cup-bearer of Na-mer, who had saved his master from death through poison; and it was in his memory that it was given at this festival until this day. For the last time, our alabaster goblets were refilled with cool wine—

> Wine that is rare enough for Pharaoh's seal
> Upon the stopper of its earthen jar;
> Wine that is stored in deep-cut rooms of stone,
> Where, in the dark, is slowly born this child
> Of clustering grapes and the hot summer sun.
> If this were used, as is the people's drink,
> To be a barrier against thought or fear,
> It were as if the Flail in Pharaoh's hand

Should of its will lash him across the brow,
Or the young lion cub, sleeping at his feet,
Should tear his flesh and show the whitened bone.
Let fools and cravens use this purple cloak
To hide their burdens from their inward sight;
But in it we drink to Wisdom, Courage, Truth,
Downfall of enemies, and furtherance of the Light.

## CHAPTER SEVEN

# DIO

When I was in the temple I used to think that after I became a priest I should find contentment in the using of the power that I was striving to gain. But now that I shared the Double Crown my heart was often filled with longing for the quiet strength of Ney-sey-ra, and after his companionship the conversation of the nobles and of my attendants was like shrill pipings on a single reed after a splendid harmony of harps and flutes.

Always must I be Pharaoh, remote and wise and undisturbed. With no one save Neyah could I put off this garment of control. I could not even be impatient when the mirror showed my hair unsmooth, nor, if the outline of my eye was smudged, could I throw the wax upon the floor, as I sometimes longed to do. Always I had to preserve an unflawed calm, as though the light around me shone like pearl instead of being flecked with the red of anger. None knew that I often felt like a harp too tightly strung, which at a touch gives forth harsh discords; that crowns and wigs and ceremonial robes were heavy after a tunic and loose hair; that to sit immobile on a throne tired my muscles, which were used to freedom. In the temple I had been much alone; but now, except when I was sleeping, or in my sanctuary, people were always with me, people to whom I must be wise and kind, people whom I might hurt by an unthinking word, which, if spoken by another, they would not heed. She to whom they gave their loyalty, whose wisdom they revered, was but an image of me that they held in their hearts. There was no one who knew my secret doubts and fears, or heard the foolish, angry words that did not pass my lips, but shouted in the silence of my thoughts. Neyah and I were together, yet I was lonely: for though I had his companionship, I longed for that double link where each to each is like the balanced scale. I could not tell Neyah of my longing, because I feared he would be sorrowful if he knew that though I ruled beside him, I still felt the loneliness of all women who do not have a man to share their lives.

Dio was often in my thoughts, and I longed for his return; he was the only person who knew me not as priest or Pharaoh, but as Sekeeta.

Five moons had passed since he had left for the quarries in the South, and the moon was again at full circle. That night Dio would be waiting for me by the lake. Soon after sunset I went to my room, telling my attendants that I was tired and wished to be alone, and that no one must come near me until I summoned them.

Then I left the palace through the private garden, where my father's herbs sent forth their pungent scent, across the vineyards, and along the little path between the reeds. Some heavy animal crashed through the night and startled me. On each side of the narrow path the water between the reeds was black as bitumen.

Then, reflected on the water, I saw a light, which shone through the open doorway of the little pavilion by the lake. There Dio waited for me. As I went through the door, he held out his arms to me. And I went into them like a tired traveller who reaches home.

Many times I met Dio there, or in the Meadow of Ra. I told him I was one of the Queen's attendants, and so he understood that I was not always free to come to him.

On the days when I could not meet him, we left messages for each other in the hollow fig tree that grew up the outside wall of the palace garden. Sometimes he would leave a drawing and sometimes a poem.

One day he sent me:

The dry pool in my courtyard
  Is filled with sweet water and blue lotuses
  Because you looked at it.
My barren garden is filled with flowers
  Because your feet trod its paths.
My vines bow down with the weight of grapes
  Because you touched their bare stems.
My abandoned fields are alive with singing-birds
  Because they heard your voice.
My broken harp pours forth its melody
  Because it heard you sing.
My poor house has become a palace
  With courts and colonnades
  Because it shaded you from the noonday sun.
And I, who am but a worker in stone,
  Should be greater than Pharaoh
  If you gave unto me your heart.

and I answered:

If I were the gentle north wind,
  Your forehead would always be cool.
If I were a jar of wine,
  Your cup would never be empty.
If I were the river,
  Your garden would never know drought.
If I were your sandal,

Your foot would feel no stone upon its path.
If I were a basket of fruit,
You would never feel hunger.
If I were a spear,
No enemy would reach you in battle.
But I am only a woman
And I have not even a heart to give you
For it its yours already.

And later I found in the hollow fig tree:

I saw my love sleeping:
A garden tranquil under the moon.
I saw my love waking:
The sun dispels the river mists.
I saw my love weeping:
Stars are the tears of the night.
I heard my love laughing:
The night-bird sings at noon.
I saw my love walking:
The cool wind from the north ripples the corn.
I saw my love open her arms to me:
So I know that when I enter the Celestial Fields
I shall find nothing that is unfamiliar to me.

Dio and I were together by the river. There was a cool evening breeze, and the water broke in little sighing waves against the bank.

"Dio, why do you love me, when all the things I tell you about you disbelieve? You could find a hundred dancing-girls more beautiful than I am. You don't believe that love is long in time; you think it's something that suddenly happens between two people, like the chips of dry palmwood that smoulder and then flower into flame at the whirling of the fire-stick."

"My Sekeeta, why do you always ponder on the reason

for things? Isn't it enough that I love you? I don't know why it is that beside the memory of you the loveliest dancer seems like a fat Nubian grinding corn; or why, when I have heard your voice, the sweetest singer is like the screaming of a chisel on a whetstone. But I am content that it is so. You are very beautiful, my Sekeeta, and if I were a great sculptor you would know that for yourself. And the stories you tell me are more beautiful than the legends of the time when Earth was young and the Gods walked with men in the Gardens of the West."

"Oh, Dio, your poor country! I should like to go there and talk to your people. Have they so little truth that what they have they believe to be but the legends of a story-teller?"

"You would love that country. They would teach you how the beauty of the present can be caught so that it seems as though it would endure into eternity, as the flight of a bird is caught for the future in stone. There would be laughter in your eyes and you would sing to the joy in your heart. I should crown you with roses and white jasmin and we should run together on white beaches in the sound of the sea. We should climb high mountains together, so high that the clouds were beneath our feet. We should sleep under the stars and walk together through valleys of wild tulips....There we will have a white house with a garden such as you have never seen, on a steep hillside, with a waterfall to sing us to sleep, and wide terraces down to the sea. We will have white doves, so tame that they shall perch upon your shoulder on their coral coloured feet: and their voices shall echo our contentment. And the walks shall be of thyme and the hedges of rosemary. And all the flowers of my country shall make that place beautiful for you in their season. If we were there now, the hills would be scarlet with anemones, and the oleanders budding over your window. We will always be together; and my eyes shall be filled with your beauty until at last I can carve it in stone. And thousands of years after we are dead, they may find my statues of you, and then they will know that, though man has searched for beauty ever since Earth was young, once it lived as a woman in Minoas.''

He was lying with his head on my lap, and I stroked his eyes so that he must keep them shut and could not see the tears in mine. He but told me of the things we had done together in dreams. I could remember the valley of wild tulips and see their pointed petals as clearly as if they grew in Kam and I had seen them when awake. Why was I born to wear a crown and but to dream of wreaths of jasmin? When he found out who I was, I might lose him upon Earth. Would he have understanding when he slept, or would even my dreams be sorrowful? This happiness might last such a little while; yet would the memory of it be a part of me always, and when at last I entered the Celestial Fields I could live this present throughout eternity.

Although I had told Dio that I would never leave the palace, he did not believe me. He thought that I was dazzled by a high position and that I set too great an importance on the friendship of the Queen. He hoped that soon the glamour of the court would grow dim for me and I should be content to go with him to his home in the Delta.

Dio hated the Queen. To him she symbolized all the pomp and ceremony that he despised. He said she must be selfish and without compassion to make me stay with her when I could find happiness with him. When I defended her and tried to make him understand how difficult was the life of a Pharaoh, he would not listen. I knew that soon he would find out that she and I were one, and I wondered which picture would remain in his heart: the Queen he hated, or the woman that he loved.

I had prayed to Ptah that I might bear his child. And when I knew that Ptah had listened to my voice, I told Dio. And he said that no longer could anyone come between us, and that he would claim audience with the Queen and demand from her my freedom to be his wife.

I would have told him then, but it was late and I had to return to the palace. So I asked him to meet me on the next day at the sunset hour and until then to claim no audience.

I knew that this interlude, when I could be with Dio in a secret garden, was drawing to its close, and I must leave this sanctuary of green quiet and walk with him in the clear light of day. For the sun does not stand still upon his journey across the sky nor can the lives of men be without change. I had rejoiced to share in the freedom of lovers, to feel my Earth encompassed by my love and to know the glad heritage that Min had given to mankind. But it is foolish not to take pleasure in the fresh green of the young leaves because one sighs for the tracery of bare branches against the moon or longs for the leafy shade of summer. Now we must work together to the glory of Kam.

I planned the pattern of our lives together....The buildings that still live in Dio's mind shall flower in stone. There shall be new temples up and down the land, where people shall be taught as I have been taught. From across the sea shall come cedarwood for doors; barges shall bring white limestone from the North and rose-red granite from the quarries of Za-an. I will gather craftsmen from the Two Lands, masons and sculptors, carpenters and scribes, and I will make gardens to enshrine this stone, with lotus pools set among trees meticulously placed. I will build a little palace in the South, where rocky islands challenge the river's flow. Even the furniture shall be of Dio's thought; it shall be flawless, out of precious woods: inlaid with the smooth sheen of oyster shell, with lapis lazuli to reflect the sky, and lines of ivory, and fillets of gold. My curtains shall be patterned with flying swans, cleaving above the reeds in their arrow flight; the plaster walls shall blossom to lotuses, and even the floors shall be of cedarwood. I will make Dio master of a great estate, as though he were a son of Pharaoh by a secondary wife. When he journeys through the land to see his buildings he shall have a barge of forty oars, and he shall drive his own horses in a chariot. I have raised him to the stature of the name of a god, for though none other shall know it, he will know that Pharaoh, Child of Horus, is his child.

How foolish I have been to sorrow that I was born to the Royal House; if I were Sekeeta only, I could have been his wife before the priests, but I could have given him nothing but my love. Had his eyes been open to the Light, I would have long since told him of my heritage, for the little things of Earth can matter not to those who know of the great wings of time and of their unhurrying sweep through space. They see mankind stripped of their earthly rank, and they know that riches may be a little fisher girl and poverty own a thousand chests of gold; that two who love each other walk through Earth in many guises, speak to each other in a hundred tongues, lie in each other's arms in palaces, or are re-united in a shepherd's hut. Yet why did I ever fear that his love would die when he knew that Sekeeta and Pharaoh were one? He will see that my hair holds the same lustre although I wear the White Crown, know that my lips are still warm under his although they have moved to speak the Oath of Pharaoh, and that my hands are still the long narrow hands he loves although their fingers know the Crook and Flail.

To-morrow evening I shall meet him, and no longer will my heart hide my unspoken thoughts. Henceforward there will be no barriers between us, and in the strength of his companionship I shall be a greater servant of the Gods. Soon we shall laugh together at his words when he used to tell me that he hated the Queen—hated her when he held her in his arms! And he will learn that for hate to live, hate and understanding must be kept apart; for if they meet, a child will be born to them, whose name is love.

Next morning, as I sat in audience, it seemed that two women sat upon one throne: Pharaoh, who gave the justice of the Crook and Flail, and Sekeeta, who dreamed of the joy that she would know when in the evening her happiness cast out fear and in its clear security she at last found peace.

The day was hot and the hours seemed very long. Then, just as I was about to declare the audience closed, the scribe read out 'Hykso-diomenes'.

The lover's phrases still echoed in my heart, which were to have told him that his Sekeeta was Za Atet. As he walked up the long room towards me, his eyes were on Natee lying at my feet. Now I should know if his love was long in time or if the hoped-for depths were a shallow pool, which the sun of truth would turn to desert. The story of the second Meniss flashed through my mind; once he had sat immobile on a throne and watched to see if they who came towards him held gift or dagger in their hands.

Then Dio stood before me. He lifted up his head and looked at me. And I saw bewilderment changed to hatred in his eyes. And without speaking he turned and left the audience room.

That evening I was told that Hykso-diomenes had left the Royal City, and that the models for the new temple buildings were lying broken in the courtyard of his empty house.

Sekeeta was no longer. The Queen was the only reality. The Queen who had amused herself with her architect.

CHAPTER EIGHT

# the laws of kam

On the first day of the new year the laws were proclaimed throughout Kam: in every temple by the High-priest; in the chief city of each nome by the Vizier; in every village by the Headman; in garrisons by the Captain-of-Captains; upon the sea or river by the Ship-master; and in the Royal City by Pharaoh.

In the first year of my reign I proclaimed the laws to my people from the steps of the great courtyard of the palace.

''Hear my voice!

''None shall obstruct the path of any in the Two Lands who seeks for wisdom in the temple or for the justice of Pharaoh.

''The people of Kam are kinsmen, and they shall do unto one another as they would unto a loved brother.

''None shall refuse succour to the sick nor food to the hungry. None shall take that which is not theirs by right. None shall make a child go in fear nor let the aged suffer from their feebleness, lest they feel the wrath of Pharaoh, who is the father of all his people.

''All who have servants shall treat them as they themselves would wish to be treated: with justice and compassion. All who are servants, be it in the house or working in the fields, shall be worthy of a good master.

''Those of you who have women in your house shall treat them with kindliness, so that they smile to hear your footsteps and your wives bear your children with joy. Those of you who have husbands, brother, or fathers, see that your tongue has honey upon it and let not your words make your home unquiet. Let all in your house rejoice that they share it with you.

''Let no animal suffer through cruelty, wantonness, or neglect. He who lets an animal starve shall be without food for twelve days, so that he may gain understanding of hunger, and knowing it, will not cause it to another. He who has an animal that has broken sores from beating or from an ill-fitting harness shall receive five lashes upon the feet and five upon the back for each animal so neglected.

''Those of you who let your plants die when water is plentiful shall give a full harvest of all your land to the temple as a free gift, so that you may know the reality of famine.

"Those of you who catch more fish than you need and leave them to stink upon the river bank shall cast no net for three months.

"Those of you who are merchants, if you lie about your wares or barter unjustly with those who have not the wit to see your dishonesty, you shall not trade in Kam for six months; and if this offence be repeated, your possessions shall be divided among the people and you shall be left with only enough land to grow food by which you may live if you work with your hands, and all your strength.

"Any official under my seal, vizier or market watchman, scribe or overseer, who is dishonest in his office and thus betrays the word of Pharaoh shall be banished from Kam.

"Any who break these laws shall find that Pharaoh is master of you all and sees that you are treated as you treat others.

"If you doubt the wisdom of any action, ask yourselves: If he to whom I do this thing were Pharaoh or belonged to Pharaoh, would I continue? And if your heart says yes, then all be well.

"Remember you are my children, and what you do unto each other you do unto me also. Speak no words that you would fear my hearing. Treat your children as though they were the children of my body. Treat your animals as you would treat this lion at my feet. Tend your crops as if they were the royal garden.

"Strive always to reach that time when you can say: There is not one who sins, there is not one who suffers, there is not one who weeps, through any act of mine. For in this there be the wisdom of the Gods and the longing of Pharaoh for his people."

CHAPTER NINE

# expedition to punt

Six months after I became Pharaoh, messengers brought news that our south-eastern boundaries were being raided by the people of Punt, who this year had sent no tribute.

Neyah set forth to teach them wisdom, and with him went ten thousand soldiers of the Royal Army. This army is under the personal command of Pharaoh, and it is called upon only in time of war. Each warrior-noble raises a hundred men from his own estate; they are his friends, for they are together from childhood, and they learn spear-throwing and the flighting of arrows from the same teachers as their overlord. If any of them are killed in battle, their wives and children are looked after as members of their master's household. Each warrior is given a house to live in with his family, land on which to grow vegetables, and as much grain from the granaries as he needs for bread, and a second measure for barter. Most nobles give their warriors a jar of beer every moon, and a roll of coarse linen and one of wool every year.

Before Neyah started he reviewed his troops. There were five thousand bowmen, a thousand men armed with the mace, and two thousand spearmen. Over every hundred there was a captain, and to each fifty captains a Captain-of-Captains. There were two thousand grain-carriers, tentmen, cooks, and others, who looked after the food, water, and baggage. All were armed with a short sword, which they wore in a sheath from their belt; it was used as a hunting-knife as well as for fighting. Each man had a linen head-dress to protect him from the sun, a simple form of the sphinx head-dress; and a woollen cloak, which on the march he carried as a pack, and in which he wrapped himself when he slept. Captains wore armlets of gold, and their sphinx head-dresses were striped in green and scarlet. Each captain had a standard on which were his emblem and the emblem of his nome; and his hundred wore these emblems upon the band of their head-dress.

No horses were taken on the expedition, for since there was no longer trade with Zuma, horses were very scarce in Kam. In the old days stallions from Zuma were exchanged for gold, ivory, perfumes, and malachite; but they would sell us no mares, lest we should breed our own horses and no longer give such high exchange for theirs. Five mares had been captured in the last battle against the Zumas, and there were now fifty horses in the royal stables. They were among our most precious possessions, and if a plague should strike the stables, there would be no horses in Kam. In time of war, the chariots of Pharaoh, of Captains-of-Captains, and of captains, are drawn by two white asses. One day we hoped to conquer Zuma and the people to the east of them, and then every noble could drive his own horses.

With the army went four healers, two young seer priests, and six looking-girls. Every day news was brought to me from the temple of Neyah's progress, and long did I pray to Ptah to protect him, and that he should return victorious.

The army travelled downstream in ninety sailing barges. At the mouth of the river they sailed eastwards to the beginning of the Narrow Land between the Two Waters. Here they disembarked, and they marched for four days until they reached the Narrow Sea, where a fleet of a hundred ships awaited them. Then they sailed south-eastwards along the coast and landed on the northern shore of Punt, which was sparsely garrisoned, for they expected that any attack from Kam would come from the desert side.

The royal city of Shebastes, their king, was four days' march from the coast. Neyah divided his troops into two encircling wings, so that they attacked the city upon both sides at once. The armies of Punt were a wild rabble, and they soon broke before the measured lines of our soldiers, who advanced upon them relentlessly as a flood. Then Neyah encircled the city and waited for their surrender, for he had gone to show them the might of Kam and not to destroy their people. On the third day Shebastes came from the city bearing tribute. He knelt down and touched Neyah's foot with his forehead in homage, swearing fealty to Kam; and he told Neyah that he would cut off the hands of two thousand warriors to show his sorrow that they had ever raised their hands against the lands of Atet. And Neyah replied that he would grieve to think Shebastes should do something that would cause him, Shebastes, to be maimed two thousand times, and that instead he must show his loyalty by making our laws the laws of Punt.

Neyah stayed in the city of Shebastes forty days, while the chiefs of every tribe and the headman of every village swore fealty to him as their overlord. Then Neyah returned homewards across the desert, for he wished to visit Na-kish. And the people of Punt, who looked upon him as their deliverer from oppression, sorrowed when he left them, and they sent two hundred bearers with the army to carry their tribute.

CHAPTER TEN

# the golden link

My people were glad that I was to bear a child, for it would be acknowledged doubly royal, as if it were not only mine, but Neyah's also. The father of the child of a queen who is married to her brother is never named. And those of my people who are children in spirit and are not yet beyond the need of legends hold that the royal title, Son of Horus, when it is borne by such a child, is not only a title, but a truth.

My body had always sat lightly upon me, but now it held me to Earth, and when I crossed the Causeway to the Gods, I brought back no memory. I prayed that Neyah might return before my child was born, so that he should sit beneath the Scales, where now I was alone.

Women whose lovers are dead think on their memories; they have but to sleep to meet their love, yet Dio had left me even in my dreams. I could not love him, lest it should fill my heart and cloud my wisdom, which belonged to my people; and I could not hate him, for I bore his child, who would be worthy to rule over Kam.

I tried to think of my little span of love as though it belonged to another woman's life; to look through other eyes than mine on two shadowy figures in a lover's song.

When I left the temple, Thoth-terra-das had come with me as my scribe. To him I was still the one who had shared his love for words. Because of his office, he knew of my sorrow; and he said to me, "Remember, Sekeeta, how I taught you to burnish joy with words, so that its radiance might be a silver disc to reflect happiness into the shadow of your troubled days. When you mould your thoughts with words, you can see them clearly and separate from yourself, see the unfading radiance of past joy beside the fleeting littleness of grief. Take not sorrow for your companion to shadow your footsteps with its echoing tread, but turn it into a statue and walk on alone and leave it, a statue beside an empty path."

And so for my sorrowful heart I sought the gentle benison of words.

In Minoas the white jasmin is flowering,
  But I will not see it wither upon its branches.
The wind blows through the valley of wild tulips,
  Scattering the petals, which have lost their brilliance.
The paths are purple with wild thyme,
  But my feet shall not tread forth their sweetness.
The beaches are white in the sound of the sea,
  But they shall bear no record of my passing.
The moon throws the shadow of the oleanders

Into a room that is as empty as my heart.
I must draw the gentle curtains of sleep,
Although no waterfall sings outside my window,
And so beyond my bitter Earth find peace,
Deeper than the drowsy contentment of doves.

When the time came for my child no longer to be housed in my body, Neyah was still three days' journey from the Royal City.

I longed to be as other women, who bear their children alone upon the bed-place with the love of their husbands to give them courage. But my child must be born upon the royal birth-chair, while I talked to the priests in attendance to show that my will was master of my body and that pain could not make me cry out against its onslaughts.

With me was Ptah-kefer, who watched to see that all was well with my body. When the child was born he would look upon those who came to speed it upon its journey; and, seeing its companions, he would know if it were one long in years or young in spirit who returned to Earth. With me also was a healer priest, ready to strengthen the child if it were exhausted by the ordeal of birth. Behind me waited Maata to take the child and bathe it in warm oil and wrap it in charged linen, even as she had once been the first to take me into her arms. With her was Pakee, who would tend my body when I could relax my hold upon it and leave it to her care.

The robe of birth, clasped at the neck by a golden winged moon, hung round me to the floor. Under its wide sleeves I drove my nails into my palms; and it was quieting to the mind like a sword-thrust that makes the heart forgetful of sorrow. I felt the sweat running down my face like the feet of moths. I never knew that Earth held so much pain; in scarlet waves it flung itself against the cliff of my will, but before I was engulfed it drew back to gather itself a greater fury. No priest who is in a man's body can know how fierce the pull of Earth can be upon a woman; yet must I talk of priestly things, my words unhurried and my breath uncaught.

I talked of the new highway between Men-atet-iss and Abidwa. I tried to think of each cubit of the road, holding my mind to the quiet peace of its shady length. I felt that my self-control was like a single flame, which I shielded between my hands while it was beset by a tempest that sought to quench it and leave me to drown in a dark sea of pain. I tried to think of all the multitudes on Earth, and to remember that what I was undergoing had been shared by the mothers of every one of them: but pain and fear are prisons in which we are alone.

I heard my voice still talking of shade-trees when, in the last onslaught of pain's white-hot swords, my child was born. I heard it crying...and the eyes of the healer priest drove me from my body, and I knew peace.

Away from Earth I was refreshed, and when I returned to my body it was gentle to me. I opened my eyes and saw Pakee watching beside my bed. She told me that Ptah-kefer had said that my child would be a worthy holder of the Flail, and he should bear the name of Den, which he had once borne as a warrior, although now he had returned to Earth as a girl-child.

My daughter's hair was the colour of pale copper, as if the copper of her father's hair had been alloyed with gold; and for this I gave her as her little name 'Tchekeea'.

As I looked at her I thought of Dio....To him a fair white wall of stone, eager and waiting for him to carve upon it until it lived beneath his hand, was greater than any gift that I could give him; and gold was but another metal to be moulded into beauty. To him a temple depended, not upon its teaching, but upon the purity of its line. Although there was nothing I could give him, to his daughter I will give a throne, and I will never bear another child who could dispute it with her. He never knew how much I longed to leave my heavy heritage and put my happiness before the guidance of a great people. Now perhaps he will laugh to think that his child has been fathered upon the Gods. Women who come to me, telling me of their hearts, wonder at my understanding, thinking it is the fruit of great wisdom; they do not know it is only that I share the foolishness of women with them.

Neyah returned when my daughter was three days old. As soon as he reached the palace he came to my room. His eyes were on the child's red hair as he stood beside the bed-place. In a voice cold and smooth as stone, he said, "Horus has grown scarlet feathers since I left."

Then he turned to leave me. I called to him, and he unwillingly came back and stood waiting for me to speak.

I was lonely for him, and yet very angry. I thought, What of his smooth women? They are like four chattering parrots, gay-coloured and stupid. They live but to put kohl upon their eyelids and to paint their nails. Their bodies are smooth, but they are empty statues. They are sensuous as cats, and much less wise. When I go to their apartements they glide into the shadows when they see me. As long as I am Pharaoh they can be nothing. Why should I mind them? To him they are like a fine bow-case, or a keen-scented dog, or a chariot that turns more swiftly than the rest; and of course he is kind to them and brings them ivory and necklases and precious oils. They fear me. I am Pharaoh of the Two Lands; its boundaries are sea and desert and mountains. My spirit can fly from my body to the threshold of the Gods. Yet I am jealous of ordinary women, women whose dominion is the four walls of their room, whose throne is but the mats upon their bed-place, whose vision of attainment is no further than the body of a man. For me to envy them is as though I longed for the contentment of oxen munching in their stalls. How he must hate this child! He has three children and I know their mothers. But he shall never know the father of my child. Three of his nobles, a captain, and his chief scribe, all have this strange, this copper-coloured hair. He shall never know which he should greet as brother.

Long had I kept these thoughts well leashed. But now, when the pull of Earth was heavy, they slipped from the well-fenced pastures of the mind. For moons and moons my body had been a prison, and the sword of my will had been deep-shrouded in heavy cloth, so that unbidden thoughts broke down their barriers and trampled savagely within the secret places of my heart.

He waited for my answer.

I was so lonely for him, yet I said, "I think you have no red-haired woman. That is stupid of you: you would find that they give you strange pleasures you have missed."

Then he left me, and I was all alone.

When Tchekeea was twelve months old, she fell ill of a plague that swept through the land; and it seemed that she must die of it. Her face and body were patched with livid blue, and first she would burn with a strange inward fire and then grow icy in my arms. She took no food, except milk and wine dropped through a reed between her lips.

Neyah stayed with her night and day, and in his arms she found peace, which she could not find in mine. And on the tenth day her dry forehead became cool and damp, and Ptah-kefer said that the danger had passed and she would live.

And when she became strong again, it was to Neyah that she ran for comfort for a hurt, or to share with him her pleasure in a toy. And the child that had once been a spear between us became the strongest link in the golden chain that bound us together.

I sorrowed to think that I had turned my face from his children, and I went often to the women's quarters and talked with the secondary wives, and I learned to understand their way of thought. I took them presents and gave them treasures; and at first, when I saw their pleasure in a bracelet or a pleated robe or a jar of some new unguent, I gave it with secret scorn. But then I grew to know them and to understand that these things were to them as a spear is to the warrior, or a tablet to the scribe. And to their children I gave love and protection, even as Neyah had given it to Tchekeea.

And so I learned that jealousy is a great evil. For, to a jealous one, love is like a collar of silver that he clutches in his hands, fearful that a thief may take it; and if he loses it he thinks that all is lost. But each one of us is like a sun; and his rays, which be love and friendship, fall upon many; and all on whom they fall shall feel no greater warmth if their brother is standing in the shade.

And this will I teach to all men and to all women who share the sorrow that once was so bitter upon my lips.

# PART SIX

## CHAPTER ONE

## SEA JOURNEY

When Tchekeea was three years old, Kiodas, King of Minoas, came to Kam upon a state visit. The bonds of friendship between his country and ours were strong, and we promised that within the year we would journey to his island kingdom.

Next year, being the fifth year in my reign, on the second day of the fourth month we said farewell to my little Tchekeea and to my mother. I wished they had been coming with us to Minoas, but in our absence our mother would shepherd our people, and I knew that Tchekeea would be happier staying with her in the freedom of the palace than she would have been, shut in by the narrow decks of a ship voyage of many days.

For a long time I had wanted to see Minoas, but there can be little joy in setting forth upon a journey when one you love is further away from you with each cubit that you travel. Kam was tranquil, for since Neyah had subdued the people of Punt, none challenged the strength of Atet; but when the rowers swept the Royal Barge downstream and I saw Tchekeea growing smaller in the distance as she stood holding my mother's hand on the quay, I almost wished that some danger threatened Kam so that I could tell the ship-master to put back.

There were six barges in our train. With us went Ptahkefer, Zertar, and two looking-girls; my four personal attendants and ten serving women; six young nobles and twenty attendants of Neyah's; Zeb and three other captains with three hundred of the Royal Bodyguard; eight musicians—three harps, two flutes, and three reed-pipes—all of whom were singers. As gifts to the king we took a tame lion cub, four months old; two cedarwood chests of gold; necklaces of lapis lazuli, cornelian, amethyst, and wine-stone; fifty rolls of fine linen; four chests decorated in gold and faience; and twelve tusks of ivory.

It took us six days to reach the coast, for we stopped each day to give audience to the assembled people, as my father had done when as children we had travelled with him to Nakish.

The people of the North are smaller in stature, though more heavily built, than those of the South; their voices have a rougher sound and their words are not so musical. Here at certain times of the year rain falls, and there is never a scarcity of water. It is the country of great granaries, and before the fields are harvested a sea of corn stretches as far as the eye can reach. The chief city of the North is on the eastern mouth of the river, near the sea. It is called Iss-an, as is the Northern Garrison, which is on the outskirts of the city, to the east; and it is from here that the Delta is administered. In the days when the Lotus and the Papyrus grew not in the same pool and the Bees dwelt not among the Reeds, Iss-an was the royal city of the King of the North.

Horem-ka, the Vizier, lived in the old palace. He was a mighty warrior as well as a man of great wisdom, and he had fought beside my father in the last battle against the Zumas. He had a son, eight years old, who was also called Horem-ka. I told the boy that he must grow up in his father's image so that one day he too should be a vizier of Kam. I gave him a model boat of sycamore wood with ivory oars, like the ones that Neyah used to carve; to his little sisters I gave toys, and to his mother a necklace of gold and lapis lazuli.

We stayed there for three days and held audience for our people, who had gathered from far across the grain-lands to see Pharaoh. On the fourth day we embarked on our big sea-going ships. The sail of the royal ship was scarlet, and the black hull was picked out in blue and gold. Five other ships of Kam went with us, and Kiodas had sent eight of his fleet to be our escort. His ships are higher in the water than ours and have two banks of oars, but the sails are smaller. The prow of each is carved like a fish, for the sea is their element.

We sailed north-east for three days until we sighted the coast; then with a fair wind we sailed north for eight days, with hills on the horizon to our right. We passed three ships of Kam south-bound with cedarwood.

I could not share with Neyah his love for ships when they challenged a rough sea. I love the sea-bird skimming of a little sailing-boat and the royal progress of a barge that travels the river majestic as a swan. But I hated the storms that now assailed us, when our ship laboured up the green mountains of the waves or troughed with despair in watery valleys. The fiercer the storm, the more the heart of Neyah rejoiced. For hours he stood at the steering-oar, and he seemed to delight in feeling his skin flailed with spray. The waves washed over the rowers, who strained at their oars to keep the bows of our ship proud to the wind. When the doors and shutters of the deck-house were closed, it was as though we had been swallowed into the belly of a fish; and when they were open the water poured in to share with our other torments. My women lay upon their mattresses and prayed to Ptah of his compassion to let them die. I was not sick, but I longed to be a god to hold out my hands and bid the waves be still.

After the long night the storm abated and the sea grew quiet. My women combed the tangles from their hair and wiped off the eye-paint, which had run upon their cheeks. They crept out on deck and sat forlornly in the sun. Now that the sea was gentle, they praised it as carefully as a man walks past the cage of a wild leopard when he thinks the bars are frail.

On the twelfth day we landed at a large island, a province of Minoas, while our ships were freshly provisioned with lettuces, radishes and pot-herbs, pomegranates, grapes and oranges; goats' cheese and butter; a little fish, preserved in oil. Here are the vineyards that yield the famous wine, of which a hundred jars are sent each year to Kam as gifts; and the fields of violets from which oil for unguents is distilled. We slept that night at the house of the governor; and when we left we gave him two gold armlets and a necklace for his wife.

We sailed north again until we sighted the mountainous coast, which we kept on our right hand for five days. Then we bore southwards, passing by the Island of Bakiss, in whose fine harbour many ships of the Minoan fleet are built. On the high ground of this island there lives a breed of goat with long silken hair, from which the finest woollen stuffs are made. The wind was fair and we did not stop, but kept south of the sunset until we saw the great island of Minoas.

As we came within sight of its shores, a fleet of fifty ships put out from the harbour to greet us. The largest of them had a sail of cornelian-red and white, which are the royal colours of Minoas.

While the two royal ships floated beside each other quietly as two oxen in a stall, a wooden bridge was put between them and we crossed over it to greet Kiodas. He wore a draped tunic of white, bordered with purple and gold; and his bronze hair, which curled to his shoulders, was bound with a plain golden fillet. His sandals were studded with amethysts, and he wore a large amethyst on the first finger of his right hand. As soon as we had stepped on deck, girls, wearing thin tunics the colour of almond blossom, played on lyres and cymbals and sang us welcome:

> The sun has risen after a long night,
> The barren trees are covered with buds,
> The silent birds are clamorous with song,
> The sea is gentle as a garden pool,
> The dry streams are silvery with fish,

As we sing our joy that the Pharaohs of Kam
Honour us with their presence."

Kiodas told me that his queen, Artemiodes, waited to welcome us at the palace. The harbour was alive with little boats, who cheered us as the royal vessel was rowed to the quay. The shore was crowded with people from the neighbouring villages, who craned over one another's shoulders to see us, chattering together in their excitement. They were gaily dressed in brilliant colours, which were not hard and clear like the dress of the people of Kam, for to each colour there were many tones. Everyone that I looked at smiled a welcome with the quick open-hearted friendliness of children; and I felt that each one of them rejoiced that we visited their country.

## CHAPTER TWO

# the palace of kiodas

It was two hours' journey by litter to the palace. Every turn of the steep road showed another vista of beauty for our eyes: white beaches of little bays, gold beside the foam of breaking waves; the sea, patterned with its changing hues, shading from green and turquoise to purple blue; an olive tree entwined with honeysuckle; and wild roses cascading down a rock. The little villages were painted white or yellow or dusty pink; it seemed that to cling to the steep slopes the houses must be as sure-footed as a mountain goat. The breeze was gentle, and sweet with the flowery scent of mountain valleys. The twisted branches of the olive trees were heavy with years: clothed in the silver green of their young leaves, they were like some old man of learning who had renewed his youth. Children ran out of houses that we passed and threw flowers into our litters; for here the hillsides were gardens of the Gods.

In the distance, the palace of Kiodas looked like a splendid city on the mountainside, or like some staircase made for giants fifty cubits high. As we approached the great entrance, Artemiodes came down the long steps to greet us. Her voice was warm and sweet as she welcomed me. She was like a lovely figurine of copper and ivory: her skin smooth as pale honey, her hair challenging the colour of marigolds.

When she showed me the beauties of her house and the flowering joys of terraces and woods, she was eager as a happy child who shares its toys with some fond playmate. The gardens, sentinelled by cypress trees, flowed steeply down to join the olive woods; and so well had man and nature shared their work that each rose, each spreading drift of violets, each army of hyacinths marching in the sun, seemed to have grown there for their own delight.

The rooms of the palace opened on to wide terraces that roofed the ones below. My bedroom had a frieze of dancing-girls in black and red; and spaced above it on the walls were the heads of bulls, carven in white stone, their horns linked with ropes of dew-fresh flowers. The bed, its head shaped like a scallop-shell, was mattressed and cushioned soft in yellow silk. Woven rugs of black and white covered the stone floor—in Minoas even their palaces are built in stone. Pink oleanders in red pottery jars stood before the pillars of three archways, which opened on to the private terrace, and filled one end of the room, making it like a pavilion open to the sun. The archways could be closed against rain by slatted shutters; and inside there were blue curtains if I wanted darkness for a noonday sleep.

My bath, not set in the floor like ours, reminded me of a stone sarcophagus. Cold water spouted into it through the mouth of a stone fish, and it was drained through a little channel cut in the floor. Pottery vases of elaborate shapes, to hold dried herbs and flowers to scent the bath, were set on shelves against the walls, which were painted with seabirds and shells and branching coral.

At one end of the terrace, walled with the distant view of sea and sky, there was a swimming pool; and at the other, an arbour invited us to rest, shaded by vines and climbing roses with sharp-pointed buds.

When I returned to my rooms to prepare for the banquet, which was being given in our honour, my women had taken my clothes from their travelling boxes and laid them away in long chests of painted cedarwood. Maata told me that she had found twelve wig stands in the room where my clothes were kept, and that she supposed the people of Minoas thought our people were bald, just because they had heard that sometimes we wore wigs for ceremonies. Dear Maata! She took much more pride in my hair than she had ever done in her own, and she felt its lustre was due to her fierce combing of its tangles when I was a child.

Her thoughts crowded each other for her tongue; and as she polished my hair she told me that the girls who brought the hot water for my bath had bare breasts and their nipples painted scarlet, "and their hair was dyed orange and yellow, and curled and be-ribboned, instead of wearing decent wigs and linen tunics like our attendants. I doubt if there is any girl in this whole country whom a husband could surprise on her marriage day."

I laughed and told her to be more tolerant of other people's customs or they would think us dull as a room full of statues.

Maata sniffed fiercely. "Sly, giggling women! Not one of them would I let work in our palace for half a day, not even to clean out the lion stalls. If the ones I've seen are not big with child it's no virtue of theirs, but because the men here are too busy painting their faces and curling their hair to have time even to remember that they are men."

"Hush, Maata. They are different from us; perhaps they

are younger than us. But they are our friends. We may be able to teach them a little wisdom—from what I know of their priests they have need of it. But frowns and disapproval lock hearts against words that might guide them. To see your face we might be surrounded by a forest of spears, and our wine poisoned, and our beds full of scorpions."

"If it is your pleasure, I will hide my thoughts. As to my speech, it matters not what I say; they can no more understand my words than I can make out their heathen chatter."

"Please me then, and smile, Maata. I also find it difficult to express myself in their language, but I am glad I learned something of it before their visit last year. It was gracious of them to welcome us in our own tongue."

Maata had left me when Neyah came to my room to see if I was ready, and I told him what she thought of the Minoans. He was in a very good humour and kept laughing to himself; as we walked down to the banqueting hall he said, "It is well that Maata has not been to my room, for when I went to bathe I found six young girls to wait on me. And when I told them to go they pretended not to understand me, and they pointed to each other and to the bed to ask which I should like to wait on me to-night."

One side of the banqueting hall was pillared, and curtained with the sunset. There were two long marble tables down each side of the room, and a shorter one on a dais at one end, where Neyah and I sat between Kiodas and his queen. Her flounced dress, of flax-blue edged with violet, was draped tightly round her waist and thighs; the bodice was cut low and showed her breasts with their gilded nipples. Her hair, piled high on her head in little curls, was kept in place by silver pins headed with amethysts.

At the King's table, also, were Ptah-kefer and Zertar; the high-priests of Minoas, Kioda's chief vizier, and the captain of his fleet. The nobles and captains sat with the women of both our households on cushioned benches at the long tables. Here each must spend the banquet with those on either side of them and cannot select those they wish to talk to, as we can in Kam.

The pale gold wine, soft on the tongue and very cool, was poured from long-necked jars with two handles of graceful shape by boys in short tunics, whose curled hair was bound with ribbons.

Many kinds of fish that I had never tasted before were served, and many sweet dishes, one being of honey, crushed almonds, and sugared rose-leaves. The table was strewn with violets and white roses. And while our tongues were beguiled with pleasant foods, musicians charmed our ears, and dancers our eyes.

To the sound of reed pipes, a dancer came running into the centre of the floor, his loins girdled with vine-leaves. He held the ends of long ropes of flowers, by which he dragged six girls, dressed as he, who were as slaves that he was bringing to his king. Then suddenly the girls whirled into a dance. He stood in the middle of them, while they danced round him, their steps weaving about each other, until he was plaited in the garlands of their ropes and bound, their captive. Then, as they rang their mockery of him, he burst his flowery chains, and they fled in pretended terror as he chased them out into the night.

Then followed two men and a girl, who though they were very graceful, were more acrobats than dancers. The men flung her to each other across the room; and as her arms back-stretched like wings, she flew through the air like a bird breasting the wind.

After each dance the company acclaimed the dancers and threw flowers to them. The first time this happened, I was startled. In Kam to praise a dancer when she has danced would be as if one stood looking at a sculptor, admiring him, and took no notice of the statue he had made. To us the rhythm of a dance is as separate from the one that creates it as is a statue from its carver; but here it is the dancer herself who is praised, and not only that thought which, through her body, she has brought alive.

I took a white rose that was lying beside my plate and threw it to a girl who had just danced, and I saw that in so doing I had pleased Kiodas. When he stayed with us in Kam, he must have thought us grudging in our praise, unknowing that for us to praise the makers of a shadow dance would be as if we sang to the moon for patterning a fig tree on a wall.

That night before I slept Neyah came to my room. He had been swimming in the pool; his hair still ran with water, and I told him to dry it before he went to bed.

He said, "I have no bed, for in it there is a sleeping girl who waits for me. I do not like this over-hospitality. I wish to sleep. If I send her from my room Kiodas may think I hold his women unworthy of me....I like to choose for myself who shares my bed."

"Poor Neyah! Tell her that on this day there is a sacred festival in Kam when all men swear celibacy for a night and leave the world of women to the god Min. She will believe anything of us. They think us magicians, who might turn them into frogs, or ride across the sky on crocodiles!"

"I am glad you threw that rose, Sekeeta; it pleased Kiodas. I found conversation difficult with his wife; it would have been easier had she been to Kam, but they were only married in the spring.

"They are such a happy people, gayer than we were, Neyah, even when we were little. They may not know who they are or where they come from or where their journey leads, but they live with laughter in that flash of time which is the present."

"Yes, but their gaiety is like foam that soon will fade."

"That may be, Neyah, but foam holds magic colour while it lasts, more beautiful than the deeps of all the seas. Though we may have the contentment of the long in years, they strain the present to their pointed breasts, closing their fingers round each grain of time as if it were a rose, fiercely distilling each drop of scent before its petals fall to free its heart."

''But they know nothing of wisdom; if I could make Kiodas fill these temples with my priests...''

''They are young, and glad; and this is good for them. To change their lives would be as cruel as if I were to take Tchekeea's favourite toy and rip it up and let the feathers out and show her that it was a linen cloth, and not a cat to whom she told her stories. Leave them. They are not evil, they are young. And when they are older they will be re-born into a land like ours.

''But it is late; the day has been long and we must sleep. Good-night, my Neyah; go to your room and in the morning tell me how you slept!''

## CHAPTER THREE

# Artemiodes

Artemiodes used to come to my room and try any of my unguents that were new to her. They had no malachite in Minoas, and she liked to colour her eyelids green with mine. I showed her how it must be made into a smooth paste with a drop of oil on the finger, and I promised her that as long as we had it in Kam she should not lack of it, and that I would send her a carved palette, such as I used, on which to grind it into a powder.

Her toilet took her a long time. Each of her many curls had to be twisted round a little stick, tied with thread, and then wetted with rose-water, before her hair was fanned dry. Her skin was very fair, almost the colour of her pearls, and every day she bathed in fresh goats' milk and rubbed her hands with sheep's cream to keep them smooth.

She had a long narrow room where she kept her dresses, each on its own wide shelf, arranged according to their colours. One that I liked specially was of yellow silk, ribboned in turquoise; and another, striped in pink and white like a tulip, was bound at the neck and hem with vivid green; and the five flounces of a third, which was the soft mauve of rosemary, were fringed with little pearls. Her sandals were as many-coloured as her dresses. When we were alone together, she often wore a simple tunic girdled below her breasts with coloured ribbons.

She would talk of clothes as eagerly as a captain would tell his fellow of a strategy for battle, and she would describe a coupling of colours like a poet who words an imagery of thought to a fellow song-maker, finding the same pleasure in the placing of an ornament that Thoth-terra-das finds in a smoothly worded phrase.

She was surprised when she saw that each of my dresses had four others that were exactly like it. I told her that in Kam most of the clothes we wore had been fashioned on the same lines for more than a hundred years.

Though she was queen to Kiodas, she did not share his rulership; and I think she was sorry for me because instead of having only the pleasures of a queen I shared the responsibilities of a king.

I had brought Artemiodes a lion cub; for knowing how much joy Natee gave me, I thought this would give her more pleasure than any other gift. She had seemed delighted, and she had said that he should sleep on a violet cushion beside her bed. But the paws of the gentlest cub are rough, and their little teeth sharp. He ate his violet cushion and tore the ribbons off her dresses. And she found that it is as difficult for the love of clothes and a lion cub to share one's heart as for a pigeon and a wild-cat to house together. So she asked me whether I was not lonely without Natee, and whether I should not be happier with the little lion to sleep in my room while I was in Minoas. As soon as he was with me he was very good; and when people whom he didn't know came near me, he used to try to roar at them in his little hoarse voice. I grew so fond of him that I decided to take him home and give him to Tchekeea; so I told Artemiodes that I thought the winters of Minoas would be too cold for him, and that I would send her embroidered linens and carved bracelets as a better token of our friendship.

Each day was a blossom on the tree of time. The cares of rulership became remote, and we had but to think of our own pleasure to delight our hosts.

We spent five halcyon days in a little summer palace by the sea, alone with Kiodas and Artemiodes. We wore such simple tunics as the fisher people wear, and cooked our food over the glowing ashes of a driftwood fire.

On rocky beaches, where the sea whispered to the moon, were little pools with living flowers that folded their feathery petals at a touch, and scarlet sea-weed like a sea-nymph's hair, and yellow crabs that scuttled sideways to a sheltering rock.

Neyah used to coil our fishing lines round his waist, and he and I would swim out to a rock that rose sheer from the deep water. Here we flung out our weighted hooks until we felt a strong fish fighting on the line. Once I caught a little octopus; its tentacles were like a nest of snakes, and evil looked at me out of its eyes until Neyah killed it with his hunting-knife. Stringing the fish we had caught through the gills, Neyah carried them slung over his shoulder as we swam back to the shore. Then I would lie basking in the warmth, while the sun burnished my skin, which glittered with the salt crystals of the sea. Not till the dusk had fallen did we wear clothes, for here even the sun at noonday was not too impetuous.

I grew to be very fond of Artemiodes, but I never knew her heart or understood her way of thought. She loved to hear of the housings of my life, but she did not ask me of my thoughts or wish to talk of things away from Earth; she liked to hear about what our people ate, how long they worked, and how they amused themselves. But when I would have told her what they were taught, I saw that she listened but from courtesy. And when I tried to find out what she believed, she would tell me of some new dish that her cooks had made, or some new whim she had thought of to please Kiodas.

Sometimes she talked of him as if she were his favourite dancing-girl, telling me how, even if his fleet were overdue, she could drive thoughts of kingship from his mind and keep him within the closed circle of an embrace. Sometimes she talked of him as if he were a beautiful youth who had still to assail her virginity; and sometimes as if she were an indulgent mother talking proudly of a wilful child. Her love for her husband seemed to change with her every mood. Perhaps it was because in Minoas they are not taught to 'know thyself', and have not yet learned that the enduring strength of love is to know the measure that the other has of good and evil, wisdom and foolishness, and, knowing it in stark simplicity, still to want to make the long journey by his side.

One night, sleeping in curtained litters, we were carried up one of the great mountains that crown their island. For the first time I held snow between my hands and saw my fingers mould it with their warmth. The gleaming white of pearl I knew, the warm white of new-cut ivory, the foaming whiteness of a breaking wave, and daisy petals brilliant in the sun; but now in my hands I cupped the heart of whiteness, the essence of all colour transmuted into purity.

The eastern sky hung out its banners of the day, and the morning breeze quenched the stars' flickering lamps. The land below us was still sleeping beneath the mist; but we, on a white island above the clouds, saw the cold brilliance about our feet turn to a throne of coral for the Gods. The horizon, mighty as the Wheel of Time, encircled us; and sleeping Earth stirred to the sound of Ra's Chariot, as to the coloured music of the dawn he returned to greet his subjects on a new day.

CHAPTER FOUR

# MINOAN ART

Just as the gods of the Minoans are different from ours, so are their paintings, their sculpture, their gardens, and their buildings. And it was not until I had been in their country for many days that I realized wherein the difference lay.

In Kam we see the ordered pattern of the universe, wherein there is no chaos and no chance; the stars plough their allotted furrows across the sky; the corn springs from the seed, ripens, falls from the ear, and is re-born, in a smooth cycle. Just as there is no stone that falls into water and makes no ripple, so there is no action, whether it is good or evil, that is not exactly balanced by the future that its present creates. Not only the universe, not only our lives, but every grain of sand that is blown upon the wind is meticulously balanced with that unflawed justice which to us is symbolized by the Great Scales of Tahuti. Our innate knowledge of this unbroken rhythm is reflected in all things that we create to symbolize the form in which we see beauty walking upon Earth.

The two opposite sides of our rooms are reflections each of the other. If there is a window upon one side and there cannot be a window upon the other, we paint its semblance upon the wall: not because we wish it to be thought that the painting is a real window, but because it shows that we realize that beauty is the twin sister of the poised scales. A plucked lotus has lost half its beauty: for when it floats upon a clear pool, the flower and its reflection unite in a balanced harmony. It is this harmony that we strive to achieve in our gardens: if there is one pomegranate tree upon the left hand of a pool, then shall its brother be upon the right hand: if the red lilies of Ptah grow by the left-hand wall, then shall their reflection grow by the wall opposite.

We see the present as the reflection of the past, or as that which creates a reflection in the future. Only thus can the present be seen in its entirety: for if one sees only one side of a balance, it is without meaning and cannot fulfil its purpose.

We know that beauty is permanent, and that, being permanent, it is beyond the confines of the five senses of the body and can be apprehended only by the spirit. We do not paint a frieze in a fashion that is expected to convince the eye that what it sees is not a painting of a man, but the man himself. But our drawing-scribes record those things that they hope will stir the spirit of the beholder, so that he can re-create with his inward vision that which the scribe saw with his spirit.

Just as writing-signs convey words, which convey thought, which conveys an image seen in the writer's mind, so do our pictures pass on what the painter has seen not only through his eyes, but in his heart. If our painting-scribes wish to record the beauty of a garden, they do not depict it as their eyes see it: for to create an illusion of reality is to create only an illusion. No one can sit in the shade of a painted tree, though every leaf were faithfully portrayed; and a flower, however beautifully drawn, can give forth no scent except of the plaster on which it has been limned. But just as corn springs from dry seed, so does the drawing-scribe plant the seeds of thought: his pool is a square space marked with water lines, and if it harbours lotuses or fish, they too are shown; his trees are formalized and show where they are placed and what kind of fruit or flowers they bear; and in the mind of the beholder these seeds of thought shall grow, until he can hear the wind stirring the leaves, see the fish flickering in the lotus shade, taste the pomegranate juice cool upon his tongue, and find contentment in this garden living in his mind.

We do not carve a statue so that men should think there is breath in the stone nostrils, we do not carve each vein and muscle, or the texture of the skin; for the exact weaving of the body is unimportant. But our great sculptors are lively of spirit, and they can convey the spirit that inhabits the body of the man whose semblance they record in stone. Just as a reed reflects a reed in the water, so does the spirit of a sculptor reflect the spirit of the man he carves. And this quality of our art can be seen at its highest in the statue of the great Meniss, which is alight with his justice and his courage; and the wisdom and compassion of my father lives on in granite.

In Minoas I saw statues carved with two kinds of vision. There were those that were but reflections of the body: each curve of muscle, the fold of the eyelids, and the fine cord of vein at wrist and elbow, were rendered as though the flesh had been turned to stone; yet they were like a lovely corpse that had forgotten the spirit that had once housed it. And there were those statues where the soul had been reflected by the soul of the sculptor; and looking upon them one could say: this man was greedy, and this man was over-fond of gold; this woman was sly, and that one riotous in love. Yet of none of them could one say: he had long thoughts, he had compassion, or, he was strong in spirit.

And in their paintings there was this same lack of the significance of the spirit. At first, when I looked upon a frieze of dancing-girls it seemed that if I turned my eyes away from them, they would move and their thin draperies flutter in the wind. And then I found that they were but a shallow pretence of dancing-girls, they were not as real as the shadows of reality upon a wall. Their image could not conjure up the sound of pipes, nor could their garlands bring back the fleeting scent of flowers; they were but empty shells in whose swift bodies blood had never coursed. They had never loved or sorrowed: for their spirit was paint and their universe was stone.

In Minoas they rejoice in the beauty of their bodies. Yet even in this they are different from the people of Kam: for to us a body is beautiful, not only for the shaping of the shell, but also because of the spirit that inhabits it. We put malachite upon our eyelids and wear fine linen as a man might build a beautiful pavilion as a background to the woman he loves. But here men love a body for itself alone, and it is as though they strewed herbs on the floor of an empty house, where dust would lie forever undisturbed by any living feet.

Yet they are happy in their youth. And to try to explain our ways of thought to them were as if one tried to tell a new-born kitten, content to suckle in its mother's warmth, of the things it would see when its eyes were opened.

## CHAPTER FIVE

# The Court of the Sacred Bulls

We arrived at the Court of the Sacred Bulls two hours after noon, while the sun was still high and would throw no shadows to confuse the players.

Neyah and I sat on either side of Kiodas on low-backed chairs painted in Minoan red and white. With us on the royal dais, which was opposite the gates through which the bulls were driven in, were members of our households.

The court was oval in shape and surrounded by ten tiers of wide stone steps, on which the rest of the spectators were assembled. Some sat on cushions and some on folded cloaks of brilliant colours. Sellers of wine, and water-carriers, and girls with flat baskets of sugared cakes and fruit and sweet-meats, went among the people.

As I looked at the crowd, who were gay as laughing children, I thought how different they were in the presence of their king from our people in the presence of Pharaoh. I saw a girl who held the stalk of a little bunch of grapes in her teeth as her lover tried to eat the fruit from her lips; and a man who was whispering to the girl beside him kissed her on the shoulder.

In Kam, though we may wear transparent linen, our bodies

are no more significant to us than our hands or feet. But here they think of their bodies not as a sword for their will, but as a vessel wherein pleasures for the senses are distilled. The girls' breasts are smooth as cups of alabaster, cups that hold enamoured wine to fire the blood. Their dresses cling like the arms of lovers to their young thighs and rounded bellies; and their milk-white bodies, gentle as gazelles, hold leopard fierceness in their silken warmth. Their men are smoothly muscled as the men of Kam, yet it seems that they gained them, not in swinging mace, in driving chariots, or in throwing spears, but in the pursuit of their swift-footed loves, whose laughter led them through sun-dappled shade to eager conquest in a murmurous grove. In Kam our bodies are but the clothes we wear on our long journey, but here their bodies are the habiliments of joy. They can hear melody in that sculptured curve from breast to thigh, clear as the notes of the night-singing bird; they speak not wisdom, yet whisper a caress limpid as white flowers in the moon-scented dark; their hair can throw a net about love's wings until they hold him captive in their arms; their feet know not the measured step of thought, yet they can dance their waking ecstasy; they walk in shadow, yet they are rose-crowned, and sleeping birds unwing their drowsy heads to join with them in their glad orisons.

Why should their hearts long for a temple's peace when they are crouched in honeysuckled bowers? Why should they dream of the Celestial Fields when golden jonquils spring about their feet and jasmin stars the night to make them wreaths? Sigh not for wisdom. You shall know its quiet when through your journey you are long in years. But while your Earth can be spanned by your arms, store memory of this honeyed happiness; gather it in the glory of your youth so that its golden sweetness may refresh your hearts when you are weary on your pilgrimage....

Kiodas broke in upon my thoughts and told me that to-day five girls and seven men were taking part in the contest. As he was speaking, a man came into the arena and read out the names of those who were to test their skill against the bulls.

Then the wooden gates were thrown open, and through them entered the procession of the players, who, standing on litters, which the bearers held shoulder high, were carried round the arena, to the cheering of the spectators. Both men and girl were naked except for protective padding, covered in gold, between their loins; and their bodies were oiled and shone like ivory. The girls' hair was cut short like the men's and covered their heads in tight curls. In front of the royal dais the players sprang from their litters and each threw a flower to Kiodas.

The three who were to take part in the first contest, a man and two girls, walked forward and took up their positions in the centre of the court. Then to a blast of trumpets the doors opened and a magnificant black bull came charging in. His forward curving horns were gilded, and round his neck was a garland of crimson flowers. Suddenly he shot out his forefeet and checked himself, bellowing with anger. One of the girls walked forward towards him. The bull charged her. As he lowered his head to attack, she seized a horn in each hand and vaulted over his head and landed, running, behind him.

The bull was bewildered. Then he saw the man to the right of him and charged again. This time the man somersaulted and stood upright for a moment on the bull's back before jumping to safety. The crowd cheered and shouted with excitement. As the bull galloped across the arena, the other girl seized it by the tail; and as it turned on her she vaulted across its back. This feat was loudly acclaimed, and Kiodas said to me, "None other in the land could have done that!"

While two cows were driven in to lead the bull out of the arena, the three victors came before Kiodas, and he crowned them with crimson roses; for they had vanquished the Bull of Roses. Kiodas told me that as this bull had been conquered by man, it was no longer worthy to be a sacred bull, and it would be taken to the pastures where the sacrificial animals were kept until such time as they were needed.

The next bull was white, garlanded with violets. He charged more slowly than the first one, and the players, who were all girls, somersaulted between his horns. When the cows led him out and the girls came to be crowned, Kiodas told one of them to stay with us. She was the daughter of one of his sailing-masters. Her body was as supply-muscled as a young boy's, and she had a long scar across her thigh. When I told her of my admiration for her skill, she laughed and pointed at the scar and said, "I sometimes make mistakes; I was lucky to be able to make more than one." I wondered whether she was ever frightened, or whether her thoughts must be kept too tightly leashed in concentration on her perfect rhythm for her to have time for thoughts of fear.

And as I talked to her, I was reminded of the red-brown people of the Land of Waterfalls. Here, in the bull court of Minoas, courage is tempered to an even finer edge. In our land we are taught that when danger bars the path along which we should travel, it must be challenged and overthrown; but here they search for danger like a hunter searching for his quarry through the tall reeds. This girl lives among a people who believe that their bodies are their true selves, and that their youth has but one flowering. Yet she is not afraid to dare her little span of youth against those sweeping horns that seek to end her strength, these pounding hooves in which she must hear the echo of death's voice.

The next bull was black and garlanded with marigolds, like the wreaths of its victors. And the one that followed it, which was the last, was red and white, and so belonged to Kiodas, as did every calf of this colour born in his kingdom. It was in a royal rage as it thundered across the arena, but two of the players vaulted safely between its horns. Before the last man challenged it, he called out something I could not understand; Kiodas told me he had declared that he would try the hardest feat of all, in which the player twists in the air as he somersaults between the horns, and lands astride the bull, facing its head.

As the bull charged, everyone was silent; the court might have been empty but for the pounding of its hooves. The player vaulted in a somersault, higher than any of the others had done; and as his body twisted in the air, the bull checked, and he landed, not on its back, but on the point of its horn. Dagger sharp, it split open his belly like an over-ripe fig; and before anyone could run to his aid, the bull had gored and stamped him to a pulp.

I found the moods of these people bewildering, for instead of the lamentation that I expected from the crowd, there was a wild outburst of acclamation for the bull. Flowers were rained down upon it, and as the cows enticed it out of the arena, the people shouted in an ecstasy of excitement. A cloak was thrown over the dead man, and I put my hand on the shoulder of the girl sitting at my feet. It must have been unnerving for her to see her companion killed, knowing that many times she would dare this death; but her face mirrored nothing of her heart.

Kiodas was delighted. He said to me, "See, the gods have taken unto themselves *my* bull. We shall have a rich harvest. None other than Zeus could have vanquished the greatest athlete in the land." And when I asked him if he were not sorrowful that such a man should have been killed, he said, "He was magnificent. It must indeed have been Zeus himself who conquered him. This bull, which the god has honoured by incarnating into it, even though for a moment, shall live in the precincts of the temple. Twenty virgins shall wait upon him and bring his food, and strew his stall knee-deep in sweet hay and flowers. He shall have a pasture and as many cows as even he can serve. As he is a royal bull, the temple must give me half of all the tribute he receives. People who bring their cows to him must pay five jars of oil or eight of wine, or the like value, for every cow he serves. And the droppings of such a bull are a strong magic against ills of the throat, and they are worth their weight in silver. In confidence, I think the priests increase their revenues by mingling the droppings of lesser beasts with what they barter; but the people do not suspect this, and some of them will even give a fine pearl for enough to plaster the chest of a sick child."

As we left the Court of the Sacred Bulls, I thought again of the man whose body lay under the cloak in the empty arena. And my heart echoed to a chord of memory, and I remembered that I had seen him in the Hall of Records while I was proving my wings. Then he had been told to seek for courage in the Court of Bulls, and now he had found her and become her son.

CHAPTER SIX

# Temple Ritual of Minoas

In the temples of Kam all days are equal, and there is no day more important than another on which to seek counsel of the priests. To think of wisdom only on a day apart is as if a man should thirst for six days and drink water from the river by his door only upon the seventh. In Kam, one day in seven a man does not labour, and fishermen leave their nets and walk in the bean-fields, and the oxen stand idle while the ploughman drinks his beer; for it is well that all should have a time for sleeping in the shade.

If a man would think long thoughts, he can think them whether his hands are working or whether he but stirs the air of a hot noon with a fan to cool his rest. Yet to the people of Minoas the Gods are not the breath of their nostrils, but are kept separate from their ordinary lives. Only on days set apart, when vintagers pick no grapes and the ships sleep at anchor, do these people go to the temple. Yet even this is not a thing of their hearts, but it is a ceremonial which they perform.

Upon such a day Neyah and I went with Kiodas to the Temple of Praxitlares. It stood on a wide terrace on the mountainside. There was no forecourt, but a long flight of steps led up to the portico, whose fluted pillars were painted a soft rose colour: and it was as though the temple were carved from dusky coral. Inside, it was like a great hall of audience, lit from above through hidden windows in the roof; the walls were painted to look like archways, and through them one could see a frieze of sacred bulls, and girls and youths playing on reed pipes. On a massive stone altar was a statue of Zeus, God of Thunder. In his right hand was a sword, and in the other, upraised above his head, he held rods of lightning. Facing the statue were the two royal thrones, high-backed and gilded and elaborately carved; upon each side of them had been placed another for Neyah and me. Behind us were the Minoan nobles in degree of rank, and the rest of the hall was packed with a dense crowd, some standing, some sitting on wooden benches.

When we were seated, the high-priest entered through a curtained doorway from behind a statue. His robe of purple silk, thrown over one shoulder and leaving the other bare, reached to the ground in heavy sculptured folds. Boys in sleeved tunics of brilliant green followed him, swinging copper incense-burners of aromatic leaves. Then came two girls carrying a double-handled dish, on which lay a freshly slaughtered kid. The blood was still dripping from its throat as they placed it before the altar. Then the high-priest began to speak his ritual prayers.

I could understand little of what he said, and I found his voice bemusing to clear thought and drowsy as bees on a hot summer's day. Time seemed as slow as a snail's track on a path. I wondered if they thought Zeus found pleasure in this prolonged and monotonous appeal, if in his murmurous words the high-priest could send a call towards the stars, or if his message died with the echoes in this room.

Then there was a stirring rustle from all the people, who must have become as somnolent as I; it sounded like an oryx running through dry reeds. I realized why interest had returned to them when, to the music of cymbals and the high clear notes of a flute, twelve dancing-girls came through the curtained doorway. They carried bows, and quivers of arrows hung at their girdles; on their heads they wore a silver sickle moon, and their thin tunics, the colour of the night sky, were caught about their breasts with silver cords. Artemiodes whispered to me that they were the hand-maidens of the Moon-goddess, and they had come to woo Zeus so that he should not challenge her rulership of the night sky with his thunder clouds. The girls danced in supplication before the statue, their arms fluid as moonlight on rippling water. The piping grew more shrill; and they feigned terror of the wrath of the Thunder-god, as the clashing of cymbals, the music of Zeus, heralded the storm. Then, to show that they had won his gentleness, the cymbals were muted, till they were like the murmur of the long waves that follow a storm.

After this the dancers and the acolytes burst into a song of praise, in which they promised Zeus that if he should keep his lightning leashed within his hands and let the almond groves be heavy with fruit, the oil jars would be filled and a thousand lamps burn in his honour; and if the vineyards were fruitful, the wine-vats would overflow and all the people should drink to his name.

It was so like a spectacle at a banquet that I almost told Artemiodes how much I admired the dancers and singers that she had got for our amusement, before I remembered that I was watching a ritual ceremony in a temple. It is not in the nature of these people to look on dancing-girls unmoved, yet they were as grave as the people of the Two Lands when they listen to the Reading of the Laws. In Kam a temple is a place where will is sharpened and thought made clear. But here the mind is dulled with ritual, so that the hearers sway on the verge of sleep, and then the senses are delighted.

On the altar stood a bowl of fine glazed pottery, painted with temple scenes in black and red. It was filled with oil, which came from an almond tree that had been struck by lightning, yet had not died, but had lived on as two trees. With this oil the high-priest anointed the King and Queen on the forehead, breast, and eyes; and he anointed Neyah and me also—after we had assented. It pleased him that we joined in his ritual. He did not know that in Kam we hold the gods of other countries in respect, unless they be of the train of Set. There is but one truth and one great brotherhood; and all gods, if they be true gods, must be of that company, in whatever form the people of Earth may picture them. And even if that which is called a god is but a statue having no spirit in the universe, still would it be against our teaching to treat that little, which is the furthest such people can attain, without courtesy.

Then in ceremonial procession the high-priest left the presence of the god as he had come. And when we left the temple I was surprised to find that it was still two hours before noon; for it seemed that the shadows of evening would be lying across the land, so long had been this ceremony.

In the drowsy hours of early afternoon, when all the palace rested, Neyah and I talked long together of the morning's ceremony. We were in the arbour of our private terrace; I was lying on blue cushions, idly watching the patterns of the leaves against the sky, and Neyah sat with his arms clasped round his knees, staring out towards the sea. Suddenly he broke in on my sleepy silence and said, "If understanding is the fruit of experience, I must be a man first born on Earth: for I can understand nothing of these people's temples. I spent two hours this morning watching their high-priest walk his part in brilliant pageantry, while he mouthed ritual prayers, and not one word of wisdom fell upon my ears, not even the simplest laws of how mankind should live among each other. He must be fool or charlatan or both. By the way he tried to bargain with his god, he might have been a huckster in the market-place: trying to buy his compassion with promises of wine and sacrificial beasts, and to beguile him with dancing-girls as if he were a rich merchant ancient of loins. There is not one among them who is winged, who can fly beyond the small confines of Earth. Though none can see a greater part of godhead than can be encompassed by the age of their spirit, they should at least allow their gods as much of wisdom as they have themselves; yet, though the vainest noble would distrust a man who praised him to his face—for the net of flattery is coarsely meshed—they praise Zeus as if he could be swayed by flattery.''

I told Neyah that when I asked Kiodas if they had temple counsellors in Minoas, he had seemed surprised and had said that when his people had disputes they kept them until one of his overseers went to their village.

Then Neyah said, ''Have you noticed that if one speaks of death these people are embarrassed? It is as if one had broken some rule of custom, which made them feel as I should if, when sitting in audience, I realized that I had forgotten to put on my beard. They seem not to fear death, yet they will not talk about it. Think of their courage in the bull court; they are careless of death for their companion, and when that boy was killed I noticed that not even the women turned their eyes away. No one is afraid to talk of what they know; so it must be that to them the face of death is veiled. What do they hope from death? A shadowy country where they can re-live their Earth, or oblivion in a pool of unending night?''

''They don't even know that a priest must be one who can say, 'I can tell you of the littleness of death, for to me its gateway has a long familiarity, and I can tell you how to live your lives, so that when once again you walk through her portals, you will rejoice at what you find therein'.''

Neyah pointed to five ships that were rounding the rocky

headland to the west, and he said, "They pride themselves, and rightly, upon their fleet, and they would not take a blind pilot upon their deck and expect him to lead them to safe anchorage; nor would they take one who said to them, 'I cannot tell you, of my own knowledge, where the rocks are hidden, but I *believe* this is the course on which you should set your oar.' If such a person dared claim to be a pilot, they would throw him into the sea—and he would have richly earned a lengthy swim. Yet they allow the course of their lives to be set by men whose gateways are not open.

"Sekeeta, though Kiodas has no conception of what a priest really is, I think that while he was in Kam he saw how much our temples mean to the people, and how we are strong in our Gods. He has a deep respect for your wisdom, although he does not understand it, and if you asked him to let us send a priest to his country to go among the people and talk to them, I am sure he would agree to it, both from courtesy to us and because he values friendship with Kam."

"Neyah, do you remember the dream I had long ago, when I visited this country in my sleep and saw the high-priest disguise himself as a swan and pleasure himself in the third sanctuary? Before I came here I knew that these temples were without light, and I hoped that we might be the spark that kindled it for them. I thought it might be that these people were old ones who were obscured, that their own knowledge was hidden from them because of some misusing of it in the past. Such people are like a heap of dry palm-wood, which a little flame can turn into a blaze. Now I know this hope was in vain; for I have been told, away from Earth, that the Minoans are not obscured, but are young. And you cannot light a beacon fire of young green wood."

"Although they are not ready to be priests themselves, we could send a teacher to them, and if they listened to his wisdom, they would hand his words down from one generation to another."

"Even if Ptah himself should come here and there were

some who listened and revered his words, passed them on to all they met, wrote down his teaching and carved his laws in stone, in a hundred years the people would have forgotten the meaning of his words unless there were true priests to follow him. For the Teaching to be alive, wisdom must flow down to Earth through open gateways, or soon it will become dead as the arm cut from a sculptor, whose fingers lose their power as soon as the master's life-blood reaches them no longer."

"But even if their memory of true knowledge were fainter than it once had been, surely that would be better than to have nothing, nothing that is permanent, nothing that lasts through time?"

"Minoas would be the poorer for hearing half-remembered truth; for if there are a few grains of gold in a bowl of sand, here are few who seek the shining grains and many who say that all of it is worthless. In these temples they have men, not priests. What would it serve them if they spoke other words? What if our priests, when challenged how their knowledge came to them, no longer answered, 'I have seen these things myself and know that they are true', but instead should say, 'Of course, I cannot know this for myself, but long ago a wise man said these things, for they are carved on a stele seven cubits high and scribed in an early papyrus roll.' If any priest in Kam should answer thus, there is not one in the land so foolish to heed his words. There is much wisdom of the past inscribed, and it is well these records should be read, for though all true teachers throughout time have taught the same, there have been some who phrased truth well, so that their words awaken the hearts of those who hear them. This one truth has many degrees of brilliance: and from all who hold it, it shines, first as from a little lamp, which can but drive the shadows from a room, until, at last, it blazes like a sun, which can drive out the darkness from a world. The lamp of light can shine on Earth only when there are priests to tend it. And when the priests are gone, for a little time the wick glows, and then it is only an empty lamp, and though its alabaster may be richly carved, soon it becomes lifeless and without warmth.

"'The time will come when these people will realise their hunger: then will their priests make praise and chant in vain, and none will watch this mockery of the Gods; and those who once looked on these ceremonies will find more wisdom in the market-place. Then will come whispers: round cooking fires, in vineyards, and in pastures, and on ships; whispers that say, 'We are alone; we know not whither we go nor whence we came: we are afraid.' And through time these wisps of words will grow, until they challenge the Gods, saying, 'We demand thy wisdom for ourselves.' And the Gods will send them children who are long in years and who can walk across the Causeway to the Gods. And the children will return and speak to these people in a clear voice; and in the strength of wise integrity they shall say: 'This is the truth, for I am priest'."

CHAPTER SEVEN

# the sorcerer

Not far from the palace there was a little valley, dark with trees; and in it was a ruined temple. None would go near this place after sunset or before the day was light; for they held that it was an abode of evil spirits, and that any who went there at the full moon would return with vacant eyes, so great was the horror that they would see. When I would have questioned Kiodas about it he was ill at ease, and I saw it was a thing of which he feared to speak. And I wondered whether there were really some evil thing in that place, or whether it were a bodiless one who was imprisoned there by his own ignorance and needed succour.

So I decided to leave the palace quietly by night and find the secret of this ruined place. Ptah-kefer thought it was well that we should go there; and so together we left the palace in the moonlight, and we went up the valley in the heavy shadow of cedar trees.

The temple was a little sanctuary, with fallen pillars, and a tree was growing through the broken floor beside the crumbling statue of a god. It had the muffled smell of musty leaves and long decay. Sodden with despair, fear clung about it like a shroud of thick grey cobwebs, and I could understand the terror of them who came here.

Ptah-kefer signed to me to be still, and covering his eyes, he looked upon this place. And he said, "There is one here who died five hundred years ago. His name was Keirondeides. He was born with some little knowledge, and if he had been patient he might have learnt something of seership. But he was greedy for knowledge and tried to force the gateways of others with the bar of filth. He knew that people who are in a weakened body, or who have a high fever, see things that are not for all men's eyes. And he brought three women to this place, young girls of little will, and made them eat of loathsomeness: of still-born children and the excrement of cats, the eggs of snakes and live cockroaches in oil. And when their bodies revolted in a great sickness, again he made them eat; until their bodies were so weakened that they could not hold the spirit, and they saw beyond their flesh, and raved in horror at the things they saw. He that should have been a priest had become a sorcerer.

"And for many years he recorded their speech, until at last one of the girls rebelled against him and put a poisonous fungus in his food, and he died in a great agony.

"He is doing but one thing over and over again throughout the years: he eats of filth that he made others eat, and then he writhes in his death agony; and then again he stoops towards the fire and watches horror bubbling in the pot, yet cannot stay his hand, which puts it to his lips. He does not know he has been here five hundred years: for, caught in an eternal now, he knows only the present, and to him this endless horror is for ever fresh."

Then Ptah-kefer told me to release him. And while he watched to see that all was well, I left my body, wrapped in its cloak upon the ground. Then I felt this clinging greyness close on me, and I drove it forth with brilliant yellow light. I knew that he whom I must release was at my feet, yet I could not see him clearly, but only as a cowering shape. And I commanded him, "You shall hear my words. Death shall be no longer in your nostrils; your tongue shall not know decay and your eyes shall no more see filth. For you shall sleep. And when you wake you shall be born again under the sun."

Then at my feet I saw, not a man old in his sorcery, but a young man as he had been before he walked in slime. And he was like a young goatherd I had seen sleeping in the sun while his flocks grazed under the olive trees upon the mountainside.

Then I returned to my body. And Ptah-kefer cleansed this place with the waters of peace; so that the memory was cleansed from it, just as the life of Ptah cleanses a poisoned wound. And we left the valley a place of peace; and the moonlight shone upon it unobscured.

## CHAPTER EIGHT

# the festival of poseidon

The day before we returned to Kam was the day of the Festival of Poseidon, when offerings are made to the Minoan god of the sea in supplication that he should send fair winds for their fleet and unleash his storms only when their ships were in safe anchorage.

Kiodas asked us to share in the festival and to wear Minoan

dress. As Maata helped me to prepare for it, I knew that she wished that I was a child again and of an age when she could command my tunics. I curled my hair in Minoan fashion and held it in place with coral-headed pins. My flounced dress was sewn with little shells and knots of seed-pearls; the bodice was edged with clusters of coral beads and showed my breasts, which I had gilded in spite of Maata's disapproval. And when she would have voiced her thoughts, I told her that it was better to be the child of courtesy than the slave of custom. "The laws of good and evil, Maata, are the same for all time and for all countries. But modesty and courtesy wear many guises. They are the products of their time and place, and their measure must be taken from one's company. If here I were to play Pharaoh, it would be as foolish as if I wore the White Crown when swimming in the lake, or sat naked upon the throne of audience.

"It is difficult to drag a ship along a dry river-bed, but it will float easily upon water; and courtesy between people on Earth is like the water between the boat and the river-bed. It may not have the scarlet of courage or the brilliant yellow of wisdom, but it is like the soft green of the meadows, against which all other colours become more splendid. Courtesy can be as cool linen when we are tired, or as the glow of a brazier upon a cold night. It may not be that great wind of experience which drives our ship upon its journey, yet it can curve our sails when other wayfarers upon the river are becalmed."

When I was ready I joined the others assembled on the terrace. Artemiodes was wearing pearls threaded in her hair, and Kiodas was crowned with coral, and I saw that in the clothes they had given us, Neyah and I were as royally dressed as they. The litters in which we were carried down the steep hillside were shaped like shells, and the litter-bearers wore masks painted like fish.

When I first saw the harboured fleet from high upon the mountainside, the ships with their sails of saffron, orange, and indigo, and the soft brown of new-cut cedarwood, looked like flower petals in a bowl of lapis lazuli.

The deck of the royal ship was banked with violets, whose sweetness mingled with the keen salt air. Green pennants streamed like seaweed from the masts, and the oars were striped in red and white. Kiodas took the steering-oar from his ship-master as we led the fleet out of the harbour. The wind was gay but gentle, and it fretted the ship with little laughing waves. Artemiodes told me that this showed Poseidon was in a gracious mood; the year before he had greeted them with storms, until they had to flee from his anger to harbourage.

I was never quite sure how much Artemiodes shared in the beliefs of her people. Did she really think the sea was a hungry god who could be propitiated by yearly gifts? Almost as though she heard my thoughts she answered them, "If Poseidon is feeling kindly towards us, he accepts our offerings; but if he rejects them, they float, and our people become most desolate: for many of them have someone they love who is a sailor or a fisherman and can be endangered by his wrath. Kiodas says that it is very harmful for the country to know when Poseidon is displeased, so now he has the royal tribute weighted so that it sinks whatever Poseidon's whim. I was afraid that this might anger the god, but the high-priest told us that the omens were propitious; and certainly the storms don't seem to have been any worse than usual, and the fleet has been more contented."

We reached a headland where there was a race of waters that had drawn many ships upon the rocks, and Kiodas made ceremonial dedication to Poseidon and cast the first tribute into the sea. Then wreaths of flowers were thrown from all the other ships, and these offerings also were sucked down by the current amidst great rejoicing. When it was seen that the tribute was acceptable, Kiodas opened a wicker cage, and from it flew three white pigeons, which circled round the ships before homing to the island with their good tidings.

Then the fleet spread out into a long line, and at a signal

from the royal ship they sped forward with a following wind, cleaving the water in their race for leadership. Far on our left a ship outwinged the line. With water spraying from her figure-head and her orange sail curved in an arc of speed, ahead of all she gained the harbour mouth. Her triumph was greeted with an echoing cheer, and Kiodas said that she had earned the greatest honour of the fleet: to wear on her prow the gold Minoan bull until at the next year's festival she was challenged for the supremacy.

CHAPTER NINE

# HOMEWARD VOYAGE

Our sails were set upon our homeward voyage, and across the gently undulating sea I watched their mountains sinking in the west. That country, which long ago I had been to in my dreams, had beauty even in reality. But now this flowery interlude was past, and I must again take up the Crook and Flail.

Ptah-kefer and I were sitting together on the deck, watching the silver furrow our ship was ploughing through the smooth water. He was wrapped in his cloak, for wind is not warming to old blood. I knew he was in the mood when his thought turned easily to words. And I asked him whether he was sorry to leave Minoas, and what he thought of these people whose lives we had shared for two months. He pretended to speak seriously, but there was laughter in his eyes as he said, "I fear the high-priest of Minoas has little respect for my double feather, for he thinks me a prodigious liar. He is a man of such small experience that not only does he fail to understand the complexities of the lands beyond the Earth, but, I suspect, he doubts whether such places exist. He treated me with the confidence of two mountebanks who would share the secrets of each other's tricks; and when he questioned me of how I deluded my people and I told him I tried to end their delusions and not create them, in spite of his politeness I knew that he thought my sincerity the deepest guile. He might have been a conjurer, who, having told another how he could make a live quail-chick seem to grow out of a man's ear, is naturally indignant because his fellow will not tell him how he makes a figurine turn into a bunch of feathers and three pomegranates.

"'And I fear he thinks the priests of Kam emasculate, for he told me, in all kindliness, of a young woman of whose discretion he was sure, and who would be honoured to lie with a fellow-priest of his; and when I refused his offer, he gave me a little flask of yellow liquid, which he assured me would make even an old man as lusty as a ram. He told me that I should not take my vows of chastity so seriously, and that it was the duty of wise men such as we to propagate our kind—of course, discreetly. And when I assured him that I had taken no vows of chastity, and that in Kam we held that wisdom was not the fruit of virginity, he thought I but tried to cloak my impotence—and pitied me!

"'Then he questioned me about my riches and about my lands. And I told him that in the palace I had two rooms, one where I slept and one where I kept the few things that I needed. But he would not believe that I had no vast hoarded wealth, and when I told him I had no need of it, he asked whether our priests were in such disrespect that none made sacrifice before our gods. I told him that our people gave a twelfth part of all the things they had in every year to the temple, as a gift. And he said, 'And you a high-priest, and you are poor? I thought Kam was called the Land of Gold'. I told him the Land of Gold was to the south, but that much of this yellow metal was in Kam, and many other things that barter highly. And I explained how our tribute was used.

"'I fear that he had made me impatient. For when he asked

me what I thought of the ceremony at his temple, I answered, 'I thought the singing was magnificent'. And as I said it, I regretted that I should have so insulted my host. But he was delighted by my words, and he said that the singers were far sweeter than when he first took office, and more people came to his temple than to any other in the country because of it, and the number of tribute bulls had multiplied exceedingly.

"'Surely they are a strange people! I felt as unfamiliar as if I were living among beautiful monkeys and had forgotten how to swing by my tail. When I spoke the truth to them, they thought me a liar; and when I told them of wisdom, they thought me a fool; and when of my impatience I insulted them, they took it as a compliment."

# PART SEVEN

## CHAPTER ONE

## Dream Warning

Every year, Neyah made a Royal Progress by river to the sea and to our southern boundary, so that throughout the Two Lands no year passed when all our people did not see Pharaoh. He would stay at the Southern Garrison for twenty days, hunting with his captains and the nobles of the South.

In the eighth year of my reign, when he was at Na-kish, my spirit, which watched over my country while I slept, brought back warning of danger. In my dream I saw the looking-girls of the temple, and they cried out that they were blind; and in my dream, also, I saw far below me the land of Kam, and from the east there came a dark cloud that swept towards it from the Narrow Sea; then I saw my palace, and towards it advanced a crawling army of black ants.

And when I awoke I knew that this dream was a symbol of what I wished my body to remember, for I had returned to it in haste. I knew that danger threatened Kam, but in what form I knew not: whether as a famine, or as a pestilence, or as an invading army. So I sent a swift messenger to the Temple of Atet to summon Ney-sey-ra and to ask him to bring with him two of the chief looking-girls, so that I might question them.

When they came into my presence I asked the looking-girls what they had seen during the past few days. And they told me that the faces of their pyramids had been empty. Then I told Ney-sey-ra of my dream and I asked him to find out what danger threatened our country. And he took a silver mirror from the table and looked at a brilliant spot of sunlight reflected in it, and so freed his spirit from his body. Then he covered his eyes with his hand, and his body spoke of those things his spirit saw away from it:

"To the east of the river there is a dark cloud. It is a cloud of evil magic put there to blind the eyes of those who would see through it. But with my will I drive back the darkness.... I see a great army advancing. They are of the Zuma people, led by Zernak, son of Sardok who perished at the hand of the great Atet.

"They have come secretly across the desert. Before them they sent spies, dressed as herdsmen, who spoke the tongue of Kam; and if they met any of the people of the land, they hailed them as countrymen; and when accepted as friend they hid their treachery with death.

"With them there is a priest of the Shadow, who is strong in power. He has cloaked these people with a cloud so that no one who has not a greater power than his can see through it and discover their evil purpose. And with him is one whose body is controlled by a follower of Set, and they call this man Belshazzardak, the 'Mouthpiece of the Gods'. None but his dark master speaks through him, for he is protected by the priest of power.

"They number twenty thousand, and with their great baggage train they travel slowly. They are still three days' journey from the river, and if they travelled west, they would reach the river midway between Abidwa and Men-atet-iss."

And as he spoke I knew that the wings of destruction hovered over Kam; for it was the time of the harvest when many of my soldiers were at their homes, and I could muster less than five thousand men. Even if Neyah or the Northern Garrison should start to-day, they would arrive too late to save my people; and my city, which I had sworn to shelter, would no longer be a place of peace, and the fields and gardens of my country would be destroyed. Each man would have to fight like a warrior god, for we would be outnumbered four to one. If Neyah were here to lead them they would follow him to the Caverns of the Underword though

Set himself should bar their path....Always has Pharaoh led his armies into battle. I wear the body of a woman, yet I have sworn the mighty oath to shepherd my people with the Crook and with the Flail to scourge their enemies. My woman's body is strong in the strength of my spirit, and Zat Atet shall lead them, though Pharaoh is a queen.

I turned to Ney-sey-ra, "We must call upon the Gods to give us wisdom to destroy the Zuma before they desecrate a single field by letting their shadows fall upon it. How many chariots have they?"

"I could not say to fifty, but about five hundred, perhaps more."

"If we use all our horses, even the mares—though I would rather pour gold-dust to the sands—we can put only a hundred in the field. So we must fight where they cannot use their chariots. A little to the south of where you said they would reach the river if they marched west, there is a great semi-circle of high cliffs, which come down to the river at each end; in the centre of it the cliffs are split by a gorge, which winds up through the hills until it reaches the high desert; and midway along it a rocky river-bed, dry at this season, joins it from the north. If we could surprise their army there, our skill might outmatch their numbers. But how could we get them there?"

And Ney-sey-ra said, "To-night at sunset, as on every night, their priest of power will listen to the commands of the follower of Set who is his master, commands that he hears spoken by the tongue of Belshazzardak. He who controls Belshazzardak is strong in power, yet I am stronger. I will overcome this follower of Set so that he makes his servant speak my words, and then I will bind him so that he cannot warn the Zuma priest of what I have done. To-night the voice of Belshazzardak shall summon Zernak and the commanders of his army, then shall they hear these words:

"'It is Set himself who speaks! You shall know victory, for I command your march. But if you dare to disobey my will, then I will send a pestilence among you so that your bodies rot before you die. You shall overthrow the temples of Ptah, Anubis, Horus, and all their train, and destroy their priests and the statues in their sanctuaries. Then shall you fill these temples with my priests and set up my image ten cubits high in stone. The land of Kam is unprepared; you will find conquest easy and harvests rich. March south for a day, then turn to the setting sun; and on the evening of the second day encamp at the head of a steep rock defile that you will see before you. It leads to a plain where herds of cattle roam in lush pastures. It is my will that you sacrifice two hundred bulls to me; half of each beast must be burnt so that in their smoke I savour a feast of flesh; the rest shall be yours to eat so that your bodies are strong to fight for me. Your chariots and the servants of your baggage train must stay in your encampment, while Zernak leads his warriors down the gorge. If you are faithful in your sacrifice, on the evening of the third day I shall give you a fresh command. Until that time you will not hear my voice. Obey! I, Set, have spoken'."

"But won't they see danger in this plan? Surely they will see that they might be entrapped in the gorge?"

"You do not know how greatly they fear Set. They would not dare to disobey what they think he has commanded them to do."

"Ney-sey-ra, that is a plan worthy of Ptah for wisdom! By their belief in evil they shall be destroyed, and so learn the retribution of false gods. Give them one more command. Tell them to start down the defile before dawn, so that they reach the plain at sunrise. Zeb with his men shall wait in the north gorge; and Maates shall fall upon their rear; all my chariots and the spearmen of the Royal Bodyguard shall be waiting for them when they reach the plain, and, as my father drove them to the sea, again shall Zuma know the strength of Kam."

"You have given Zeb and Maates their commands, who will command the warriors on the plain?"

"The Chariot of Pharaoh leads the battle line. Often have I thrown spear at crocodiles or loosed my arrow to a flying bird, now I shall have a quarry worthy of my skill. I call upon the gods to let a shaft of mine drink Zernak's blood. Ney-sey-ra, you taught me wisdom so I could rule, would you have me fail my people in leadership?"

"To other women I should say this were unwise, but on your brow your father set his seal, and you shall lead his chariots worthily."

CHAPTER TWO

# the amphitheatre of grain

There was no Captain-of-Captains of the Royal Body-guard save Neyah. When I became Pharaoh I had appointed Zeb my standard-bearer, and during the expedition to Punt he had won the rank of captain. Maates, the other captain to whom I now gave command, I had known since the days when he used to go swan-shooting with Neyah and me in the reeds. He was the only son of Maata's brother, the Overseer of the Grain-Lands of the Royal City.

Within the hour soldiers were filing down to the quay. Since the time of the Zuma invasion led by Sardok, swift river-boats, on which three thousand men could be em-barked, were kept fully provisioned with grain and wine, arrows, linen for wounds, and other things for war. Six trade barges were at the Royal City, and these were added to our fleet for the transporting of the horses and chariots and the remainder of our army. I ordered that another barge should follow us with two hundred jars of burning-oil so that the bodies of the Zumas should be burnt, for they were unworthy to have Kam as shroud.

I went to the Room of Seals and took my father's great war helmet from a chest where it had lain, wrapped in fine linen, since he had worn it into victory.

When I said good-bye to Tchekeea she clung to me—the noisy preparation for battle is frightening for a child. Her cheek was smooth against mine, and as I held her close, I thought that soon my body might be mine no longer, but in my child it would still live in Kam, while my spirit journeyed on through time. I picked up a ceremonial flail and put it in her hands, "See, Tchekeea, till I return you shall rule for me, and then you shall sit at the banquet and no one shall send you early to bed."

"Mother, you are dressed as a warrior, and warriors are killed."

"Zeb will look after me; how can I be hurt when I have my soldiers round me? We shall drive the Zumas from our country and they will scuttle like guilty puppies from the goose-tender's wife when she finds them nosing round the nests. Smile, my Tchekeea, and be worthy of the Flail....Now I must go, but come with me and see the warriors start."

Within three hours all my soldiers had embarked; followed by Zeb, I galloped my chariot to join them at the quay. The news that Pharaoh would lead them into battle had reached their ears, and they greeted me with our battle cry, 'Atet and Light', as in one great voice they proclaimed their rejoicing in my leadership.

The rowers bent to their oars as the ships were unleashed from their moorings, and we swept upstream to the song that the steersman sang to keep them to their rhythm:

> Pull on your oars, my rowers!
> Pull on your oars,
> So that the boat cleaves through the water
> Like an arrow-head of wild-swans
> Returning to the reeds at sunrise.
> Blow strongly, wind!

Blow strongly,
So that my weary rowers may rest
In the shade of the swelling sail.

The Goddess of the Winds smiled upon us, and when the wind fell idle at evening, our rowers had rested and we swept on up-river. I talked long with Zeb and Maates, and with Ptah-kefer, who together with Zertar and five healer priests accompanied us. Our battle plan was shared among all. The boats were near enough for a strong swimmer to take messages from one to another: diving from the stern of one boat, he would swim to the one behind, and to return, a rope was thrown to him and he was pulled back to the leading boat.

When I was a child I had longed to be a warrior and follow Neyah into battle; now in my heart I prayed to Ptah that I might not fail my country. I could remember when I had fought with the sword and lived the life of a warrior in Athlanta; but that was long ago, and it is difficult to keep the warrior scarlet in a woman's body. What if I should be afraid and instil with my fear those to whom the courage of Pharaoh should be as a standard and a battle cry?

It was the dark of the moon, and the sky was singing-bright with stars, which the smooth water mirrored as though they had rained down from the heavens and been unquenched. The sleeping villages were silent as we passed. Faintly across the still air I heard the shrill bark of a hunting jackal. The reeds rustled as an animal that had come down to drink fled from the sound of our oars. Kam was tranquil as a sleeping child, who breathes quietly though a cobra slides towards it across the floor. Suddenly I knew that I should be fearless in battle. Even a water-rat has courage when its young, nested under the bank, are threatened; the people of Kam are my children and the Two Lands are the shelter wherein I must house them in safety. Hound-dogs can drive a lion out of the reeds, but a lioness with cubs is a match for six of them, and Kam shall be tranquil in the shelter of our swords.

We travelled for two days and two nights, and upon the third day, an hour after high noon, we reached the Amphitheatre of Grain. Here are two great granaries, disused for nearly a hundred years. Before the Two Lands were reunited, this place had been one of the chief grain-lands of the Lotus, but now that the corn came from the Land of the Papyrus, it had returned to pasture and none lived here but a few herdsmen. It is here that our finest bulls and cows are put to roam so that the best of our cattle multiply themselves, and the young bulls are sent throughout the country to beget strong calves.

Our boats could not get close in to the bank, for there was no quay, so the horses had to walk along landing planks. Some of them squealed and reared until their charioteers calmed them and could lead them to the bank.

Ptah-kefer told me that the Zumas had not yet reached their encampment, and that, not daring to seem to doubt the commands and promises of Set, they had sent forward no outposts. So instead of waiting for the cover of night, we marched across the Amphitheatre of Grain and encamped near to the foot of the cliffs.

Five hours before dawn, Maates with his twelve hundred macebearers left to take up his position in the battle plan. He was to climb a path up the cliff to the south of the gorge and wait as near to the head of it as he could without danger of being heard. Then, when the last of the Zumas had entered the gorge on their way down to the plain, he would block their retreat, so that when we drove them back towards him they would run their heads against a wall of stone.

Zeb with his archers went up the defile to hide with his men in the north river-bed, which joined it midway between the Zuma camp and the plain. He would let half their army pass and then assail them with a burning rain of arrows, until their columns writhed like a snake whose back is broken by a stick.

Before the warriors left, I spoke to them, "We are outnumbered four to one, so we must fight like warrior gods. This is a battle of Light against Darkness, and in each man you kill, you kill an evil one, and in their death the Gods rejoice with you. At dawn I will lead you into victory as the great Atet led your fathers."

CHAPTER THREE

# Battle against the Zuma

Where the cliffs are riven as though the Gods had cleaved them with a sword, we waited in the deep shadow of early dawn. The ruddy sky was pennanted with clouds like smoking torches flaring in the wind, as our chariots were drawn up in their battle-line, with the spearmen behind them and on either side.

Then the chain of our hidden outposts passed down word that Zernak was coming towards us down the gorge, and our charioteers stood at their horses' heads, soothing them so that they should not stamp or neigh and so betray us.

Muffled by the distance, I heard the droning of the Zuma chant as they marched to make their sacrifice to Set.... Soon, soon their blood shall match this angry dawn! Soon it shall fertilize these fields, which they who lose it would have laid in waste. And there shall be a column of smoke and fire; not of a bloody sacrifice of cows to Set, but of their own bodies, which would have pillaged Kam and now whose ashes shall mingle with our earth.

As I waited in the centre of the chariot line, I prayed to my father, who had been so great a Pharaoh, that I might wear his helmet worthily. Loud in my ears I heard the Zumas chant and I knew that in a moment I must loose the battle line....

''Father, hear me! If I am to die, let it be proudly and on victory.''

Then before me I saw his chariot, no longer empty, for in it he rode in splendour.

And as their ranks advanced upon the plain, he waved me onward, and I gave the battle cry, 'Atet and Light'. And the chariot of Atet led me as in a wheeling wave we swung upon this mighty footed host.

Our chariots thundered to the charge, and we flung the first flight of our throwing-spears. I saw one impale their high-priest through the groin, and he died in the spouting of his evil blood. They tried to scatter before us, but from each side, like the two wings of a hawk, the ranks of our spearmen closed upon them. The chariot on my right was overthrown, the belly of the screaming horse split open by a sword. I saw a captain sever a Zuma's head, and the blood upjetted from the empty neck before the body crashed forward on the ground. I saw a charioteer rein back his horse while the warrior leapt out to pluck his spear from where it was wedged between the ribs of a man who had fallen under the chariot wheel. I saw a young captain still fighting on, though his left hand was severed at the wrist.

Then before me in the swaying press of men, I saw Zernak, dressed in the insignia of a king. He sprang on to the hub of my chariot, striving to cut me down with his sweeping sword. I drove my spear downward, downward through his throat, and its haft drank deep of Zuma blood, which drenched from his mouth and veiled the hatred glaring from his eyes, eyes that had hoped to see Kam vanquished....Now if I die I would have killed my enemy and tasted the strong wine of victory....I felt the wild surge of triumphal joy as when the cobra crumbled in my hands. I pulled off my helmet and let my hair stream free, so that before he died he should know that a woman Pharaoh was a greater warrior than a Zuma king.

When the Zumas saw their king was slain they became a

rabble without ordered rank and tried to retreat to safety up the gorge, but their way was barred by their own soldiers beaten back by Zeb.

Our chariots could not follow up the rocky defile, so I halted them while our spearmen pursued the fleeing enemy.

For nearly an hour the gorge echoed with the tumult of battle. Then again I heard our battle cry, and from the gorge came Zeb in victory. I had been wounded after Zernak's death, but when our chariots drew back to the plain I had put on my cloak so that none should see that I had been hurt. But now that the victory was safe, I looked at my wound and found a broken arrow through my left arm near to the shoulder.

When Zertar came to tend the wound, he said that he must cut out the arrow-head, and asked me whether I could bear the pain or whether he should call a Horus priest. But I said, no, that an arrow was a clean sharp pain, far easier than the bearing of a child.

CHAPTER FOUR

# the stele

Over fourteen hundred of our warriors had been killed. The severely wounded, who numbered nearly five hundred, lay on folded cloaks in the shade of the cliffs. I went among them with the healer priests, and told them how their children would rejoice to know themselves so magnificently sired.

Then I heard that Maates was dead, killed by an arrow when nine Zuma heads had split under his mace. I said that he should have the burial of a prince and lie beside my tomb in Abidwa, where one day my own body would be laid: both resting after battle in the Light.

Of the invaders, all were dead save three hundred wounded. Though of Zuma blood, they should stay here until their hurts were healed, and then escort the embalmed body of their king back to his country, so that Zernak's people should see how a king returns when he has set forth to conquer the Two Lands. The two thousand servants of their baggage train should be kept in Kam for a year. They should work in the brick-fields under the same conditions as our own people. This same thing we do to all prisoners of war, and when they return to their own country, they take with them a memory of the compassion of Kam. There was little of value to us in the Zuma encampment, excepting four hundred and eighty horses, and they were all stallions. And twenty of our mares, which had been born of those captured by my father from Sardok, had been killed.

In the evening when the sun was low, the wounded were taken from the groves of trees and carried down to the boats to return swiftly to Men-atet-iss. I was tired and my wound was burning my flesh. I sat with Zeb leaning against a tree, beyond the shadows of the cooking fires. He told me more of the battle. The Zuma ranks had broken when they were surprised by his archers; and though some had stood their ground, many had fled, only to find their way barred by Maates. I knew that Zeb's heart was sorrowful that Maates had died, for they were long friends, closer than many brothers. I told him how my father had returned to lead us to victory, and that now Maates followed him as in his golden chariot he outstripped the sun. And I talked to him of the days when we were young; of how when we had first met he had taught me courage; and from my anger friendship had been born; of how he had saved Neyah's life on a hunting expedition in the South when a wounded leopard turned on him. And I said to him, "The two who were once an angry child and a lion boy have become Pharaoh and a Captain-of-Captains."

When he realized that I had given him the highest rank to

which a warrior can attain, he tried to tell me of his gratitude, but I said, "So often have you risked your life for me and those I love."

And he answered, "But when you were a little girl I gave my life into your hands, and always it is there to do with as you will." And I knew that Zeb would serve me if I were not Pharaoh, but a herdsman's child.

All that night the sky was lit by the burning bodies of our enemies. And at dawn our warriors who had died in victory were laid in the earth that they had protected with their lives. Wrapped in their cloaks, their weapons in their hands, they slept the deep sleep that the body knows when it has released the spirit to walk in peace. And over their graves I spoke these words:

"Mighty Ptah, who gave life to these your children, welcome them back to your country from whence they came. Theirs was the Scarlet of the God of Warriors, and their swords reflected the Light. Proudly they lived and splendidly they died, and the memory of them shall dwell in our hearts even as they dwell in your country."

And I decreed: "To mark this resting-place a great stele shall be erected, and on it shall be carved, 'Here lie the bodies of fourteen hundred and eighty-six warriors of Kam, who died to give peace to the Two Lands and to shield her from the Shadow'. And then shall be their names and mine, and the time of their victory, 'On the twelfth day of the fourth month of the Harvest in the eighth year of the reign of Zat Atet, Nekht, Sekhet-a-ra Meri-neyt, Daughter of Anubis, Bearer of the Golden Lotus of Wisdom, Keeper of the Scales of Justice, Holder of the Crook and Flail, Ruler of the Two Lands, Keeper of the Boundaries of Kam, Pharaoh'. It shall be cut deep into the stone, so that it shall endure through the span of many lives. And it may be that some whose names are recorded upon it will see this stele when they are re-born in Kam. And they may remember, and smile, and say, 'Once I was buried here'."

CHAPTER FIVE

# the homecoming

News of the battle had been given forth from all the temples; and as we sailed down river, the people crowded the banks to see the return of Pharaoh and the Royal Army in victory. We reached Men-atet-iss on the fourth day. On the quay stood my Tchekeea, dressed as a warrior prince and holding the Flail, which I had put in her hands to lighten the moment when I had left her.

Grave as a vizier she held out the Flail to me and said, "While you have been gone I have kept your city safe and I have held the Flail truly for you. Now it is yours again—and I need no longer be so very good." And so, casting her dignity aside, she flung her arms round me.

She came with me in my litter to the palace, and on the way she must hear all about the battle. She questioned me on every detail, and sighed to think she had not seen my spear kill Zernak.

"When can we have the banquet? I shall stay up all night and no one can send me to bed, because you promised." And I told her we would wait for Neyah's return, which I expected within two days.

Tchekeea said, "When you were away I behaved just like you. When anyone argued with me I showed them the Flail and said you had put it in my hands and so all must obey me. And every morning I asked the Gods tremendously hard to look after you and to let you win very quickly; and I asked them four and five and six times a day so they couldn't possibly forget. Do you think if I had asked oftener you wouldn't have been wounded? Was it a very hurting arrow?"

And I told her, "It didn't hurt any more than cutting your knee does when you fall down in the middle of an exciting game; and if you hadn't asked the Gods so very hard, the arrow might have hit me somewhere it really mattered.''

''First I thought I would dress like a queen and have malachite on my eyes, and sweeping eyebrows; and then I thought as you were being a king I would be a prince, and I wouldn't dress myself or let anybody else do it until they brought me princely clothes. And I commanded that all should call me Den. I took Natee out for all his walks and practised with my bow and throwing-spear until Benater *had* to say that I was as good as a boy of twice my age....And Silvermane has had a little foal, and it's a mare. Neyah promised he would give it to me, and she is to have a meadow of her own, with trees and a house thatched from the sun....And Mother, while I was out I met a little girl who had fallen down and tore her only dress. As I was prince I didn't like girls' clothes, so I gave twelve of my tunics to her. You don't mind? Nekza wasn't very pleased, but I didn't listen to her while I held the Flail....And when they sent from the temple to tell of your victory I went to the market and told all the merchants to give everything on their stalls to the people and to take no exchange for it, but to come to the palace and I would give them twice the value of all they had given away. I told Rey-hetep. He looked surprised, so I said, 'It is the royal word'. And so he did it, and everyone was pleased. Will you promise to tell Neyah, the first moment you see him, that he mustn't call me Tchekeea any more, but always Den?''

When I reached the palace, the hot south wind was stirring the brilliant folds of the flags, which flew from triumphal masts that columned the full length of the white painted walls and, on the pylon, rested in deep grooves like a rack of spears.

Zertar said that I must rest in my room for three days, for the muscle of my arm was deeply torn and unless it was kept still the flesh would not heal without scar. It was good at last to put off my warrior dress and to lie in hot water strewn with orange-flowers, to have my body soothed with healing oils and feel the weariness seeping from my bones. The linen of my bed was smooth and cool, yet my body was too tired to sleep. So I sent for Maata, who with her strong gentle fingers soothed the muscles of my head and neck, until under her kind hands my body grew quiet and let my spirit go.

CHAPTER SIX

# Neyah's Return

When Neyah reached the palace early next day, he came straight to my room. His brow was lined with the burden of his thoughts, and I saw that he was weary from swift travelling. Before I would talk of all that had befallen us, I sent for broth and wine and made him eat.

He said, "I was on a leopard hunt two days north-west of Na-kish, when you appeared to me in a dream. You said to me, 'Return; journey swiftly down river. Kam is in danger'. Then you put your thumb upon my forehead and said, 'Remember'. When I awoke I set off north-east and reached the river on the morning of the next day. I took a fast river-boat of thirty oars, which belonged to a noble, and travelled downstream, journeying night and day with relays of rowers. I knew that the seer of the garrison would have received news of the danger and the Captain-of-Captains would have already started north, so there was no need for me to send a messenger to Na-kish to warn them. At midnight on the third day I reached Nekht-an, where they told me that it was the Zumas that threatened us, and that at dawn you would give battle with them in the Amphitheatre of Grain. Never again will I journey without a seer, for not until we came in sight of

Abidwa and saw the flags, did I know that we had won a victory. The Vizier came out to meet me with the news that the Zumas had been destroyed and that the Southern Garrison had turned back from Nekht-an.

"When I reached the Amphitheatre of Grain, the bodies of their dead were still smouldering. The stallions of Zernak were pastured on the plain, and my patience outpaced the rowers' arms, so I took the king's chariot and the swiftest of his horses, and in thirty hours I reached the Royal City, only halting when my horses must be rested."

Then I told him the story of the four days when Kam was balanced in Tahuti's Scales. And when I told him how our father had returned to lead me, Neyah said, "I thought my army would fight leaderless, but I should have known that Atet left two sons, two Pharaohs whose chariots could lead the van of spears. Never was man so blessed in his wife, my sister, my brother, Pharaoh, and Priest of Anubis!"

CHAPTER SEVEN

# Belshazzardak

Two days later news was brought to me that Belshazzardak had not been found among the Zuma dead. I sent soldiers to search for him, and they found him three days' journey across the high desert towards the sea, hiding in the tent of a herdsman whom he had killed; and he was brought to the Royal City.

Next day, a thousand people assembled in the Hall of Audience to hear me give the judgment of Pharaoh upon this follower of Set. When he was brought into my presence I knew that here was no great one of the Darkness, for he did not possess that strong shield of pride with which they challenge the onslaught of the Light; for his eyes, heavy-lidded as a crocodile's, were dull with fear.

And I pronounced judgment upon him:

"Belshazzardak, Mouthpiece of the Gods of Zuma, hear my voice!

"If you had been a priest of power, even though that power were used in the name of Set, then I should have challenged your will with mine; and if you had conquered, then you would have returned to your country unmolested. If you had been a true priest, you would have been our honoured guest, even though our countries were enemies, and you would have returned in peace to your home. If I had found that you were a strong man, worthy of my hatred, then should I have put my condemnation upon you for daring to lead your people in an attempt to desecrate my country.

"But you have so little knowledge, even of evil, that you have made yourself a weapon in the hands of a Princeling of the Shadow.

"I do not prophesy, neither do I condemn; I but tell you the workings of the Law, I but tell you what harvest you will gather from the seed you have sown. To add my condemnation to what you have already brought upon yourself were to drive a thorn into a man's foot when there is a sword twisting in his heart.

"You have allowed your body to be used by another's spirit. If you had a hundredth part of the knowledge that you claim, you would know that no one who is not evil would use the body of another for his own.

"If a man plunges his hand into a cauldron of boiling bitumen, then will that hand be crippled and no longer obey his will. The will of one who allows himself to be possessed is so weakened that for many lives thereafter he is born insane. When you are re-born, in sleep you will look down on the prison of the body to which you must return, knowing that, when you wake, that drooling figure will crawl upon the ground and scream in terror of the hideous shapes that do surround it.

"You were a priest, although in name alone, over a great multitude. You should have been a light unto their twilight, but you were a heavy shadow upon their darkness. For this, you will experience all that these people suffer because of you.

"An army of many thousand men trusted you to guide them to victory, but, because you are a false priest, your tongue ordered them to their death. When you die you will return to that moment when you led your host from the pass through the cliffs, and saw, not a herd of bulls for sacrifice, but the wheeling chariots of Pharaoh, and, seeing them, knew that you had betrayed your people. Caught in the moment of your betrayal, time will stand still for you, and yet seem endless, between the death of a madman and the birth of an idiot child.

"Six days ago the body of your king left on its last journey to your country. To-morrow, as though you were a true priest, my soldiers shall escort you to the outposts of Zuma; for if you had been a true priest, your people would have needed you to guide them in their tribulation. The news will have gone ahead of you of what befell their army because they listened to your voice, and you will find a welcome worthy of you—in Kam we do not torture prisoners.

"And when you are again re-born in Zuma, still may you hear them telling round their fires the story of the humiliation of their smooth oracle, Belshazzardak."

CHAPTER EIGHT

# the safeguarding of the two lands

Twice had Zuma challenged the strength of Atet and twice had Zuma been driven back from Kam, and now Neyah and I sat in council with our Captains-of-Captains and with the Viziers of Men-atet-iss, Abidwa, Iss-an, and Nekht-an, to decide how our boundaries were to be made safe for our children.

It is easy to make a decision when it involves only one's own life, but when the lives of many thousands of people will be altered, then is the yoke of responsibility heavy upon one's shoulders. Though everything that we do changes our future, some actions show their reflection in a day and others stretch far ahead of us. Before setting forth to climb a high mountain, it is well to think not only of the precipices that must be scaled, but also of the new vistas that can be seen when the summit is reached.

With a great army of two hundred thousand men Neyah could scourge the people of Zuma with a mighty flail, so that, as long as memory dwelt in them and in their children of many generations, they should never again assail the might of Kam. But what if our armies crowned victory with victory and swept through the Land of Zuma as easily as a sword cuts honeycomb? Our boundaries would be thrice increased, yet if we were Pharaoh of Zuma as well as of Kam, would our people be happier when we wore this triple crown? What do our people lack in the Two Lands? We have enough grain for none to go hungry; each man has land for his garden; our vineyards give us wine, and our flax fields are blue lakes among the corn and our linen-weavers know not empty looms.

What can the land of Zuma give to us? Its grain-lands are like oceans to our seas, yet if we owned them our fields would lie fallow and our people would no longer need to work for their bread, and in their idleness they would find discontent. Only the men who walk the warrior's path are in our armies; but if we had these vast boundaries to keep, then would our ploughmen, artisans, and scribes, have to change the pattern of their lives and join the ranks of our fighting men; and they would hear no music in the battle cry, for only they of the Scarlet rejoice in the sword.

If a man steals a bunch of grapes from your vineyard, by the Law of Scales you can take a bunch from his, and so adjust the balance. But one bunch of grapes looks like another, and the one stolen from you may have had ninety grapes on it, and the one you steal may have a hundred, and by taking it you have placed yourself in the debt of another thief. The wise man whose vineyard is raided by a thief will not turn thief himself to right the wrong, for he knows that there is another way in which the Scales can be made true: the thief will have to become an honest man to repay the debt that he in the past incurred.

But a man who finds his house has been robbed is a fool to set no watchman. The Zuma gateway into Kam is the Narrow Land between the Two Waters. So we decreed that, five days' journey from our north-east boundary, there should be built a chain of garrisons set two days' march apart, and that our fleet in the Narrow Sea should be increased to guard our eastern shore. The Minoan fleet is master of the Northern Sea, and our fleet joins with theirs in its guardianship, Punt has acknowledged us her overlord and Na-kish secures us from the Land of Gold. When this mighty north-east gate is built, then will our country be tranquil through the years.

If we went as conquerors to their land, the people of Zuma would hate us and hate our Gods; for though we gave them our justice and our laws, they would see in them the Flail and not the Crook. But the time may come when the people of Zuma shall hear our voices in the south-west wind; then will they put to the sword their evil priests and overthrow the tyrants who are their kings; for they will have heard that contentment flowers in Kam and they will wish us to be their overlords. If that day comes, then shall we have won a mighty victory, not by the sword in our hand, but by the sword of our will.

# PART EIGHT

## CHAPTER ONE

## noonday of my mother

When my mother died, I prayed to the Gods that I might not shadow her noonday by my sorrow. She left Earth smoothly and quietly as a sailing boat drifts downstream on the cool wind of sunset. It was as if she had lived in a house with closed shutters, and had opened the door upon a garden where dreams were flowering in their glory, for she had walked out into the Light and seen my father waiting for her.

Her body joined my father's in their tomb at Abidwa. Beside her, as she had wished, was placed a painted wooden chest, which long ago Neyah had made for her. In it she had kept the presents we had given to her and to our father when we were children: little slips of ivory on which I had written her name while I still found it difficult to scribe; pieces of broken limestone on which Neyah had practised carving; and two ivory game pieces of a set that he had started to make for her and never finished. In her sarcophagus she still wore the bracelet that we had given to her when I was nine. And with her were put many other things that she had been fond of: a little statuette of Shamba, my father's lioness; and some painted pottery which we had brought home from Minoas when we stayed with Kiodas.

When the tomb of the great Atet was opened, the flowers that I had put there when I was a little girl, like soft brown shadows still held their petals' shape. Before my mother joined her husband, the room was filled with fresh garlands as for a bridal. And their bodies slept beside each other even as their spirits rejoiced together.

CHAPTER TWO

# Children of Pharaoh

Though I could meet my mother in my spirit, on Earth I was often lonely for her counsel and her understanding. I had always told her of the things that troubled me, and the light of her wisdom had driven forth the shadows of my uncertainty, so that I knew my own heart and could see the path clearly before me.

While Den was still a child, I thought that, as she grew older, I should find with her that same harmony which I shared with my mother. But though we loved each other and our thoughts often reached the same destination, we travelled there upon different paths.

I have always wanted to know the reason for things. All my life I have had dreams and visions and known their reality, but I was never content until I learned how I saw them; for I wished to know the laws and not only to see them in action. If I see a tree beautiful against the sunset, I see it not only with my heart but with my mind; I know why I find it beautiful, which line it is that gives the rhythm that to my mind is beauty. But to Den a thing is beautiful or ugly, an action is good or evil, not because of reason, but because she knows it in her heart. Sometimes she used to laugh at me and say that to try to explain why the curve of one jar was more satisfying than the curve of another was as if one should pull a flower to pieces to discover the secret of its perfume.

I hoped that she would go to the Temple of Atet as I had done, but she was impatient of priestly things, and I knew that to force my will upon her would be as useless as to try to tame a wild leopard by shutting it away behind bars. Yet she had wisdom, without knowing from whence it came, and she could weigh hearts without knowing the Scales.

From the time she was twelve years old, she often sat beside me when I was in audience; and before I gave judgment she made a private sign to tell me whether she thought the one before me was innocent or guilty. I weighed hearts with the facts of Earth and the wisdom of the spirit, but many times I found that Den had known the truth before I had. At first I thought that she must be a seer, but that was not so. She would say, 'I know things, but I don't know why I know them—and I don't mind'. Though she would not undergo the training of a priest, as time went by I was sure that her judgments would be worthy of the Scales under which she would sit when she was Pharaoh.

Den always went with Neyah when he made his yearly progress to the garrisons. He used to take her hunting with him in the south, and he said that no lion-spear sped more truly than hers and no arrow was more swiftly judged. Although she was Dio's child, I think she was more Neyah's son than she was my daughter.

Neyah had four daughters by his secondary wives, but his only son was Seshet, who had been two years old when I became Pharaoh. Until he was seven he lived with his mother in the women's quarters, but after she died he shared with Den the Apartments of the Royal Children, which had been ours when we were young. He was like his father as the shadow of a tree is like a tree, and I think that he used to pray, not to the Gods, but to the image of Neyah that he held in his heart. He would have found happiness in the life of a healer priest or a man of learning, but because Neyah was a Warrior Pharaoh he longed to follow in his path. He spent much time in the Room of Records. He would climb up to a high shelf and bring down a papyrus that for many years had not had its sealing threads untied, and unroll it as eagerly as a child listens to a story-teller. He would read old judgments of Meniss and of his grandfather, and lists of the ways in which tribute had been expended in different years. The scribes' plans for the building of a new road or for a new system of water-channels, which long ago had become familiar to the people of Kam, were as fresh to him as the day on which they were born in the minds of the men who had designed them.

Neyah was always very gentle with his son, and he used to take him wild-fowling, though he thought that he had very little skill with arrows. But once I saw Seshet practising at a target of a flowering papyrus reed that was swaying in the wind. He transfixed it with three arrows before he saw me watching him. Then I realized that when he missed a flying swan it was not because he could not hit it, but because he hated to destroy its perfection. I told him to explain to Neyah that he didn't like killing birds, but he made me promise to keep his secret. And I did so, for I knew that it would give Seshet more pain to admit to anything that he thought a weakness than to be laughed at for being unskilled. I told him that there are many roads to freedom, and that he who attains freedom in the way of a scribe has as splendid a courage as he who attains it in the way of a warrior, but I could not make him realise that what he possessed was not cowardice but compassion.

His present was always overcast by his future, for Seshet could see the shadows that would be thrown by everything he did. If Den swerved her chariot too swiftly and it was nearly overturned, she never thought of what would have happened if it had tilted a little further; but to Seshet, who watched her, what might have happened was almost as vivid as if it had come to pass, and his bones ached, so keen was his vision of the hurt that she might have received. Yet deeply within him shone the flame of true courage that does not run back although it can see the unmasked face of danger.

He had given his heart to Den ever since she was a baby, and Neyah and I always hoped that they would marry and rule after us together. Den was the Royal Heir, and unless she married Seshet, she would rule alone and he could not be Pharaoh. If I had not had a child, Neyah could have declared any of his children the royal heir; and if he had had no children, he would, after consulting with his seer priests, have declared one old in spirit to be the next Son of Horus.

When Den was fourteen, the time came for her betrothal to Seshet to be announced to the people, so that all should know them as their rulers when Neyah and I handed on the Crook and Flail. To Seshet, Den was the sun of his noonday; when she was with him there could be no shadows, and when she was away from him the sky was without stars. But she loved him only as a brother, and within her heart he could not kindle the brilliant flame that lovers know. And because of his love for her, he saw her heart; and he knew that, as his wife, she would never find the happiness at full circle that another man could give her who was not only a brother to her spirit, but also the lover that her body had chosen. To Seshet, marriage with Den meant to have her who was the breath of his nostrils for his wife, and the crown of Pharaoh. But he loved her beyond possession and beyond power; and greater than this, he loved her beyond pride. He longed to be Pharaoh, because the Crook that he would then hold would have been Neyah's, and because the crown that he would then wear would have been worn by Neyah. He knew that he would have been forbidden this denial of his heritage if he told his father that he gave up the succession to the throne because he loved the woman that he would have shared it with. So Seshet told his father that he could not be Pharaoh because he dared not lead the Royal Chariots into battle. Neyah loved him, and as he listened to him, his heart sorrowed that he would have no son to follow him. But he knew that the boy was long in years to have gained humility, which so few gain until in the gaining of it they are almost at the end of their journey. And he thought that Seshet was wise beyond the understanding of scholars to have weighed his own heart, and knowing that he was not a leader of warriors, to have put off the war helmet of Pharaoh and laid down the Flail. So Neyah made Seshet the Vizier of Nekht-an, and the Land of the Lotus was shepherded by his compassion.

CHAPTER THREE

# Den and Horem-ka

The passing years brought beauty and strength as gifts to Den. Her hair shone like new copper, and her body was as slender as a young boy's. She used to go on expeditions to far countries, searching for new animals and birds to bring back to Kam, just as my father had searched for plants and trees. She was the pride and the fear of the Master of Chariots, for if danger stretched out his hands towards her she laughed him into the shadows. She was beloved throughout the Two Lands, for whether she was with an old scholar or a young noble, a captain-of-captains or a hound-boy, she made each feel that he was her equal and that she had chosen him for her companion. Her anger was swift, but it was outpaced by her sympathy and her generosity.

One of her favourite companions was Horem-ka, son of the Vizier of Iss-an. He was a captain of the Royal Bodyguard, and except when he was in attendance on Pharaoh, he lived on his own estate, which was near to the Royal City. He was a strong man both in heart and in body. His skin was red-brown with the sun, and his hands had the broad palms of a warrior; his brows were level as the wings of a hawk, but his mouth was the friend of laughter.

Though there were many who loved her, when Den was nineteen she had still not chosen her husband.

One day news was brought that a lion, which was no longer swift enough to catch antelope, had taken a child from one of the villages, two days' journey to the south of the Royal City. Den went with Neyah upon the lion hunt. And she returned, not in a chariot as she had set forth but in a curtained litter. The wheel of her chariot had broken while she was challenging for the quarry, and she had been thrown out and kicked on the head by a following horse.

For four days she lay as though she were dead. Only the faint beating of her heart showed that the silver cord was still unsevered. So slender was her hold on Earth, that it seemed that her spirit was like a bird that rustles its wings before its last flight. She breathed embalmed in sleep, and neither seer nor healer could stir her from this strange tranquillity.

Her body was quiet as a statue as I watched beside it. Then I heard someone come into the ante-room and the voice of Horem-ka demanding to see my daughter. The servants told him that he must not enter. But he swept them aside, and they parted before him as reeds bow before a great wind. The curtain of the doorway clattered on its rings as he pulled it back. The room was dark, except for the dim light of one alabaster lamp, and I think he never knew that I was there. He knelt beside Den and held her hand, calling her by the little soft names that lovers use. And his voice followed her to those far lands where her spirit wandered; and her spirit heard his voice, and she returned to her body. She opened her eyes for a moment and smiled at him, murmuring his name contentedly as a drowsy child. Then in the shelter of his arms she slept, no longer in sleep in the semblance of death, but to the refreshing of her body.

On the third day of the second month of the Harvest in the twenty-first year of my reign, Den and Horem-ka were united before the Gods.

As Horem-ka was not of the royal blood, he would not be Pharaoh, but only the Royal Husband, when Den came to the throne. Neyah announced him to be the first in the line of succession after Den, if she died before she bore an heir; for though Horem-ka had not the blood of Meniss in his veins, our tradition lived in his heart. He became the Royal Vizier, for Rey-hetep had grown weary of office, being seventy-six years of age. In the armies he ranked second only to Neyah, and in all save name he was the son of Pharaoh.

He and Den together had the strength of the two sides of a

pylon, and they were balanced each to each like the two sides of the Scales. Now that Den had found peace, which the beloved dweller in her heart had brought to her, she was no longer impatient of the ways of wisdom, and she listened to the voice of her memory, from which her knowledge of people had been born. Ney-sey-ra gave her of his counsel, and in the voices of priests she found that joy that once she had found only in the swiftness of chariots.

With Horem-ka she travelled throughout Kam. They talked with the viziers, and they went among the people in the market-places; they talked with priests and temple counsellors, with vintagers and with women gathering in the harvests; so that our people knew that when the Crook and the Flail passed into her hands, they were the same ones that Neyah and I now held, and the contentment of their lives would be unbroken by our death.

Nearly two years after their marriage, a son was born to them and Den asked me to choose a name for him. And to my grandson I gave the name Seshet-ka, after him who was the son of my heart, though his body had been fashioned by Neyah and Sesket.

CHAPTER FOUR

# the death of neyah

When I had been on Earth forty-six years, the sun no longer rose over the horizon of my days and sorrow hid the stars from my sight. For Neyah, who had gone upon a journey far to the south of Kam, died of the fever of the swamps.

He told me in a dream that his body was ill, twenty-seven days' swift journey from the Royal City. And he told me that

I could not reach him upon Earth, for within two days his body would be an empty house.

Away from Earth death is a rejoicing; but to waking eyes it shadows beauty, flowers lose their perfume and the singing-birds are dumb. Yet although all the people of Kam could show their sorrow, in my eyes the tears must burn unshed. For to my people I must speak of the littleness of death, tell them that they should rejoice that their Pharaoh drove his chariot in the Golden Army of Horus, tell them that he had but gone ahead of them and waited to greet them when they too should die.

Neyah was their shepherd and the avenger of their wrongs, and they loved him as they loved their Gods, for to all of them Pharaoh was the symbol of what one day they would become. But to me, Neyah was the little boy I played with when I too was little, the one with whom I had always shared the secrets of my heart, the one with whom my tongue could be unguarded and heart unwalled.

And I was so very lonely.

CHAPTER FIVE

# the evening of my days

For a year after Neyah's death I stayed in the Royal City, and Den and I ruled over the Two Lands.

My little grandson was dear to me, and I would tell him the stories that Neyah used to tell to me: of the scarlet fish, and of the oryx who challenged the North Wind to race to the horizon; of the monkey who wanted to be a man, and of the tortoise who was proud. With him I re-lived the days of my youth, and I thought of how, when he grew older, I should tell him legends of the Gods and of the strong in heart who lived upon Earth through the old years.

My spirit still watched over my country; and I saw the land spread out below me as though I were poised above it like a hawk. Where the water-channels ran not freely, though the crops were still green to the eyes of men, I saw it as a desert. Where there were speakers of evil to the people, I saw it as though there were a great cloud of flies. Where there were those who opposed their servants or their animals, I saw blood over the lintels of their doors. And about the houses of those who would destroy their fellow-men, I saw not shade-trees, but skeletons springing from the ground along their path, for they walked in the shadow of death.

And when I saw those things that were not well in our country, I would tell of them to Den, so that although her own lotus was but an opening bud, she was a Ruler of Maat and there was no wrong in Kam that was hidden from the eyes of Pharaoh.

When there was one of great guile or strong in his evil, still did I sit in judgment upon him; and while he slept the night before, I listened to the words he repeated to himself, with which he hoped to bewilder me. Then, when he came before me in audience, I said to him, 'Listen and I shall speak your words for you'. Then a great fear would fall upon him, for he knew that I heard the words of his heart as though he had spoken them in a loud voice upon a still evening. Then would I give judgment upon him.

As time passed I saw that Den was following the pattern of my life as one lotus flowers like another, and that in her hands the Crook and Flail were secure. So, when I was forty-seven, I went to live with Seshet, to pass the gentle evening of my days at Nekht-an. Mirrored in its lotus pools, the old palace of the South stood upon the east bank of the river, and my windows opened to the setting sun.

Though Seshet was their vizier, the people of the South came to him with their troubles as if he were a temple counsellor. He went among the people of the little farm-lands, and a man who told him that the lettuces in his garden were wilting felt while they talked together that they were the two masters of a great vineyard. The linen-weavers knew that he understood the trouble brought by a roughened finger in the setting of the fine threads upon their looms. And the soldiers loved him, for his words could unseal the wine of laughter. His people called him Nekht-ab, 'the great-hearted', for they flourished under the sun of his compassion.

We talked together of things that are far away from Earth. We explored the crystal uplands of clear thought and scaled unfooted pinnacles where we could capture some image of the spirit with words. In old papyrus rolls of forgotten song-makers we heard whispers of lovers whose bodies were long dead, yet whose memory still walked through leafy avenues.

In the evening he would call for his musicians, who plucked from their strings the melodies of his thoughts; strange music, clear-cut as shadows on a wall, its harmony spaced into measures meticulous as the lines on the pillars that mark the river's height. The silver of flutes wound through the green of harps, as brooks awake quiet pastures in valleyed hills.

The spirit of Neyah shared my sleep, and his son was beside me through the day.

When Seshet had become Vizier of the South, he caused a new temple to be built at Nekht-an upon the west bank, opposite to the palace. When it was ready to be made a place of peace, I spoke these words to the assembled people.

''Hear my voice! For the Gods have made my tongue of silver so that your hearts shall echo to its words as a bell echoes to the striking of the hammer.

''Remember always that the things which befall you are but your own actions reflected in a true mirror. No flail shall fall upon your back unless your hand has been upraised unjustly. Your belly shall not be taut with hunger nor your throat parched with thirst unless you have suffered another to know these things. You shall not journey across the wilderness in darkness unless you have closed your eyes to the Light when it would have shone upon you. Your feet shall not bleed because of the stones upon your path unless you have heeded not the voice of one who told you to make sandals for yourselves of your own wisdom. You shall not cry upon the wind for loneliness unless you have been false to one who was your proven friend. You shall not fear death looming in your path unless you have denied the glory of his contenance.

"'Think only this of anything you do, 'Would I be glad if this were done to me?' Then shall you travel swiftly in the Boat of Time along the River of Eternal Life, and set no course upon the stream of tears that flows through the Caverns of the Underworld."

CHAPTER SIX

# the heart of kam

Up and down the great river of Kam our temples stand like an avenue of torches. The voices of priests are heard in the sanctuaries, and the courtyards whisper with the feet of Sandal Bearers. But the priests of our children are still in the bodies of children. So, on the seventh day of the seventh month of each year, all children who are in their seventh year are taken to the temples for the seers to look upon their gateways. And children whose bodies sit lightly upon them and who, in the great journey, travel along the pathway of a priest, return to the temple for their further training when they are twelve years old: so that in their turn they can become the life-blood of the heart of Kam.

Those among them who remember their dreams clearly, or

who have a mark within them which shows that before they were born they had begun to fly, are taught how to grow stronger wing-feathers so that they can become dreamers of true dreams. They shall become Pathfinders of the Jackal, and when the gateway of sleep is as an ever open portal through which the Light shines, they shall lead others through the dusk of Earth, even as Anubis has led them across the Great Causeway.

Those children who, when they sit beside the river looking upon bright water, see it coloured more vividly than dreams, are trained to leave their bodies and to go to and fro over Earth while they describe what they see upon their wanderings as though they saw them pictured in a polished bowl, or in a mirror, or upon the silver faces of their pyramids. They shall become the Lookers, who, swiftly as clear-sighted birds, watch over our country so that under their protection its tranquillity is undisturbed. And among them there are those who shall become Lookers of Maat whose tongues speak while they travel to the far realms of the spirit.

Those children under whose eyes life beats strongly are trained until they become Priests of Ptah and can cause life to flow down through their gateways. Just as the water-carriers fill their jars at the river to restore the young green to their gardens, so shall these healers draw water from the river of life to give it to those who thirst for it. And they shall give health to our people even as the inundation brings life to our fields. Among them are those who follow the Leadership of the Hawk. When in their hands they hold the sword of a Horus Priest, they shall sever the bonds of those who are enchained in the furthest Caverns of the Underworld, and about evil they shall put a noose of fire. They shall war with the great overlords of Set, and with their power beat down the challenge of destroying eyes.

Those children who see through the dark curtain of their lids are trained as seers. But only those who are in men's bodies are chosen, for this is the hardest of all line of temple-training, and a body must be a strong citadel to encompass this burnishing of the spirit without being injured. Their bodies cannot be unto them as a gentle pavilion, for while they are awake they see those things that other men see only while they sleep; and though they return to their bodies, they cannot escape from the multitudes of the beyond-earths or from the demons of the Underworld. When they have worn the Scarlet Feather of Maat, there shall be no curtains drawn to them on Earth. They shall look upon a sick man and know what has caused his sickness. They shall look upon a man and see his *ba* as though he were cloaked in colour, and so know the tempering of his heart. They shall see the memory of old evil, which stains the place where that evil was done; and they shall see where an ancient wrong or a forgotten sorrow has left its mark upon a room, clearer than bloodstains upon a floor. They shall see men who walk bodiless as clearly as if they were clothed in flesh, whether such men are free in their spirit or bound to earth by their own ignorance or by a condemnation. They shall read the records that are held in stone that is unscribed, yet which has been made lively with memory and can bear witness to those who can give it speech—and this power they share with the Lookers of Maat. And they shall fight mightily against the Hosts of Darkness, for they shall be Warriors of the Scarlet upon Earth and away from Earth, and seeing truth they shall fight for it in splendour.

These legions of the Winged Ones, who in their several ways have trained their will, shall join that mighty panoply of spears which protects us from the black destroying wave that would engulf us in the name of Set.

CHAPTER SEVEN

# the tomb of meri-neyt

In the twenty-ninth year of my reign my tomb was ready to receive my body when my spirit need return to it no longer.

I shall lie at Abidwa in the City of the Living Dead, among the beloved of my family in the last garden of Za Atet. Round me will sleep the companions of my journey: Ney-sey-ra who taught me to fashion the Golden Sandals so that the Causeway to the Gods was smooth under my feet; the viziers who gave me of their counsel; the captains who have been a flail in my hand to scourge the enemies of my country; Maata who sheltered my childhood; Harka who made me wise in the ways of chariots; Benater who taught me to weigh the spear that killed Zernak; and many others who have worked with me in the shepherding of the Two Lands.

The Gods made me their Vizier, and Ptah put the lives of his children into my hands. The scroll of my life is nearly scribed, yet within me are housed all that I have been since I was born in the Royàl City: I am the child to whom my mother brought sleep when she sang to me in the dusk; I am the daughter of Atet, whose image has been a standard that I have followed; I am the girl who went into the Temple to learn of wisdom, and the triumphant one who has proven her wings; I am the woman who rejoiced in her lover, and who sorrowed until the tears of her heart were stemmed by the slow healing balm of time; I am the Pharaoh who gave justice to the Two Lands, and the warrior whose chariot led the van of spears.

With me in my tomb shall be those things that will show our followers in time the manner of people who once dwelt in Kam. There shall be the things that I have used during my life: the sandals and cloaks and head-dresses I have worn, and the chest wherein I have kept my necklaces; the furniture from my apartments, and the little vase that held my flowers when I lived in the temple.

These things will show the surroundings of my life. But it matters little what people wear, what houses they live in, or what things they use. It is their thoughts which should endure through time; the span of their knowledge, their burnishing to Light. So with me there shall be long papyrus rolls on which shall be recorded by the scribes under my seal the wisdom I have learnt, the prayers I have said, the laws I have kept in Kam. They shall be with me in my sarcophagus; for as my body held wisdom while it walked on Earth, so shall these records hold it still. They shall be tied with threads of the warrior scarlet and sealed with my priest name, Meri-neyt.

With me also shall be the legend of the Creation of Earth and the story of the Journey of Man. When man sets forth upon his journey, he has learnt the strength of mountains and the gentleness of plants, and become wise in the ways of animals. Yet if evil is upon the one hand and good upon the other, to him their faces are as one statue reflected in two mirrors, for his *maat* is an empty jar. But through long time he finds that the voice of evil, though it beguiles him with smooth words, brings pain and sorrow to him. And thereafter it may be that for many lives he listens to no counsel. Then the voice of good falls upon his ears, a voice calm as clear water, unhurried as a hill of stone; and it tells him of the end of his journey, and the traveller listens and he goes on his way refreshed. But the things of Earth are still heavy upon him, as though he carried a great burden upon his shoulders. He seeks wisdom in many countries and in a multiplicity of tongues. Sometimes he travels across stony deserts, where his footprints are scarlet upon the sand, and sometimes he walks by the river beneath the shade-trees. But whether his day has been a rejoicing or a tribulation, always at night he shall sleep, to awake refreshed on a new dawn.

He left the Gods to go upon his journey, and he thinks that

he has travelled away from them; and for many lives this is so, for he journeys upon a circle. And in time he becomes a pupil of one of the twelve pupils of one of the twelve pupils of a Luminous One. Now he has joined a brotherhood, each of whom is part of the Gods as the filaments of the feathers are part of the Hawk of Horus. When this time comes, it is upon the other semi-circle that he travels, returning from whence he came. And when the end reaches the beginning, his circle will be completed. Then he will be one with the father, brother to the Gods who gave him life.

Upon the same scroll shall be recorded the Weighing of the Heart by the Forty-two Assessors of the Dead.

When the traveller reaches the end of his journey, he finds himself upon the bank of a river, and before him he sees a boat, which is the Boat of Time in which he must take passage. But before the decks allow him to set foot upon them, he must call them by name; and he must name the oars, or they will not row him; and he must name the prow, or it will not lead the boat along the river. He journeys in the boat over the dark water until the river down-plunges into the Great Caverns. Here he is beset by demons, which assail him in their shapes of terror, but if he is without fear, they cringe back into the shadows. Then he disembarks upon a quay where seven steps lead up to a great door. He must call upon the bolts by their name, and the hinges by their names, and he must know the secrets even of the planks that make it. At the hearing of their names, the door opens before him, and he passes through into a great hall of audience, where, seated on their thrones, are the Forty-two Assessors of the Dead. They soar above him into the shadows and their faces are beyond his sight, for he is in a valley among the mountainous Gods.

Each in his turn shall challenge him; and if he cannot answer them in truth, saying, 'By the Feather of Truth, thee have I conquered', then shall the floor open under his feet and he shall be in darkness until he emerges from his mother's womb. And in his conquering, the virtues shall enter into him and the evils shall enter the strength of their overthrowing into his heart.

Upon the four sides of the hall are the Assessors upon their thrones.

And the first shall challenge him, saying:
Hast thou treated thy body wisely and considerately, even as thy creator cherished thee in the days of thy youth?

And the second shall say:
Hast thou lived out the full span upon the Earth that the Gods allotted thee?

And the third shall say:
Hast thou kept thy body as a clean garment unstained by the River of Filth?

And the fourth shall say:
Hast thou lain only with the woman whom thy spirit loveth also?

And the fifth shall say:
Art thou free of the knowledge of the body of thy mother or thy daughter or thy sister or thine aunt?

And the sixth shall say:
Hath no man been unto thee as a woman?

And the seventh shall say:
Is there any animal that can call thee husband?

And the eighth shall say:
Have thine hands taken that which was not theirs to hold?

And the ninth shall say:

Hast thou eaten of food until thy belly was tormented
and cried out against thee, or taken of strong
drink until thy will was the slave of thy body?

And the tenth shall say:
Hast thou severed the silver cord of any in violence?

And the eleventh shall say:
Hath thine anger been just, and the flail in thine hand
been as the Flail of Pharaoh?

And the twelfth shall say:
Hast thou looked upon the rich and the skilled and
known not envy?

And the thirteenth shall say:
Hath thine heart been untorn by the claws of jealousy?

And the fourteenth shall say:
Hast thou spoken no evil except of evilness itself?

And the fifteenth shall say:
Hast thou left no plough idle in the furrow when the
seed was ready for sowing?

And the sixteenth shall say:
Hast thou lusted after knowledge for those things
that were not for thine ears or for thine eyes?

And the seventeenth shall say:
Hast thou seen thy giant shadow upon the wall and
thought thy semblance mighty?

And the eighteenth shall say:
Hast thou turned from the right path when it was
beset with danger?

And the nineteenth shall say:
Hast thou chained thyself to Earth with fetters of gold?

And the twentieth shall say:
Hast thou looked upon the things of Earth until thine eyes were blinded?

And the twenty-first shall say:
Hast thou been upright in thy dealings in the market-place?

And the twenty-second shall say:
Hast thou shown gratitude to all who have befriended thee upon thy journey, whether it be thy companion, or the pomegranate that refreshed thee when thou didst thirst?

And the twenty-third shall say:
Hast thou given bread to the poor and the fruits of thy vineyards to the weary?

And the twenty-fourth shall say:
Hast thou closed thy mouth against falsehood?

And the twenty-fifth shall say:
Hast thou been so prideful of thy wit that thy wisdom was clouded?

And the twenty-six shall say:
Hath thy friendship been a strong rock in a desert of shifting sands?

And the twenty-seventh shall say:
Hast thou chained thyself to no man with the shackles of hatred?

And the twenty-eighth shall say:
Hast thou known no sorcery nor polluted thyself, and hast thou kept thy body thy dwelling-place alone?

And the twenty-ninth shall say:
Hast thou brought contentment to the heart of thy mother and honoured thy father's house?

And the thirtieth shall say:
Hast thou honoured all true priests?

And the thirty-first shall say:
Hast thou remembered the Gods throughout thy journey and asked their counsel?

And the thirty-second shall say:
Hast thou closed thine ears to wisdom that speaks in a loud voice?

And the thirty-third shall say:
Hast thou quenched with thy wisdom the thirst of the parched for truth?

And the thirty-fourth shall say:
Hath thy power been used only for the Light?

And the thirty-fifth shall say:
Hast thou been a sword in the Army of Horus?

And the thirty-sixth shall say:
Hast thou led any man upon the path that leadeth not to freedom?

And the thirty-seventh shall say:
Hast thou a vision of thyself in thine heart in honour?

And the thirty-eighth shall say:
  Hast thou known thine own heart and been a true
    scribe of all thy works?

And the thirty-ninth shall say:
  Dost thou know that the end of one journey is but
    the beginning of another?

And the fortieth shall say:
  Hast thou remembered the plants, which were once
    thy brothers, and quenched their thirst and
    tended them so that they flourished?

And the forty-first shall say:
  Hast thou been to all animals as thy master is to thee,
    using wisdom, kindness, and compassion unto them
    who were once thy brothers?

And the forty-second shall say:
  Canst thou say in truth, 'I have never worked man nor
    beast beyond its strength. I have known that all upon
    Earth are my fellow-travellers and I have succoured
    them upon their journey'?

Then he shall no longer hear the sonorous voices of the Gods, and in silence his own voice shall ring forth, saying, 'Thee have I conquered, for upon Earth there is no sinful one, no sorrowful one, no suffering one, through any act of mine.'

Then this Hall of Truth shall be as the noonday, made luminous by the pure clear flame of his spirit; and if all the winds of Earth shall gather their forces upon this flame, still would it burn serenely undisturbed. He no longer sees the Gods towering above him, for he has become of their stature, and to him their faces are as though he looked in a true mirror and saw his own countenance, for he is a brother in their semblance.

Then before him he sees the Great Scales of Tahuti. Upon the one side is his heart in the form of the jar of his *maat* and upon the other side is the Feather of Maat. And they are poised each to each in perfect balance, for upon both sides there is Truth.

And the walls open before him like a great gateway, and he walks forward into the light of the Celestial Fields, where the corn that stands seven cubits high awaits his garnering.

CHAPTER EIGHT

# Return from Exile

When I had lived four years at Nekht-an, a pestilence swept through the Two Lands. Though the healers went among the people, many there were who found freedom from pain only when death released them. The doors of the palace were open to all who needed succour, and with my women I went among the people, tending them in their sickness. Then the plague fell upon me also, and all thought that I must die. I was grateful that this should be so, for I was weary of my exile. Yet when I thought that the next turn of the path would show the gateway of my home to me, the hold of my body grew stronger upon my spirit and kept me captive.

No longer was my body my willing servant, but it was an oppressor that tormented me with pain. No longer were my bones sheathed smoothly in my flesh, but they kept sharp and brittle as the dead branches of a tree, and my skin was brown and withered as forgotten leaves. To walk across the court-yard needed all my strength, and to keep my mouth closed against lamentations demanded all my will. I prayed to Ptah that I might bear my pain proudly as though it were a spear-thrust gained in battle. Age had come upon me in the space of one moon, and she had brought neither peace nor quietness in her hands.

For two years I lived in the body of an old woman, and often before I returned to its prison, I stood beside my bed, looking upon the crippled earthly shell to which I must return. Free in the semblance of my youth and strength, I would touch my smooth and shining hair and think of the wigs and head-dresses I must wear throughout the day to cover its sad greyness upon Earth.

It might be that while I slept Neyah and I had been reliving our childhood together, had climbed a high mountain, or swum in moon-green lakes. And while my feet paced slowly beside the palace lotus pools, I would think of my dreams, and it was as if I were a night-singing bird shut in a wicker cage that hears its brother wing towards the sky.

There are many whose bodies are old and heavy upon them who shun the face of death. Why are they frightened to renew their youth? Why are they frightened of release from pain? Grant that the day be soon when falling sands shall mark the ending of this little span, so that my body can sleep and need not wake, and I may be free as youth and wise as age.

When I was fifty-three years old, I saw the gates of my home open before me. I walked with my mother, and Neyah, and Za Atet, and he that was Ney-sey-ra, in the Gardens of the Setting Sun, and I knew the joy and peace that are one. Far below me I saw Earth as a little cold room that had opened its doors and let me free. Then faintly I heard a cry, like frightened children who are alone, and it was the sorrow of my people who knew that I was dying. And though I knew I need return no longer to that body wherein pain housed with me, down through the shadowed depths I went, and for the last time I made my body speak unto the people that I loved, so they might share my happiness with me and not be sorrowful that I had died. As I felt my body close on me, I prayed for strength that my last message to them should be clear and silver-tongued:

"I have seen the splendour of the evening veiling the sky in the colours of the universe, when the great Sun-god Ra journeys beyond Earth to hold converse with his brothers. Yet shall I see a greater glory than this pageant of the west.

"I have heard a thousand thousand singing-birds whose throats cry out the melody of life. Yet shall I hear far sweeter songs than this, nearer the heart of music than a harp.

"I have led chariots in the battle line and set victorious banners on the wind. I have found peace in temple colonnades and listened to wise counsel from true priests. I have kept my country's ploughlands deep in grain and shared with them my people's quietude. Yet do I know the glories of the Earth are fleeting shadows on a misty day beside that moment when, ahead in time, I shall at last unbar death's final gate and walk in the Fields of the Long Standing Corn."

Then like a sun-shaft breaking through a cloud I left the shadow-land of tears and pain, to walk with my dear companions in the Light.

The End

# Joan Grant

Joan Grant was born in England in 1907. Her father was a man of such intellectual brilliance in the fields of mathematics and engineering that he was appointed a fellow of Kings College while still in his twenties. Joan's formal education was limited to what she absorbed from a series of governesses, although she feels she learned far more from the after-dinner conversations between her father and his fellow scientists.

When Joan was twenty, she married Leslie Grant, with whom she had a daughter. This marriage ended soon after *Winged Pharaoh* was published in 1937—a book which became an instant best-seller. Until 1957 she was married to the philosopher and visionary Charles Beatty, who is the author of several books, including *The Garden of the Golden Flower,* a treatise on psychiatrist Carl Jung. In 1960, Joan married psychiatrist Denys Kelsey.

Throughout her life, Joan has been preoccupied with the subject of ethics. To her, the word "ethics" represents the fundamental and timeless code of attitudes and behavior toward one another on which the health of the individual and society depends. Each of her books and stories explores a facet of this code. As Denys Kelsey has written, "The First Dynasty of Egypt once knew the code well, but lost it and foundered. Eleven dynasties were to pass before it was recovered, but those were more leisurely times when the most lethal weapon was an arrow, a javelin and a club. We feel that in the present troubled days of this planet, these books must be presented."